# THE
# GIANT'S
# ALMANAC

Also by Andrew Zurcher:

*Twelve Nights*

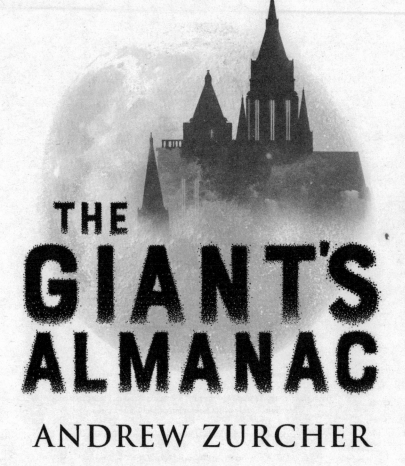

# THE
# GIANT'S
# ALMANAC

## ANDREW ZURCHER

PUFFIN

PUFFIN BOOKS

UK | USA | Canada | Ireland | Australia
India | New Zealand | South Africa

Puffin Books is part of the Penguin Random House group of companies
whose addresses can be found at global.penguinrandomhouse.com

www.penguin.co.uk
www.puffin.co.uk
www.ladybird.co.uk

First published 2021
001

Text copyright © Andrew Zurcher, 2021
The moral right of the author has been asserted

Set in 10.32/16.34pt Adobe Garamond Pro
Typeset by Jouve (UK), Milton Keynes
Printed and bound in Great Britain by Clays Ltd, Elcograf S.p.A.

The authorized representative in the EEA is Penguin Random House Ireland,
Morrison Chambers, 32 Nassau Street, Dublin D02 YH68

A CIP catalogue record for this book is available from the British Library

ISBN: 978–0–141–38564–8

All correspondence to:
Puffin Books
Penguin Random House Children's
One Embassy Gardens, 8 Viaduct Gardens,
London SW11 7BW

*For Davara*

*To the nobleman Khwaja Kalan, who held the fortress at Kabul, the emperor Babur wrote in 1528. He was on campaign far to the south, near Etawah, in what is now Uttar Pradesh, India. Dismounting in a strange land, he called for a melon, cut it, and wept as he ate it. How, he asked his friend, could one forget the pleasures of one's home? How could one forget both melons, and grapes?*

# Author's Note

Every word has a history, and most of them are ancient. Just as the water poured into a cup has reached that cup only after circling the skies in a cloud, only after raining from that cloud upon the soil, only after seeping through that soil to trickle into a river, only after running down that river to pool in some reservoir; so a word reaches your mouth, or your hand, only after thousands of years of arduous travel and continual exchange, crossing frontiers and propagating by the whispers and songs and poems and conversations of thousands on thousands of people we have never known, and can never know. At last it comes to you, a scribble on a page or a fleeting thrum sounded on the air: its being so light, and the time of its use and sense so brief! There are few lives so fragile as that of a word, and few histories so miraculous. And yet words are all around us, impossible and fecund and every one of them a marvel. Tens of thousands teem in you, only waiting to serve your need – that is, to express yourself, to say what you mean. Like pilgrims, or like birds on impossible migrations, they have reached you still on the wing, and your speech is but the flitching of their feathers as off, still flying, they pass into the future.

Among many words that I cherish, there is one I love most – perhaps because over the course of its journey it has acquired so many meanings that have to do with journeys, with the past and with the future. It is a word that has rubbed shoulders with mathematics, and with distant stars, with longing and with the seasons, with love, with generals plotting wars and with farmers planting fields. *Almanac*: this word came into English from the Latin spoken across Europe in the Middle Ages, and from French, but it had in turn been borrowed from Spanish, and the Spaniards had themselves had it from Arabic – that is, the Arabic spoken by the Muslim conquerors who occupied Spain between the eighth and the fifteenth centuries. In Spanish, in French, and in Latin an *almanac* was an astronomical calendar used for making astrological predictions; farmers turned to almanacs for advice on when to sow their seeds, or breed their livestock, and lovers, and merchants, and sailors loved, and traded, and set sail according to the almanac's recommendations. But the Arabic word spoken in Spain, *al-manak* ('the calendar'), had itself come from some other source, possibly the Syriac term *lĕ-manhay*, 'the year to come', or perhaps the Classical Arabic word *al-munāk*, 'the place where the camel kneels', thus 'the stopping place', or 'the end to the day's travel'.

I like to think of people long ago – people just like you, and me – reaching at evening the end of their day's tiring journey, and gathering beneath the constellations and beside their kneeling camels to pass the night in talk, in song, in planning for more days yet to come. It was from these people, nestled among their tired animals with their eyes upon the stars, that this plotting and keeping of space and time, the *almanac*, first arose. It is the map of the heavens, the guide to life, and the end of the journey, still whispering of the desert, and of the sky, of light and of night, of setting out and – at length – of coming home.

# MOTHER'S

I

# *Forget it*

Hanging from a corner of the roof, his hands like claws all muscle strapped to the leaden drainpipe, his now aching heels ground into the old wall's gritty mortar and still more gritty, crumbling brick, Fitz would normally have taken a wide view of the garden around him. Most days, he climbed the Old Friary half just for the privilege of this moment, the space of three or four deep, steadying breaths in which he could feel himself, though only a boy, the lord of it all. To one side, flanking his own humbler cottage, within the compass of the tall hedge, was the orchard where Clare once stole, she said, at evening for apples. To the rear of the Old Friary stretched the stately lawn, scored on either side by arcing beds of cadent roses. And beyond the gable to which he clung, beneath a red western sky, stood the ancient great maze cut from privet, its frustrating paths one of his earliest memories, its plan like the map of his own palm one of his most enduring. All of it – the orchard, the rose lawns, the maze – lay beneath him now, the disregarded petty kingdom of the house.

Had he paused to think, Fitz would have thought about the house: this house, this great house, that was almost his own. He would have thought it strange, maybe, to find himself breaking into a place so familiar. After all, he might have gone in by the front door. Often in the past he had gone in by the door. He had a key, given him by Mr Ahmadi Senior, with strict instruction to visit the library every day. But since Mr Ahmadi Senior had died, and his son and heir had come to live in the Old Friary, since everything had changed, Fitz had tended to climb the drainpipe. Something about Mr Ahmadi Junior unsettled him; where his father had been slow, kindly and gentle, his son by contrast strode into every room with an abruptness, a restless immediacy that made Fitz jump. He seemed always about to step out from behind the door, always ready to deliver one of his mordant rebukes. So different from his father, and yet, somehow, alike, the son had slipped into his father's place as a knife might a wound. As Fitz hung from the edge of the roof, digging his heel hard against the ancient brick wall, he might – had he thought about it – have made a resolution to avoid Mr Ahmadi Junior altogether, and evermore.

But today his hands and feet seemed to climb by themselves and, oblivious to the grounds around him, blind to the house and to the man who sat at its centre as a spider tends its web, Fitz had only one thought on his mind. He certainly wasn't intending to borrow a book. Instead, tucked inside his shirt, close against his skin, lay the crisp, rigid square of an envelope. Where his body hung, slung against the wall, it seemed to arch instinctively away from the paper's cool surface, from the sharp corners that dug into his flesh when he moved. As for the letter within the envelope – he wished he had never read it. He didn't want anyone else to see it.

4

Above all, he didn't want Clare to see it. Ever.

Fitz kicked his right foot against the hard brick wall. He was here. For a second the pain in his leg surged into, and joined with, a flush of something hot and vital that rose in his neck and swept down his back and hips. It was the sharpest, fullest feeling of presence.

*For every presence, an absence. For every end, a beginning. For every height, a depth.* The words of his old neighbour thrummed in his ears. *Every zenith, my eyes, has its nadir.*

Now he was losing his footing. Fitz turned to the heavy stone casement of the second storey gallery. Capped with an alcove almost entirely freestanding in cut stone, it had been added long after the friary was first built. Its high windows were always locked, but like most things that surrendered to the ingenuity and persistence of an eleven-year-old boy, these locks for the right fingers had a trick to them. *Anything – even an impossible thing – can be open to you, if only you have a method.* Fitz swung his left foot on to the ledge, heaved his body round the drainpipe and stood on the ledge. He pressed the warped iron pane, slipped his finger against the catch inside, then swung the window silently open. Like a cat he sprang to the floor, the pads of his feet making no more sound on the floorboards than water slipping into water.

Fitz was going to lose the letter in a place where it would never be found. *When you come into my library, any library, you leave all the cares of your life behind you. You shut them out. When you are in the library, you are safe.*

Mr Ahmadi Senior had been right enough about that. The library made Fitz feel safe. But it wasn't the books, exactly, or

5

the quiet afternoons which, undisturbed and lost to the world, he passed in reading at the decorated walnut table, beneath the room's high windows. What made him feel safe were his words. *Zenith. Nadir. Algorithm. Albatross*. He recited them, often, like an incantation to ward away spirits, threats and curses, and when he had once run through them he circled back and pronounced them to himself again. Now, stepping down to the wooden boards of the gallery floor, each step was a syllable, each pace another. He stalked silently up the gentle slope of the long gallery floor. His gaze he focused on the little stairs that led from the far end of the gallery to the main hall and staircase, and beyond the stairs to the library. As he passed by, intoning his words with religious care, he dared not look to either side, where on his left and on his right hung grand portraits in full length and dress of the family's illustrious ancestors: men swathed in strange, sumptuous fabrics, their hands resting with comfortable assurance on heavenly orbs or mariners' instruments, on the hilts of swords, or smartly tailored in the long, formal clothes he knew marked them as Janissaries, elite soldiers of a vanished empire. Their precise *moustachios*, their beards and weapons and tools all placed just so, their unremitting eyes, and, above all, their likeness – these things, these things and so much more, so drilled into Fitz each time he had looked at them, that he had begun to think that their places had been reversed, that he was the portrait, and they the harsh critics who had come to inspect him.

Onwards: making no noise against the little steps, no noise on the cut marble landing at the top of the grand staircase, no noise in the corridor that led to the south wing of the Old Friary, he pressed towards the library, holding his breath only as he crept past old Mr Ahmadi's study – where, perhaps, his son even now sat behind the antique desk, working beneath the countless small cupboards that opened on the wall above, like eyes, in which every odd thing had its home.

Fitz padded softly into the library. His breath was still, his pulse calm, each beat of his heart a syllable. *Zenith, nadir.* Now, reaching for the wooden steps, he repeated those syllables again. Now, climbing to the top of the steps and turning to the highest of the room's shelves in the greatest of its fine, carved oak cases, he said them yet once more.

*Albatross, the diver.*

Fitz ran his index finger along the leather spines of Mr Ahmadi's ancient library. The top shelf held the smallest volumes, but notwithstanding their size, he knew they were just as precious as the taller, more imposing folios below. Perhaps even more precious. For the last several minutes, climbing, stealing through the house, ascending the steps, drawing through the air with his hand, it was as if Fitz had been making a single motion, extending his body in a long sweep as a dancer might, to this perfected gesture.

His finger stopped.

Beneath it, in a gap that should have held a wider book, leaned a little card-bound volume. Its cover, a faded yellow, was spotted and on its back a little mouldy. Fitz had lighted on it, pulled it from the shelf, and found himself holding it before he meant to. From inside his shirt, buttoned close against his chest, he drew the thin, folded sheet in its plain white envelope, holding it by thumb

7

and forefinger as if it were a snake or spider, or any venomous thing.

He remembered the letter's short words well enough without reading them.

'It is now past time. He is not your child. I will come for him.'

Fitz shuddered once, then thrust the letter into the gap, a white shadow cast into a dark recess of ancient, tanned leather. For a moment he watched it, willing it to be still and not to spring back, to fall into his hands as it had that morning. In the shadow between two books, deep within the shelf, he could still make out the simple address on the envelope, the curt and aggressive strokes that were the start of Clare's name. It had never been meant for him.

He didn't care. In the silent audience of his own thoughts, his words repeated: *zenith, nadir, algorithm, albatross*.

He was safe. More importantly, Clare was safe. Very soon he could forget all about it. He could look away, and forget it. It would be over.

Fitz took a deep breath. He turned to the little book in his hands and thought he might borrow something from the library today, after all. It was a thin and a beaten book, a sudden and impulsive and an ignorant choice. That pleased him; but he didn't stop to open it, to swim as he usually did with big strokes of his eyes across the title and the first pages, taking in those delicious opening words like sugar on the tongue in the late afternoon. He had simply dived in and snatched it; now he clutched it hard to his side, and slipped down the steep wooden steps to the floor. The act was done, the mission nearly ended; now he needed only to cross the landing and the gallery, slide down the drainpipe, and cross the garden, and that letter, those terrible words, would be out of his life for good.

From down the darkening hall came the sound of a muffled voice. Something about its tone made him freeze, straining to hear. It wasn't anger, but an edge more serious, a tension that stopped only just short of cruelty. He crossed the library to the door, caressing the floor with the pads of his feet as a dancer might, or a cat before pouncing, and listened again. He could almost make out the words: intermittent, animated, punctuated by long pauses. It was Mr Ahmadi Junior, speaking on the telephone.

Fitz wouldn't remember, later, the delicate steps with which he crept down the hallway. He wouldn't remember the careful placement of the balls of his feet on the dead and silent centre of every floorboard. He wouldn't remember the gloom shed by the far window, where the gathering storm outside drizzled in its failing light. He was drawn as if in a dream by a thread, and his gaze lay along that thread focused and intense, ignorant of any other sight or sound, any other touch. He might have floated.

'I remember very well whose son I am!' barked Mr Ahmadi. The sudden clarity of his voice, roused with impatience, broke Fitz's trance. His left hand shot out, by instinct, and gripped the frame of the study door. The door itself, thick and solid, stood firmly shut before his face. No one had heard him. He steadied himself.

'That's just the problem,' Mr Ahmadi continued. 'That's just it.'

There was another pause, then some muttered words, too low to make out. Fitz strained his ears, tightening his jaw and leaning towards the door until his forehead nearly rested on its deep-grained panel.

'I will kill him if I must,' Mr Ahmadi said. The words hardly carried into the hall, if they did at all, no more than syrup through a cloth.

Fitz started back from the door as if electricity had surged suddenly through it. Had he heard what he thought he had heard? His heart leaped and stuttered.

'Anything –' Mr Ahmadi continued – 'to keep him out of play.'

The hallway whirled in the stillness that followed. Fitz, planted on his feet, felt as if he had been plunged into the depths of a great and current water, whose swells waved through him in irresistible shocks of surprise and nausea. Though he feared to make even the smallest movement, he had the impression that his legs, stamping wildly for purchase around him, staggered. His hands, still at his side, seemed to be swimming in the air. The skin bristled along his neck and shoulders, and pricked down his arms. A burning, painful feeling grew in his chest, and he realized that he had been holding his breath; for fear of gasping, he held it still.

'I will kill him if I must.' It couldn't have been that. He must have misheard. Fitz closed his eyes, preferring blindness to the juddering spasms that had begun to shake his field of vision. *Forget it. I heard him wrong.*

But there was no mistaking his neighbour's next words. They sounded from the study clear as the peal of a bell.

'I must go,' Mr Ahmadi said. 'He's here now. I saw him from the window only a few minutes ago.'

For a second or two, nothing happened. Then, from within the study, behind the great mahogany desk Fitz had glimpsed so often while passing down the hallway towards the library, Mr Ahmadi Junior set the bone-handled, antique receiver down in its cradle. Fitz heard it settle into place, and then the familiar, extended crackle of dry wood stretching its limbs as Mr Ahmadi leaned back in his spindled chair.

Every nerve in Fitz's body, acute and sensitive, seemed to prickle. He choked with agitation on the air, his jaw thrust forward like that of a fish snagged on a drawing hook.

And then his fingers twitched, and he dropped the book.

He had forgotten that he was holding it. *The Giant's Almanac*: fifty or sixty pages, manuscript, card covers, written in a free and open hand. It was almost nothing. It hardly slapped the floor when it hit. It hardly made a sound. It hardly dented the silence.

But it was enough. Immediately, from within the sealed study he heard Mr Ahmadi push himself back from the desk and rise to his feet. And he heard another noise, the sound of hard, powerful claws scrabbling against granite. Fitz didn't stay to hear more. His eyes snapped open. His arm swung to the floor to retrieve the book, even as his legs, charged with fear, uncoiled down the hallway. He knew he wouldn't make it to the gallery window. There was no time to waste.

As he scattered himself down the hallway, round the corner and into the Friary's grand, central hall, Fitz could almost feel the touch of Mr Ahmadi's grip on his neck. His words, his strange words, his threatening words, seemed to chase him like a demon or a fury, tightening round his collar. But his mind, calculating, told him that his neighbour was not the most immediate danger; the long iron handles of the Friary's panelled doors would present no obstacle to the house's oldest resident, the huge Alsatian Mr Ahmadi had inherited from his father. Fitz had raced Aslan a hundred times, and knew his footing in the halls of that house as well as he knew his own. And he knew, as only a friend really knows, just how quickly the dog would take up the chase, and how relentlessly he would pursue it.

At the top of the broad and turning stairs, Fitz drew up and inclined his head. He was a hunted animal scenting the air. The moment he reached the ground floor, he would have a choice: to let himself out of the front door, and circle round the back of the big house, through the kitchen garden and orchard; or to reverse, sprint down the back hallway, negotiate the complicated kitchen, and try his luck with the servants' entry. He imagined both routes, almost simultaneously, with geometric precision.

He didn't reach a decision.

From the other side of the first-floor landing, the door he had yanked behind him was now rattling violently. It wouldn't hold for long. Fitz wedged the book firmly under his arm, and when the latch finally gave way, he sprang.

Often he took the steps of the grand staircase two at a time. Today, with one hand gliding on the wide oak bannister, he stretched for three. He calculated, leaping: the curve of the descent would deposit him, with a bound, halfway across the lobby on his way to the front door. Momentum knew this was his preferred route, but, with sudden resolve – hearing fast legs on the steps behind him – he twisted, swinging his legs clear over the bannister and into the back hallway. Through the dim light, between heavy shelves crammed with dusty instruments, he tried to lengthen his pace. The hallway opened on to a high-ceilinged, panelled dining room, framed with more portraits of black-bearded fathers. Every one of them seemed to frown at Fitz as, without a break in his gait, he propelled himself across the surface of the room's heavy walnut dining table – holding his feet high to be sure his trainers wouldn't scuff the polished finish. On the other side, as he darted through the doorway, he let it swing closed behind him; this might buy him the second or two he would need in order to locate the back door keys.

There was no need. The cook had left them hanging, as she often did, on the old disused chimney breast beside the kitchen's elaborate range. Tonight was her night off, and the cold meats she had left for Mr Ahmadi's dinner lay, covered, on the broad table that stood between the hearth and the door. Fitz snatched the keys from their hook, tossed the book on to the table, vaulted it, caught the book as it slid off the other side, and just managed to plant the right key in the ancient lock of the house's heavy back door. For a second he felt gift and magic surging through his body, as if he were an arrow nimbling through a still air, at once both rising and falling. Light lay on the other side of the door, and freedom.

Then Aslan crashed into the kitchen door. It hadn't even slowed him – and, unlike Fitz, he could go straight under the table.

With a heave the boy shouldered open the massive door. There was no time to shut it behind him; everything would now depend on his sprint. Flying across the gravel yard he kept his tread light as a dancer's, trying not to create the traction that on loose stones might slow him. When he had gained the grass, he pushed his feet more firmly into soil. The skies were gathering with thick storm clouds as the day gave way to red gales, but the grassy lawn over which he now dashed lay firm and dry beneath his feet, and with every pace he added speed. Thirty metres from the crumbling stone walls of the Old Friary stood an ancient stone well – covered, with a stone roof. To either side tall hedges stretched away, impenetrable as thickets, bristling with boring, thrilling thorns. Clambering on to the stonework, Fitz reached high and placed the book delicately on the roof above him. Fast hand-over-hand work took him up the carved wall of the well house, and he just managed to sling his legs out of reach as Aslan ground to a stiff halt, all slather and barking, on the lawn behind him.

Fitz stood on the roof looking down. There was nothing menacing in the dog's stance, or in his eyes. The fear that had closed round Fitz's throat, squeezing his shoulders even as it loosened his stomach, now started to drain from him. He had got away with it.

'Not this time, my friend,' he said, and smiled at the panting and good-natured dog. He loved Aslan, but with a wariness. He had always shuddered to think what the impetuous Alsatian might do to Mr Ahmadi's books if he ever managed to catch Fitz in one of their chases. He had seen discarded piles of feathers after a hawk's sudden plummet from the sky. It didn't bear thinking on.

Fitz was about to jump down off the back of the well house, into the strip of wood that bordered this and his own cottage's garden, when he heard a window opening behind him. It was a delicate sound, barely audible over the rising wind – but even whispers, when dreaded, can cut the air like a knife. The boy froze. For several seconds, nothing happened. Aslan had stopped smearing his muzzle into the dry grass.

When Fitz turned, he saw Mr Ahmadi framed in the broad casement. He'd swung the window wide after unlatching it, and stood now in the red storm light, his arm still extended. Even from this distance, Fitz could see the starched elegance of his tailored shirt, the heavy wool weight of his suit, and his neatly trimmed black hair. Everything Mr Ahmadi Junior did, he did with precision. It was no accident that he had opened his window just at the moment Fitz had thought to turn his back on the house, just at the moment he was about to drop down into the wood and make a safe escape.

Somewhere in his stomach, buried deep, Fitz wanted to scream, and run away. But the man in the window seemed the same man as always – precise and severe, but proper, even kindly. He quailed. 'I borrowed a book,' he called out. His voice sounded brave.

Mr Ahmadi said nothing in reply. Larks dared the air between them, and quivered into the hedges on every side.

'I will bring it back,' he shouted, with less conviction.

'Always you take the wrong ones,' answered Mr Ahmadi. He didn't need to force the resonant, deep reed of his voice; it carried. 'Always you mistake. Always you turn simple things into adventures.'

'Mr Ahmadi Senior said I could borrow any book I wanted,' Fitz protested.

'A power to do wrong is not the same as an obligation to do wrong,' said Mr Ahmadi. After a pause, almost too faintly to hear, he added, 'Quite the reverse. You should read better books.'

Mr Ahmadi was not looking at him. He was scanning the woods behind the hedge. Fitz thumbed the flimsy cover of this slim volume that he held wedged beneath his arm.

Aslan, who had been watching the conversation with detachment, suddenly stood up and barked. He had heard something over the wind. As a rule, Mr Ahmadi frowned at Aslan's antics – when he noticed them at all – but now he seemed to smile. In this way, Fitz heard Clare's voice before he heard it.

'Supper is on the table, Jaybird,' she shouted. The soprano tilt of her voice seemed to summon the little birds again from their hidden hedges, and they flurried in the air over the lawn. Mr Ahmadi, the voice on the telephone, the plotter, the murderer, had broken into a wide and benevolent cheerfulness. Fitz felt the last tension drain from his legs.

With his free hand, Mr Ahmadi carefully shielded the protruding lens of his telescope where it stood against the casement; with the other, he slowly drew the window closed behind him. 'Bring it back tomorrow,' he said, almost inaudibly as the window shut and the latch turned into its seat.

'I will,' Fitz called, almost over his shoulder as he turned and slipped down the back of the well house, scrambling lightly over the cords of dry wood Mr Ahmadi's gardener had stacked against the winter.

In the friary garden, even under the riot of a threatening south-westerly wind, even under the severe gaze of Mr Ahmadi Junior, all that it contained was eternal, blessed, a kind of paradise enclosed and shut off from the rest of the world. But beyond the hedge, everything changed, and today more than ever. He felt it the moment he jumped down on to the hollow bare earth of the leaf-strewn path: something awry, some slight shift or turn that made the whole of the wood strange.

Fitz hesitated to raise his eyes to the expanse of trunks before him; whereas normally he would have passed without a second thought by the wood, or stalked eagerly into it, today his nerves recoiled from it like an alien thing. Maybe it was the strange light of the coming storm. Behind every tree something unknown and invisible today, newly, stood concealed. Within every shadow sheltered some inscrutable and inarticulable fear. Fitz felt a dead weight rise along the top of his spine and creep up his neck. His arms dangled.

*Don't be stupid. Don't be a baby.*

He started to cross the little stretch of wood that lay between Mr Ahmadi's garden and his own, between the friary's sunken, ancient grounds and the patch of scrabble and vegetables that stretched behind his own cottage. It was at once the long way round and a shortcut, at once familiar and the border of something strange and menacing.

He hadn't taken ten steps when it struck him, more forcefully than before, that something was wrong. The voice of the wind still roaring in the garden seemed, in the wood, instead muted and green. At this time of the year, in this weather, no birds sang. He expected the deep quiet and, at a distance, the lean and moan of the taller trees. What he didn't expect – he couldn't put his finger on it for a moment –

*Whispering.*

Ahead, just past the gate to his own garden, a drystone wall ran round a little churchyard attached to a ruined chapel. Once, the chapel had served the family in the Old Friary where Mr Ahmadi now lived, and the toppled headstones that crowded the yard recorded what Fitz had always assumed were their names. Illegible now and crusted with lichens, anonymous and neglected, the stones were the closest thing Fitz had to old friends. Tottering between them was one of his earliest memories, and there were few days, save in the worst of winter, when he didn't stand for a minute or two among them, or watch them from his window, among the yew trees that now dwarfed and overgrew the derelict building. Tonight he ought to have stopped at his own gate and gone inside. He should have shut it behind him and gone right into the house. Instead he found himself in the churchyard, his hands on a cold plinth of stone, the collapsing weight of the wall standing between him and the whispering woods beyond.

The evening's strangeness scared him, and yet he couldn't quite give it up.

The blood strained tight in Fitz's skin like a fist in a glove. He almost expected to see faces peering from behind, or within, the wood's shadowy trunks. He couldn't tear his own stare from them. Of course there was nothing – just the familiar moss-crusted texture of the trees, the bark here grey, there brown, coated in the shadow of high leaves, as far as the eye could see. He drew a deep breath, lifting his lungs till they ached against his ribs. With the cool stone under his hand, he thought perhaps he had imagined the noise, that it was just some unusual effect of the storm blowing overhead.

But there it was again.

*Whispering syllables, dusk-words, a soft sibilance between shifting leaves.*

For the second time that evening, terror raced over the little hairs that velveted his taut skin. There were too many trees before him, too many places where those voices might be hiding. He suspected one, then all of them. His eyes leaped erratically across the scene like a drop of water crazing on a hot pan. His heart, his whole chest, cramped, squeezing the wind out of him. The whispers crawled on his neck. They worked towards his ears.

'Boy.'

Fitz had been watching the woods, his back to the cottage. Now he spun round, pressing his legs flat against the tombstone, and almost throwing his free hand before his face – throwing it down against his side, instead.

The man before him was a little taller than he was, a little heavier but not much, grizzled. His short hair and neat corduroy jacket gave him an air too dapper for the woods. His left hand rested on the silver head of an ebony cane.

'Where is your mother, boy?'

'Inside,' Fitz answered. His eyes darted at the cottage, at its windows. 'Inside the house.' The words stole from him and were gone before he could stop them.

The man peered at him, as if in disbelief. 'Aren't you forgetting something?' he asked. His voice was insistent, near a sneer.

The wind that gusted along the hedge and through the churchyard swept also through Fitz. He opened his mouth to answer, but had nothing to say. The backs of his legs, stiff against the headstone, wanted to run, but he had almost trapped himself between the chapel and the stone wall, and when he glanced towards the trees the man's cane shot out, warding him back.

'Now,' he said, 'what's this you are holding so tight?'

With his cane he prodded at Fitz's leg, forcing him to move towards the corner of the chapel wall.

Fitz saw that he had been gripping the headstone hard enough that his fingers, cold in the wind, ached as he released them. It was the only new stone in the yard. He had never looked at it.

The man scanned the inscription. 'Another relation of yours, I suppose.' He lurched forward and grabbed Fitz by the arm.

Paralysed but for a shaking in the back of his skull, Fitz watched the man's chin as the words hissed out of him.

'I'm a friend,' he said. 'I expect we'll meet again later.'

The pain in Fitz's arm had still not subsided as he watched the man – who certainly did not seem like a friend – disappear round the hedge the same way, five minutes earlier, he himself had come.

All the tension in his body abruptly recoiled from him. Without thinking about it, he sprang to the length of his legs and sprinted for the cottage gate. This distance of twenty metres, dodging stones and stumps, he could cover in a few heartbeats and in any darkness. He had done it a hundred times, a thousand. He could probably have run it in his sleep. Every root, every patch of dirt, every thin clump of weak and whitish grass he knew, or his feet knew, and they hit the earth like a hail of stones. Before he could make sense of his fingers or their well-practised movement, he had slipped the bolt from the gate, opened the door, let himself through, and shot the bolt again.

He stood panting, safe, looking out at the wood beyond the garden. In the distance darkness collected between the trunks. If there really had been whispering – surely there hadn't been, surely it had been a trick of his imagination – but if there had, then perhaps it gathered there now, as shadows sometimes fell together at twilight, murmuring. He looked back the short way he had come, where the ordinary stone well stood at the edge of Mr Ahmadi's ordinary hedge. The man had passed beyond it; he too was gone, curled and sunk into shadow.

'What was all that noise, my little prince?' Clare stood out of sight, just inside the door, rummaging in a cupboard for something heavy. Fitz made the fear flush from him before he answered. *Forget it.* It wouldn't do to make Clare upset.

'Nothing, Bibi. Just Mr Ahmadi loaning me a book.' He looked down and was surprised to find the book still in his hand.

'He is such a dear man. Come inside and eat your supper.'

Fitz picked a blackberry off the cane as he went in, and chewed its hard and bitter seeds with precision, one by tiny one until he had dealt with them all. He swallowed them. He put the book on the table next to his plate, and sat down. He told himself he was going to enjoy *The Giant's Almanac*.

Clare came into the kitchen. She stood next to Fitz's chair.

'Aren't you forgetting something?' she demanded.

He froze, his hand on the edge of the table. It was a long way back.

'Fitz?'

A little amusement played on her face as she turned it towards him. Relieved, Fitz jumped up and kissed her cheek, and then together they ate their meal.

## tabiyya

'Come here, my eyes, and sit down beside me, for I would tell you a story.'

Though it was afternoon, and nearly summer, the room was dark. Heavy wooden shutters with close slats had been pushed across the enormous windows, nearly covering them. In the two narrow shafts of bright sunlight that still pierced the gloom, brilliant motes of dust sparkled and danced, swirling in an apparent chaos of constant motion. The boy took one of the two little stools that stood by the door, and placed it beside the old man's chair, far from the swirling motes. He sat down. In his hand he held the shāh, and turned it over again and again against his palm.

'Many years past when I was young like the vine in summer, I made a journey into a far country.'

The old man's white beard had been trimmed that morning, but his eyebrows grew as wild as ever with bristling tufts. In his last, weak days, he had grown gaunt, and his faintly purple skin sagged beneath his eyes and in his cheeks. With a careful and deliberate motion, he rearranged the coarse wool blanket that covered his lap and legs.

'I went there to trade, and I brought many valuable things with me for the market: leather and metalwork, porcelain and silk, spices, carpets, and dyed cloths of many colours. A man who goes to the market must be well furnished with many things of many shapes, and hues, and textures, if he is to be noticed at all. The market is so busy, and so full of diversions and entertainments, that a merchant with poor wares can easily be mistaken for one of the many beggars who set up their blankets beside the tables.'

The boy heard that the old man's voice was growing weak. He went to the table that stood in the light, and from a glass pitcher poured a cup of water. The cup was black and of a high glaze, set with a ring of lapis lazuli just beneath the rim. He handed it to the old man, in order that he might drink.

'If he is fortunate – and I have always been fortunate – a merchant spends his days trading away all the things he has, for money. In the morning I would set out my wares on the tables in the market, carefully positioning each thing to its best advantage: the gold in bright shadow, just beyond the light of the sun when in the long afternoon it fell full upon my stall; the spices where the breeze might wanton with them, coyly, both offering their scent to passers-by, and snatching it away again; the carpets flat, one set upon the other, so that the coarsest lay above and the finest below, tempting but resisting the eager touches of my customers. There is an art to laying out merchandise, and I was such an artist: not a day passed but I cleared my tables, in every city I visited. I became very rich.'

The old man took a drink from the cup with the ring of blue stones.

'It was my custom in those days always to keep moving, to buy wares at a cheap rate in one place so that I might sell them at a higher price somewhere else. But one day when I set up my tables in the market of a new city, I had the fortune to meet another merchant whose stall was set beside mine, and when the day's trading had ended, and my tables as usual were bare, he laughed, saying I had given away all my worldly possessions, and invited me to his house to eat with him. I was proud, and pecunious, and I thought I would enjoy helping him to load his mules – for he had many goods at the end of the day unsold – and I eagerly desired to eat freely what he would freely give me, rather than part with a single dinar in the purchasing of a scanty meal.

'This merchant lived in a modest house in the city, neither poor nor opulent, but the homely gifts of his friendship were many and offered without stint: ass's milk and sweet dates, spiced lamb and eggs baked with herbs, flatbreads, sweetbreads and candied peels – more, my eyes, than I could eat, and I was well satisfied. When we had pushed away the meal and sat together in the cool part of the evening, the merchant turned to me.

'"Brother merchant," he said, "your trading today has reminded me of a story that is known to everyone in this city but which I think you, as a foreigner, will not have heard. I would like to tell you this story."

'In those days I was as eager to gather stories, my eyes, as I was to buy new wares, and I urged my new friend to continue.

'"There was a great king from this place, who became king over many kings. It was his custom to pass the winter in feasting, and the summer in campaigning, fighting wars to extend his kingdom and to bring riches back to his city. At the end of one long summer, he returned from campaign, bearing in his train a mass of treasure the

25

likes of which no eastern or western monarch had ever seen, more than historians, more even than poets could begin to describe. My words, brother merchant, cannot do justice to such wealth. With this treasure he planned to make his capital city the centre of the world, a city more fragrant and luxurious than ancient Babylon, grander and more elegant than Rome, more famous for learning than Athens or Alexandria, a city to rival Carthage, Persepolis or Tyre or Antioch. He had sent before him orders to his masons and artisans, to construct a palatial temple surpassing the scope and beauty of any building ever constructed. To his temple he summoned a thousand kings and emirs, the princes of the lands lying between the Bosphorus, the Asian steppe, the great eastern gulf, and the deserts of Egypt. These princes would he feast in his temple, and they would acknowledge him the shāhanshāh, the king of kings.

'"This conqueror rode to the Feast of a Thousand Kings upon his favourite stallion, alone, without his guard, dressed in a common soldier's garb and bearing at his belt only his sword, for during the feast the kings his vassals were to confer upon him his rich robes of state, with all the ornaments of power and rule. He alighted on the steps of his new temple, and was about to enter the great hall when he was stopped by a beggar – by a little boy, no more than twelve years in age. This boy stood on the steps in his rags, holding in his hand the brush with which, for a few common coins and a great number of painful kicks, he had cleaned the feet of the kings as they had arrived to take their seats for the feast.

'"'Great king,' said the little boy, 'great king and lord of land and sea, pardon my insolence, and suffer me to speak the space of a single breath.'

'"The king was irritated by the child's forwardness and thought at first to strike him, but the boy was at once so humble and mean, and yet so well-spoken, so lowly and yet so courteous, that he paused; and that pause saved his life. For the boy told him that every one of the thousand emirs had borne into the temple a dagger strapped to his leg, concealed beneath his gown. Only the beggar boy, grovelling in the sand and dirt upon the steps as he ran his brush over their feet in exchange for copper coins, had noticed these weapons. By these daggers surely the princes intended some harm to the king of kings, and not to crown him but to kill him.

'"A few simple orders were quickly given, and the king entered the temple as planned – to the smiling faces and the loud cheers, but to the hollow and the faithless hearts, of his subject lords. Walking the length of the hall, and taking his seat on the throne set highest above the expectant audience, he called for the servers to carry in the feast – a thousand men bearing a thousand platters, to be set at once before a thousand revelling kings. Glasses were lifted and a salute began to rise. But at the signal – for these men were not servants, but soldiers, trained and obedient – the platters were uncovered to reveal not a sumptuous feast, but shackles. Before they could rise to defend themselves, every prince seated at the feast found his neck bound in a collar of iron. They had entered the hall as kings, but they would leave the hall as slaves.

'"To each of the soldiers who had served him on that day, the king granted a kingdom for his service. But to each of the kings who had sought to betray him, he gave a punishment. Their beards were shaved, and their royal garments exchanged for coarse cloth. Their sandals with buckles of beaten gold the king caused to be cast upon the fire, and from that day they went barefoot. Chained by the collar one to the other, they were beaten into the desert, and set to work in a secret place building the king's tomb.

'"Meanwhile the king sent forth a decree that the beggar boy who had saved him, whose sharp eyes were even sharper than those of the shāh himself, should be his heir. And his decree was that the shāh's temple full of treasure should be his inheritance, along with the allegiance of a thousand petty captains, who had won kingdoms only by this boy's sharp eyes, his faithful heart and his bold tongue. But the boy could not be found, though the king had his decree proclaimed in every city where the sun falls upon the sand, though he caused the decree to be carved in stone and set up in the markets of a thousand kingdoms. Year after year, growing old, the king waited; year after year, growing old, he was disappointed.

'"At last, after many years of fruitless searching, the king found that all of the joy of his heart had dried and was consumed, like water in the desert, leaving only the salt trace of his tears. On that day, from the desert, came the thousand kings who had become his slaves, each still chained to the other, to say that his tomb had been completed. Then the king ordered that his treasury, containing all his gold and silver, the fine cut jewels as numberless as the stars in the night sky, the rich hoard of metalwork, of carving, of stuff in horn, and leather, and coral, or worked from the bones of great whales and from rocks fallen from the sky – all this, that was to be the inheritance of the beggar boy, he caused instead to be borne into the desert by the kings who had betrayed him, and buried in his tomb. And it is said that the slaves who buried the king's hoard in the desert also buried themselves with it, in shame at the lives that they had lived, and at their faithless hearts, so that no man knew where the king's treasury lay concealed, not even the king himself."'

The old man's voice had dwindled, in this telling of this story, to almost a whisper. Now, with a shaking hand, he held out his cup to the boy, who took it to the pitcher and filled it. When the old man had drunk again, he set the cup down on a little table that stood by, and closed his eyes for a while.

'It is very important to me, my eyes, that I should tell you this story, which the merchant told me in my youth, and which I have always carried with me, through all of my life after. I would like you to remember it, and think of it, as I have done. But I am very tired, and I cannot go on today. Come again tomorrow, and when we have played a little of our game, I will tell you more.'

The boy stood, and closed the shutters against the light so that the old man could sleep. He raked up the glowing embers in the hearth, so that they should keep their warmth for many hours after, and he pulled the table, with its great chessboard still open, carefully into the corner. Around him, a thousand ancient books stood on a hundred wooden shelves, their covers closed, all dark, all quiet. He pulled the door closed behind him, and made his way silently down the great staircase, across the hall, and out of the house.

2

*The jewel*

Fitz woke in the night. At first he wasn't sure where he was; then he recollected this was a sensation he often had, when he woke in the night – in his own bed. He fanned his arm beneath his pillow, feeling for the book he had earlier stowed there. *The Giant's Almanac*. Taking it between his thumb and fingers, he squeezed its covers hard.

*I know where I am.*

He had gone to bed almost immediately after dinner, before the light had faded – what light there was, under the heavy black anvil of clouds striking northwards at dusk from the sea. Clare had been tidying his clothes away into his little chest while he read his book, a book nothing like the old books he usually read. Mr Ahmadi's tall, Victorian volumes were not so much covered as cased in leather, their spines ribbed and tooled with gold, books with two or three title pages framed by elaborate and ornamental architectural designs, hand-coloured like the illustrated plates tipped in at regular intervals between their stately laid sheets. These books he carried back to the cottage not as a conqueror might in triumph his captive, not as a pirate spoil, but like lamps digesting genies. Sacred, splendid, solid, they asked reverence, and Fitz read them with devotion. This book was different. Light, slender and shabby, to its narrow spine a slip of paper had been glued where the title, scrawled in pen, was almost illegible. Inside the covers, if anything, matters were worse – and better. It wasn't a book at all, but a kind of manuscript or journal, every chapter drafted in the same loose, sloping hand. While Clare arranged his few clothes, Fitz hadn't hesitated to take the book to his bed and slide it under his pillow.

'Mr Ahmadi Junior was very angry with me today,' he had told her. He was impatient to tell her everything about what he had heard – or thought he'd heard – and about the man in the woods, and the whispering and –

'Nonsense,' she had answered, her hands full of his three shirts. 'Mr Ahmadi loves you, Jaybird. He's just a little fussy about his father's books.'

'I know. I think he was cross because I saw him at his telescope again.' Mr Ahmadi had a habit of allowing his antique spyglass to drift towards the cottage next door, and Fitz liked to make mischief by implying that the man in the grand house was deeply in love with his impoverished lady neighbour. This little lie, lie though it was, was safer and kinder than going through the real events of the afternoon. It was an unspoken rule of the house that Fitz should never under any circumstances talk with strangers, and any kind of danger made Clare – though she tried to hide it – intensely distressed.

Clare had snorted while wrestling the drawer back into the chest. 'Don't start telling tales.'

31

'You tell so many stories,' Fitz had said. He had already been half asleep, snugly tucked against the warm inner wall of his room.

'I tell so many stories,' Clare had agreed, 'and every one of them is true.'

As he had fallen asleep, Clare had told him his favourite story, the story of how she had come to be his Bibi: how she had been standing by the shore of the sea, weeping, when she had noticed his little basket floating on the waves; how she had plucked him from the water and hung up his little blanket on a gorse bush to dry against the wind; how in the basket she had found by his side a great ruby, the size of her fist, along with a delicate bone-handled brush, and a letter – a letter that revealed he was a little lost prince, a letter that spoke of a deadly enmity between two brothers, the one a just king and the other a villainous usurper, how the villain had triumphed and the good brother had been driven to despair, how the villain had sought the prince's life, how his mother had roused him in the night, and dressed him, and hurried with him wrapped in her arms through the city, to the shore, and how – even as the howl of dogs and the tramping feet of horses had sounded in her desperate ears, even as the searchers had found her and were drawing their swords from their scabbards to cut her head from her shoulders – she had launched his helpless little body on to the waves with a prayer.

And Clare had told him the rest of his favourite story, that his mother, the young queen, had loved to brush his infant head with the soft bristles of the bone-handled brush, that she sent with him the great ruby that was once the king's, and that she had prayed to all the genies of the earth and sea and sky that they would guide and shelter her little boy upon the waves to the waiting arms of his new Bibi. And she told him that a tempest must have swept him across the oceans as if under full sail, and carried him for thousands of miles past strange and terrible coasts, past jungles that trailed their hanging vines longingly into the salt sea, past cliffs of granite and chalk on which the tides crashed and were crumbled, past cities and great trading ports, past nations and creeds and wars and through the lives of millions upon millions, past colonies of seabirds and the nurseries of great whales, through forests of bizarre seaweed and the wrecking and contorted reefs of colourful corals, until he drifted on a clear blue day on to the shore here, in England, not half an hour's walk down the shady lane from Clare's own tiny cottage.

'Am I really a prince?' he had asked her. The questions were part of a litany, a time-honoured ritual that they both loved.

'You are, you are,' Clare had answered, hushing him. 'Such a ruby as your mother sent, as big as your fist and as red as wine, could only be the gift of a king.'

'And where is the little bone-handled brush now, Bibi, that my mother sent with me?'

'It is here, my little prince, it is here,' said Clare, and she had stroked his hair with the five fingers of her white hand, sliding them through the thick strands and tufts of ink, lightly rubbing the delicate skin of his head. And she had sung to him his favourite song, a lullaby which like a great and gaudy jewel always crowned the little ritual of reminiscence.

*'Over the sea, the green, green sea,*
      *beyond the swelling throes,*
*where sun and spray at last agree*
*with gold to pave the skies, and rose,*
      *though the hour be late*
      *still does he wait —*
*he waits there still, my prince, for me.*

*Be gone, you winds, into the west,*
      *be gone, you sailing stars,*
*be gone, bright moon, unto your rest,*
*be gone all longing, strifes and jars:*
      *though the hour be late,*
      *still will he wait,*
*my prince, my peace, and all, my best.*

*Upon an island all of stone,*
      *within a golden hall,*
*there lies my true love's burning throne*
*with pearl and lapis crusted all.*
      *A kingdom he*
      *will give to me*
*when I am his, and he my own.'*

And Clare had kissed him, and said to him the words she had always said to him every night, her arms enclosing him, and the warm green scent of her hair draped round him: 'I will keep you safe forever.'

Now his room lay dark around him, and he was alone. Now, outside the low window, on the other side of the room, the wind was howling in the hedges. He could almost feel it running its rough hands under the slates of the roof above, unsettling them, pushing for a way in. Every few moments it seemed to stamp at the single-paned window, like an impatient visitor, its blunt force knocking the whole casement flat against the wall that held it. The violence of it made him shiver.

Fitz drew the duvet over his head and reached his hand down into the corner, where the bedpost met the wall, for the little lamp he kept hidden there. Mr Ahmadi Senior had given it to him one afternoon, not long before he died, with strict, conspiratorial instructions to conceal it from Clare. *A child should read in the night*, Mr Ahmadi Senior had said. *When your dreams rise to the surface, like silt stirred in the quiet pools between light and light* – that *is when you must read. Read as if your life depended on it.* The torch wasn't the sort of thing you could buy at the shop. It wasn't much of a torch at all. Oblong, about the size of his fist, it lay in a case of tough, leathery hide scribbled about with geometrical figures. The strap from which he hung it, on his bedpost, also fastened this cover; releasing it, the leather case fell away easily to reveal a luminous, perfectly polished, crescent-shaped jewel set in a heavy stone wedge. This rough chunk of stone, blacker than the night, sat solidly wherever you placed it, as chunky as granite. From the milky and phosphorescent jewel that stood a little proud of its surface, almost hanging in the stone as the new moon does above the sea, arose a glittering light. It didn't extend very far, and it wasn't very bright – but here, beneath the huddled covers, close and warm, it was enough to read by.

Fitz hunkered down further beneath the duvet. He didn't want Clare to see any kind of glow from beneath the door, and anyway the wind had carried a chill off the sea, and he was cold. He reached under his pillow again and pulled out his book. Feeling carefully with his fingers, he opened it to the place he had marked, earlier, with an envelope.

*That other letter.* The one he had found on the mat after dinner.

He let the book close, and turned the letter over in his fingers, almost afraid to touch it, handling it as if it were a dangerous thing – maybe dead, maybe not. The return address had immediately caught his attention. It was printed in small, stately capital letters across the back of the envelope: 'KEEP HOUSE, DUNURE, AYRSHIRE'. *Just like the first one.* Even now the words felt to his fingers like little stings, like the taste of a battery, sharp and acidic against his tongue. After the ordeal of the afternoon, he would have torn it up, or burned it without opening it, but for one thing. The first letter was addressed to Clare, in a neat, anonymous hand. This one was different. On its front, in an almost illegible scrawl, only their own address appeared.

*That scrawl.* It was from a different person.

*Not now.* He would open it tomorrow.

Fitz was tucking the unopened envelope back into his book when he heard a sudden, sharp, violent rapping. With practised fingers, he slipped the light back into its leather sheath, then drew the cord tight to seal it. He slid it under his pillow, pulled the duvet close round his neck, and lay flat. No one knocked at this hour. He strained to hear, willing himself to be alert, to catch every sound. Below, just audible above the roar of the sea wind, he thought he could hear Clare stepping on the old floorboards of the cottage's front hallway.

Again: three sharp, angry blows echoed through the house. It sounded like something metal beating against wood.

*The front door.*

Fitz slipped from his bed, keeping his head and body low, leaving the duvet and blankets behind him lying flat and warm. Between his bed and the bedroom door nothing lay in his way, and he knew which floorboards creaked, and which didn't. He stepped only on the latter, picking his way like a cat across snow. The door never latched properly; he had only to draw the handle with a single, fluid tug, and it swung noiselessly open, wide enough for him to slip through into the brighter darkness of the first-floor landing. The light was on downstairs. Fitz could see Clare's feet where she stood at the far end of the hallway, by the entrance. She was slipping the chain across the door.

He had only just taken up his perch, squatting at the top step, when she was suddenly thrown back. She stumbled and nearly fell. She was shouting, something incomprehensible. Fitz grabbed the painted newel. His fingers bored into it. The wind was rocking the house as if it were a ship heaving on swells, as if it were a bough tossing in a gale. He fought his stomach, and his eyes, trying to stay still, to force or wedge himself into safety, to make the rocking stop. He couldn't have said whether he was pulling on the newel post, or pushing it away, but somehow his head was craning lower, and lower, down the staircase, trying to make out what was happening.

Clare had stumbled to her feet and thrown herself at the door. She was shouting again, her frightened voice a descant above the roaring southerly wind that gusted through the opening. Only the chain was holding the door now. Fitz could see through Clare's frantic hands the splintered wood where the lock had been broken. Someone must have forced it open, kicked or battered it down. Someone had to be pushing against it, trying to sever the chain, trying to topple Clare over. In the glare from the ceiling light above, the muscles of her lower calf bulged where she had braced her turned ankle against the floor.

For a long moment, nothing moved: the heavy oak door, poised between opposing forces; Clare, planted against the floor like a strut, pushing and striving with every muscle just to stay still; and Fitz, gripping the newel, contorting his neck, holding his breath, willing his eyes like hands to heave against the door and slam it back into place.

In a lull of the wind a voice came through the opening. It was reedy, strong and low, a man's voice, and angry.

'I said I would come for him. He is my jewel. It is time. It is past time.'

*My jewel. The letter.* Fitz felt his stomach heave.

The man was sticking something through the crack of the opening. It appeared slowly, effortfully, as if he were trying to drill through a stone. Its tip caught the light and Fitz realized it was the silver tip of a staff or cane, hooked and gleaming. It advanced, stiffly prodding, inches from Clare's face. She stared at it, redoubling her strength, trying to drive it back.

*You. The man from the wood.*

Suddenly everything changed. The wind roared through the house as the kitchen door swung open, creating a powerful draught. Fitz tasted salt on the air, mingled with the blood his front teeth had drawn from his lips. Clare fumbled on her feet, dropping almost to her knees. She fought to hold the chain as the front door began to shake, the cane swerving wildly like a pumping lever against the inner wall. Now from the back of the house a heavy tread sounded, beating like a drum against the loose floorboards as a man strode down the hallway. Fitz shrank into the darkness, scarcely tethered to the stairs, scarcely daring to look as the man's body engulfed the light, filled the hallway, as he drove towards the door, reaching out for Clare.

It was Mr Ahmadi.

His strong hands hit the door palms flat, slapping against the oak in perfect percussive unison. The door cracked heavily against the trapped cane. Clare scrambled to her feet and, taking up a position beside her neighbour, she put her shoulder to the wood and heaved.

For an agonizing interval, the intruder seemed to withstand them. The cane swivelled slowly, prising against their combined, blunt weight and force.

Mr Ahmadi braced his foot, and said something Fitz couldn't make out – something fast and commanding, his words as hard as hammers, but unintelligible, as if in another language. With a last push, he forced the door hard against the cane; as it suddenly withdrew, the heavy oak collapsed back into its frame.

'Go,' said Mr Ahmadi.

'I will come for him,' said the voice outside, barely audible over the rushing gale.

*Those five words.*

Fitz's neck suddenly clamped shut. He struggled to breathe.

'I will come again for my jewel.'

A massive chest of drawers stood at the foot of the stairs. Clare and Mr Ahmadi dragged it directly in front of the door. Mr Ahmadi spent a long while prodding and shifting it, until he seemed reluctantly convinced that it would hold against the door. Clare watched him silently. Beneath the light, seen from above, she looked much smaller than she was, and haggard. Fitz was used to thinking of her height and broad frame the way he thought about a light-house, or a sea cliff: strong, unshakeable, capable of withstanding anything. Winds, tides, storms broke on her, and she withstood them without a thought. Now, beside Mr Ahmadi, she seemed instead a little frail, uncertain of her stance as she settled and unsettled her feet in a suppressed agitation. Pulling breaths from his chest as he might a hook from a wound, Fitz tried not to look at her.

When he was satisfied with the position of the chest of drawers, Mr Ahmadi stood awkwardly in front of it, his hands at his sides. Fitz had retreated into shadow at the top of the stairs, silently inching his way back towards his own bedroom door, but he could still see Clare's back, and Mr Ahmadi's feet, and their voices carried easily across the wooden floors. His neck felt damp and cold, and he had started to tremble.

'I have to thank you,' said Clare.

'You don't have to,' said Mr Ahmadi. 'Any neighbour would have done the same. I was in my garden when I heard you shouting. Luckily I had my key to the gate and –'

'Habi.'

He stopped.

'The kitchen door was locked. I locked it myself.'

Fitz listened to the wind outside. It was gusting now in waves. He counted three heavy swells. Each of them broke across the house suddenly, with a roar, then flourished in a long and frittering tympany of tossing branches and trembling leaves.

'It is very late,' said Mr Ahmadi, 'and the story I have to tell is a long one. It will be better to tell it tomorrow.'

'Tell it now,' said Clare.

'Tomorrow.'

'Then I must ask you to leave.' Clare stood back against the wall, and held out her arm to direct Mr Ahmadi to the kitchen. Her voice had sounded severe; her gesture, straight and rigid as metal, was no less so. He passed in front of her, and Fitz heard them both walk quietly to the back door. Nothing further was said, but from the top of the stairs he heard each minute click as Clare shut and locked the door behind her neighbour, and then slid the heavy bolt into place – a bolt they had never, so far as he could remember, used before.

Fitz stole back into his room then, and from his window watched Mr Ahmadi walk the length of the gravel path that ran alongside their cottage garden – the path that connected his own garden gate to the little lane in front of their house. At the gate Mr Ahmadi paused, and he stood there for several minutes, his hand on the gatepost and his head, partly turned, cocked to the wind, as if he were listening. Over the wind, back on the other side of the house, came the sound of a train passing in the night. As it faded, Mr Ahmadi opened the gate, turned to lock it from the other side, and then disappeared beyond the hedge.

Fitz slipped back into his bed, never taking his eyes off the window. After a few minutes, across the trees and the hedge and the garden that lay in its way, the faint gleam of a light illuminated the sliding beads of water where they had begun to run in spasms again down the glass. Fitz thought of Mr Ahmadi standing at his lighted window, watching over the garden, surveying the tossing trees and the tides of wind where they flooded and ebbed under the shifting clouds. Again and again his thoughts traced the steady beam of light that connected their windows, running over it with his eyes as if it were a rope. The wilder the weather became, the tighter this rope stretched, the tauter, and the dizzier he grew watching it.

So fixed had he become on the window, he almost didn't notice when Clare slipped into his room, draped in a blanket and carrying a pillow, and took up her post as a sentry might, at the foot of his bed. Maybe he felt a little warmer. Or maybe he was already asleep.

3

*Michaelmas daisies*

By the time he'd woken in the morning, the sun was already streaming through Fitz's window, and the bare white walls of his room had dazed his smeared and smarting eyes. He had known even before he heard the hoe scratching in the garden below that it was late – that Clare had had her breakfast, and that she had already dressed in her work clothes and set about her chores for the morning. While the sun climbed the wall, Fitz had curled in his bed, reading from Mr Ahmadi's book. Piecing the words with his finger, letting them soak into his tongue, he had read until his back began to ache.

Now he turned over and slipped from the bed. From his window Fitz saw, first, the havoc that the night's strong winds had made among Clare's trellises and beanpoles. Then, as she stood, holding her hip, he saw her, too; she was trying to restore order. When she looked up, he waved. She smiled and briefly struck her familiar farmer pose, which almost made him giggle – but then she went straight back to her work, all muck and twine.

At the foot of the stairs Fitz regarded the chest of drawers where it still stood butted against the front door. He had forgotten. A piece of the lock hung broken from the door frame, and a cool breeze whistled through the gap. Now, by the late-morning light flooding through the glass above the door, the hallway seemed smaller, less consequential; the door had gone back to being just a door; and Fitz noticed the knot in his stomach, which had tightened quickly, begin to subside. Maybe it had been a misunderstanding. Maybe the man had just been troubled, or confused.

His thoughts were interrupted by an abrupt knocking. Fitz started. At first he thought it was Clare, somehow locked out in the garden, asking to be let in, and he set off towards the kitchen. But when the knocking sounded again, he realized with alarm that it was the sound of someone's knuckles beating against glass – the glass of the broad bay window in the cottage's front room. The door to this room stood open, and he picked his way gingerly behind it, to a place from which he could almost see the window.

When he finally dared to look, there was no one there.

He crossed the room, and pushed his way in silence between the table and one of the chairs that stood before the window's broad view. Outside, the short lawn led over a hedge to a little lane. Beyond that a stand of old oaks, mixed with hazel and birch, hid the railway line beyond. Fitz almost didn't notice the little blue car parked behind the hedge.

But he did notice the sudden rustling beneath the window. He was already retreating when a tall, sandy-haired man, his glasses half fallen off his nose, stood up only inches from the windowpane. He was holding three snails in his left hand; with the other, he fixed his glasses, inadvertently wiping little trails of snail slime across the lenses. He was beaming, despite the slime.

'Snails!' he announced.

This was evidently not the intruder with the cane. Fitz smiled back.

'You have slime on your glasses,' he said, speaking in an exaggerated way in order to be understood through the glass, and pointing.

The man crossed his eyes, squinting hard, as if he was lost in deep contemplation of a particularly complicated mathematical puzzle. After a little of this computation, he set the snails on the window sill, drew out the tail of his shirt from beneath his belt, and started to wipe his glasses with it.

'I'm Ned More,' he said. 'You must be –'

'Fitz,' said Fitz. 'Fitzroy, really, but that's a stupid name, so my mum just calls me Fitz.'

Ned finished wiping his glasses and restored them to his nose. Probably his hands had been soiled with dirt from picking up the snails; somehow or other, it had got on his shirt, and his glasses now looked as if he had deliberately spread them with mud. He sighed.

Fitz laughed. 'Wait a minute,' he said, and dipped a napkin in a vase of fresh flowers that was standing on the table. He flipped open the old lock, lifted the sash window, and handed the napkin to the man, who cleaned his glasses again.

'Thanks,' said Ned. 'I've had a long night.'

'Me, too,' said Fitz.

Clare's breakfast still stood on the table – a pot of coffee and a jug of milk, a loaf of bread turned on its side and covered with a cloth, a small plate holding a slab of butter, and the last jar of plum jam from the summer before. Fitz touched the coffee pot and, finding it warm, fetched a cup and saucer from the shelf beside the fire. He poured out the coffee without spilling a drop, and presented it to Ned over the sill.

'Coffee is good after a long night,' he said.

They agreed about a lot of things, beginning with the medicinal properties of coffee. Fitz wasn't quite sure how they got on to the subject of Tamburlaine – something about summer storms coming off the sea like cavalry off the plains at dawn – but within a few minutes they found themselves swapping stories about the difficulty of using elephants to attack fortified positions in the Hindu Kush. Mr Ahmadi's library had taught Fitz much about worlds far away from his own. Ned More was easy to talk to; he seemed to take as much frankly delighted interest in stories about obscure discoveries and forgotten explorations as Fitz himself did. His eyes, a little wet with excitement – or perhaps it was fatigue – pursed with merriment whenever Fitz began to stretch the truth and embellish his encyclopedic enthusiasm for tales with his own imaginative additions.

'Fitz.' It was Clare. She stood in the doorway, wiping the tips of her fingers on the already-muddy bib of her dungarees. She was speaking to her son, but her eyes were on their visitor. He had been holding his empty coffee cup, as he leaned with both elbows upon the window sill, but now he drew himself up, and set the cup down on its saucer.

'There's some coffee left for you, too, Clare,' said Fitz.

He always called her 'Clare' in front of strangers. He fetched a clean cup from the shelf and poured the coffee out neatly.

She thanked him. And then, 'Could you introduce me to your friend, please?'

Fitz understood her tone. He bowed as if he were the leading actor introducing a new play at an old theatre, or a troop of clowns at a circus. 'Dr Ned More,' he said, 'it is my honour to introduce you to Clare Worth.'

'I'm pleased to meet you,' said Ned More, holding out his hand – ludicrously – over the sill and across the wide table. Clare couldn't have reached it without climbing on a chair.

She sipped her lukewarm coffee, letting Ned drop his hand and retreat into a slightly baffled expectation.

Fitz followed her gaze out into the front garden, where her eyes had picked out the car standing in the sunny lane.

'That's not a very surgical parking job, for a doctor,' she said. 'You're all over my Michaelmas daisies.'

The kind-eyed young man was clumsy, too. As he reached in to set down his coffee cup, he turned his head too fast towards the car and knocked it on the window sash above him. Despite the pain, he laughed with embarrassment. 'Oh, I'm so sorry,' he said. 'I was looking for the house number. As you can see, I'm not always a very coordinated sort of person.' He rubbed his head, and walked in a little circle in the garden outside. Fitz noted, as he knew Clare also had noted, that Ned More was certainly trampling the bed of pansies by the window.

'No,' she said. 'Apparently not.'

'I'm not that kind of doctor anyway,' continued Dr More. He now leaned into the casement again, and briefly rested his forehead on his forearms. 'I'm a historian, but I haven't actually taken my degree yet. Well, I'm not properly a historian; I'm more of an archaeologist. Who doesn't do fieldwork. Not yet, anyway. Oh, I don't know what I am.'

'You appear to be lost, for one thing?' ventured Clare. Her coffee was gone, so she tried the pot, and got the last of it. Normally she would have offered the last cup to the guest; Fitz thought it likely she was preoccupied with her trampled pansies.

The young man looked up, his face suddenly a picture of earnestness. 'No,' he answered. 'I'm not lost at all. I've driven all night to get here. I'm found!'

Clare looked at him blankly.

'I hope you received my letter?' tried not-quite-Dr More.

'No,' said Clare. She put down her cup and folded her arms across her chest.

'Yes!' cried Fitz. 'From the castle!'

Fitz ran upstairs and retrieved Mr Ahmadi's book from under his pillow; the unopened envelope still marked his page among the blotted sheets. When he had flown down the stairs and into the front room again, he found Clare still watching Ned More, her arms still folded across her chest in distrust. With considerable ceremony, which he hoped might distract Clare from his role in concealing the letter in the first place, Fitz drew it from the book and presented it to her. 'Madam,' he said.

'That's it!' Ned More was beaming again.

'No,' said she. 'Somehow it appears I hadn't received it. I haven't read it yet, anyway.'

The young man frowned.

Fitz had slid into one of the spindled chairs at the table.

'But since you are here, Dr More, Clare needs the letter no longer. She has the sender on hand, to explain everything to her!'

Clare had turned the letter over in her hands. The sight of the return address had a pronounced effect on her. Tightening her clutch, she narrowed her eyes, and she looked up sharply at their guest in the window.

'Fitz,' said Clare, 'have you finished Mr Ahmadi's book yet?'

'No, Clare, not even close.' He held it up and opened it at the place the envelope had marked – only a few pages in.

Clare wasn't looking. She held Dr More's eye very firmly as she spoke, as if he might suddenly produce a large hook, catch Fitz by the nape of his neck, and heave him out of the room never to be seen again.

'Well, I think you must return it to Mr Ahmadi this morning anyway. Can you please take it back to him now, tell him that I sent you, and ask Cook to make you a cup of chocolate while you choose another.' This was not a question.

'But I don't want a cup of chocolate –'

'But Mr Ahmadi will be very pleased to give you one, when you ask him. Off you go.'

Fitz rolled his eyes at Ned More, then backed out of the room as if from the presence of a monarch, averting his eyes and waving the book flatteringly in the air over his head. He ran down to the kitchen door and opened it – but he didn't go to Mr Ahmadi's. Instead he tiptoed back to the hallway and, just beyond the doorway, stood listening.

'I came for your son,' Ned More was saying.

In an instant all the blood in Fitz's body leaped into his head. His ears and eyes throbbed, and he had to fight to keep from gasping.

'For his sake, I mean. I recognized him at once, the moment I saw him through the window.'

'You recognized him,' said Clare. Fitz knew the shape of her voice; her arms were still crossed, and she would be staring sceptically across them.

'Yes. I don't know how it's possible –' Dr More was scrambling. 'No, it's just too strange to make any sense at all – but it was obvious to me. As plain as ink on paper.'

The thoughts in Fitz's head swirled, flying before him like rooks in a gale.

'Look, I'm bumbling around out here – it's been a long night – but the truth is, I think he is in danger,' said Dr More. 'Very great danger. Perhaps you both are.'

With his fingertips pressed against the wall to try to take the weight off his feet, Fitz inched closer to the front room, until he could just make out Ned More's face through the crack between the door and its frame.

'I think we were in fairly serious danger last night,' retorted Clare. Her voice had cooled; now it clanged like iron.

'Last night –?' Ned seemed puzzled. Or maybe he feigned it.

'Was that you beating at the door?' asked Clare. She didn't usually tolerate sneering, from anyone, but this tone and curl

50

seemed to well up out of her lips neither bidden nor checked. 'Was that you threatening me? Or was it a friend of yours? How many of you are there?'

The colour drained out of Dr More's face. Fitz had read about this in books. It was one of those symbolic and exaggerated descriptions to which writers turned, when they wanted to express a character's dismay or fear. He had always thought it was a bit like one of his embellishments – the sort of thing you wished into possibility, because it made for such a good story. But here, here in the front room of the cottage, it happened. The young man, still bathed from behind in the dappling brilliance of the late-summer sun, turned absolutely, chalky white.

'What kind of danger are we in?' said Clare. Ned's stunned silence had obviously convinced her of his sincerity; where before her tone had been menacing, now she sounded matter-of-fact, honest.

'If Professor Sassani is here,' said Ned, quietly, 'I think your lives could be at risk. I believe he has killed before.'

'Tell me what you know, then,' she said. 'Quickly.' And she sat at the table, putting her hands out in front of her, where Fitz could see them. She had interlaced her fingers, and was gripping them hard, in a tight ball. 'My son will be back soon from the neighbour's, and I don't want him to hear a word of this. Why have you come to my house, and what do you want with him?'

'I'll have to start pretty far back,' he said.

'Then do,' she answered.

There were brushes lying all over the house. Clare liked it that way, because the decision to paint was one that she preferred to take capriciously. She often painted with watercolours in this front room, especially in summer when the light flooded in through the large window, and the garden and lane beyond were deep with thousands of shades of green. No one ever purchased her green paintings, but she did them in their hundreds; some of the oil canvases she had painted five, even six times. Now she took up a delicate brush and dipped it in the jug, and as Ned talked, she painted – thick strokes of deep black – across a scrap of heavy paper that lay handy.

After graduating from university with a degree in Middle Eastern Studies, Ned More said, he had been asked to join an army mission to support archaeologists in Iraq. The Americans had sacked Baghdad, and in the disorder a great number of archaeological treasures had been stolen from the museum there, and from collections and sites across the country. This was a crime. The looters had been organized. They had known what they wanted, and they had taken some of the most valuable and most beautiful objects – statues and carvings, coins and jewels that were two and three thousand years old. European scholars, who knew the collections well, made plans to go to Iraq to support their colleagues in trying to clear up the mess, and to protect what was left. Young More was proposed by the master of his college at Cambridge, a retired diplomat, as an able and obliging sort – and, besides, he was a fluent speaker of Arabic who might prove very helpful to the group. And he was an orphan. And he hadn't yet found a job. Despite the danger, Ned had quickly resolved to go.

*An orphan.*

The expedition was a failure: thwarted by security problems, fighting and violence in many areas of the city, and in the whole country; the archaeologists and historians who had flown out from Paris never even set foot in the capital's National Museum. After two weeks they returned home, disappointed and frustrated. But even though he had not once left the hotel, and notwithstanding the failure of the expedition, something remarkable had happened to Ned – something he had kept entirely secret.

Early one morning, hours before the others had woken or come down to eat, an old man had sat down next to him in the lobby of the hotel. Ned was reading an old newspaper. The old man was grizzled and apparently very poor. He wore only a dirty cotton *thawb*, the long common robe usual in the city. His face was cracked and leathered from the sun, and some of the lines that crossed his cheeks showed dirt. Ned admitted he had at first been worried, and looked to the guards standing duty inside and outside the hotel's front door. But the man behaved like a king fallen on hard times, and he spoke flawless English. What he said, and did, astonished the young English student.

'I have a document in my possession,' he told him, 'that the museum looters are desperate to find. They must not succeed. It reveals a secret, a magical secret, the means to locate a great treasure, carried out of the north by the Persians thousands of years ago, and concealed in a vault, buried in the ground not many miles from this place. The bulk of the treasure is so much gold, so many precious stones, such carving and metalwork as this world has never seen. Thieves have taken some of it already, hundreds of years ago' – he waved his hand in the air, dispensing with this inconsequentiality – 'but where they missed the main chamber of the vault, the bearer of this document will not, and will recover the hoard. But of much greater importance' – and here the old man leaned in further, and spoke in the lightest of whispers – 'it will permit the bearer to find a far greater treasure, even, than that: a set of instructions for the construction of one of the most beautiful machines that the human mind has ever devised. Indeed, it is the work of no human mind.' And then he drew a paper from within his shirt, and pressed it into Ned's hand, and said, 'I am in danger. I may die very soon. Take the manuscript, and go to my brother, Professor Sassani, in Cambridge. Yes, young Mr Edward More, he said, I know you well enough. He is my brother. Tell no one about me, tell no one about this manuscript. Trust no one. But go to Sassani. He will take you on as his student. Study what I have told you. But be careful of my brother; he too is a thief, and a wicked man.'

And then the old man shuffled out, pushing weakly through the hotel's battered door, past the armed soldiers and into the glare and dust.

Ned did as he had instructed: concealed everything from the archaeologists on the mission, and everything from Sassani – who did take him on as a graduate student, and supervised his doctoral dissertation on Near East antiquities. For four years Ned studied the ancient Persian military campaigns in Bithynia, in what is now north-east Turkey, and the various surviving objects they were thought to have brought back with them, which once stuffed the royal treasury in the Persian capital city of Ctesiphon. He was determined to learn everything he could about these artefacts, for he hoped that, one day, he might begin the great work that had been thrust upon him by that nameless and shabby old man in the hotel in Baghdad – the recovery of the lost treasures of the *shāhanshāh*, the Persian king of kings. Meanwhile he kept safe the manuscript he had been given. He could barely read it, the writing was so ancient, and the calligraphy so fluid and ambiguous; but he concluded, through long study, that it was only one scrap of a larger paper, a paper that had been torn in at least two pieces.

At long last, Edward More had finished his doctoral research two months earlier. He had planned to go to Syria, to consult a well-known scholar there whose work he admired. But then three things happened, all on a single day. First, he went to the British Museum in London to see a manuscript, one he had meant to consult during research for his thesis. He recognized it immediately as the lost and torn piece missing from his own document. When he returned to Cambridge that night, however, he found his flat had been burgled, and his own manuscript was gone. He immediately suspected Sassani; but when he called at Sassani's rooms that very night, to challenge him, he found that the professor had suddenly withdrawn from the college and the university, with plans to retire to his country house in Scotland – on the coast of Ayrshire.

'Keep House,' said Clare, looking up from her painting.

'Yes,' said Ned. He put his cup down. 'I drove up there last week. Unannounced. It's a big place, much bigger than I had imagined. The housekeeper said Sassani was abroad, but because I was his student she let me stay the night. It was lucky I did.'

He reached in his pocket and took out a folded piece of newspaper. 'I found this on Sassani's desk,' he said, as he leaned forward through the window to place it on the table before her. It was a photograph on newsprint of an old, bearded man, with some sort of article written beneath – Fitz could barely see it through the crack in the door. 'That was the man who approached me in Baghdad,' said Ned. 'He was found murdered. Someone drove a long knife into him.'

Clare picked up the cutting and turned it over – and there, on the other side, she saw something. She had stopped painting; now she dropped her brush and her hands sprang away from it, as if she had been stung. Even from the door, Fitz could see the heavy drops of black, shed from the brush, soaking blots into the paper in front of her.

'That's the address of my mother's cottage,' Clare said. 'My cottage. Written there. That's our address.'

'Yes,' said Ned. 'The address I was looking for when I ran over your daisies.'

'What's that word beneath it – it's in –'

'*Yāqūt*. It's the Arabic word for ruby.'

*I will return for my jewel. As big as your fist and as red as wine.*

Fitz shuddered; the noise of thrumming in his head was so loud that he was sure they could hear it in the next room.

Clare was thinking, tapping one of her long fingers on the table. 'So you wrote to me from Keep House. That day.'

'Yes,' said Ned. He was staring at her, from the window, with intense interest.

'I see. Professor Sassani's house. And now he is here. I think I should leave. That Fitz and I should leave the cottage right away.'

'If you had opened my letter,' he said, his face breaking into a smile, 'you would have found that that was my suggestion, too. I would like you to come with me to London, to meet a friend of mine there. And I would like you to bring Fitz.'

Clare said nothing.

'Of course, if you think it's best, we can go to the police on the way, and tell them about the threat to your son –'

'Fitz isn't my son,' said Clare. The words were not ones Fitz had ever heard her use; they seemed to spring out of her, unbidden and unlicensed. Her back had gone rigid. From under the green cardigan she was wearing, Fitz could see the sharp edges of her shoulder blades and the hard, round knucklings of her spine. She had slapped the full length of the brush down on the wooden surface of the table; it was hardly less rigid than the tendons in her hand. He saw every individual strand of her thick hair. He saw the minute quiver in her ankle where it suspended the heel of her right foot above the floor. He saw everything about her, about the room – the light – the prints framed on the walls – the books stacked on sagging shelves – the scuffed table – the chipped grandeur of the huge window – the dirt and mould that, try as she might, Clare could never quite scour from the latch – he saw nothing less than everything. Everything. What he would not have given to have seen more, to have heard less.

'She left him with me. His mother.'

*She.*

'I see,' said Ned More, softly.

*Left him.*

57

'No, you don't,' said Clare. 'I might as well be his mother. She gave him to me. I was just a student. My own mother had just died. They showed up on my doorstep.'

'His mother?'

'She left him with me.'

Ned was holding her, but from where he stood Fitz could see well enough, though he could not see her eyes, that they refused to be held.

'His mother?' Ned repeated softly.

'I think she was his mother. She left him.'

*She. She. Left.*

'It's just – I've always half expected someone would come for him. Waiting for that knock on the door. The letter in the post.' Clare suddenly seemed to slump, or to uncoil; all the tautness left her, and her hands dropped to her sides. Almost in a whisper, she added, 'I think he's always half expected it, too.'

Fitz put all these words into his thoughts in just the way that Clare tidied up his room at night, before he slept. He could picture her closing each of the drawers of his little chest, one by one, until the room felt entirely clean again.

'And now, look, here you are,' said Clare.

There was a flash of wings, and a large, heavy bird settled in the side garden; after only an instant it let out a huge and piercing shriek. For the second time that afternoon, Ned More jolted, and cracked his head into the hanging sash above him. On this occasion there was neither embarrassment nor good humour. He simply crumpled on to the sill.

Clare jumped to her feet, knocking over her chair, and rushed forward to help him. She took another cloth napkin and poured water from the vase to dampen it, then held it to his head.

'I'm grateful,' he said, his words muffled by his arm. Fitz thought he was biting his shirtsleeve.

Clare dabbed at his head with the wet cloth, letting the cool water ooze on to his hair until it began to trickle down the nape of his neck. Then she put the cloth by.

It seemed like an age that they stood like that: Ned folded over the sill, Clare staring down at him without seeing him at all, and Fitz, alone in the empty hallway, reduced to little more than a crack in the door.

'You'd better come in,' Clare said.

It shouldn't have, but it caught Fitz by surprise. Surprised to find that his legs moved when he willed it, he almost tripped over his own feet, stumbled, and caught himself silently on the wall. There hardly seemed any point in doubling back to the kitchen door, but he did it anyway; and when Clare turned into the hallway, he tried to make it seem as if he had just walked in.

For her part, she looked the same as always.

Fitz's heart fortressed.

'That was quick,' she said, looking him up and down.

Fitz's face smiled brightly, as bright as the green light that fell on one side of the hedge in the friary garden, a green light that was gold, as golden, or more, than gold.

'You still have the book, you rascal.' Clare pursed her lips theatrically at him, as if she were deciding whether or not to scold him. Her eyes weren't up to the ruse, though, and she let it pass. She looked away. 'Now come and help me with this chest.'

Together they dragged the chest of drawers away from the door, gouging the dark wooden floor despite Fitz's best efforts to lift it. When the front door swung open at last in the still-rising wind, Ned More was standing behind it, holding the wet cloth up to the back of his slightly unsteady head. They got him seated in the armchair in the front room and – partly because there was a new chill beneath the massing clouds, and partly because he had nothing else to do – Fitz made a fire in the stove while Clare put on some tea. He knew just how to do it so that the paper would light the kindling, the kindling the logs, and every last piece of combustible material would flame, glow and ember, consumed into ash. He worked methodically. The silence suited them, but when the fire began to draw and crackle without heat, Fitz distracted Ned with stories about Shapur the Great, one of the old Persian kings Mr Ahmadi Senior had seemed to specialize in.

'Here,' said Fitz. 'Wait a minute.'

*This will surprise you.*

From the cupboard by the fireside he extracted a large wooden case, tough and dark-stained, gleaming with thick shellac. At its corners it had been finished with leather pads, and along its long, top edge a carved handle revealed exquisitely precise craftsmanship. Fitz knew Ned had been indulging him by listening to the stories of his old neighbour; behind the spectacles, behind the eyes, Ned's focus had been on something else – the pain in his head, perhaps, or maybe he was still tired. Fitz's own thoughts had been elsewhere, too. But now, by quick glances as he settled the case, opened it, and began to unpack it, Fitz could tell – and he observed it with satisfaction – that Ned had woken right up.

It was a chessboard. But it wasn't like any other chessboard Ned had ever seen. Fitz watched him take it in. Two feet along each edge, opened, it contained a raised playing surface of sixty-four squares, the dark squares cut from polished obsidian, the lighter foiled with beaten gold. Between the squares a grid of carved wood latticed the board with intricately cut figures, words flowing in all four directions in some ancient script along which Ned couldn't help but trace his fingers. At every corner of this lattice a miniature sapphire, cut round, was set, the wood setting cunningly dimpled to allow the gem proudly to catch and dazzle the ambient light. They glittered in the sunlight now, like stars of day. In a trough carved all the way round the board, the pieces lay couched as if in moulds perfectly shaped to take them, eight along every side. Half had been cut from whole rubies, the other from whole emeralds, and each was set on an ivory base. The workmanship was exquisite, and the board – though evidently ancient, scuffed here and there by centuries of use – in almost pristine condition.

Ned was still trailing his finger across the inscriptions carved into the playing surface, mumbling syllables, when Clare appeared in the doorway, bearing a tray heaped with tea and sandwiches.

'Fitz,' she said, 'aren't you forgetting something?'

He looked up sharply, and Clare motioned to the table with a nod of her temple. Without protest or much attention he set out a few cups and plates from the shelf in the corner. His eyes never left the board where it sat before their guest.

'*Shatranj*,' Ned said. 'The Persian ancestor of chess. Where did you get this?' Without waiting for a reply, he added, 'This writing is Middle Persian – how old is this board? I've never seen its equal. This should be in a museum.'

Fitz smiled. While Clare set down the tea, he began to remove the pieces from their cradles: two greater thrones, each a *shāh*; two lesser thrones, the *wazirs* or counsellors who guided them; four chariots, four elephants, and four horsemen, the full sum of each *shāh*'s council; and sixteen foot soldiers – half in red, the other half in green. He arranged them carefully on the board, each turned precisely according to the training he had received from Mr Ahmadi Senior.

'Battle formation,' he said. They all looked at the board for a few moments, while the fire took up a slow blaze beside them. 'Mr Ahmadi Senior gave me this set, before he died. He was our neighbour. He taught me the ten *tabiyyaat* of the Arab masters, and many famous *mansūbat*.' And then, his speech over, and almost as an afterthought, he added, 'He told me he was given this board by his father, who taught him.'

Ned looked for a second as if he might say something, glanced up at Clare, and then changed his mind. Moving quickly, he removed several pieces from the board, and rearranged others, trying to keep the orientation of the remaining pieces in just those attitudes in which Fitz had originally placed them. 'A *tabiyya* is a fixed opening position,' he said to Clare, as he worked. 'It's a state of the board that two players will recognize has balance, a point of departure from which the true action of the game can commence. And a *mansūba* –' here he paused, and with care disposed two

62

pawns, moved them, then moved them back – 'is a set problem, a kind of riddle.' Ned seemed happy with his changes; he leaned back from the board, holding his hands out over it, as if over a warm flame.

Fitz smiled, again. He had recognized it. 'The greatest *mansūba* of the Persian masters,' he said. 'Dilaram.'

Clare had pulled up a spindled chair, and now seated herself next to Ned. She looked as perplexed by Fitz's arcane knowledge as Ned was. Without withdrawing his eyes from the board, he explained her son's allusion. 'It's said that a rich Persian nobleman, a master at *shatranj* – this was hundreds of years ago, a thousand – he was on an unfortunate day outplayed by his opponent. Distracted by his love for his favourite wife, Dilaram – who sat, as the custom then was, obscured behind a screen – he agreed to ever wilder wagers, even as his opponent manoeuvred him into ever more difficult positions. Before long he found he had staked against his win not only his whole wealth, but his estate, his palace and all his ancestral lands. Unable to continue the game unless he found a further prize to which his opponent would agree, in an evil moment he staked Dilaram herself – and, on the very next move, found himself in a position – just as you see before you – that he considered inescapable. He began to weep.'

'But he was wrong to weep,' said Fitz, proud of his knowledge. 'Because Dilaram had watched every move of the match. Through the screen. And she saw a solution that her husband didn't see. She couldn't advise him – that was against the rules, that would dishonour him – so instead she made up a set of verses, a song that would suggest a move on the board, a move her husband could use to reverse the tide of play, and save them both. She sang the verses

63

to her maids, and her husband – he was already paralysed by the misfortune he thought would destroy them both – and her husband heard her voice, and he understood her meaning, and he evaded the trap laid by his opponent. And so,' Fitz concluded, reciting the story just as it had been told him, 'she saved him, and their love, and all his wealth and estates.'

'It is the most famous *mansūba* in the history of *shatranj*,' said Ned. 'He would have lost everything without her.'

'But it also has a meaning,' Fitz said, excited. 'In order to save his queen, the nobleman had to sacrifice his two chariots, his most valuable pieces. We learn from this *mansūba* that our situation is not always what it seems, and that sometimes when things look their worst, we are at our strongest.'

Clare's mouth was hanging open.

'Is something burning?' asked Ned.

'No,' Clare answered. She hadn't taken her eyes off the board. 'I'm warming the oven for dinner, that's all.'

Fitz was looking out of the window, where smoke appeared to be rising from something in the lane. He cocked his head, and saw through the grey, rising billows a flash of blue: Ned's car.

Then it exploded. They all had time to watch the fireball rise, incredibly slowly, on its pillar of black, choking smoke.

Clare was first to her feet. She leaped for the hallway, and was about to open the front door when someone rapped on it, hard, from the outside. She froze.

Ned and Fitz joined her in the hallway. All three of them stared at the chest of drawers, then at the door, still swinging slightly open, held only by its chain.

And then it came again – three short raps. Fitz's pulse pounded in his neck.

No one knew what to do.

The door flew open, kicked hard, and the heavy oak hit the wall of the hallway with such force that, with a thud and crunch, it stuck fast, embedded in the plaster.

Mr Ahmadi stood on the threshold. He was dressed in a suit and a black riding cape, and wore a tall, formal top hat on his head. This he removed as he stepped forward and offered his hand to Ned.

'Habi Gablani Ahmadi,' he said. 'I am sorry about your car.'

Ned stared vacantly at him, shocked and wrong-footed, while they shook hands. He was obviously confused.

'That is to say, I am sorry I blew it up. It was necessary.'

Ned was obviously still bewildered. They all were. 'Why?' he asked, weakly.

'To distract the man who has set fire to the roof.' He gestured up the stairs, where thick black smoke was starting to curl round the ceiling.

'We have a few minutes at most,' said Mr Ahmadi. 'Take what you need, what you love, but only what you can carry.' He turned to Fitz and placed his hand on his shoulder. 'What you love, little prince, is the *shatranj* board, and the crescent lamp. And my book. Be quick.'

Before Clare could protest, Fitz had sprinted up the stairs and into his room to fetch the lamp where it hung from the inner post of his bed. Keeping low, he retrieved it easily, along with the book from beneath his pillow, without disturbing the thin film of smoke that had already begun to seep from the loft hatch. From the hook behind his door he grabbed his hooded jacket, then dashed down the stairs again, taking them two at a time.

Ned had packed the pieces back into the board, closed it, and carefully stowed it in a cloth bag that Clare usually used for knitting. He held it tight to his chest while he peered down the hallway towards the kitchen, and through its windows to the garden. In answer to a look from Mr Ahmadi, he shook his head.

When Clare rejoined them in the hallway, she was holding a notebook and a sketch pad under one arm, while wrestling to get a raincoat over her other shoulder.

'I called the police,' announced Mr Ahmadi. He still held his top hat in one hand, and was knocking it against the other as if to beat out the seconds while he waited. His eyes moved with purposeful precision across the hallway, into each of the rooms, and up the stairs while he waited. He was assessing everything.

Clare stuttered to a full halt, and with her arm still tangled in her coat reached out with it to pull Fitz close to her. 'The police – they can't –'

'I understand,' answered Mr Ahmadi. He placed his hat on his head. 'That's why I gave you only a few minutes. I want to get you into those trees before they arrive.' He gestured out of the front door. 'You will be gone, but they can take care of the fire. Now, we go.' He stepped lightly to the door and nodded towards the trees across the lane.

'It's our only move.'

The sun had dropped behind the steep hillside down the lane. As they crossed it, skirting the billows of smoke still pouring from the car fire, Fitz noticed a little clutch of Michaelmas daisies, turned into the mud and now coated with ash and soot. The smoke would conceal their flight, but it also blotted the light that would normally be glowing through the narrow gap between the crowns of the tall trees. That was a light he loved, that he knew as surely as his eyes knew day, his skin the summer, his feet his home. As they hurried into the undergrowth and the damp air of ferns and moss brushed against his ankles, Fitz felt distinctly that they had passed from day into a long night.

Before them, the shadows clustered round the trees, cool and quiet. He never looked back.

## 4

## *The shāhanshāh*

Clare put out her hand to help Fitz up. He had tripped on one of the brittle, fallen branches that the winds had shaken from the dry trees. It had been a hot summer after a warm, rainless spring, and dead limbs lay strewn over the floor of the wood. Mr Ahmadi, twenty or thirty metres ahead in the fast-gathering dusk, hadn't broken stride; he seemed to move silently across the dense mat of leaves, sticks, parched moss and yellow grass where the others were struggling – noisily.

'Are you all right, Jaybird?'

Fitz tried to smile.

'Hurry.'

Clare's eyes searched him for a moment, prising at him, but he hardly noticed. As he tumbled forward, the crescent lamp clutched hard in his palm and its strap wound round his fingers, Fitz kept his own eyes on Mr Ahmadi. The gusts blasting through the dense wood – even here – swayed the tall trunks, which seemed to sing in deep moans with the motion, and in fretful, alarming cracks. Ahead, the gusts of wind played tricks with the ruffling cut of Mr Ahmadi's heavy cape, swirling through it as if, having made the trees their orchestra, they would have Mr Ahmadi for their dancer. The even glide of his hat through the leaning trees Fitz found mesmerizing, and on and on, pace after pace, he followed him as if drawn by a thread, or upon a track.

They called this the Bellman's Wood. Fitz knew every stump of it. Long after it had become his favourite haunt, long after he had learned to recognize its spring flowers by their January leaves, its secret mosses and lichens in their hundreds, and its occasional, spectacular summer ferns – long after all that, an older girl from the village had told him that it was named for the old undertaker, hundreds of years dead, who still stalked it. She told Fitz she had seen him: a figure with a cape and a tall hat, who floated through the trees searching for dead men to drag off to their graves. Fitz had scoffed and told the girl he didn't believe a word of it; but he never lingered in the wood, after, in the way that once he had.

Now, following Mr Ahmadi, he wasn't sure if he believed her or not. After fifteen or twenty minutes of plunging through sometimes thick growth, the air up ahead seemed to lighten, and Mr Ahmadi began to dip out of sight, then disappeared altogether. Fitz knew that they were coming to the edge of the wood, to a gully where the train ran north and east towards London. He had watched it sometimes at the place where it vanished from view, into a long, dark tunnel. He had never seen this tunnel's other side, and regarded its brick arch with respect and suspicion, as if perhaps it were not only the entrance to a tunnel, but to something stranger, and more permanent.

Clare caught him up, latching on to his shoulder. Ned was just behind her, heaving a little with the difficulty of walking so far, so fast, with so little falling over.

From behind them, very far off, came the sound of sirens.

'Where is he going?' Clare asked.

'To the train, I think,' said Fitz. 'There's a tunnel just up to the right, past that big oak.'

At the edge of the wood a single, massive oak stood sentry on an embankment above the railway line. A little group of yews around it gave off a sticky resin as they pushed through the low boughs.

Mr Ahmadi was standing down the line and just out of earshot, beside the entrance to the tunnel. His face bore no expression at all. Haggard and stubbled, his cheeks would, had they been fuller, have sagged; his eyes looked as remote as the moon, and as baleful, as if they had gazed on a secret so sad that no common sight could ever content them again. But as the three of them broke out on to the embankment, and began to run towards him, his face changed.

'Come quickly,' he called, and beckoned to them with animated urgency. 'The next train is due in less than twenty minutes,' he said, as they reached him, heaving for breath. 'We may not have time.'

'Time for what?' Ned asked.

Mr Ahmadi looked at him with incomprehension. 'Time to get through the tunnel.' And then he turned on his heel and disappeared into the darkness.

Fitz didn't wait for permission, and once in the tunnel, he could hardly have turned back. Violent in the gully outside, the wind was amplified by the constricted space, and it drove him on, fast, as his eyes adjusted to the near darkness. The vault above was punctuated at regular intervals by weak lamps, the light from which seemed to dissipate or hang in the gloom, and hardly reached the single track below. Fitz rushed along the verge where the way was clear, the tough but regular gravel a relief to his feet after the sharp, uneven ground of the wood. Mr Ahmadi, ahead, drifted in and out of visibility like a day-thought glimpsed in a dream, occasional streaking flashes of his white cuffs the only marker of his black figure in a deeper shade.

When Fitz finally caught up, he nearly collided with him. Judging from the distant, pale glow hanging beyond a bend ahead, they hadn't come halfway. Mr Ahmadi had stopped before a place in the tunnel wall where even in the low light the bricks looked fresher, the mortar whiter. He had an iron stake in his hand, thick and pointed, with which he had begun to batter the bricks. To Fitz's surprise, they seemed to crumble easily, and in only a few moments he had opened a generous hole.

'Help me,' he said.

Together they pulled the bricks from the wall, leaving an opening as broad as a barn door. Within, Fitz could see only dark, from which protruded the low gleam of a highly varnished wooden bar. At its head, only inches away, was fixed a large, iron ring, engraved with a circle of wildly writhing snakes. All round the ring, too, as if the snakes cut into the metal had escaped from their iron beds, wrought serpentine forms coiled and lashed into the air. The menacing energy of their ferrified jaws and near-quivering tails struck Fitz like a bite.

By the time Clare and Ned had caught up to them, Mr Ahmadi – drawing on the iron ring – had pulled out what looked like a cross between an old-fashioned carriage and an antique wooden sleigh. He drew it directly on to the tracks, aligning its metal wheels on each side with the rails, and then – working a crank set low at the vehicle's front – locked the wheels into the track. He ducked back into the darkness, and returned in seconds with a heavy pile of folded black cloth in one arm, and in his other hand a long wooden pole, the sort of rod you might use, Fitz thought, if you wanted to go fishing for a whale. Mr Ahmadi handed the cloth to Clare while he fixed the rod at the back of the gig, driving it into a socket and then securing it with two metal pins that stood near. Only then did Fitz notice that the pole was connected to the cloth by a myriad thin, strong cords.

*Halyards.*

'Get in,' said Mr Ahmadi, gesturing as a magician might, to a woman about to be sawn in half.

'Where are you taking us?' asked Clare. Her voice half demanded, half beseeched.

'Away from them,' said Mr Ahmadi, with his eyes on the wood at the opening of the tunnel.

Behind them, shifting shadows jostled against one another in the day's last, grey light. A trick of perspective made them seem impossibly tall and sinuous. Fitz couldn't count them – there were too many, it was too dark, or both. He couldn't count them; he could hardly see them; but he could hear them.

*Whispering. Hushing.*

'Who are they, and why are they chasing us?'

'They're called Wispers,' answered Mr Ahmadi. He offered his hand to Clare to help her step up into the gig. 'They're scouts, spies. I'm not sure why they're after you. But if we don't move – and quickly – you'll have to ask them yourself.'

Clare took his hand and stepped into the gig. Ned followed, leaping on to its wooden floor, then settling uneasily on its intricately carved, rolled wooden bench. As the gig shifted beneath him on the track, he grabbed an ornate knob beside him, and grimaced.

The wind was already whipping at the corners of the cloth where it lay in Clare's arms. Fitz, perhaps alone among them, could see what was about to happen. He glanced again at the Wispers, at their silent, elongated figures loping down the track towards them. Some dread he couldn't have explained pushed him back against the tunnel wall – until the moment Mr Ahmadi took him under the arms and lifted him into the gig to sit between Clare and Ned.

'Don't worry, little prince,' he said in Fitz's ear. 'I have been dancing with the snakes since before you were born.'

The hard oak bench cracked against his arching shoulders, and Fitz crumpled. Mr Ahmadi hauled up on the wooden bar at the front of the gig, until it had risen, like a lever, to stand upright. As it shifted into place, the whole gig seemed to condense or go rigid, the way a cloud of bees will of a sudden swarm. The iron ring at the bar's end now hung a few feet away, but level with Fitz's gaze; in the eyes of its eight wrought-iron snakes, dark jewels were set that, like covered fires, seemed to smoke and promise burning.

73

He shuddered. Somewhere in the distance, a train whistled.

Mr Ahmadi leaped in to stand before them. He stared full into their faces, his expression a wild blank. 'Hold on to whatever you can,' he said. In a single fluid motion, he reached for the cloth where it sat in Clare's lap and, hurling it like a discus as he spun forward, unfolded it into the accelerating, tumbling, hungry wind that roared down the tunnel. It soared and spread against the dim light before them, until with a barbaric snap that pierced into the very base of Fitz's spine, the sailcloth flexed into its full figure, and the carriage lurched ahead. Mr Ahmadi gripped the iron ring, and leaned back until the top of his black hat, a sleek silk oval, hung before Fitz like a black moon.

It was at that moment that, as if a thought remembered in the nick of time, in a blur of fur and muscle Aslan – bounding beside the accelerating gig – sprang on the boards beneath Fitz's feet. His momentum, hurtling forward, would have bowled his big front shoulders directly into Mr Ahmadi's legs, had his hindquarters not caught on the gig's edge and braked him. Scrabbling as the wind shot them forward, the big dog strained with every claw, tearing at the air with his bulging eyes. Fitz lunged at him with a cry, and arms, and hands, grabbing at his fur, his flesh, his legs, somehow hauling on his tail until, with a sound like a stifled howl, he was in.

The next few minutes passed in a rush. Ignorant of the commotion behind him, Mr Ahmadi drove the gig down the tracks as if before a hurricane blast, ever faster, ever wilder. The buffeting air that had smacked and pummelled them began, as the gig picked up pace, to howl in its creaking sail;

through it all Mr Ahmadi, erect and unbowed, held his hat high, his only concession to the torrents of wind his unrelenting, morbid grip on the iron ring before him. Peering forward in terror over the nape of Aslan's neck, Fitz soon realized that each of the eight snakes dancing off the iron ring was a lever or winch, and each one controlled one of the eight halyards by which the huge spinnaker was tethered. As Mr Ahmadi adjusted them to respond to the turbulent gusts, he studied the telltale ripples and dimples that appeared and vanished as quickly in the face of the sail before him. From instant to instant his hands struck the outer surface of the ring, darting first to one, then to another of the long, sinuous iron heads, racing to slacken or tighten one or another of the halyards by twisting here, or releasing pressure there. Always the black face of the sail, flung out pregnant and swollen before them, stood featureless, taut, tight as a drum.

Then, suddenly, they burst out of the tunnel. Fitz clutched Aslan hard by the haunches and pulled him even nearer; Clare held him, in turn, by both shoulders as she braced her feet on a wooden bar that ran low round the side of the gig. The motion of the wheels on the tracks seemed to change in the open air; where before the tunnel running with bricks had rushed around them, the sail billowing within inches of its walls, and every moment a deafening alarm, now they seemed to be flying, almost suspended, in a huge and noiseless expanse. Night was falling, and the sky vaulted among its evening lights, russet bars crowding behind them, and before them the heavy pall already part-spangled with stars of night.

'What is this thing?' Ned called, trying to get Mr Ahmadi's attention.

'I call it a hopper,' called back its pilot, without turning.

Ned braced his arm on the hopper's side. A stand of evergreens was approaching on the right, beyond open pastures; he stared at it, turning their impossible speed over and over in his mind.

'Why?'

This time Mr Ahmadi let go one of his hands from the iron ring, and unfolded his body backwards, so that, like a dancer on the arm of the straining machine, he was for an instant extended.

'I fervently hope,' he shouted against the blast of air, 'that I will need neither to tell you, nor to demonstrate.'

For a long while they watched the countryside pour by them, night gathering and settling in its turns and folds, a little deeper with every bend. The wind stayed almost right behind them while they shot on before, their speed hardly flagging even as they drew up the long, rolling land swells, hardly gaining as they cascaded down the gentle slopes beyond. From time to time one or other of the sail's corded extremities rippled and began to fold; then Mr Ahmadi drew the snake-headed winch from its socket, and holding the wayward halyard limp and fluttering at the length of his arm, whipped it like a lash in the air, beating and again beating the sail until – sometimes with the greatest reluctance, like a mule cudgelled into service – it took the wind again, and flew.

Moments after they sped howling past a deserted station platform in a little town, the track came round a bend and suddenly joined a second, then a third track – all three of them running in parallel. Mr Ahmadi spun to face them.

'I'm going to need your help,' he shouted. Aslan barked, and Mr Ahmadi shot him a scowl, as if noticing for the first time that he was there. 'There's a low bridge coming – in a minute, or less. When I tell you, all of you lean to the right – hard.'

As they neared the bridge, the problem was obvious: the pole set at the rear of the gig, from which the spinnaker flew, would be too tall to clear the underpass. A lump began to rise into Fitz's throat, as he realized just how fast they were hurtling down the track; then he understood that the lump was his stomach.

'Now!' cried Mr Ahmadi, and he dropped to the floor of the gig to release the handle that locked the wheels. Clare tumbled on to Fitz, and Fitz on to Ned, lurching sideways with Aslan in his arms, and the whole of the buggy seemed to topple rightward for a long, sickening arc of a moment, accompanied by the squeal of metal ripping and shearing against metal. Just as they passed under the bridge, clearing its squared span by inches, Mr Ahmadi shouted again, and all three of them, dragging the dog, pushed back against the lean, climbing upward until the gig crashed down again on the rails, locking into place.

Mr Ahmadi bellowed into the wind before them, iron snakes shaking in his hands. To Fitz's terrified eyes, with the black sail unfurled before him and the light of the moon glazing his silhouette from top to toe, he seemed an otherworldly form, a prophet or shaman of exorbitant power sent to conduct them into unintelligible wonders. And yet, as the gig settled again into its regular carriage, Ned and Clare looked relieved almost beyond words; for the first time since they had climbed aboard in the tunnel, Ned relaxed enough to take a look around.

77

'Habi,' he said. Mr Ahmadi didn't hear him. 'Habi! Habi!'

He didn't need to point. The moment Mr Ahmadi turned, he saw the train bearing down on them from behind. The driver must have seen them, too, for the train – now very near, and gaining with every second – let out a piercing whistle.

'Again!' called Mr Ahmadi, over his shoulder, and he took the top two halyards into his hands, shaking their snakes at the sky. At the signal given, he again swooped down to release the wheels just as his three passengers rolled to the right; but this time he sprang to his feet and hauled dramatically on the upper stays, changing the angle of the envelope so that the wind began to lift the gig straight into the air. For the space of one terrifying instant Fitz was sure that the whole of the carriage – which shuddered as it rose – would flip. But then Ned heaved upward, taking Fitz and Aslan into his enormous embrace as he shifted and steadied their weight, and the gig crashed sideways, directly on to the adjacent track. It skidded slightly, jolted, and buckled, then slid with a grinding of metal into its groove just as Mr Ahmadi locked the wheels again.

Seconds later, the train slipped past them on the right side, an eruption and riot of light and sound. Clare pulled Fitz to her and held him, sobbing into his mass of dark hair. Over her shoulder as the train screamed past, Fitz watched the big empty squares of the lighted windows as they flicked by, frame after frame, like the film of an old projector reeling from the machine.

*It's empty. The train is empty.*

It wasn't quite true. He had seen the driver clearly enough: a woman with a brown bob, dressed in a suit of blue, and over that a brilliant red cloak. Her gaze had been fixed on the track dead ahead, with something – strange enough that Fitz doubted his own eyes, doubted the distance, doubted the jumbling speed and the light – something like a smile playing at the corner of her cheek.

'That's why I call it a hopper,' said Mr Ahmadi, to no one.

That was to be the last of their adventures on the gig. For a time, through an uncannily empty gloom they sped, past silent stations with their stifled lights looming overhead, through still villages behind drawn curtains, between deserted, endless yards piled high with shadows. As it drew into the outskirts of London the direction of the line altered, and Mr Ahmadi had to trim the sail. For a while the buggy rolled on, more sedately than before, between hedges and houses and walls and – at last – the intermittent tunnels of the capital's perimeter, but the sail didn't begin to give out, at last, until they had reached almost the centre of the city. Here, as the cloth sagged and ruffled, beside an unmarked and unlit service platform at the edge of a desolate waste of tracks that ran away as far as Fitz's eye could see, Mr Ahmadi pulled the gig up and to a final stop. In a great sweeping of his arms he drew the sailcloth, while it still fluttered windily in the air, through the ring, and folded it as it came.

Working fast, Mr Ahmadi stowed the gig in thick bushes growing at the side of the tracks, then – vaulting easily on to the platform – rejoined the little huddle of his shaken passengers. The wind still licked at his cape, and his thick black hair, raked this way and that by its gusts, revealed in his face a complicated tangle of fatigue, fear, exhilaration, intelligence and brooding. 'I will come for it when the wind changes,' he said. 'For now, we go down.' He cocked his head to a stairway at the end of the platform, which disappeared into the ground.

The stench from the stairs hit before they reached them; as they descended, it only grew stronger. Rotting, festering leaves had been blown by the wind into small clumps in the corner of every tread. Soaked with rain, or worse, they stained the air with must and the promise of vermin. Broken lights hung from the sloped ceiling, among flaking paint and crumbling concrete. Aslan stumbled, and Fitz caught him by the collar.

'The lamp,' said Mr Ahmadi. He had drawn Fitz with him to the front of their orderly file. Fitz looked down at his hand, as if it were a landscape on the other end of a telescope, and was surprised to find that he still had the lamp-strap wound about his left wrist, and that the lamp still sat snug in his palm. As he unbound it from his locked grasp, his fingers ached in the tough, swollen grooves where he had almost entirely cut off his circulation. But the crescent pearl of the lamp, when unwrapped, shone brightly enough to show them where they were going – down another steep flight, and on to a platform that ran along underground tracks. As they neared its end, Mr Ahmadi turned and stopped them.

'This is a tube service line. The platform will continue on a narrow ledge for another few hundred metres; after that, we're going to have to walk on the tracks. Keep to the right and do exactly what I do. There won't be any trains on this part of the line, not tonight. It will take about a quarter of an hour.' Mr Ahmadi made as if to turn, but saw the question, hot and severe, in Clare's eyes. 'He's safer down here than he is up there,' said Mr Ahmadi.

At the end of the platform, a little ledge about a foot in breadth continued alongside the track. Single file, Mr Ahmadi still in the lead and Fitz behind him with the lamp, they carried on into the darkness. After a while the ledge sloped down to track level, and the ground became rougher, dirtier, at times studded with huge bolts and concrete slabs that seemed designed for no other purpose than to knock, bruise and scrape them as they passed. Once or twice Fitz thought he noticed in the corner of his eye a flash or sudden darting movement, as of eyes or the quick flick of a tail, but he kept his feet moving forward, right in Mr Ahmadi's footsteps, one tread after another; not even Aslan, usually ready to chase anything that twitched, was distracted. For ten or twelve minutes, for longer, they trudged beside the tracks, once or twice merging with, then dividing from, other lines. The metal rails seemed to slope ever downward, towards a rumbling sound that came intermittently and afar off from beneath their feet.

Fitz had counted their way past four dirty arches of sooted brick when Mr Ahmadi stopped abruptly in front of a heavy steel door. They crushed together in the darkness, like half a worm, thrashing. 'Help me,' said Mr Ahmadi to Ned, and the two men pushed their shoulders against the metal until with a heavy and grating reluctance it shifted inward – just far enough to allow them all to slip through. They climbed an interminable circling staircase, this one clean, well-lit and clinical. It issued through a small service lobby on to a broad, dark street.

Fitz had never seen a city, and was completely unprepared for the rushing air, the moving lights, the knots of people, and the tall buildings that suddenly surrounded them. But he had hardly a second to take it in, for Mr Ahmadi had already begun to rush them across the broad road, down to a corner where black cars coasted through green lights, and into a large walled park edged with dense shrubs and canopied with trees. 'Go, go,' he urged, nearly pushing them through the gates of the park – first Clare, then Ned, and last of all Fitz – as he scanned the surrounding streets and their traffic of pedestrians, buses and cabs.

The park muted the enormity and clamorous bustle of the city, and Fitz tried to match his stride to Ned's as his leather heels rang out on the paved path that ran diagonally through the park's centre. Iron benches were dotted along the lanterned ways, but they sat empty, deserted like the park as a whole – with the exception of a small group of men laid out and sleeping, surrounded by cardboard boxes, round a dry fountain at the park's very centre.

As they passed, one of these men jumped to his feet and walked directly up to Ned. Ned stopped. The man held out his hand, smiling. Half his teeth were gold that glittered beneath the lights almost as brightly as the grease in his matted, dark hair. Despite the heat he was wearing a heavy padded coat with a furred hood over what looked like thick canvas trousers and an even coarser shirt. He looked dirty. Ned tried to circle round him, holding his arm back to ward off Clare and Fitz, but the man dodged with him at every step, holding his pace and his gaze – and always smiling.

Still ten or twenty metres behind them, Mr Ahmadi had stepped up his pace to catch them. Fitz watched him anxiously.

'Look,' said Ned to the man. 'We don't –'

Aslan trotted up, sat in front of the great, hooded man, and barked.

'Shut up, Aslan, old mate,' he said, and laid his huge hand like a mitt on the dog's eager head, scuffling him hard on his neck between the ears. Aslan was evidently delighted. 'We've got quiet work to do.'

By the time Mr Ahmadi reached them, the other three men were on their feet, stretching and groaning but in good humour.

'Habi,' said the big man who was their leader, 'you're useless at introductions.'

'We've not met proper–' began Ned More.

But Mr Ahmadi cut him off. 'Arwan Abramanian, Ned More, Clare Worth,' said Mr Ahmadi. To Ned he added, 'Behind you are Athos, Porthos and Aramis – but deal with Arwan. You'll get the most English out of him.'

'And the most sense,' said Arwan, laughing.

Even his laugh, thought Fitz, was too large.

'I want to get out of the open,' said Mr Ahmadi. He was standing off from the little group. His gaze still shifted round the park, watching the paths, checking the trees in succession, as if he expected someone to dart out from behind one of them at any second.

Arwan stopped laughing. 'Are you taking the boy in?' he asked. Fitz shrank instinctively against Clare's side. Mr Ahmadi nodded.

'Then step inside my office.' Walking quickly, Arwan led them to the far corner of the park, where a boarded doorway blocked the entrance to a disused toilet. He reached his huge hand through a gap in the wood, up to the elbow, and released some sort of catch; the whole barrier swung open easily. As Arwan turned to usher them in, Fitz realized that Mr Ahmadi was not with them.

Lingering by the fountain, not far from the piles of cardboard boxes draped with quilts and sleeping bags, he stood, legs apart, his head cocked to one shoulder, deep in concentration. Before him in the air his hands danced, fingers seeming to pick from the darkness with extraordinary agility minute motes – or not to pick them, but to shift and move them, as if he were rearranging in the raked light of the lamp above him the little dust that swirled before his rapt and attentive gaze.

'What is he doing?' Clare asked Arwan.

'Thinking,' said Arwan. He frowned.

Suddenly Mr Ahmadi looked up. His eyes shot across the space between them as if he had loosed them from a sling, and Fitz felt them hit as hard.

'He's here,' he said. Softly though he spoke, his voice seemed to carry, and Fitz realized that the noise of the streets around them – muffled before by the lush foliage of shrubs and trees, by the distance and darkness, but still there, a comfortable cocoon – had died completely away.

'Who?' said Ned. 'Who does he mean?'

But Mr Ahmadi had begun to sprint towards the little hut. Head inclined so that the top of his hat tipped towards them, his black cape fanning behind as he ran, the cloth spread dark against the wider cloth of the darkness, he seemed to fly at them.

As Arwan muscled him into the shadows of the little building, from the corner of his eye Fitz thought he glimpsed wide wings soaring above the park, thought he saw forms shifting in the thick undergrowth to every side, thought he caught on the hush of the night a quiet descant of whispering.

That, or something, had spooked Aslan. Threading Fitz's legs as a rope through a needle he barrelled into the light, growling and baring his teeth. In all their years of playing Fitz had never seen the dog angry in earnest, and he shrank behind the thick board of the door – but only to a place where, through the rough-cut hole that Arwan had used for a handle, he could still see.

Mr Ahmadi had almost reached them. Now turned, he backed towards the hut, towards Arwan whose stance – set and heavy as a fighter expecting the first punch – promised cover. Out in front, Aslan advanced on a near tree, snarling, his thick coat of golden fur transformed into the bristling hide of a boar. He seemed to know something that the skittering eyes of Mr Ahmadi had not yet determined, and by the rigid line of his tail Fitz read the danger before the men had seen it.

Fitz never saw the arm that threw the knife. He was aware only of a flash as its blade sliced through the torchlight, and of the heavy spring of the coiled dog as Aslan leaped – impossibly high – into the night air.

Mr Ahmadi hadn't had time to twitch, much less avoid the blade, and the knife would have sunk deep into his neck if it hadn't sunk, instead, into Aslan's. Before any of them understood what had happened, the dog dropped from the air on to the unyielding ground. Fitz knew from the way the body fell, already as heavy and formless as a wet rag, already as silent as the earth against which his head slumped without rebound, that Aslan was dead.

Fitz's eyes gagged. Where his hands gripped the heavy, rotting board of the door he retched with anger and pain, every joint in his arms and hands and fingers no joint, but breaking, convulsing, tearing from the inside the very buckles by which he stood, and held, and watched.

*And watched.*

Where he drew the knife from Aslan's neck, Mr Ahmadi's hands were stained dark with blood.

*And watched.*

A spasm ripped through the dead dog and from its blood-curded throat a cry through the night. Mr Ahmadi dropped the heavy blade against the grass, kneeled, and sank his fingers into the dog's flank and fur, kneading it back into stillness. Through the gap in the door, alone of those inside the little hut, Fitz watched the man ease the dog away.

*And watched.*

'Habi,' said Arwan. He had gathered Aslan in his arms, and laid him by a tree. 'Habi.'

No words more – time must have passed – the men had moved – Fitz felt the door push haltingly against the stiff pain in his arms – he felt nothing but – Clare's hand against his forehead drawing him towards her – he remembered he had gasped.

Space was suddenly tight inside the toilet, suddenly bright. By the light of Arwan's torch he saw for the first time the little room's walls, which had been papered throughout with huge sheets scrawled over with minute equations. These equations, studded with numbers and operators and strange symbols he had never seen, gathered in clumps, and were connected by a complex network of lines and arrows. He watched them, fixing on them, pulling himself back to focus. They had been written and rewritten, revised and developed in different colours of ink, but always in the same, small, feverish writing.

Arwan and Mr Ahmadi shoved their shoulders against the stubborn door, jamming it shut; Fitz kept staring at the numbers flowing and clotting in the shadows as if they might explain something, as if they might account for the hollow thud of his friend against the ground, or the hollow thud of his heart against his ribs. On and on they went, like shoulders against wood, inscrutable and inconclusive. Ned and Clare, pressed against the wall, were craning their necks to see over Mr Ahmadi's shoulder. Clare's eyes stood wide, white in the pale wash of equations. She had seen Mr Ahmadi's hands where he was wiping them on a rag.

Fitz noticed the bright edge of the torchlight against the numbers. He noticed Arwan's thick, resonant breath. He noticed a feeling like metal against his neck. He noticed anger and sorrow in his fingertips, in the tight ball of his foot above his toes.

The door was shut. Mr Ahmadi turned.

'Today, this is Arwan's office,' he said. His voice was flat, steady, brittle as a reed. 'He is a mathematician.'

Mr Ahmadi regarded them all for a moment: Ned, who was still scanning the walls with curiosity and surprise; Clare, who had backed against a sink with Fitz's hand squeezed between both of hers, and pressed to her tight stomach; and Fitz himself, his thoughts as blank as Mr Ahmadi's face. 'Arwan is always hunting for prime numbers. But we're not here for mathematics. I have to get you into the museum,' he said.

Ned's eyes started, then widened.

'I have a friend there,' he said. 'He's expecting us – I was going to bring Clare this afternoon –'

Mr Ahmadi raised his hand. 'I know. Unfortunately, your friend Professor Farzan is shortly going to be arrested.'

Ned's lips moved, and he seemed to be squinting, but nothing came out of his mouth. Eventually, with great effort, he managed to say, 'Why?'

'For abetting thieves in the theft of a priceless ancient artefact.'

'Professor Farzan is an eminent scholar,' snapped Ned, angrily. 'He's never helped a thief in his life.'

Clare put her hand on his arm.

'No, not yet,' said Mr Ahmadi. 'Follow me. I'm afraid I have to ask you to put up with one more difficult climb.'

From outside they heard the sound of raised voices. Arwan blew air out of his pursed lips in a sigh. 'The boys will take care of it,' he said. 'For now. You must hurry.'

He pushed them all back into a corner, then lifted a corrugated metal sheet from the floor. Beneath it gaped a hole, from within which, by the light of his torch, they could see the rungs of a ladder. A heat and stench rose from within, warm air and something like leaf mould. Arwan got his legs into the void and on to the rungs, then started down, hand over hand.

'Now you,' said Mr Ahmadi to Clare. 'I'll bring the boy.'

Ned followed, then Fitz, and Mr Ahmadi above him. They made slow progress in the dark, descending a narrow and airless square shaft with rusted metal on every side. The rungs under Fitz's hands, cool and wet to the touch, had sharp edges that seemed to cut into the insides of his knuckles, so that every step quickly became an agony. For three or four minutes they climbed in the dark, labouring to breathe, until the shaft gave out into a low, hot tunnel. Pipes ran down its ceiling, and thick electrical cords.

'Run,' said Arwan, shoving Fitz to the front and handing him the torch.

Fitz ran. The utility tunnel lay straight for about a hundred metres, then dog-legged to the left and right, then ran straight again. Fitz could hear the others pounding behind him, trying to keep up with the light. Passing the powdered ruins of a rudimentary wall, he came into a broader passage; here the ceiling rose, and the pipes, lagged, radiated less heat. At the end of the passage, a sharp turn opened on to a metal gate, locked with a heavy chain. Fitz almost crashed into it. He held the bars of the gate with his fists.

For the first time that night, as he heaved for breath through his burning lungs, he felt tired.

Behind him the others arrived, panting, and at last Arwan – whose loping, lumbering strides almost made running unnecessary. They made way for him as he drew a little key from his coat pocket and opened the padlock.

'So,' he said, turning. 'I will leave you here.' He made to leave.

'Arwan,' said Mr Ahmadi. 'Tell her I'm on my way.'

The big man nodded – a heavy, serious motion of his massive, bearded head.

They watched the reflected light from Arwan's torch fade as his footsteps also faded, one after the other, down the far passage. In the darkness their own breathing mingled for a few moments before Fitz reached for his lamp.

Mr Ahmadi put a hand to his arm. 'No,' he said. 'Wait.'

Sure enough, before much longer a door opened somewhere in the distance, and they heard a new sound of footsteps approaching – coming closer, fading, then closer again – then a click, and a droning, buzzing noise heralded the yellow dawning of a glowing electrical light that, as it brightened, revealed a large room beyond the metal gate.

A tall, bearded man appeared suddenly from the side. Dressed in an oversized tweed jacket, corduroy trousers and brogues, and with one pair of glasses on his weathered nose and another hanging from a loop of twine round his neck, he looked as if he had just stood up from his carrel in a dusty library crammed with illegible manuscripts. He set his hand to the gate, and pulled it open with all the force of his large frame, dragging the chain noisily through the bars. He put out his hand.

'Habi, Ned,' he said to each of them in turn, shaking their hands with firm warmth. 'Clare,' he added, turning to her, and putting out his hand. 'I'm Farzan. Welcome to the British Museum.'

The adults stepped lightly through the gate. Fitz alone had stepped back – back the way a thing might go back in its box. He was retreating into the passage – until Farzan caught his gaze, and he stopped.

The Professor looked at him for a long while, with a tightening of his gaze gently pinning the boy in his place, as if he were a specimen being fixed in a display case. One corner of his mouth turned up in a smile as he recognized where Fitz himself had returned his gaze – and he followed it.

There, in the centre of the room, alone and now bathed in yellow light, stood the statue of a boy, full size, cast in bronze. In places green and stained by the centuries, in other places shining with the smooth polish of long handling, the figure was obviously ancient. He stood legs parted with one arm by his side, the other extended as if to beckon or summon someone. Over his eyes, now blank, seemed to hang the shadow of a brightness to which his parted lips also spoke, as if he were on the cusp of an invitation or command, some articulate regality that, for all his slender proportions, his whole form communicated. He wore a rough tunic over trousers, and round his neck hung a massive chain of something like gems, or metalwork. A graceful coronet on his head suggested crenellations. But none of this held Fitz's attention.

What had seized his attention, what dazzled and terrified him, was that the boy was familiar to him in every detail, from the shape of his chin to the length of his arm, from his graceful wrist and delicately jointed fingers, to his mass of thick hair. In attitude and expression, in his stance and in his gesture, in every point of his appearance, one boy answered the other's eyes as a photograph might, or a mirror. He was looking at himself. The boy was Fitz.

'Ah,' said Professor Farzan, turning back to Fitz. The other adults had fallen silent, caught for a moment between a thought and its catastrophic consequence, and Farzan stepped a pace from them, stuffing his hands into the pockets of his tweed jacket. 'And welcome to you, too, my boy. Welcome to the British Museum. Welcome to the *shāhanshāh*, the king of kings.'

5

*Dilaram*

Ten minutes later, they all stood in a long panelled drawing room, lit by a single standing lamp. All the curtains were drawn, and many of the armchairs at the far end of the room were shrouded in deep shadow. At the near end, upon a broad mahogany table surrounded by high-backed and ornately carved chairs, Professor Farzan had spread two ancient, yellowed manuscript leaves and a grand, leather-bound book – a huge, thick tome, its cracked covers stamped with decorative patterns. The book's spine bore no title, but as he pulled out chairs for his guests to be seated, he told them that the three texts were early records of European travel to ancient cities in what was now Syria – chronicles that recorded the position and condition of ancient monuments that had long since been rifled, reaved and ruined.

Fitz took his seat at the table by Clare's side. Ned sat across from them, with Mr Ahmadi to his left. Professor Farzan locked the heavy panelled door through which they had entered, and then placed the key, carefully, on the end of the table. Beneath the glow of the lamp, the gold key cast its image deep into the polished surface of the mahogany table.

'I understand you've all had a difficult day, and it is very late,' said Professor Farzan. 'I am sorry to have arranged our meeting in this way, and I am sorry to keep you from your beds. For reasons that will become clear, it was necessary that we should meet when the museum was closed. And necessary that you should enter the museum without being seen – neither by the guards, nor by the cameras.'

Ned was looking at the key, thinking, Fitz thought, what he was also thinking.

*Why had Farzan locked the door?*

'Many people have recently developed an interest in our young friend –' he gestured to Fitz – 'and some of them are dangerous. I want to explain to you what I know, in the hope that it will help you to stay safe – in the hope that it will help all of us to stay safe.'

Clare had taken Fitz's hand beneath the table. Fitz thought that her hand was very cold. He looked at her and was surprised to see, for the first time in his life, that her cheek had no colour in it at all. She looked grey.

'The situation may not make sense, and yet it is actually very simple. A few weeks ago, the British Museum received a rather important delivery: almost a thousand objects, each one of them a priceless historical artefact, from the collection of a fabulously wealthy magnate, recently deceased. These pieces were acquired abroad, and have only just been brought to this country; the dead man's estate has offered us a limited opportunity to study the collection, here in the museum, as a courtesy – though naturally any detail we can add to the understanding of the items it contains will only increase their value. Once we have finished our work, the objects will return to the family, and disappear again from view – maybe forever.'

'The heir to a collection like this will become very rich,' said Ned.

'He is heir to much more than this,' said Mr Ahmadi. His lips were as thin and tight as nails. 'You cannot possibly imagine.'

'Quite,' said Professor Farzan. 'But for now, this is our chance. We'll be allowed to keep one or two things for our permanent collection, but only that. One or two. For the rest, we have about three weeks to catalogue them, describe them, study them, photograph them. Most of the museum's curators were transferred to this project – the collection contains objects of all sorts – paintings, sculpture, funeral plaques, precious stones, clothing, books, coins, even mummies – everything. Some of it is comparatively modern, some of it older, some of it impossibly old. Some pieces are European in origin, some Chinese, some African; but the most interesting part of the collection – and this is where I come in – dates from the Sassanid period of Persian history, about seventeen hundred years ago. The moment I began to work on this material, I discovered something very unsettling.

'There are two manuscripts here. They are two copies in Middle Persian of the same text. They are old – more than a thousand years old – and were themselves copied from an older original, now lost. They tell of a great treasure buried in the desert in what is now Iran. They don't say *where* it is, but they describe *what* it is – a hoard so extensive, so diverse, that it would tell us unimaginable things about ancient history – about the Greeks, about the Romans, about the ancient Parthians themselves, and all the cultures that bordered anywhere near the Silk Road that ran through Persia between Europe and China, for millennia. It's the sort of thing that archaeologists and museum curators fantasize about. According to these manuscripts, the hoard was buried by a group of slaves who were themselves buried with the treasure; not a single person survived to speak of its location – not even the king who ordered it to be buried could find it.'

'Surely you don't believe stories about buried treasure,' said Clare. 'You're a scholar, working in a museum.'

' "The treasures of time lie high, in urns, coins and monuments, scarce below the roots of some vegetables",' answered Professor Farzan. 'Much that this museum contains was once buried treasure. The tombs of the Pharaohs, the graves of countless Egyptians, Assyrians, Romans, Greeks – all of these were plundered by Victorians hoping to strike it rich in one way or another. But you're right, in a sense. I don't usually believe stories about buried treasure; however, that's only because I reckon most of that buried treasure has already been dug up. But then, last week, while I was working on another part of the collection – completely, as I thought, unrelated, I found something shocking.'

Farzan picked up the large, leather-bound book from the table, and turned it so that the others could see. He opened its cover to the title page.

'This is a volume from the early sixteenth century. It was printed in Basle, in Switzerland. It's a rare annotated copy of a famous work by the Roman writer Cicero. It's worth tens, maybe hundreds of thousands, solely on account of the person who owned it. I was excited when I noticed it, because this person, like me, was interested in Near East antiquities. Which is what makes the coincidence I'm about to show you so very bizarre.'

He put the book down, and gently closed the cover. From the inside of his jacket, he drew a pair of wooden tweezers.

'It was the practice in the early days of printing, when binding books in leather, to stuff the inside of the binding with pieces of old manuscripts – whatever waste material happened to be lying around. Pages from much older manuscripts, sometimes cut into little pieces, can for this reason be found inside later books. Now, what a Swiss printer in 1500 considered to be worthless – it boggles the mind. Because he couldn't read Middle Persian, for example, he packed this manuscript page into his copy of Cicero.'

Using his tweezers, Professor Farzan carefully drew from inside the leather cover of the book a sturdy sheet of parchment, which was entirely covered with neat, small writing – in an elegant script that Fitz couldn't recognize at all.

'When I saw this last week, I immediately phoned Ned, because it reminded me of something he had told me about years before. In fact, it is the other half of a document once given to him in a Baghdad hotel, which –'

'I told her,' said Ned, cutting him off. 'And I think Fitz might have heard it, too, if I'm not mistaken.'

Professor Farzan turned over the manuscript page. Clare only had eyes for Fitz.

– 'which, as I was saying, includes a drawing of a statue you have now seen.'

Fitz's heart began to pound. The drawing on the reverse of the manuscript page, like the statue itself, so closely resembled him that he felt he could be looking in a mirror. Executed in black ink, it was indistinguishable from the portraits Clare so often did, absent-mindedly, whenever they were sitting together.

'The moment I saw this manuscript – perfectly preserved, undisturbed, for the last five hundred years in the binding of this book – I knew it would help us to understand the statue. What I didn't know is that it would help us to understand *you*.' Here he turned to Fitz.

'The manuscript contains a long passage about the statue. I have composed a rough translation of the central portion of it. I will read it to you.'

Professor Farzan replaced the manuscript in the binding with care, and retrieved a folded piece of lined white paper from his pocket. He straightened it and began to read, stumbling here and there over his own crabbed handwriting, and once or twice adjusting his glasses, or raising them to peer under them at something especially illegible.

'The Great Hoard of the *shāhanshāh* is his Kingdom. It will not be recovered by any man. It is the joy of his heart that he has buried in the sands and in the rock far from the tread of any man, and belongs to no man but to the *shāhanshāh* alone. But even the tamarisk that grows in the desert may bloom, and its roots drink the salt of many tears. So if the son of the king shall appear, at any time, before the eyes of his father, he shall inherit the Kingdom, and having the Great Hoard he shall be known to be the *shāhanshāh*.'

Professor Farzan folded the paper again and placed it back in his pocket. He took off his glasses, and wiped the sleeve of his coat across his bushy, greying eyebrows, then replaced his glasses. He blinked at them all, searching their faces for something that was not in them.

'Don't you understand?' he said. 'They cast the statue and placed it on a plinth in Bishapur, so that when the heir of the *shāhanshāh* was found, he should be known. At any time.'

No one said a word.

'The heir,' insisted the Professor. 'The statue is the figure of the heir, the *shapur*, the son of the king of kings.'

'You don't seriously think –' started Ned.

'Of course I don't,' laughed Professor Farzan; his voice was merry, Fitz thought, but his eyes were hard. 'But it doesn't matter what I think. What matters is that there appear to be a great many people who have suddenly become interested in this young man. And you can't deny the likeness. For many people – ignorant, superstitious – that will be more than enough. Many people want to find the Kingdom. They have wanted to find it for years. They think the boy will lead them to it.'

Ned took off his glasses and with two fingers rubbed his eyes, then pinched his nose and squinted, hard. Fitz wondered if he was wincing from the difficult thoughts he was thinking, or from the pain he was causing himself.

'And how is a boy supposed to find this Kingdom, this treasure, he is due to inherit?'

'How old are you, child?' asked Farzan, turning suddenly to look Fitz full in the face. 'Answer carefully.'

'He's twelve,' said Clare.

Mr Ahmadi, watching the Professor, shook his head.

'Are you?' Farzan asked him. His eyebrows lifted.

'Nearly,' answered Fitz. 'At the end of next month.'

Professor Farzan leaned back in his seat, folding his hands across his lap. He looked at Mr Ahmadi. 'Tradition has it that the heir will find the Kingdom when he comes of age.'

'And tradition has it that he comes of age when he is twelve?' asked Ned.

'Yes,' answered Mr Ahmadi. 'Then he will be a man. Hence the appearance, now, of Sassani – and all of them.'

'Grave robbers as a rule are fairly superstitious, and they are a nasty bunch,' added the Professor, 'whether they work in museums or in the dead of the night. And when time is short, and thieves fall out with thieves . . .' He stopped, and pursed his lips, causing the spiky hairs of his beard to bristle sharply against the light.

Fitz looked at Clare. She still sat stone-faced beside him, not blinking, hardly even breathing. It was as if she had been cast in bronze.

'What do you recommend we do?' said Ned.

'I want to leave here,' said Clare. She was speaking directly to Ned. 'Surely you know a place where we can go, somewhere out of all this. Somewhere Professor Sassani can't find us.'

Mr Ahmadi cut in. 'This Sassani is a problem. He sets fire to things. But he is nothing near the greatest danger that you face.'

'He's right,' said Farzan. He still stood before them. Now he leaned forward, spreading his hands on the table. His voice was grave, and steady, and the twinkle in his eye had completely dried. 'The forces surrounding you are powerful, and they are watching this place above all. Sassani smoked you out of your hole. He set the fox running, but the huntsmen chasing this quarry are many, they are skilled, and they mean to succeed. Habi torched your car because they were watching the roads; indeed, most of the roads into London have been cordoned off tonight – it's mayhem. Trains into London – the same. Did you notice that the tracks were quiet? Did you see the carriages standing still at the platforms? Why do you think you weren't flattened by a tube train, as you walked down the Piccadilly Line? Only two out of eight lines were running tonight, and they weren't stopping in central stations. London is locked down tighter than bark on a tree. If you try to leave the building – if you try to leave this room – they will see you, they will follow you, and they will take your son.'

Clare was unconvinced. 'We got in. We can get out.'

'You got in through a wartime evacuation tunnel, which the police believe to be closed – indeed, they think it has been filled in – and you only got in that way because I created a diversion.' From his pocket the Professor took a pair of gold, griffin-headed armlets, and placed them gently on the table. 'When these disappeared from a case in Room Fifty-Two, tonight at about ten p.m., it created for a brief time a great amount of interest, both inside and outside the museum.'

Ned's mouth opened.

'Part of the Oxus treasure. Fifth century. I will return them, Ned, don't worry. But I had to get you all inside. All three of you had to see the statue for yourselves, or you never would have believed us.'

Clare seemed to crumple, as if she had had all the air sucked out of her. Beneath the table, she pulled her hand from her son's, and placed it, palm broad across her chest, just beneath her neck. She tried to breathe deeply.

'What, then?' She was staring at the table in front of her.

'These are grave robbers,' said Professor Farzan. 'They want treasure – and if this manuscript is anything to go by, they're going to want lots of it. They want your son to help them get it. Give them your son, help them find their treasure, and then they will leave you alone.'

'This is a ruthless enemy,' said Mr Ahmadi. 'He will not stop. This is the only way you can save this boy.'

'I'm here,' said Fitz, sitting up. 'You can talk to me. I'm here.'

'Well said, boy,' said Professor Farzan. He sat down in a tall chair, with arms, that stood at the head of the table. He settled deeply into it, never taking his eyes off Fitz. 'And what do you say? What will you do, to save yourself?'

'I will do whatever is required,' said Fitz, 'so that we can all go home.'

'No,' said Clare.

'I will do what is required,' said Fitz.

'What is required,' said Mr Ahmadi, 'is that you come with me to meet the most skilful, the most powerful, the most dangerous, and the wealthiest thieves in all the world.'

'Who are they?' asked Fitz.

'They are the ones who own these manuscripts, this book – the statue, all the coins and gems and metalwork, the priceless things on loan to the museum here. They are the most accomplished grave robbers the world has ever known. They are called the Heresy. If I am the one to bring you to them, I can protect you. I give you my word that you will come home.'

*Zenith. Nadir.*

'How can you protect him?' said Ned. 'What makes you think they will listen to you at all?'

*Algorithm.*

'I know they will,' answered Mr Ahmadi. His top hat sat on the table in front of him. He shifted it carefully between his fingers, and stared at it while he spoke. 'Because I am one of them. Like my father before me, I am a member of the Heresy, and not the least of them.'

*Albatross. And the roots drink the salt of many tears.*

No one dared speak: not Mr Ahmadi, who had lured them to this place only to betray them; not Professor Farzan, who had connived at it all; not Ned, whose trust in his old friend lay in pieces on the table; not Clare, who had lost her whole life in a day, and was surrounded by enemies; and least of all, Fitz thought, himself – for he intended to break Clare's heart in order to save it, and the words stuck in his throat.

*Dilaram.*

There was a knock at the door.

'Habi,' whispered Professor Farzan, 'how long do we have?'

Mr Ahmadi's hands danced in the air before his face. He seemed to be picking out invisible threads, weaving his fingers in intricate patterns across the face of some idea only he could see. His face expressed intense concentration, and his eyes sifted great matters like grains of sand.

'A few minutes, no more – then the Director will arrive, and they will force the door. With him will be – enemies. They are not here to bargain. We must move quickly, or we must surrender.'

Professor Farzan stood up from the table, crossed the room, and using both hands threw open one of the sets of heavy curtains. Where Fitz had expected to see a window, instead the curtains parted to reveal the door of a vault. At its centre was set an antique combination lock – a heavy black dial, circled by minute markings.

'I don't have the combination, nor does the Director – but Habi can open it. He will conceal himself inside, with you –' Farzan had crossed back to the table, and was speaking directly to Fitz – 'while your mother, and Ned, and I confront the people on the other side of that door. They're going to try to arrest me, but they won't be able to make it stick. When we've gone, when everything is quiet, Habi will take you to the Heresy. Help them find what they want. We will come for you when the time comes. On the day of your inheritance – on your twelfth birthday – we will come for you, and we will bring you home.'

Mr Ahmadi had already slipped from his chair to the safe. Holding his hat at an angle over the lock, with his ear cocked close to the mechanism, he crouched beside it, turning the knob with delicate precision. They all held their breath.

Again, there was a knocking at the door. Now Professor Farzan stood behind his chair at the end of the table, his head bowed. Still seated, Clare was fumbling at the back of her neck for something. Fitz knew what it was: the silver jay, its wings spread as for flight, that had been her mother's, and that she wore always on a thin leather strap round her neck. With the practised fingers of an artist, within seconds she had unfastened the knot and refastened it, again, round Fitz's own neck. She slipped the bird inside his shirt, where it lay cool against his skin, and put her hand against his chest.

'Don't be long, Jaybird,' she said. There were tears running down her cheeks. 'We will come for you.'

Mr Ahmadi stood up, replacing his hat on his head with a flourish, and drew open the door of the vault. It was a narrow opening – only about a metre – but, within, the vault seemed to lie deep, extending to three or even four metres into the walls and soil. Along the shelves that ran down each side, Fitz could see small grey card boxes, each with a descriptive label, stacked neatly in row upon row. He stood up from his chair, circled the long end of the table, and paused at the vault's door. At the far wall, in part shadow, stood the gold-painted cover of an Egyptian sarcophagus.

'It's a fake,' said Professor Farzan, gesturing towards the gleaming gold case and shaking his head dismissively. 'In you go. And quickly.'

Fitz took hold of the corner of one of the shelves and stepped with care through the opening. Mr Ahmadi stepped in behind him, his hat in one hand and the other with his finger to his lips. He turned and drew the door closed behind them, shutting out the light, just as Fitz settled into the dust that coated the floor.

'Is it really a fake?' whispered Fitz to the black stillness of the inside of the vault. His own body, with the blood in it, appeared to make a kind of electrical sound.

'No, of course it's not a fake,' said Mr Ahmadi. 'It's the three-thousand-year-old death mask of a great king. You don't put something in a vault unless it's valuable. Now be silent, and very, very still.'

For what seemed hours – agonizing hours – they waited in silence. Every bone in Fitz's legs began to ache. The ache spread into his back, where it burned, then into his shoulders. He dared not stretch his legs, or shift his weight, for fear that he might make a noise – scuff the floor, knock one of the shelves, dislodge one of the small grey boxes, disturb the slumber of the three-thousand-year-old king – anything that might alert someone outside that the vault was not empty. In the darkness he thought from time to time that he could hear Mr Ahmadi's breath, but then thought that he was imagining it; certainly Mr Ahmadi never stirred, never shifted, never made the least sound. All the while, in Fitz's bones and muscles, the tearing ache seemed to grow into a fever scream.

'They still have not left the room,' said Mr Ahmadi, in a whisper. 'We have only a little time left.'

Fitz pondered this for a few moments, then whispered back. 'Only a little time until what?'

'Until we run out of air,' said Mr Ahmadi.

He must have begun to turn the lock mechanism again, because Fitz heard it click. A few minutes later, he heard it again. Mr Ahmadi said nothing further, but Fitz thought he must be poised over the third number, postponing the moment when it should strike, the moment when the bolt that bound them in would spring free and release the door again. If anyone were in the room, without a doubt they would hear that.

The vault had become stiflingly hot.

And then the moment came.

'Now,' said Mr Ahmadi, more loudly this time. He turned the lock, the bolt withdrew, and he pushed the door open.

The room now stood in almost complete darkness; the only light came from under the panelled door. From beyond it, they could hear movement. Mr Ahmadi carefully closed the safe, crossed the room, and pressed his ear to the door while Fitz waited. After a few minutes the noise receded, and the light in the corridor outside was switched off.

'Now we climb,' said Mr Ahmadi. 'Go exactly where I go, do not lag behind, and above all, trust me.'

They slipped out of the room, leaving the door as they had left the vault – shut firm behind them. Down a corridor, up a quiet stone stair, through countless doors and from room to room, shifting unobserved between passages and staircases, they rose within the fabric of the building, never putting their heads needlessly beyond a corner, never setting their feet but lightly where they meant to go. At length they emerged into a huge hall or courtyard of white stone, luminously bright, magnificently deserted. In its centre stood a round tower; above, a ceiling all of glass. Fitz checked the gasp as it rose spontaneously from his throat, absorbing his shock in a shudder that stuttered through his chest like a deadbolt catching.

'Now,' said Mr Ahmadi, 'we will run. Very fast. Remember, everywhere and exactly where I go.'

He set off at a sprint for a paved ramp that coursed, ascending, round the outside of the tower. Fitz followed, matching his stride to that of his guide, throwing his legs out before him at every step. Up the ramp they sprinted, circling the building. Fitz's chest heaved as he struggled to take in ever larger breaths. As they rounded the tower for the second time, Fitz thought he could hear commotion below, the report of heavy soles on stone. From the corner of his eye, beyond a ledge, he saw a black form moving, and heard from somewhere the sound of lift doors closing.

They reached the top. A grille had been pulled down over the large entrance to a larger room. Through the glass Fitz could see chairs, tables, colourful displays. Mr Ahmadi had drawn aside, and was picking at the lock of a small, nondescript door – almost invisible against the white walls of the tower. The pins in the lock made a tiny scratching sound, and Fitz strained to hear it, to hear the lock turning. But in the silent emptiness of the huge hall, he was suddenly conscious of another sound, instead: a lift rising, slowly but surely, somewhere in the walls away to his left. Turning, scanning the open air, across a high walkway he saw the lobby where the doors would open.

'Mr Ahmadi,' he said, his voice tentative.

With a heave of exasperation Mr Ahmadi pushed himself to his feet. 'I know', he said; his eyes had immediately swung to the far, blank wall, within which the lift rose. It was nearly at the top.

'Follow me.'

Abandoning the door, they ran away from the lift, round the tall tower that dominated the courtyard, and across a second high bridge. The close, bright room on the other side was stacked with mummies.

Mr Ahmadi stopped in front of a huge stone chest, carved and set on a massive plinth. He paused, judging it for an instant, then stepped lightly on to the plinth and began to rotate the chest's heavy stone cover.

'In,' he said.

'What is this?' asked Fitz, climbing too slowly, catching his feet clumsily against the faces, the outstretched arms, the raised swords, the shaggy hams of satyrs.

'Sarcophagus. Imperial, Roman, second century. Pentelic marble. Try not to break it. In.'

Inside the chest smelled of chalk and walnuts. Mr Ahmadi didn't waste a moment slipping in behind him. His hat he tossed into Fitz's lap. With his back hunched against the marble, he shimmied the cover back into place, and in the last slice of light as the lid closed, Fitz saw on his face a dramatic scowl – as twisted and horrible a face as any carved on the stone exterior – commanding him to be silent.

'These are not museum guards. They are much worse, so – not a sound,' whispered Mr Ahmadi. They crouched side by side in the darkness.

Footsteps ran into the room; they could feel them through the stone like a distant drum of war – two or three large men. Fitz imagined them, perhaps security officers, perhaps something worse, armed, looking for him. They wanted to kill him.

*But I'm already in a tomb.*

As the footsteps died off down the long room, Fitz tried to picture the last person to have lain in this stone box with its cover closed: wrapped in white cloth, the body pale, eyes open, staring at nothing but eternity.

He shivered. Mr Ahmadi, sensing the movement, put his hand firmly on Fitz's shoulder.

'No,' he whispered, so quietly that the word was almost as still and quiet as the close and warming air of the sarcophagus itself. 'Only two walked away. One –' he paused, breathing, and his voice when it came again was if anything even more silent – 'is still . . . here.'

Just then they heard the light tread as this last man – this guard, this hunter, this assassin – paced the museum floor. The footsteps seemed – were they? – to be getting closer. Fitz felt his body shrink inside his clothes, felt the breath squeeze from his constricting lungs. The cold of the stone rose like a spreading vein of ice in his bones. The footsteps came to a halt. There was a tap, then another. Then a third. The man was pacing the length of the sarcophagus. A fourth tap. Something was in his hand. It sounded metallic where it rang gently against the edge of the plinth – metallic and solid. Every muscle in Fitz's body hardened.

From a distance, there came a shout – a muffled oath – and the footsteps ran off. Before they had faded completely, Mr Ahmadi had stood, bowed, to the cover, and was starting to push it open. Fitz didn't need to be asked; the moment the gap was wide enough, he vaulted through it, straight off the plinth and on to the wooden floor. Mr Ahmadi, as nimbly free, didn't bother to set the stone to rights but sprinted past Fitz, back towards the courtyard.

Two, three moments after he had squatted anew before the little white door, tools in hand, it swung ajar.

'Up,' said Mr Ahmadi. Fitz rushed up the narrow flight of stairs while Mr Ahmadi drew the door quietly closed behind him. Fitz hadn't climbed halfway before the man's long strides caught him up; pushing past him, he easily fiddled the lock on a hatch at the top.

The hatch swung open in a wild whirl of wind. Fitz saw at once, saw with a lurch in his guts, that it led on to the roof: an expanse of glass panels in a heavy metal frame, lit from below, gave on to the glowing, throbbing darkness of the city sky. Beyond, as far as his eye could see, there were only roofs, buildings, and more roofs.

'There is no time to wait, child,' said Mr Ahmadi. Outside the door he climbed on to a ladder that ran up the wall. As Fitz followed, looking only ahead, only at the individual rungs, at the wet stone behind them, Mr Ahmadi leaned down from above and gently swung shut the door after them.

They climbed, first up the stone face of a little cupola, and then, by another ladder, across the cupola's dome. Always the wind tore at them, knocking, wheedling, inviting, departing in a huff one instant, only to return the next with a new invitation. Fitz fixed his mind on his fists, and one by one he locked them to the rungs of the ladder. Step on step, handhold on handhold, they rose. No one followed them now; no one saw them crawling, like ants, across the sheer face of the museum's highest, sheerest roof. It never occurred to Fitz to ask where they were going – all he knew was to move his fists, one upon the other.

When they could go no further, Fitz stopped. He looked up. Mr Ahmadi crouched on a wide ledge. From a large case sitting on the ledge he was removing pieces of equipment – Fitz could hardly see against the glare from below, and in the wind that seemed to rise in surges, like fast swells breaking on the shore, from the dome below. And then all of a sudden he knew. He had only to draw himself over the ledge.

'Put this on. Put your arms through the loops, and buckle it round your chest. Pull the straps tight.' Fitz did as he was instructed. In a few moments more he had been clipped to Mr Ahmadi's harness.

'There is one thing I know,' Mr Ahmadi said, as he lashed himself strap by strap into the heavy frame. 'The wind never lies. It may whip and crush you, but it serves no master but itself. It may never be your friend, but it will never be your enemy, either. The wind never breaks faith. The wind is free.'

*Don't be long.*

And then Mr Ahmadi stepped off the cupola's shallow ledge into the wind, and they flew.

# THE HERESY

6

*The Heresy*

The room was small, but bright. His bed, hardly more than a pallet laid upon a board, stood to one side of a tight square; on the other wall a little desk had been placed beside a window. Before it stood a wooden stool, round with four legs. Against the adjacent wall, opposite the door, there was a second window, square, like the room. Otherwise, everything about the space spoke only to its emptiness. No carpet covered the bare boards of the floor; no light dangled from above; no curtains framed the windows. The walls were white, and rose high and blank to a lofty ceiling. Apart from his bed, the desk and the little stool, the only furniture in the room – the only thing – was a trapdoor in the ceiling. This was the tower room, and Fitz knew that the door opened upon nothing but the sky.

Everything was exactly as he would have wished.

Fitz sat on the edge of the neat bed and rehearsed his memories of the last day's events. It seemed to him like a dream, or a thing that had happened to someone else.

He began with the moment Mr Ahmadi had leaped from the cupola above the museum. The wind must have been crashing hard into the dome, because it had splashed up as waves do on the shore, and the updraughts had rocketed the wing into the sky, higher and higher as Mr Ahmadi circled in a narrowing gyre. The world had become dizzy then, and coursed by as on a carousel, roof after roof, and broken, slurred lights, red and white in a dark haze, swam. At last he had become aware that they were gliding – but only after they had been gliding for some time. His stomach pushed into his ears, and when he wiggled his fingers, he was sure he felt his toes. Tense, compacted, his body ached in its harness and seemed to stagger through the heights of air. Falling, they had risen by lurches, shuddering and surging ever higher. He could remember the cold, the surprising affront of wind like ice that slipped into his clothes, then into his skin, that held his bones in unyielding hands. He could remember fighting to keep his neck straight, to push his head up, and back, to strain his eyes forward rather than allowing them to fall upon the ground – to fall upon the rushing streets, the people and cars and buses that seemed at once impossibly far, and far too near. But if the ground held terrors, so too did the sky: jolted and buffeted by gusts, Mr Ahmadi struggled to keep the wing steady, and again and again, teasing the updraughts out of the dark canvas of the night, he curled into their sickening towers and they rose, tumbling, until Fitz had thought he might scream.

Perhaps, battered by the wind into a kind of blunted sleep, he had dreamed. Maybe the elevation had undone him, or the cold, a cold that drowned every thought. Whatever the cause, he had somewhere between the rushing dark clouds and the wheeling lights of the city below found himself suddenly aware – again – of a flash and spreading of wings, white wings, wings like sails thrown out as wide as the eye's own horizon. At first they had seemed to scythe the air around the fixed arms of the glider, cutting into the night in halting and in speeding bursts, keeping time with the blasts and howls of the sky's tearing voice as it sang its strains of insane music. But then, gradually, the white flashes of wings seemed to settle, and Fitz became aware of great birds around them, not as a harrying or as a haunting, but as a presence. From moment to moment as Mr Ahmadi sought to climb into the wind, striving against the draughts and blasts where they knocked and shook and shuddered the glider, the birds appeared to be accompanying them, tracking them, at times near and at times far, but always there. Fitz had dropped in and out of consciousness so often he hadn't known what was sleep, what waking; but always in the pale light rising from the land below he sensed the wings over him, wide and weariless.

How long they had flown, like froth foaming at the fountaining head of the wind, he had no idea. All he knew was that their bodies, arced and rigid, had been pushed across the answering arc of the sky, speared hurtling across the dome of night until with the night, at last, they dropped.

They had come to rest at the top of a broad grassy slope by a wide river. It could have been the hour, or the repeated shocks of the day, but Fitz hardly seemed to remember the details of the landing; it was as if they had simply stood up, and found the ground beneath them: Mr Ahmadi shuffling on the grass before him, Fitz shuffling behind. Once they had unstrapped themselves, and Mr Ahmadi had broken down the glider and packed it away, each of them taking a handle, they had walked briskly down to the river. A little pier or dock stood at the river's shore, and beside it, for the river or the tide was low, a little beach lay in shadow. On the beach – as if someone had prepared for them – a wherry had been drawn up on the stones and sand, with oars set ready in the locks. Mr Ahmadi had jumped down, and Fitz behind him. They had stowed the glider in the transom and had together pushed the boat out, Fitz scrambling in before the river water began to lap at his ankles.

'Sleep if you can,' Mr Ahmadi had said, as he pulled on the oars. And, nestled in the bows, Fitz had slept – for how long, he didn't know. All he could remember was the pull of the oars against the wind and, when he opened his eyes, Mr Ahmadi's silhouette against the lights, his tall hat dipping forward, then leaning back, again, and again, framed by the dim air above the syncopated surging of the riverbank.

Day had overtaken them. Guiding the wherry close to the bank, where the current was weakest, Mr Ahmadi had pulled, and pulled again in an almost musical motion – but Fitz had felt that his strength was flagging. They had passed through a lock, where the bank shifted – now lower, grassier, draped with willows and longer, more ample. The water of the river, which earlier had heaved with gusts and slapped at the little boat, now lapped and lingered at its edge, lisping with the strokes of the oars and the tissuing breezes among the leaves of whispering trees. Fitz had drowsed in the dim light, his sense of things displaced, dispersed, fragmented. Hours might have passed.

And then – for the first time – the boat had struck the bank.

The steps running up the bank were broad, ten or twelve feet across, cut from single slabs of stone and weathered by centuries. A small man in a porter's uniform had hurried down them to take in the boat, drawing its painter through an iron ring that hung from a post, and lifting the glider easily from the transom. The manner of his movement was hushed, deferential and efficient.

For the first time in days the wind seemed to have subsided, and the morning, the bright morning, the clear and dew-fresh morning was laced with birdcalls and cut with an astringent fragrance of lavender and verbena. The scene like a thread brushing the air had drawn him: he had risen to his feet, and stepped ashore.

Now, sitting at the edge of the bed, his gaze fixed before him at the whiteness of the wall, Fitz grasped at a feeling – the feeling of his arrival, of those first steps on the grounds of the Heresy. For all of his fatigue, for all the dirt and rust and sweat and soil that had stained his clothes, for all the rumpled and rattled anxiety of the day before, he had immediately registered – there, on the steps – the encompassing and seductive peace of the place. His senses had been in tumult, startled at the novelty, so that even now he could taste the luxurious emerald of the grass, and hear the bright crystalline ringing of the pearled drops of dew that tipped its blades, could all but touch the lark's tight trills, and stub his fingers in the musk of purple buds; and yet, instead of that riotous congestion of sound, and sight, of touch and taste, what Fitz recalled above all was the sense that he had not been there at all, that even as it had happened, it was no more than a memory, that he was no more than an exciting tale told by another.

He didn't dare admit to himself how much he had liked it.

Between rows of roses huddling their blooms he had trailed Mr Ahmadi, himself trailing the short porter, up a wide path and through an evergreen hedge. Beyond the hedge, lawns like ample skirts lay spread round a rambling sprawl of buildings, dressed in places with stone, some tall, some broad, some timbered and twisted, others soaring with geometrical precision into arch and buttress, turret, tower and spire. Each shouldered another, and in their juxtapositions the centuries, and the eye, jostled; but Fitz had found again that with every step he took towards the sandstone gatehouse, his unquiet heart settled, his straining nerves relaxed, and every taut and aching sinew in his body relaxed.

The porter had left them at the gatehouse. Inside, another man stood between them and the door to the open court beyond. He wore a heavy felt coat all in red, belted with a black sash, that dressed him to his knees. On his head was a matching round cap. With his legs planted wide, as wide as his wide shoulders, he seemed to occupy the whole of the passage. There was no getting round him. Above him, in the flat stone wall of the gatehouse was carved a huge, single eye. Unadorned and uninterpreted by any text, by its openness it seemed to Fitz to express unsleeping vigilance; but there was something strange to it, too – a kind of formlessness, an emptiness.

*It has no colour, no pupil.*

The eye sat directly over the man's head as he accosted them.

'As Registrar to the Heresy,' he had said, 'I require you to register your visitor.'

'He is not a visitor,' Mr Ahmadi had answered. 'I present my Apprentice, Fitzroy Worth, and challenge the Heresiarch to break him.'

'The game is already ended,' said the Registrar. He stepped aside to let them pass.

'The game is already ended,' said Mr Ahmadi, with a nod of his head, inclining the tip of his tall hat. Then he had stridden through the inner door.

The strange words had swept over him like water at the shore; dumb and senseless as the sand, Fitz had felt them rush over him, cold and foreign. And yet like water, too, they drew him; where Mr Ahmadi went, as in a dream he followed.

All the rest, almost, had been a blur. They had passed from one court to another, some open and grand, others small and intimate, some arcaded, others austere, here a Gothic tower wall blanketed in ivy, there a low courtyard that might once have stabled workhorses. From path to path, through arches and doors, Fitz had tried to hold pace with Mr Ahmadi, never attempting to do more than follow him; from the deference and formality with which others treated his neighbour, he had understood his place. The man who had loaned him books, who had admired Clare – that man now appeared completely gone. This man was obviously something else entirely: someone before whom others scattered, suddenly furtive and unsure. He had swept through crowds as a wind through dry leaves.

In one court, almost the last, they had crossed a complex pattern of hexagonal paths to join a little knot of children, who were clustered round a well or some sort of fountain. Their heads bowed, they were deeply absorbed in a hushed conversation. For the first – and only – time, Mr Ahmadi had broken stride, stopping beside the oblivious children with the start of a stern look in the corners of his eyes. One of the children – a girl maybe Fitz's own age, or a little older – had turned her head and stared at him with such idle curiosity, such relaxed intensity, that he had almost blushed as he looked away.

'What is this?' Mr Ahmadi had said, holding up a loose coil of something like wire, or thin cable.

From within the thick cluster of children's faces – Fitz hadn't seen her – another girl's voice had answered. 'Retractable arrows,' she said. 'I've fitted my crossbow with cabled harpoon spikes.'

Mr Ahmadi had held out his arm. The little clot of children had opened, and into his hand first the heavy iron spike itself, and then the heavy crossbow had been placed – with ceremony, with respect. For a moment he had weighed it in his palm. As he had turned it back over to outstretched hands, his face – briefly inquisitive – had again grown stern. 'Be careful with it.'

'Don't worry,' said the tall girl. Her face radiated assurance and power. 'She's an excellent shot.' For a second Fitz stared at her, awed by the confidence with which she spoke. But her face, like those of so many others, had, as Mr Ahmadi had turned again on his heel, striding off, instantly been lost.

'I know,' Mr Ahmadi had called over his shoulder. And muttered, almost to Fitz, 'that's exactly what worries me.'

At the foot of a tall, round tower Mr Ahmadi had left him. 'Go to the top of the stairs,' he had told him. 'There you will find a room that is yours. The door is unlocked – few doors here are locked. Wait there. Wash. Sleep, if you can.'

Fitz had slept in the tower room; by the time he had reached the top of the high stairs, his legs had failed him and sleep the only thing he could do.

Judging by the position of the sun, now colliding with crags and hills on the horizon, he had slept for hours. No one had come for him. No one had seemed to want him at all, for anything. He found a basin on the window sill, full of water, and beside it a cloth. Slowly, methodically, as if the movements of his arms were the rising and falling of his chest, as if the slow circles he described on his chest, his arms, his legs were the returns of a dream, he washed himself. Then he dressed.

'Hello,' said a voice, stabbing through the peaceful insulation of his reveries.

Fitz felt as if his heart were not beating, but tearing a path out of his chest. He hadn't heard a tread on the tower stairs. He hadn't heard the door open. He hadn't seen so much as a mote of dust shift in a sunbeam. And yet here was a girl – the taller girl from the courtyard, the confident one – standing before him. In his alarm and surprise, Fitz now noticed everything about her with flashbulb clarity: her height and slender delicateness; the brushed bronze of her skin beneath a loose cotton dress, and the folds of her long hair, brown as a knot in oak; the length of her arms, a flat tilt to her jaw, a quirk of the face like a smile that hovered always in her cheek; a fragrance like leaves in autumn; her bare feet. But he noticed above all, as he had noticed no other thing in all his life – cleaved to it with a distraction that stunned and paralysed him – the ice in her eyes, neither blue nor white, but the colour that air itself would take, were it to freeze and float in a sky of light.

'Hello, I said,' said the girl.

Fitz stood up.

'You're in my room,' said Fitz.

The girl looked around now, appraising it, taking it in.

'I am in the room,' she said, as if conceding something. 'The Master sent me to get you, to come to your Enrolment. After that it's dinner.'

'You haven't got any shoes on,' said Fitz.

'I'm practising,' said the girl.

'Practising for what?'

'Making no impression on the world.'

'Maybe you'd be more successful if you didn't stare at people,' said Fitz.

'Fair,' she said. Fitz thought she might be blushing. He was wrong. 'I'm Dina. You're new.'

'I'm Fitz,' he said.

'I know,' said Dina.

'Who is the Master?'

'Surely you know him already?' Dina asked. Her brows furrowed with incomprehension. 'He's the reason you're here.'

'You mean Mr Ahmadi.'

'The Master. Here, everyone is known by their role in the game – except for the Prents, of course. Apprentices. We're still students. We don't have offices yet.'

Fitz felt as if a light had been switched on in his head. The baffling exchange between Mr Ahmadi and that man at the gate – the Registrar – came back to him again. Mr Ahmadi had presented him as his apprentice, a student, someone without an office – yet. They had spoken of a game.

'Hello in there,' said Dina.

'Hi,' Fitz answered, his eyes focusing again to take in the girl who stood before him, her head slightly inclined, the look of idle intensity, almost cruelty, once again in her frozen eyes.

'You looked for a moment as if you had disappeared somewhere far away,' said Dina, 'and right now – past now – we need to be in the Porch. So, even if you have another forty thousand questions, follow me.'

She pivoted on her toes, and disappeared through the doorway and down the stairs, as quietly as a cat. Fitz watched her go, as if from behind a window or from a great distance.

'Now,' she called. Her voice echoed on the circling stone of the stairwell.

There was nothing in the room to take. He shut the door behind him and raced down the stairs, taking them two and sometimes three at a time. He reached the bottom in a fluster, conscious of his heavy stomping and dizzy from the torrent of turning. Dina was standing outside in the courtyard. By the time Fitz was able to see straight, she was almost laughing.

'Lesson one,' she said. 'Your eyes don't necessarily have to follow your body. Next time, fix them on something that doesn't turn, and you won't lose your balance.'

It was Fitz's turn to blush.

'When you're sure you're ready, follow me,' said Dina. She strode off with her light step, touching the hard gravel of the courtyard with only the ball of her foot. Fitz didn't hesitate. Even through his shoes, the gravel seemed to bruise his heels.

Through an arched passage they reached another court, this one the low, timbered square with walls all of white daub. Here steep thatched eaves hung low over a one-storey hall, at the centre of which stood a wide oak door. In the middle of the door hung an iron knocker, in the shape of a large, closed fist.

Fitz, following Dina's eyes, saw that this must be the Porch. Inside, through small, thick panes of glass that distorted everything, he could see a warm light, and the richly dyed gowns of the Officers.

'Not yet,' she said. She didn't break stride.

Fitz frowned, faltering. 'But you said we're already late.'

The older girl walked straight on, as if he hadn't spoken, and ducked through a low passage. Fitz hurried to catch her. After the humility of the little court they had left, he hadn't expected what now greeted them. A sweeping stone staircase, with a narrow base but fanning wide to both sides, rose steeply at the far end of the court towards a little round building, a palace entirely faced in the softest pink marble and capped with a gleaming golden dome that – rising above the shadows of the court – caught the last of the evening's sun. To both sides steep marbled walls rose into the evening sky, tall and magnificently carved, crowned with ornamental battlements leaved with gold. Dina was already walking up the grand stairs, taking them two at a stride.

By the time Fitz caught up with her, she had reached the top. He was out of breath, his lungs rasping with pain from the climb. Dina seemed relaxed and easy.

'Second lesson,' she said. 'Keep up, newbie.'

'What are we doing up here?' said Fitz, between breaths. 'What is this place?'

'Turn round,' she said.

He did. The entire Heresy lay unfolded at their feet. If he had had any breath in him, he'd have caught it. Instead, he looked out gasping in stupid wonder. It was like the view from his tower room, almost, but wider, grander, all in a single piece, and behind the jumbled courts and halls and towers and squares of the Heresy, behind the smoke lifting from their chimneys and the evening sun where it glanced on their vanes and downspouts, lay the lawns and gardens, the great walls, the river, the valley, and green and rocky hills all around – the sea –

'Before you go in there, you need to know what you're up against.'

Dina stretched out her arms, as if she were a sorcerer summoning the vision before them.

'These are the courts and halls of the Heresy. There are sixteen courts in all, and eight halls. Over each of the halls a single Officer presides.' Dina moved to stand behind Fitz and, taking him firmly by the shoulders, steered him to the right. 'The far courts to the east contain the Hall of the Sweeper. The Sweeper is a general, a planner, a surveyor. He deals in logistics, espionage, and on the financial side, everything from purchasing to investments. His hall is a giant arena called the Model, larger than a warehouse, ten times the size of the largest hangar you can imagine. It's the biggest enclosed space in the world. And here he puts on simulations of every kind of system that interests him, from wars and diseases to financial markets and migration. He is shrewd, cunning, calculating, passionless. Never cross him.

'Next to the Sweep, this side of the big court, there's a much smaller court, dark and darkly towered. Do you see it?' Fitz nodded. 'That's the Rackery. The Rack is basically a torturer, an artist of pain. He teaches all physical sports, along with the arts of fighting and of war. He teaches politics. He is mean, wary, violent. A tiger. You can trust poison; you can trust fire; you can trust a knife; you can trust him. His court is much smaller than the others, but he does all his work in the tower cells, which are these two towers just over there. In the tower cells or –' Dina stopped, and raised her eyebrows. Fitz almost thought a smile touched her cheeks. 'In other places.

'Next over, the large court with the gorgeous brick palace, that's the Registry. The Registrar you probably met when you arrived. He's an archivist. He keeps records of everything that is, or has been, and his library – besides the seven storeys you see here – is mostly underground, built into the rock of the valley floor. The Registrar presides over all formal ceremonies in the Heresy, but we Apprentices know him more for the animals and fish he keeps. There are stables and stalls by the hundreds in his forecourt, and in the Registry itself a giant aquarium that rises six floors within the central staircase. Don't fall in; it's full of sharks.

'The Master you know already. Truth is, we've hardly seen him for the last several years; he's been off on Heresy business –'

Fitz cut her off. 'He's been living next door to –'

'On Heresy business,' repeated Dina. Her tone was final. 'But all the central courts make up the Mastery, and they are all his – except for this one. His are the three towers in front of us; the far one, as you know, is yours.'

'Who lives in the other two?' asked Fitz.

'He does.' She tightened her grip on his shoulders, so hard he winced. 'And I do. The Master is second only to the Heresiarch. He leads the Officers. He teaches all forms of play. Language is his province, and literature. Music. Stories. Poetry. Dreams. Ethics. He gets into other people's heads. Believe me, he already knows you better than you know yourself. And so he cannot be trusted.'

Fitz recoiled from this as from a snake. He looked away, towards the west, towards the sea, to the far, light-spangled halls of golden stone, with their tall windows like a cathedral's, and turned spires.

'The last courts, on the west, are the Keeper's. In the Keep she teaches arts of all kinds, anything to do with hands. She has a vast library, studios, galleries. Some of the Apprentices will tell you she dabbles in magic. But that's nonsense.

'The middle courts on the west side are the Jack's. The Jackery is a place of illusions, paradoxes, impossibilities and contrafactuals. He's a logician, a mathematician, a sceptic. You can't imagine the things he knows – and neither can he, because he doesn't believe any of them. The Jackery itself is in the court with the giant atrium, just there –' she pointed to it, where the glass roof still glittered as the light finally dropped behind the sea cliffs – 'but the Jack spends most of his time meditating, outside, under the plane trees. He'll work anywhere, on any surface: paper, walls, blades of grass, whatever. You've seen him. He looks solid enough, but he's slippery.

'And last but not least – especially not if you're as hungry as I am – the Commissar. Her main house is the Refectory, which is this huge beamed hall just below us here.' She gestured to the steeply pitched leaden roof in front of them. 'Technically speaking it's the Commissary, but we usually call it the Lantern Hall. That's where we have all our meals. The Commissar is in charge of food, stores, nutrition, health, everything to do with the body. She's a biologist, really, and a chemist, and knows everything about the living and the physical world. She studies drugs and medicines, surgery, psychology, the brain, that sort of stuff. But she also knows everything there is to know about plants, trees, geology, whatever. She's another one you can trust. You have to. If you don't, she might poison you.'

Dina poked him, hard, in the back, and he startled, jumping, so that he teetered for a moment on the very edge of the steps, and thought he would fall. He spun round, meaning to protest, but the sight of the gorgeous temple behind Dina took his breath away. It was the only bright thing in the whole of the Heresy now, still illuminated by the setting sun, still glowing with veins of pink and white.

'And here?' he said. 'What is this? Is it some sort of church?'

'I like that,' said Dina, nodding and pursing her lips. 'But no. It's the Heresiarchy, the court and judgement chamber of the Heresiarch, the centre of the whole place, its heart, its core.'

'What happens here?' asked Fitz. He had taken a few steps towards the building, raising his hand as if he would lay it on the stone.

'No one knows, really,' said Dina. 'It's a mystery.'

'Why don't you find out, then?' said Fitz.

'No, I mean, it's a mystery in the proper sense of the word. There are rites, arcana, occult ceremonies. These are the hidden, most secret rules of the game.'

'Everyone keeps talking about this game,' said Fitz. He had stepped to the wall of the Heresiarchy, and was running his hand over the polished pink marble. It drew him like a magnet. 'But I haven't seen anyone playing any games.' Following a streak of white that writhed through the stone slab, his fingers brushed towards the entrance to the Heresiarchy, towards its great oak door, towards the iron handle that stood at its centre.

Dina stepped to him, light as a cat, and covered his hand with hers.

'What's the game?' asked Fitz. He had fallen into a kind of reverie. His heart swelled in pulses of tide, and his vision swam. Something urgent, a kind of throbbing that was almost a shaking, began around his ears.

'What *isn't* the game?' whispered Dina. Her mouth was very close to his ear. 'We're born into a world of rules. Pick something up and drop it, and it falls. That's a rule. Love someone, and lose them, and it hurts. That's a rule. Do some things well, and you become rich. Do other things well, and you go to prison. Everything, every action you might take, every word you might utter, every thought you might entertain, is governed by rules. You could wake in the morning and go outside without dressing — why shouldn't you? Because wearing clothes is a rule. Otherwise you might as well tie shoes to your head and wear hats on your feet. You drive down the street and come to a traffic light. Red means stop, green means go, and you stop, and you go, because those are rules. Don't kill. Don't take what isn't yours. Don't go where you don't belong.'

Fitz pushed his hand towards the big iron handle at the centre of the oak door. 'I want to go in,' he murmured.

'No one goes in there except the Heresiarch,' said Dina. Her voice in his ear was like her eyes: cold, blue, vast, far. Then, suddenly, her hand tightened on his, and she yanked it backwards, pulling his arm painfully across his back.

'All you need to do is learn the rules,' she said, her voice hardly more than a breath, 'and if you play by them – *exactly* and *perfectly* by them – then you win the game. Every time. In the end, you don't even need to play it. It's over before it begins.'

*The game is already ended.*

Fitz wrenched himself away, spun, and stared at Dina. He half expected to find her transfigured, changed into some monstrous shape; but she was the same girl: her body at once relaxed, and ready, her eyes level and serious, a little twist of mockery at the corners of her mouth. He knew he should fear her. He knew he should be angry. And yet the moment he looked at her, all he felt was her spell.

'No one goes in there but the Heresiarch,' she repeated – as if none of the rest of it had happened. 'Only there isn't a Heresiarch at the moment,' she added. 'Not since he died. We're in an interregnum.'

Fitz wanted more than anything to keep looking at Dina; he wanted to watch her, to study her, to find out who she was, how she worked, and what she meant to do. But he couldn't bear to do it; he felt instinctively that the closer he got, the more he knew, the greater would be the danger. His eyes swerved, and he looked out over the whole of the Heresy, trying to find in its courts and their geometry, in its towers and domes, its roofs and ridges, instead, some explanation for the way Dina's touch had turned from tender to torture.

'Lesson one, remember?' she said quietly.

Fitz sighed, a long and heavy breath that allowed all his tension to float out of him. He felt for a breath like he was hanging from the roof of the Old Friary. 'Shouldn't we go?' he said.

Dina didn't answer, but she led the way. Skipping down the grand stairs of the Heresiarch's court, down to their narrow outlet and the low passage that led back to the Porch, Fitz had the distinct sense that he was being funnelled, as water into a jug. It made him uneasy, so uneasy that when he caught up with Dina at the Porch door, he hesitated, half in mind to go back to his tower – no matter what the Officers wanted from him. From within the Porch, he could hear them talking in animated voices, and the glow now – against the settling evening – was much brighter than earlier.

Dina cleared her throat.

'What should I do?' he asked.

'What do you think you should do?' Dina replied.

*Fine.*

Fitz stepped up, took the knocker in his hand, and brought it down, hard, on the wood of the door three times.

'Not what I would have done,' said Dina. She seemed almost amused. *That mockery.*

133

The Registrar opened the door. Dressed in the same, long belted coat in which Fitz had seen him before, and wearing his round red cap, he now struck Fitz anew. For one thing, he stood taller by a head than any man Fitz had encountered in his life, totally out of keeping with the low-raftered room in which he stood. Beneath his cap, his heavy eyebrows, moustache and beard all of black gave his face, and his impatience, an imposing definition.

'As Registrar to the Heresy,' said the man, 'I demand by what right you knock at the Porch door.'

Fitz looked at Dina. She shrugged. Her cheeks still held their wry cheer, her eyes their distance.

'I have no right,' he said to the Registrar.

The Registrar scowled. 'You're late,' he said. He drew the door open wide, and stepped aside with it.

Inside, the long, low hall was illuminated with hundreds of black lanterns, which hung thick from the twisted rafters on chains of iron. The wood of the floor and the high roof blazed all around them, gleaming with the lantern-light, and burned in the two hearths, one at either end of the room, where logs crackled on high-piled andirons. At the far end of the hall, seated at a long table, facing them, sat six people on eight chairs. Near the centre of the table Fitz saw Mr Ahmadi, and – to his surprise – the homeless man from outside the museum, Arwan. Of the other four, two men and two women, at first he recognized perhaps two faces from earlier in the day. One – a woman with soft features and a face pale as cream, her short hair tucked beneath her cap and her hands resting easily in her lap – seemed familiar, but Fitz couldn't immediately place her. They sat in silence, watching the two children approach them down the length of the hall, trailed by the Registrar.

Fitz stared at the familiar woman as long as he could, trying to read her features as they approached.

*I know I know you.*

When they were about ten feet away, Dina touched Fitz's arm, gently at the elbow, and he stopped.

The Registrar went to a desk that stood by the wall. He raised the desk's cover, and from it retrieved a large book bound in brushed leather. With this under his arm, he took his place in one of the empty chairs behind the table. Fitz noticed that the chair almost at the centre of the table remained empty.

*The Heresiarch. We're in an interregnum. Keep up, newbie.*

The Registrar opened the large book that he had carried to the table, to a page very near the end. It was blank. He looked up. Where before, at the door, his expression had seemed almost that of anger, now his eyes narrowed in something more like interest, as if he regarded the children before him as a difficult problem to be solved.

'Your name,' said the Registrar.

Fitz gave his name. The Registrar wrote it down at the top of the large, blank page, in the centre, but without formality or embellishment.

'Who will offer to stand surety for this boy?' the Registrar asked.

Dina took his hand. Fitz very nearly pulled it away. No one but his mother had ever touched him, there.

'I do,' said Dina. The Registrar entered Dina's name directly beneath Fitz's.

135

'*Ignorantia sapientia*,' said the Registrar. He looked directly into Fitz's eyes. Even from this distance, Fitz could see that his pupils had dilated into encompassing, black pools, almost blotting his eyes completely. 'In ignorance lies wisdom. It is said that a foolish man once challenged a prophet, demanding the secret of life and the best thing for man. Hear his answer.'

'The best thing for man,' said Dina, 'is never to have been born at all.'

Fitz tried to pull his hand from Dina's. She gripped it more tightly, and with a slight, powerful shake of her arm, forced his own hand back down. Fitz was startled by her strength.

'What will you give,' said the Registrar, 'for indemnity against his default?'

'My life for his life,' answered Dina.

'Your life is not yours to dispose,' said the Registrar.

'Nor is anyone's,' answered Dina. 'And yet it may be taken.'

'*Placet*,' said the Registrar. 'A good answer. You may stand surety for this boy. He is matriculated.' He made a note in the ledger. Then, having set down his pen, and using the tips of his fingers, he pushed the book very slightly away from him. He sat back in his chair and regarded the two children as the other adults also did – with detachment.

Mr Ahmadi leaned forward slightly. He set his hat on the table before him.

'We may now proceed with the enrolment. You have entered into the mother; now you must choose how you will be delivered to the father. For the game is already ended.'

'The game is already ended,' repeated all the others, including Dina.

'Ignorance,' said Mr Ahmadi, 'is the greatest privilege. A step taken in ignorance, like flying on the wind, is a kind of blessing. And yet you may, if you choose, ask each of us one question. But only one. After that you must choose from among us.'

Fitz looked carefully at the man who had once been his neighbour. His face, still drawn and sunken from the trials of the day and night before, reminded Fitz of his father's – of the austere portrait of Mr Ahmadi Senior hanging in the dining room of the Old Friary. But there was in his features, now, none of his father's kindness, nothing of the gleam that, even in the milky confusion of the old man's eyes, had animated him. Fitz wondered if he were already dead, if the light that made the heart bright and the eyes merry, that struck music into the voice and kindled nimble fire in a man's actions, had in Mr Ahmadi Junior already gone out. The events of the night before swam in his eyes, and he wished he had been able to see Mr Ahmadi's face while he was driving the gig, lashing at the winds, or later, when they had driven upward on the night's gusty convections. Then he might have known.

Fitz wanted to ask what he was meant to choose. He wanted to ask what this was all for. He wanted to ask why a man he knew, from whose library he had borrowed books, a man who had spent the night saving him from fire, wind, earth and water, now sat before him like some sort of judge of the underworld, severe, uncompromising and final.

*That was it, wasn't it. The game is already ended. They think they know what I am going to do.*

He looked at the row of adult faces where, ranged before him, they sat. As his gaze ran along the table, even before his eyes settled on her, with a jolt as if struck he remembered where he had seen that woman's face before – *she must be the Commissar*, he thought. She looked familiar.

*I almost remember.*

'There are many things you do not know,' Mr Ahmadi prompted him. Fitz's gaze snapped back to him. The others looked at him, too, and sharply. Fitz thought he must be breaking with tradition. They were expecting something.

'There's nothing I need to know,' Fitz said. 'I don't want to ask any questions.'

At that, most of the adults at the table sat up. They looked at each other, clearly unsettled. Dina began to crush Fitz's left hand in her right. Mr Ahmadi, alone, remained impassive, though Fitz thought perhaps a smile had started at the corner of his mouth.

*So you* are *there.*

'That is also your right,' said Mr Ahmadi. 'But now you must choose.'

The adults at the table now regarded Fitz, and Fitz alone, with interest. They studied him as he did them, each appraising the other. Fitz took them in turn: at the table's right end, the Registrar, tall and meticulously barbered, his thick moustache trimmed at hard angles round his mouth, and on his head the round cap of red; at the table's left end, also capped in red, the Commissar, of middle age and height, stout as a barrel, her face flanked by brown curls tucked behind her ears; to her left another woman, the Keeper, sharp and small like a tack, every stretch of her skin and long felt gown taut, as if pulled and twisted tight by the plait of gold she wore beneath her green cap, that lay across her shoulder as might a snake; opposite her, next to the Registrar, also wearing a green cap, the Sweeper, a fat dollop of a man whose gold buttons, down the length of his blue felt coat, seemed on the verge of popping off, and whose thick chubs of hands lay holding one another, on the table, like raw sausages extruded from their cases; beside him Arwan, the Jack, as massive and as powerful as a tower, his face all granite, heavy and impassive, capped in blue; his double, the man they called the Rack, ancient and wiry, his jaw stubbled with white, and white the wisps of hair that fringed his wrinkled face from beneath his loose blue cap; at the centre of the table, Mr Ahmadi – the Master – still in his cape and tall black hat; and beside him, the empty chair.

'I choose Dina,' said Fitz.

Arwan stood up, upsetting the table with his enormous legs. He wasn't alone in his evident shock; all of the adults – save only Mr Ahmadi, who now really was smiling – seemed to have had the wind knocked out of them. The Keeper turned to the Rack, putting her hand on his arm, but her mouth, though it moved, made no words. The Sweeper crushed the flesh of his fingers together, muttering. Arwan, finding himself on his feet and his head knocking among the pendant lanterns, recovered his dignity by flattening the creases in his felt coat, then rounding the table and stalking off. He left the courtyard door standing open; in the draught the fire roared.

'So be it,' said Mr Ahmadi. He turned to the other Officers, meeting their gazes one by one, and then leaned back again in his chair. 'I will train him,' he announced. His eyes, like the fire, seemed to crackle and flame as they settled on Dina. 'But because he has chosen you, it falls to you to take him in to the Sad King.'

The Registrar picked up his pen with reluctance, and added a note to the foot of the page on which he had written Fitz's name. Fitz noticed that the greater part of the large white leaf he had left blank.

'Your death is enrolled,' said the Registrar. He unbuttoned his cassock and slipped his pen into a pocket within. 'You have much to learn, but nothing left to lose.'

Mr Ahmadi stood, and took up his hat and placed it on his head. Leaning a little over the table, hands splayed, he balanced his whole weight on the tips of his fingers.

'Now you must go in to the Sad King. Dina will show you the way.'

Mr Ahmadi nodded to the Registrar. The tall man in the red coat had already risen from the table. Without ceremony he pulled open the low wooden door in the corner, and stood beside it so that the two children could pass through. His hand in Dina's, his eyes on her flushed face, Fitz followed her past the table, past the Registrar, past the old and uneven door hinged and studded with heavy iron. As they stepped through the passage into the room beyond, the Registrar was already closing the door; Fitz heard it shut snug upon his heels.

And then he hardly cared.

Fitz had followed Dina into a hall of light. The room itself was huge, an open and cavernous, high-beamed space that, like the low Porch from which they had entered, was lit by lanterns hanging chained from the ceiling – but here, by hundreds and by thousands how much greater, both brighter and more golden! Lights washing across its steep nave, lights trickling and in cascade, lights pendant on long and sinuous chains that swept to peaks only to plummet heavy with their deep glow once more, tides of lights, swells of lights, lights that gathered by folds on folds, cramming the heart. The space was dizzy with light; his thoughts, his eyes, swam. Each of the lanterns on its own chain hung slung from some far fixing in the ancient rafters, invisible above. Fitz had a sense of the hall's height, of its length, of the black, carved wood of its walls and the high pitch of the ceiling's ridged peak, its almost intolerable expanse and capacity. Dina relinquished his hand and he wandered alone into the gold-burnished brightness. Fitz found himself tracing a tightly defined path that wound to the right, then scythed in a long spiral anticlockwise into the centre of the hall. Faster and faster he circled in the shifting, fascinating, disorientating candlescape of the hall, driving towards the midst of all until, like his own heart high and hurling with its sense of arrival, the lights leaped on three sides in a towering, fluting convection that girded the hall's innermost enclosure.

Dina drew up to his side where Fitz had come, abruptly, to the lanterned path's middle end. Leaning to the floor she lifted by its handle a heavy oak door, and dragged it aside; together they stared at the hole she had exposed, paved around with rough stone and jewels of many colours. Circular, five or six feet in diameter, its maw of darkness shrouded with a rising mist that swirled and dispersed into the wide, warm hall of honeyed light, it seemed like the question to which the hall was the answer, the doubt to which the hall asserted its spectacular hymn of reply.

'You weren't supposed to pick me,' said Dina. 'You were supposed to pick *him*, the Master.' She said it as a matter of fact. Her voice cut through the light and magic that surrounded them, and hunkered like the black of the hole before them, down, flat. It was as if they inhabited two different places, two different worlds, Fitz trembling at the centre of a gyring hive of illumination as encompassing and assuring as he had ever known, cocooned by its splendid brightness, while Dina, beside him, stood in an empty room with the lights on.

'What is this place?' Fitz asked. Still awed by the majesty of the space, his voice, hushed, barely registered over the slow hiss of ten thousand wicks alight.

'The Lantern Hall was built over a kind of well,' Dina answered. 'The well we call the Sad King.'

'Why?'

'The king who built the Heresy, who was the first Heresiarch, had lost something that was very dear to him, something that disappeared into the earth and never returned. This – *feels* – like that.'

'What is the feeling,' Fitz murmured. His eyes closed, but the light seeped through his eyelids gold and gorgeous like butter melting through gauze.

'All of this –' Dina gestured around the hall – 'grew from that. All of this can only ever grow from that.'

Fitz looked at her. She didn't seem to feel like anything. He considered how he felt. He had been excited at first entering the Lantern Hall, eager when rounding the lit way that led him to this place. That excitement had, like a taut string bowed, and bowed, sounded in him with so much resonance and heat that he had felt he might burst. Now, here, staring into the darkness of the void in the floor, listening to Dina, it ran from him as suddenly as the yolk from a cracked egg.

'Third lesson,' said Dina. 'Never forget to forget yourself.'

Fitz watched the mist spiralling in the well hole of the Sad King. The shapes changed and changed again, changed into and out of themselves.

'Everyone who comes here, everyone who is matriculated as an Apprentice, has to come to the well of the Sad King. It's a ritual. You're supposed to bring the thing that you love the most in the world, and give it away. Only after you have given away what you love most, can you begin your training.'

Fitz was immediately conscious that he had only one thing with him to give. He wouldn't.

'What did you give?'

'Maybe one day you'll find out.'

Fitz remembered that icy, distant look in Dina's eyes, and thought it unlikely that he would ever find out anything about her. Her eyes were like an empty room.

'Did you just drop it in?'

'Sort of.'

Within the swirl of mist rising from below – maybe two feet down, maybe less – the interior of the well went dark. That was where the water was. Fitz put his hand to Clare's silver jay and felt the tiny metal of it cool between his thumb and forefinger.

'What if I don't? Give something up.'

'Then you can't stay in the Heresy. You have to make the choice. That's why we're here.'

Fitz's eyes strayed from the swirling mist and its unknowable shapes to the hard paved edge of the well head, mortared with dark jewels like scabbed wounds. He knew what it would mean to leave the Heresy. Here at the centre of the web, maybe, he might be safe; but out there he knew what awaited him. He had seen the fires, the shadows of strange forms moving in the trees; he had heard the threats, and the whispering that moved like wind among the leafless trees. He remembered Aslan.

His fingers, almost of their own volition, began to tug at the jay.

*No. This is mine.*

A lump stood out in his throat and lifted involuntarily towards his mouth. Beneath it the blood in his veins seemed to dance with air, to blow and puff as it sputtered in his chest. An idea was forming just out of reach of his conscious thought; he could feel it beginning to protrude from somewhere almost hidden within him, swirling out like the mist that rose towards him. He was afraid to look at it. He forced himself.

*I'll give myself but I won't give that.*

*How hard can it be?*

'I've made my decision,' he said.

'So quickly?' Dina was smiling at him. Her eyes flicked to his hand, which still hovered at his breastbone.

She was still smiling as he stepped into the well. She didn't protest, or move to stop him.

He had assumed he would hit the water instantly. He was braced for it, for the chill promised by the rising mist that had played invisibly on his skin and in his nostrils. It would engulf his shoes, his trousers and his shirt, but he would feel it on his hands and face before the shock of it penetrated his clothing. He was petrified, but his fear he could sacrifice.

He didn't hit the water. Nor did he have time for confusion, alarm, fear or regret before he hit something else entirely. It was five seconds, ten seconds, even fifteen before, in the well-night dark as pitch, tearing through the thick vapour rising in shreds and clouds all around him, he realized what had broken his fall – what continued to break his fall as down he dropped, scything through black, through cold, and through his own surprise.

*Arms. Bare arms, arms in sleeves, in coats, dirty arms, clean arms, strong and skinny and hairy arms, arms bent and straight. Countless, endless, cradling arms.*

It seemed to Fitz as he fell on and on down the shaft, tumbling through a forest of outstretched arms, that it might just continue forever. It didn't hurt at all – in part because he leaned into the slap and scrape of skin against his body by curling or sitting down into the impact, in part because he began to fall ever more slowly as the web and lattice of arms continued to ease his descent. But if he fell more slowly, still he fell, on and on, ever downward, ever through a mass of arms.

And then, at last – when he had forgotten to expect it – his feet hit water, and he plunged into the well. At once, like a coiled spring, in a spasm of reflex his body extended – his feet kicking down in search of purchase, his right arm thrusting into the misty air above him. The water on his skin was warm and salty, like a bath of tears, and Fitz had just time to notice its strangeness before his hand, groping in the open as he sank, closed on another hand. As he had fallen the arms sustaining him had dropped away like leaves before drops of rain. Now this fist, finding his, grasped and held him, but had strength only to halt his further fall, not to lift him clear of the water. Fitz thrashed his head, still submerged, and fought to bring it clear of the surface. His body writhed, groundless, as beneath the hot sorrow of water he struggled to fight down the panic in his chest and the tumult in his ears.

*No. No. No. Not again.*

Then, moving with the tentative tapping tread of a spider, another hand sought out his arm and, finding it, took hold of it – then another, and another, and more, until his arm like the under-hull of a seasoned boat was crusted up with clinging – and in a concerted moment they lifted Fitz gasping clear into the dank and heaving air. Now he began to fall upward again, each hand to a hand handing him and hand by hand rising. The socket of his shoulder seemed to tear with pain, but into the tangle of wrists and gripping he managed to push his second arm; instantly a dozen other hands closed round it, and Fitz felt himself roughly but surely dragged towards the glow that, as his blinking eyes cleared against the shifting damp and drops, revealed itself at last as the Hall of Lanterns, and the last hand upon his was Dina's. He kicked out his foot, finding the jewelled ledge. She pulled him clear of the well.

Fitz found himself on his knees. The rough rock of the well's edge had crunched into his shinbone as he crawled clear of the swirling cloud of vapour, and now he collapsed round his legs, the adrenaline that had been coursing through his body spent, and every corner of his skin coarse and raw.

Having hauled him from the well head with surprising force, even with ease, Dina had relinquished his hand almost as if it were a soiled thing. Now, while Fitz rubbed his shin to no purpose, all the while – equally vainly – struggling to make sense of the succession of physical sensations he had just experienced – she took a step back from him, as an artist might, while painting, to get a better view of the canvas.

'Why did you do that?' she asked him.

His awareness of Dina had been jostling in his consciousness with attention to himself. Now he stared at her. All the pain in his legs seemed, suddenly, to have been an illusion.

'In the well – there are –' He was going to say that there were people. It would sound ridiculous, and he checked himself before the word formed on his lips. 'There's –'

'A lot of water, by the look of it,' said Dina. 'Why did you throw yourself into the Sad King?'

As if Dina's words were flies buzzing round his face, Fitz pinched his eyes and shook his head to clear it. 'No, there's more than that. Not just water. I mean, before the water – there are *arms*.'

As he looked up at her, around Dina's head thousands of lit lanterns glowed, in such a way that her face seemed to emerge from the great brightness around and beyond it, at once into a clarity and a darkness.

'People's arms,' Fitz said. He started to push himself up. 'There were –'

But Dina's eyes had hardened. All the horizons of sky they had contained she now compressed into two tiny balls of crushed glass.

'Don't be crazy,' she said. 'You fell in the water.'

Dina pulled him to his feet and clapped her hands to his shoulders, as if she were knocking sense into him, or stamping out some sort of lunacy that – running its thickening tendrils beneath his skin – now threatened to shoot and twine out of his body.

Dina shook him once, hard, then left him to stand and shiver while she turned on her heel and strode away from him, down the spiralling avenue of lanterns. He watched her go. After about twenty paces, she stopped, and turned.

'You came to the Sad King, and you gave yourself. A good choice. That is all,' she said.

As she spoke, all the lanterns in the hall began as if pulled by a single steady arm to rise. Their movement was silent, and still, but every light strung from every chain seemed to travel at its own pace, so that they burned in and past and out and among one another as they lifted, flexing and rippling Fitz's wondering eye.

'We'd better get you cleaned up,' she said. 'And then it's time you met the set. If we dawdle much longer, we'll miss First Feeding.'

Dina held out her hand. While the lanterns rose, he walked to her and took it. Down the clear stone floor she swept him, and out by the giant doors.

7

# *Dina*

'Is it true you knocked at the door of the Porch? Russ said he saw you knock.'

'I asked the stupidest questions at my enrolment.'

'Dina, what did the Jack say, when the new boy chose you?'

'Why don't you have your proper clothes?'

The questions and comments came so fast, the moment he sat down at the table, that Fitz didn't know where to look first. Eight places had been laid for the eight Apprentices; and Fitz observed that his was the last, across from Dina's. Now she took her seat opposite him, swinging her legs deftly over the bench without catching them in her long black gown.

'Let him be, rabble,' she said with authority. 'He's just been chucking stuff into the Sad King.' She nodded down the hall to the place – beneath and between the long tables that had been carried in and laid for dinner, among the hundreds of people sitting, eating, conversing, laughing – where the well lay silent, waiting, full of a mystery that none of the children seemed to understand.

*A mystery they wouldn't believe, if I told them.*

'And besides, he hasn't eaten all day.' Dina took a bowl of bread that sat on the table between them and held it up to Fitz. His stomach had been cramping with hunger, and he seized at two crusts a little too greedily.

'Evidently,' said the quiet girl beside him, who hadn't yet spoken. She held out her right hand – thin and cold as a sheet of glass, and as brittle – without extending it past her other elbow. Fitz put down the bread and tried to take it, but felt he was intruding. 'Payne,' she said.

'And this is Russ, who is apprenticed to the Jack; Padge is with the Commissar and Navy with the Registrar ('The tall, arrogant one,' added Navy, a bright-eyed girl mopped with waving red curls). On this side,' said Dina, numbering them off with her long index finger, as if tapping each one on the pate in turn, 'Dolly, who shadows the Keeper; Fingal follows the Rack, and Payne the Sweeper.' Fitz took them all in as fast as he could, circling the table of their eager and curious faces. 'Introductions done,' concluded Dina, nodding her head once for formal emphasis. 'Let's eat.'

'And who do you follow?' asked Fitz.

Dina already had a piece of the tough bread in her mouth, and was chewing vigorously. 'The Master, obviously,' she said, between gobs.

'Then we both –'

'Yes,' said Navy. 'It's strange. We haven't had eight before, and nobody's ever doubled up.' Navy, alone of all the children at the table, didn't seem interested in the baskets of bread. Instead, she remained entirely focused on Fitz, staring at him with round eyes and her lips a little parted, as if always about to say something else. Usually she did.

'I wish someone would double up with me. There's more than enough to go round in the Registry.'

'Eat,' said Dina, taking up the basket and reaching across Russ and Padge to put it in Navy's face. Navy took a piece of the bread and placed it on her plate.

'But it's nice that you two will be together,' she said to Fitz from across the length of the table. 'Maybe you'll be close.'

Dina picked up the bread basket again, and with a look like murder shoved it with more violence across Russ and Padge, nearly knocking Navy in the nose.

'Eat more,' she barked. Navy took another piece of bread and set it beside the first.

'Well, at least working with the Registrar I get to be with the animals,' Navy said. She added, 'That way it isn't so lonely.'

'If only you were lonelier,' retorted Fingal, and then retired into a kind of sullen introversion. He was tall, with sharp features and a long fringe of heavy blond hair that almost concealed his eyes. Fitz thought he looked about sixteen.

'We have a kind of farm in the Registry,' Navy explained, as if she hadn't heard him. 'And a *huge* aquarium. I have to muck everything out about every five minutes.'

'Perhaps you should go and do it now,' offered Fingal.

'Moodies,' said Navy, philosophically, to the table as a whole. And then to Fitz: 'Everyone gets the moodies at his age.' Silently, she mouthed a number to Fitz: 'Seventeen.'

Dina rolled her eyes, and Fitz felt for a moment like giggling. In all his life he had never seen, much less met, much less been part of, such a strange and dysfunctional and intimate group of children, so obviously dissimilar and yet so obviously familiar. The children he had known at school were nothing like this: distant, formal, and suspicious, or – occasionally – thick as thieves. But these children were different. He could see already that they couldn't be called friends; the way they carried themselves, the way they interacted, was hardly friendly. Fingal seemed to be shuttered in his own world, contemptuous of the others. Navy's heart she had pinned to her sleeve, but no one seemed to have any time for it at all, apart from Fitz. Russ, shy and amiable, was absorbed in a quiet conversation with Padge about a book Padge had propped in his lap against the side of the table. They both looked to be about fifteen, Padge a little taller and stronger, and with a great deal more freckles. Dolly – whom Fitz recognized as the girl with the crossbow – was probably Fitz's own age, and had the darkest skin he had ever seen, with dense black curls that cascaded over her back and shoulders, hiding her face from his view – except for the brief moments when she stole a glance at Dina, whom she seemed to revere, or mistrust. And then there was Payne – was that her first name, or her second name? – who was using a knife to cut her bread into minute and identical squares, and lining them up in orderly rows on her plate. These children didn't seem like friends at all, but they had something else.

*Family. They're one another's family.*

The recognition hit Fitz like a brick. He looked around the hall in which they sat, trying to understand how this little knot of unlike hearts and ill-matched minds had come to share so much. Their table sat on a sort of raised wooden platform at the end of the long, lofty hall. It was a long table, but only covered half the platform; beyond his end stood another table at which the seven Officers were seated, each of them engaged in animated conversation with her or his neighbours. At his end of the table, not two metres from theirs, Fitz could hear a little of what Mr Ahmadi was saying, and he tried for a moment to parse it – something about research, needing to spend days in the library, something about requiring the Keeper's aid to solve a puzzle. But servers moved between the two tables, laying down plates of food and taking others, and in their bustle Fitz lost the thread; and so his thoughts and attention shifted back to his own table, to the way Navy and Dolly – who might well be friends, on second thoughts – were pulling ridiculous faces at one another, at Dina's unquiet silence, as she pushed through her food, her eyes ranging restlessly over the other children, picking out details and harvesting observations. Behind her, below, on the hall's broader floor, three long tables ran the length of the room in parallel, each flanked by long wooden benches. At these benches sat hundreds of men and women of all ages – some as young, almost, as Fingal, others as old as the Rack. The same servers moved among these tables, shifting bread, platters of meat, and bowls piled with steaming vegetables, pouring water and wine, and watching the diners closely in order to anticipate their next needs.

'Who are they?' Fitz asked Dina, gesturing behind her to the benches crammed with diners.

'Fellows of the Heresy,' she answered. She was halfway through Second Feeding, as she had termed it when the plates of meat arrived. Dina had been served first, Fitz last. 'They all work here, and live here. Each of them has an Office – like a department, working under one of the Offs – but they all eat together.'

'Offs?'

Dina pointed at the Officers at the next table. 'Offs,' she said. She swivelled her finger so that it pointed, almost with disdain, at their own table. 'Prents.' Then she gestured behind her, vaguely. 'Fells.'

'And, those people, were they all students, before they were –'

'Fells,' said Navy. 'No.'

'Yes,' said Dolly.

'But not like us,' Navy said. 'Some Prents go on to be Fells, some go to do Society work somewhere else. But we're the real Prents. We're training to be Offs. That's different.'

Fitz nodded as if he understood.

'As if you'll ever be the Registrar,' said Fingal.

'Like I said,' said Navy. She put her fingers at the corner of her mouth and dragged her cheeks into the caricature of a frown, miming her derision to Fitz from down the table. 'Moodies.'

'And what about the –' Fitz was staring with interest at the commotion and hubbub in the hall below them. His eyes followed particularly the graceful, almost dancelike min-istrations of the black-coated servers who dodged between the tables and seemed to skip about the hall, delivering and removing platters, pouring from great jugs, and clearing plates and cutlery.

'Servers,' said Navy.

'Serfs,' corrected Dina.

'It's not a nice word,' Navy protested.

'And yet it's what we all say,' Dina said, while she chewed, refusing to look at the girl who looked so earnestly at her. 'Even you.'

'They mainly work for the Commissar,' Navy said, 'and the Sweeper. But every Office has its Serfs. You'll see them all the time. They're extraordinary.'

In among the orderly, mathematical movement of the Serfs in the lower hall, something had caught Fitz's attention. At first he wasn't sure what it was – a ruffle, or disturbance that he only noticed out of the corner of his eye, a kind of burr in the smooth lines of the service. For a moment his eyes searched the floor, and then like the wind moving on a water the problem disclosed itself again, this time to his notice. A tall, gaunt figure moved among the Serfs, dressed in the same felted and belted coat as the Officers, but this one of many colours and irregularly stitched to form a kind of motley. His movements were awkward, parodic, at once perfectly in line or keeping with those of the Serfs, and yet somehow extraneous to them.

'Who is that?' Fitz asked, of no one in particular, and therefore of all of them.

Dina turned on the bench and followed his discreetly directed index finger.

'The fool,' she said, and went back to Second Feeding.

'We call him the Riddler,' Payne said, from his left. She spoke softly, and with crisp articulation. 'He isn't an Off, but he does this and that in the Sensorium. He is not –' she paused – 'exceptionally bright.'

'He's bright enough to truss you like a pig, rip you neck to toe, and turn you out on the table,' said Fingal, hardly looking up from his plate.

'That's disgusting,' said Navy, leaping to the defence of Payne, who looked appalled.

Padge put down his book. 'The language may be colourful,' he said, 'but Fingal has a point. The Riddler presides over the most ancient Office in the Heresy, the Sensorium. Up here he doesn't make much sense, but down there – when he's in his element – let's just say he can find your pressure points pretty quickly.'

'Nonetheless and moreover,' said Dina, still occupied with her food, 'the fool.'

Around them the food was changing again. The Serfs moved with incredible agility and speed between the tables and the kitchens, which were situated at the end of the hall, furthest from the Prents' table. As they had been eating, the night had darkened, and Fitz looked again with wonder at the lamps that lit the hall, now retracted high among the beams of the pitched ceiling, hanging on their chains. Now he noticed, as he hadn't before, that each of the lamps had a variety of coloured glass panes – red, blue and green – that seemed to wash through the air above the tables with floods of mingling hues.

'It's pretty, isn't it,' said Navy. She was still watching Fitz's every move.

'Don't get used to it, though,' said Dina. 'They only light the lamps on a wedding night.'

'Is there a wedding tonight?' asked Russ, looking up for the first time from Padge's book. 'I hadn't realized.'

'They hold weddings, here?' Fitz was incredulous. Somehow the Heresy had seemed so closed, so withdrawn from the world.

'Not weddings like *that*.' Fingal was sneering again. 'A Black Wedding. It's the ceremony in which a student or an apprentice formally and finally renounces the world and all that is in it.'

'You should know,' said Navy.

'Enough,' said Dina, severely. From the stunned look on Navy's face, Fitz thought Fingal might have kicked her under the table. To her credit, she didn't protest. She didn't make another peep.

A gong sounded, nearly knocking Fitz off the bench. When he turned round, he saw why. The massive brass gong – still vibrating from the tremendous walloping one of the Serfs had just given it – stood only a few feet behind him. He had just begun Third Feeding, but he put his fork down, and stood up with the rest of the room.

The Fells filed out of the hall, one row after another, in silence. Almost everyone had been interrupted in their meal – some were in the midst of Second Feeding, others not yet done with Third. The plates lay as they had been left, the food in places still steaming.

Fitz half whispered, half mouthed to Dina, 'No one's finished eating!'

Dina raised her eyebrows.

'But everyone has finished,' she said. And added, 'Don't worry. The food won't be wasted.'

No sooner had the Fells left the room than the Serfs took their places and began to eat from the half-finished plates. Dina gave a twitch of her head, and Fitz realized that he was supposed to do something. For some reason he looked at Navy, who was gesticulating wildly with her hands for him to go, out through a door on the dais beyond where the Offs were sitting, back out into the room they called the Porch. He and Dina led the two short columns. As soon as they were through the door, all the Prents pulled off their gowns and hung them on the hooks from which they had taken them on their way in.

'Where do I put mine?' asked Fitz.

Padge hung it for him on the last of eight hooks. It was covered in dust, and on a wooden plaque above the hook he read a name: 'Nazir'. He must have been staring at it. He'd seen the name before. *But where?*

'My grandfather,' said Dina. 'He died the month before last. He was – special.'

'I'm very sorry,' said Fitz, coming to himself. The other Prents – even Navy – had already dashed from the long, low room, and only the two of them were left.

'No, I mean, he was special to the Heresy. No one has used any of his things for a long time.'

Dina held the door for him as they stepped back into the dark courtyard. Only one lamp hung from an iron fixing outside the hall, five or more metres away, and the stars cast little light. As Fitz brushed past Dina, he smelled that warm scent of leaves that he had noticed when he first met her – like the Bellman's Wood in September, full of must and rain. For a few instants, disorientated in the dark, he thought he could see by the light of that fragrance, and the trees of the wood reared all around him.

Fitz was brought back to his senses by a mewling sound. It came from the centre of the courtyard. He peered into the darkness, and saw the outlines of a heavy cage, the sort of reinforced box in which they moved animals in cartoons, or in zoos.

'Is that a cage? What's in it?'

'It's a kind of broad-nosed lemur,' said Dina. 'It's rare – one of the rarest animals in the world. We were studying it today with the Registrar.'

'If it's so rare, why is there one here?' Fitz had approached the cage cautiously, but he need hardly have worried. It was tiny, not much more than a baby, and was sucking its thumb.

'Search me,' said Dina.

Fitz could barely make out the shape of the animal's body where it cowered in the back of its cage; but its face mesmerized him: in its proportions and movements so close to human, but furry, and at completely the wrong scale. As he crouched, watching it suck its tiny thumb, he realized that something else was bothering him about the lemur. It had Dina's smell.

'Listen,' said Dina, cutting into his thoughts with a light touch to his shoulder. 'The wedding will begin in a few minutes, and you have a pretty spectacular view of the hall through the big east window. From the tower room, I mean. I don't have to be in my House till ten bells. I'll race you.'

There was no contest. Even in shoes Dina would have outpaced him, but by her head start and in the fleet freedom of her naked feet, she left Fitz so far behind he might have walked. By the time he had climbed to the top of the tower stairs, utterly spent and out of breath, she had already pushed his bed over to the west-facing window, and was kneeling with her elbows on the sill, watching the hall below. In the west, the sky still showed a smudge of day, and the last of the evening's stars glimmered faintly in the high obscurity above green-black hills. Above the lead and thatch and slated roofs of the Heresy's many courts, bats sliced silently through the shadows in their erratic flights. The precision and purpose of their movement struck Fitz as beautiful, the more so for its unpredictability.

'There,' said Dina, pointing.

The Serfs had pushed the long tables to the sides of the hall. Now they were scraping heaped platters of scraps and leavings into the hole of the well at the centre of the hall. Fitz thought of the arms extended in the blackness of the shaft below. 'Don't worry,' she had said.

*The food won't be wasted.*

Through the clear glass panes of the large east window, Fitz and Dina watched the last preparations taking place, as Sweepers began to push long mops across the tiled floor, while Commissaries extinguished half the lanterns, lowering them by the rack and snuffing them wick by wick. Fitz's eye went back again and again to the black hole in the middle of the hall's long floor. It was a place of which everyone was conscious, and to which no one paid the least attention, a kind of constructive absence.

Sensing his preoccupation, Dina jarred him.

'It was supposed to be Fingal's wedding tonight,' said Dina. 'He's been working towards it for two years, at least. That's why he was in such a foul temper.'

'What happened?' asked Fitz. His eye drifted to the methodical snuffing of the lanterns; from this distance, the Commissaries seemed to swarm to their tasks like ants, so organized and orderly that they almost appeared to be the several bodies of a single, distributed consciousness.

'He wasn't ready.'

'What makes a Prent ready?'

For a while they were silent. The bats were not troubled by the darkness that huddled ever closer around the buildings.

'Let me ask you this,' said Dina. 'Have you ever seen anything truly beautiful?'

'Yes, millions of things,' said Fitz. 'The Bellman's Wood, at home – it's full of gorgeous things, gigantic beech and lime trunks like –'

'No,' said Dina. 'Listen more carefully. I mean something truly beautiful. Trees can be cut down. They rot. Things crawl in them. They burn. Char and ash. I mean something more substantial, something more enduring.'

Fitz wanted to say that the scene unfolding before him, as the Commissaries swirled in arcs between the dancing racks of rising lanterns, while the Sweepers traversed the floors in orderly patterns around and between them, was beautiful – in its precision, its effortless, silent symmetries.

'Clare is beautiful,' said Fitz. Dina turned her head to him. Her eyes seemed to punch through his own, so that he recoiled. 'My . . . my mother.' His voice cracked on the word. For a second, or more, he stalled, self-conscious, and in his determination to conceal it, revealed it. 'She tells beautiful stories, as good as anything you might read in a book. In her voice –'

'No,' said Dina again. Her posture beside him at the window hadn't changed, but her voice had; it hit the glass of the window like pebbles or grit on a road, strict and staccato. 'I don't mean your mother, either. Your mother may be your mother today, but tomorrow she may not be. Today she may be beautiful, but already the marks of her death lie upon her. Her stories may appear to be beautiful, but they're not real – only fantasies. I am asking you if you have ever seen anything *truly* beautiful.'

'But to me –'

'Not to you,' said Dina. 'Not beautiful just to you. Something that is in itself, as a property of itself, always and forever, without compromise or loss, beautiful. Something that you can show, can point to, that is truly there, and will always be there.'

'Can there be a thing like that?'

*Would such a thing be beautiful anyway?*

'It's hard to say,' said Dina. 'Your Apprenticeship has two parts. The Commissar, the Sweeper and the Rack together make up the three Houses of Disillusionment; they are the Disillusioners. That's a mouthful, even for Navy, so for short we call them the Losers. In different ways you practise with each of them the skill of seeing through illusions, or understanding appearances of all kinds for what they really are – just appearances. The Registrar, the Keeper and the Jack are Incoherentists, and theirs are the Houses of Incoherence. We call them the Breakers. The Breakers teach a harder thing than the Losers – not just how to give up on your feelings for beauty, but how to surrender your arrogant judgements about truth. The goal of your training is to accept, with peace and resignation, that beauty and truth may not exist.'

'And the Riddler? Is he a Loser, or a Breaker?'

'Neither,' said Dina. 'And both. By the time you've finished your work in the Sensorium, you can't be sure whether you, yourself, exist.'

'But some things are true,' Fitz protested. 'Ice is cold. And one and one make two.'

'If ice is cold, why does it seem to burn?' asked Dina. 'And one and one make two when you're adding, I don't know, sticks, but not when you're adding rabbits.' She smiled, but she hadn't yet looked at him; they both still watched the preparations in the hall below. 'I'm being silly, I know,' she conceded; 'but the more you push against apparent truths, the more they seem to crumble and give way. Even one and one.'

'Don't you believe in anything?' asked Fitz.

'Of course I do,' said Dina. Her voice had now grown sharp, and it stung him like fat from a pan. 'Of course I do. Listen. You saw the gatehouse on your way into the Heresy. You saw the blank eye. When the Sad King left his kingdom, when he gave it all away, relinquished everything of value and took to the waves with his counsellors and his generals, accompanied by only a few servants and friends, it's said that they were driven by a storm into a strange harbour – lush, overflowing with grapes and olives and every kind of fruit that is sweet and nourishing to the taste. There were fat herds on the hills, no end of grass, and the water where they rode was deep and – fed by a cascading stream – fresh. The king put his people ashore; they thought they had reached a land of plenty, a promised land. No sooner had they put their foot to land, though, than a hideous colossus stalked over the mountain, a monster covered in grime and blood, at his side a heavy barbed truncheon with which he threatened to crush and powder them all. But the most strange, most terrifying thing about him was that he had only a single, round eye in the middle of his forehead. The sight of him turned them all to jelly. There was nothing they could do to defend themselves. He shut them up in his cave, where every night he returned from his day's labour among his herds and vineyards, and every night he plucked one or other of them from the cowering crowd hunched by the wall, and stripped him, and ate him whole. They would all have perished in that way, had the Sad King not devised a plan for their escape. He gathered every piece of metal that they had – little knives, ornaments, brooches, rings, each forged or hammered thing of use or beauty, and while the giant was out, from the alloy fashioned in the giant's fire a single, strong shaft tipped with a fine point. When the monster returned that night from his toil, even where he stood in the mouth of his cave, the Sad King thrust the spear through his eye, and he and his people fled to their ship, and escaped.

'*That* is the blank eye. Not until you have relinquished sight, until you have surrendered the false promises made by every sensation, not until you have begun to see not with your eye, but with your *new* sight, your *blank* sight, your blindness, can you find anything truly true, anything actually beautiful.'

In the hall below them, things had suddenly changed. Six of the Officers had filed in, wearing their heavy black gowns drawn close round their long coats, but instead of the usual caps they were wearing what looked like hook-nosed bird masks, grey and engorged, with huge black eyes. Moving as one, as a single line, they stepped down from the dais at the end of the hall, and advanced towards its centre. The floor had been cleared before them, and the lights dropped; even from this vantage and distance, in the safety of a tower room through two windows, Fitz found their synchronized advance, their surreal garb and their poise both enthralling and unsettling.

But he was completely unprepared for what happened next.

He and Dina were unable to see all the way to the far end of the hall, but it was clear that, down by the kitchens, a commotion was stirring. Black-coated Serfs, repulsed or battered by something, someone, were being flung across the floor towards the Officers, some staggering backwards as they tried to regain their balance, others sprawling along the floor as if they had been pushed, slung or kicked. Over and over again these figures rushed back out of sight, back towards the end of the hall, only to find themselves, again, knocked or fought back. Their motions were large, theatrical, like caricatures in human form, the swirls and arcs of their arms balletic, the exaggerated movement athletic. It was theatre. It was dance. All this Dina and Fitz observed in complete silence, mesmerized; the muted action below them, however strange and violent, elicited not a murmur from either of them.

At first. After a minute, or maybe two, Fitz thought he could hear a kind of rhythm or chant rising from the hall below. It was then, for the first time, that he noticed that the Officers – still occupying the centre of the hall – had begun to shake their arms, at first only gently but with increasing force and violence, in an accelerating rhythm that matched the now unmistakable sound of their chanting. What is more, beside him Dina began to move against the window sill, apparently unconsciously and only very slightly, rocking back and forth on her knees, as if her body yearned to participate in the dance, in the primality of ritual that was unfolding below.

Fitz felt himself paralysed. He was embarrassed even to be aware of Dina's involvement, anxious about the nature of whatever was happening in the hall, and uncertain about how he should react to the things he was witnessing.

*She seems to be* enjoying *it.*

And then the figure appeared. Surrounded by a mob of black-suited Serfs, pushing and shoving one another to be nearer to the centre, a small group hove into the children's view, carrying a kind of mast or cross, on which hung the shape of a man – or not the shape of a man but, Fitz realized, a man. An actual man. He was tall, fair-haired, and dressed in a loose white gown. His hands and feet had been strapped to the mast on which he was carried, his arms pulled back over the crossbar and tied behind him. He looked delirious, as if he, too, were chanting in time with the monody rising from the Officers before him and the shouts and acclamations made by the rout that surrounded him.

Now for all his fear and anxiety, Fitz couldn't help but break the silence.

'Is that a cross?' he asked. 'Are they crucifying him?'

*It's revolting.*

The men carried the mast into the centre of the hall, immediately adjacent to the Sad King, and set it down. There it stood, as the servers backed away like cats fought into a corner, and the Officers advanced. They circled the mast and the man, his head now down, chanting and shaking their fists in time, stepping sideways in a revolving procession, leg over leg, ever faster, ever more violent, their chanting now ringing high and low registers in call and response, while the Serfs, fought back, returned, poured round the ring of Officers circling, so forming an outer ring of heckling cacophony that sounded to Fitz like brittle sticks rattling in a tempest, or like fire ripping through a dry wood, every instant a new explosion of sound: relentless, undiminishing, eternal.

'No,' said Dina. She still rocked on her knees, and Fitz wasn't sure, now, if she weren't forcing her forehead into the iron mullion of the window before her, gently but with deliberation making that oldest motion of suffering. 'It's not a crucifixion. There's an old story about sailors sailing in the Mediterranean past the island where the Sirens sing – terrifying, beautiful women, partly human, partly fish, scaled but also voluptuous, their music like the salt water from which it's partly made – the more you drink it, the thirstier you become. It's said these sailors coveted the song of the Sirens, yearned to hear it, to know it, to have it revealed in all its awesome clarity, while at the same time to resist and to reject it, to preserve themselves from it. So they had themselves tied to the masts of their ships, so that even if they cried to be released, to be allowed to drown and die in the throes of enchanting sea rhapsodies, the cords round their wrists and ankles would protect them. From themselves. He isn't being crucified. He's being pushed to the limits of his reason. He climbed that pole willingly, I promise you.'

167

Fitz's attention was so fully engaged by the square of light before him, and all it contained, that he didn't hear the tolling of the hour bell – from a belfry two courts behind – until it had stopped ringing.

Dina stopped rocking.

'That was ten bells,' she said. She sprang up from the bed and was across the room in what couldn't have been more than a single step. 'I'm late. Good thing I'm quiet on my feet.'

She stopped in the doorway, as if listening down the dark tower stairs. Then she turned, and her face, catching only the palest shadow of a light, floated in a void.

'Little brother,' she said. 'Promise me that you'll not watch any more of it. Not on your own.'

She wasn't making an appeal; this was an instruction.

'Promise.'

*Rules.* He nodded, and turned away from the window, sitting down heavily in the darkness.

And then she was gone.

Fitz lay on his bed, turned towards the bright shape of light cast on the high opposite wall. Now that he could no longer see the form and motion of the ritual below, he could barely resolve the patterns of near-inaudible music that reached him, and he wondered how much of what he had heard before he had only imagined. A low thrum or drone was all he could be certain of, a noise like cicadas that seemed to rise, perhaps, or fall – though as he listened on, the rising seemed to become the falling, and the falling the rising, until he wasn't sure what he was hearing, or if he was hearing anything at all. In frustration he turned over, drawing the blanket round him and trying to think of some more familiar, some more empty and undisturbing thought.

He had watched spiders at rest in their webs. They were not at rest, but vigilant. No matter the hour of day or night, the size of the web, the rain, the wind – if a fly were to become entangled in the sticky cords, it could only be a matter of time before the spider scuttled to the place. The movement was mechanical and the response programmed, as regular and reliable as the shape of the web itself, spun from some plan kept in an old book on a back shelf in the dusty archive of time. But twitch the web, and the weaver could not help but answer.

Fitz got to his knees, drawing the blanket round his shoulders in the cool night. He kneeled again before the bottom pane of the leaded window, and looked.

The young man with fair hair, still dressed in his white gown, still hung from the mast in the midst of the hall. But around him the Serfs and Offs had fallen quiet or almost quiet, and were circling, two concentric rings in opposed motions. From the room a sort of murmur rose, as of a colony of birds at rest – a white or a blank sound, presaging fury.

Suddenly the revolutions stilled. The room for a long breath – Fitz held his – stood static. From the back of the hall, someone was approaching. All eyes were on him. The Serfs parted to allow this figure in, then the Offs. Dressed in a scarlet gown and wearing an outsized headpiece, the figure seemed to shuffle forward in great pain, or with great deliberation, gaining ground in little surges and casting glances to left and right as he went. When he stood before the mast, he turned, and Fitz saw the face of the mask clearly – the grossly caricatured figure of an old man, shrivelled by age and experience, and yet swollen, too, as if the very troughs in his skin had enlarged it, as if the grey pallor of his cheeks also gave them life. In the centre of the mask, immediately above his pendulous nose, was set a single, round eye, bulging, gorged and washed with milky white. It was disgusting, engrossing, disarming, enraging. Fitz gagged to see it. With faltering strength – or was it the trembling of a huge power in the summoning? – he lifted his cupped hands into the air. He was holding something. Fitz strained to make it out.

It was the baby lemur.

As if it were a signal, one of the Offs stepped forward. Judging from his height, it had to be Arwan or the Registrar. He had a long knife in his hand, and seemed to dance, swirling with it within the circle, turning round the old man, reversing and sliding behind the mast. With a single, sharp upthrust, he seemed to plunge the knife into the young man's back.

Fitz stifled a shout; the noise sputtered out of him like the mewling terror of some innocent creature.

But the knife thrust hadn't harmed the man. It had cut through the cords that bound his hands. Now he spread his arms and arched his neck as if in pain. He brought his hands together before him, accepting from the old man the tiny, huddled form of the animal, holding it in the air as the other had done. All eyes, including Fitz's, were on it.

And then, as if he were opening a jar, turning his hands in contrary motion round its neck he strangled it. Hours seemed to pass until the moment when he let the lifeless body drop, almost weightless, silently to the floor. The young man had never once looked at the tiny animal; his eyes were fixed on the old man before him.

*How.*

*How. Howl. Howl. Howl. Howl.*

As if lurching on a swelling sea, as if his body were being tossed against the level, as if he were on a boat adrift in a storm and had lost all sense of orientation and proportion, Fitz began to retch. His head burned and sweat beaded on his temples, at the back of his neck. He smelled a heavy dead stink of salt.

Lurching in the darkness, without knowing where he was, shoeless, sightless, without meaning or understanding, he stumbled out of the tower room and down the stairs. His body dropped from step to step as if falling, the only imperative in his head to take that wretched and defenceless little body from the floor and hold it in his warm arms.

*It was sucking its thumb.*

Fitz's eyes burned in the darkness, and tears dropped on his bare arms as he ran.

At the bottom of the staircase he tripped across the cold stone landing to the gravel courtyard. As he staggered across the stones, he felt nothing – neither the cool air on his arms, nor the jagged stones beneath the soft pads of his feet. His bleared eye was fixed on the light coming from beneath the arch ahead; when he reached it, turning right, he fixed himself on the next arch, the next lantern. On and on he drove himself, past too many arches, into too many courts, until finally he stopped, wheeling and bewildered, aware of himself and that he was lost.

A hand grasped his shoulder, hard, from behind. He might have screamed, but another covered his mouth.

'Be still, little prince.'

It was Mr Ahmadi. Not the Master, but Mr Ahmadi.

Fitz was still.

'Where are you?'

Fitz turned round and looked at his old neighbour, searching his face for its long and bony beak, its inhuman black pools for eyes, its cold raptor skin.

'I don't know,' he said. 'I don't know where I am.'

'You look as if you've seen a ghost,' Mr Ahmadi said. His hands lay on Fitz's shoulders. They held him in place. Fitz thought that, without them, he might break into ten thousand pieces.

'I saw – through the window – Dina. In the tower. That old man.' The words came halting out of him, discrete and disconnected.

Mr Ahmadi's thumbs tightened on Fitz's collarbone. The pain checked the tears that were starting in his boy's eyes.

'Who *was* that?' He might have asked a question, but it passed through his throat like a shuddering expulsion. He wasn't sure if he had asked the question, or if the question had asked itself through him. He felt he had shifted an awful mass from his chest.

'It *should* have been the Heresiarch,' said Mr Ahmadi. 'The Heresiarch is the leader of the Heresy, its head and director. In the Black Wedding, the Heresiarch gives the initiate a choice. It's a kind of trial, a test. The initiate has to renounce something, something impossibly dear. It is the fulfilment of the renunciation promised at the well of the Sad King. It's different for everyone.'

Fitz tried to wriggle free. Mr Ahmadi loosened his tight grip, but still held him with one hand.

'We're in an interregnum,' he said. 'Which means we have no leader until a new one has been chosen, and accepted. So tonight it fell to me to break him. I wore the mask of the Heresiarch. It was only me.'

Fitz stared at him. *Whoever you are.*

'But that tiny creature,' Fitz protested. He was staring at his toes, trying not to blubber, but knowing that he still couldn't control his own words. 'It's so rare. It was in danger. It was a *child*. It was a *baby*.' Spasms tore through his ribs and his mouth emitted a kind of rasp and creaking, as of wood grinding wet on wood. 'Who would *do* that?'

Mr Ahmadi sighed. 'It had lost its mother, child. It wasn't going to survive anyway. The species isn't going to survive. There is nothing that you, or I, or any one person can do about that. Its time had come. For that poor, desperate creature, what we did to it was a merciful end. I made sure of that. I wouldn't have allowed it otherwise.'

*The game is already ended.*

'I wish you hadn't seen that tonight. Not yet. Dina should have stopped you. But if you are to survive in the Heresy, even for a short time, you will have to make yourself ready for what is to come. You will have to learn very, very quickly.'

*You have nothing left to lose, but much to learn.*

Never letting Fitz out of his touch, Mr Ahmadi had rounded, and now was guiding him, by the shoulder and out of the courtyard where they had been standing. They walked in silence into the deeper quiet within one of the passages. Fitz didn't recognize it – didn't recognize any of it. The buildings around him were shadows, and the shadows buildings. He stepped from darkness into darkness.

Suddenly, in the deepest of the shadows – in the shadow cast by other shadows – they stopped.

'Allow me to show you something,' Mr Ahmadi said. His voice was no more than a whisper.

He stooped to the ground beneath them, and from the path retrieved a handful of pebbles, the sort that lay everywhere on this side of the Heresy.

'Tonight you feel very alone. And it's true that I can't always be by your side. But you are not alone. Watch.'

Mr Ahmadi peered into the darkness above them. He seemed to be searching for something. What it was Fitz could hardly have guessed; he saw nothing at all, only thick, unyielding darkness. But, satisfied, Mr Ahmadi examined the stones in his left hand, picked out a handful of the largest, looked at Fitz with a smile, and then – drawing his right arm back like a catapult – launched them into the darkness of the empty sky.

Fitz waited for the stones to strike something: a window, the roof of one or another of the Heresy's countless gables, perhaps just the paving on the far side of the court. But there was no report – only, he thought, a rush on the air like the sound of feathered diving, of swooping, the whistle of wind across the pinions of great birds in flight.

And then, like a dream, like a wish summoned, they came, one after another: six white ghosts sailing with wings outstretched through the broad black canvas of the night, each of which settled on the lawn immediately before them, a pebble gripped tightly in its beak. Mr Ahmadi stooped again, and with a gentle reverence, like kings dispensing gifts, they laid the stones in his palm.

'Albatrosses,' said Fitz.

'Albatrosses,' agreed Mr Ahmadi, simply. Fitz stood gaping, astonished at these silent creatures, and remembering their wings—only a few nights before—when they had come to the Heresy—

But something was troubling Mr Ahmadi. He turned abruptly to the boy at his side.

'I have a feeling,' he said, 'that he is waiting for you.' In Fitz's hand he placed what was, clearly, the largest of the pebbles he had picked up, the size of a walnut, and heavy. Mr Ahmadi nodded towards the sky. 'Hard as you can,' he said.

With all his strength Fitz hurled the stone at the night. Now the rush of a wing on the wind was unmistakable, and from a great, dark height a white form above them plummeted into view, planed out, circled, and drew up on the grass, alighting before them. The other birds shuffled out of the way to make space for his giant wings.

'As I thought,' said Mr Ahmadi. 'Go on, take it.'

Fitz crouched, held out his hand, and held the black eye of the enormous bird for what seemed an age, before with a simple dip of its head it dropped the stone again into his hand.

'These are my friends,' Mr Ahmadi said. 'And now I think they will be yours.' In a long and fluid lunge, he swept his extended arm in a wide arc to the ground, and the greatest of the seven albatrosses hopped to a perch on his sleeve. As he turned and turned in the quiet stillness of the courtyard, the others fanned out around him, taking flight each on its own bearing, until the last – still holding the Master's eye – loosed his wide and delicate wings, his trembling wings, and lifted almost without effort into the night.

'You may not always see them,' whispered Mr Ahmadi. 'But they have sharp eyes, and a way of knowing when you have most need of them. And so you see you are not alone, even here at the Heresy, benetted round with villains though you may be.'

It might have been the sound of one of the birds, touching down on the tiles of a roof across the court. Or it might have been something else, someone else. But at the sound of the sharp, clear crack that echoed from the walls, Mr Ahmadi's face changed instantly. His eyes had been light with magic; now his brow set hard as iron.

'You're not supposed to be out at this time of the night,' he said, taking Fitz painfully by the arm, and steering him under a near arch, 'and I mustn't be seen talking with you. Already some of the other Officers suspect me. They think I have brought you here for my own ends, that I wish to make myself Heresiarch, or even – who knows what they think. Maybe they will attempt to take you from me. So keep close, move quickly, and I'll get you back to your room. Tomorrow, follow Dina to lessons. I'll need you to do this for a while – I don't know how long.'

'But why?' Fitz protested. 'I thought the Heresy wanted me for something, that you were going to help me to go home –'

'You are not yet of age,' Mr Ahmadi snapped, as if impatient with the complaint. He looked anxiously over both shoulders, and then, catching himself, went on more gently. 'Child. The Heresy has many hands. Some would draw you in; others would cast you out. I know that much, but only that much. Whom I can trust, how to act – of these things I am not yet sure. It may be that, before long, I will wear more than the Heresiarch's mask. Then perhaps we can put a stop to this once and for all – to all of it, for both of us. But whatever happens to me, soon you will come of age; then we can give the Heresy what it wants, and what it wants is the Kingdom – you remember: the Great Hoard of the *shāhanshāh*. I must discover where it is. I search every day. I will not give up the search until I have read every book in the library, every record in the archive, every last scrap of paper or parchment in the Heresy. For now, follow Dina; she has a head on her shoulders, and she can keep you safe. She practically runs this place. Let her teach you. No matter what the Officers of the Heresy want from you, the more you learn, the stronger you will be when the time comes.'

Mr Ahmadi had begun guiding Fitz again, down the narrow brick passage. They moved across a lawned court and between two tall buildings and into the court below the Mastery, which Fitz already knew well.

'Child, do you still have my book? The one you took from my father's library?'

Fitz nodded.

'Keep reading. When you understand, you will be safe.'

By a light shove on both shoulders, Fitz felt himself propelled across a bed of gravel towards the stone staircase that, even in the pitch of a moonless midnight, he now knew was his. He placed his right hand on the stone column at the centre of the round stairs, then looked back. The courtyard behind, dark and silent, was already empty. He began to climb.

## mansūba

*O*n the next afternoon, when the boy opened the door to the library, he found it still dark. All through the night, and all through the morning, he had waited for the moment when he might visit the old man, and hear the remainder of his story. But he was not disappointed to find him again asleep in his chair. With a light step he crossed the floor, and in near silence he kindled a fire among the ashes that remained in the hearth. When the sticks had begun to burn well, he covered it with two logs that stood in a buchet nearby, then crouched before the fire, waiting for it to grow and give off heat.

At length the old man woke up, and opened his eyes to the flames burning on the hearth.

'You have come again,' he said, after a while.

The boy pulled the table near to the old man's chair, and for an hour or for many hours, they studied the ornamented board that lay spread upon it, working together through the many problems that the board presented, and the meaning of those problems.

After a long time, the old man sat back from the board, and adjusted the wool blanket that covered his lap and his legs.

'Come, my eyes, and sit beside me, and I will continue with the story that I was telling you yesterday.'

The boy went to the door of the library, and picked up one of the two stools that stood there, and brought it near to the old man so that he might sit. But before he sat down, he said, 'Tell me, please, why do you call me "my eyes"?'

When the old man looked up at him, the light from the fire did not gleam in his eyes as the boy had expected. Instead his eyes seemed to swirl with milk, and their colour was dim.

'Because there is nothing dearer to a man than his sight, which is confined in the tender ball of the eye. No part of the body is more delicate, no part more valuable.' He was quiet for the space of several breaths. 'But this is not the only reason why I use these words for you. An old man, if he is not to die within himself, must see the world as if through the eyes of a young boy. It is all too easy for the world to lose its freshness and its wonder; it is only by seeing through the eyes of another that we may avoid dying while we are still alive.'

The boy went to the table by the window, where he opened the shutter a little. But today clouds had covered the sky, and no sun fell upon the pitcher as he poured water into the black cup, and lifted it by the ring of lapis lazuli that ran beneath its rim.

After he had drunk, the old man continued with his story.

'I told you yesterday how I travelled into a distant country, in order to trade, and befriended another merchant; and I told you, too, how this merchant invited me to his house for a meal, and afterwards recounted to me the story of the king of kings, the beggar boy and the fate of his wondrous treasure hoard. This was all I heard of the story that night, as it was all you heard yesterday, for the evening had grown late and I had much to do before the morning. I therefore returned to the inn where I was staying, and prepared the second part of my goods for sale on the following day. When the morning came, I took them to the market, and laid my stall out cunningly as before, so that by the time the market closed there was not a single item left upon my tables. My friend the merchant of that city happened to be passing at that hour, and laughed to see my stall again so empty.

'"Brother merchant," he said, "again I find that you have given away your worldly goods, so that you have not a scrap of silk to your name! It is a great sadness to me, each day to find how trading has driven you to beggary!"

'I laughed at his jest, remembering how he had invited me the evening before to his house, and fed me, and given me drink. But on this day he did not invite me to his house; instead he said, "After you have returned to your inn, and eaten your evening meal, meet me at the gates of the city, for there is something in the desert that I would like to show you."

'I did as he invited me to do, and before an hour had passed I met him again at the gates of the city. Beyond the gates there was a waste place that stretched for many miles in every direction – dry, dangerous and deserted. In the early morning, just as the sun was rising, many people set out from the gates on the road, for it was possible to reach the next city on foot in only a few hours; but in the evening the road was empty, and as we set out through the gates, we were alone.

'We circled round the walls until we came to a place where the ruins of an old well stood. Here the merchant told me to sit, for in this place he would continue his story from the night before. He said I would understand later why he had asked me to come to this place.

'"Brother merchant," he said, "I told you yesterday how the king of kings looked in vain for his heir, the beggar boy, but I did not tell you what happened to the boy. Behind his disappearance lies another story. The king of kings, who was an accomplished soldier, was not a scholar. When he left his city to go on campaign each summer, in his place as ruler he left his chief counsellor – his wazir, who was also his brother. Now the king's brother was wise and knowledgeable, but like his brother he was ambitious. From year to year in the king's absence, he developed a taste for the power that was vested in him, and he conceived a great desire to be king in his brother's place. Understanding that his brother was returning from campaign with an inestimable hoard of treasure, he saw his opportunity; when he sent emissaries to his brother's vassals, commanding them to assemble at the Feast of the Thousand Kings in order to crown his brother king of kings, he found a way to insinuate in their minds a conspiracy to murder his brother and put himself in his place; however, he did this so cunningly that each of these princes believed the conspiracy to be his own design, or a plot hatched by one of his confederates. Thus it was that, when the conspiracy was discovered, no man spoke against the wazir.

'"And yet the king's brother was bitterly disappointed, and very angry. He exercised his fury by arresting the beggar boy and torturing him, before shaving his head and sending him into the desert as a lackey to the king's slaves, who had been commanded – as I have told you – to construct the king's tomb. For the wazir had convinced the boy that his information, though it had saved the king's life, had caused him an incurable sadness, for among the thousand vassals whom the king had enslaved, many were men of his family, the close companions of his youth and his dear friends. So it was that, bound to the slave gang, collar to collar, the boy trudged into the desert, dejected, cast out and surrounded by enemies.

'"For months the boy toiled with the other slaves to build a sumptuous tomb fit for a shāhanshāh. The king's prisons had been emptied to furnish architects, masons and artists, and these were the celebrated men of the slave camp that sprang up in the desert; to them was given the choice of tents, with the best of the food. To the kings now made slaves, little was offered, but from them much was demanded: hard toil in the hot sun with little water, digging, hauling, lifting without end. All the precedence of former days was quickly forgotten, and among these slaves he was most celebrated who could lift the most or dig the deepest. In this company, the boy was almost lost: scrawny and stunted after a life of poverty, his child frame was no use in a test of strength and endurance. He was fortunate each night if for his supper he was grudged the grease in the pan, and to shield him from the wind and the cold they offered him the largest tent of all – the vault of the night's open sky. These hardships the boy tolerated with fortitude, for he remembered the great sadness into which he had cast the king of kings, and he was abashed.

'"But it was not long before the slaves of the camp found a use for the boy. Their camp in the desert was secret, the site of their underground tomb hidden from the world; the king had forbidden travellers to enter the desert, but it was often necessary for the architects and masons, for the smiths and even for the labourers, to make journeys from the camp into the city, or to the quarries, or into the mountains to hunt or trade. What was to stop these men from revealing the site of the king's tomb, and trading the knowledge of its location for money or for their freedom? The secret could only be protected if the location of the tomb was hidden even from those constructing it; and yet they must have a map to guide their return, whenever their business called them away. The boy was agile and quick, but – above all – he was both clever and good. Hear the ingenious solution that he devised. Working with a blacksmith at the camp forge, the boy created a marvellous instrument – a kind of map – made up of four circular bronze plates. These plates were not at all solid, but composed of a beautiful, delicate lattice of tracery; and yet they could be mounted one upon the other, by means of a central pin that bound them. When they were assembled, and each turned in exactly the right way, their configuration revealed a map that represented the site of the tomb in relation to the king's city and to three other landmarks that lay at the edges of the desert. Using this instrument, craftsmen and labourers working on the tomb were able to travel freely to and from the site, and no man was ever lost.

'"But there was a trick to configuring the instrument, and in this trick its cunning truly lay. When the king's brother had first caused the boy to be shaven and shackled, he discovered about himself something he had never known before – that beneath his thick, black hair his scalp was disfigured by a cluster of irregular marks, like stars that had fallen from the sky and burned themselves into his skin. The shape made by these marks upon his head was not unlike the constellation known as 'the Giant', and so the men of the camp took to calling the boy by this name. When designing his ingenious instrument, the boy had the blacksmith cast the four bronze plates so that they could only be configured correctly by taking a sighting, through the instrument itself, of the marks on his own head. By aligning eight particular points with the eight stars of 'the Giant', the four plates could be brought into the correct configuration, and the map would be revealed; without this alignment, the plates would be useless. For this reason, the boy was required to accompany everyone who left the camp, for they could not find their way back without him. But because the marks by which the instrument was configured lay upon the top of his head, the boy could not take a sighting by himself.'"

'Here my friend the merchant paused with his tale. He said he wanted to be satisfied that I had understood it, for much that happened after depended upon it. By this time night had fallen, and the stars had begun to appear above the sky of the desert where, down beneath the hills of the high city, it lay quiet with mystery. Looking out upon the desert's hidden treasures, I pondered the ingenious contrivance of the boy, and the care he had taken to protect the dignity of the king's tomb. Little did he know that, while he was toiling as a slave to serve his master with such secrecy, the king himself was scouring his kingdom to find him! I marvelled at this quirk of fate, and told my friend that I had understood his tale very well.

'"Years passed, brother merchant," he said, "in the building of the king's tomb. The slaves of the camp grew ever more artful in their business. Many kings were apprenticed to crafts that, in days gone by, they would have scorned, and in those crafts they grew to be great masters. Beneath the sands they created a palace as gorgeous as any built above them: hall upon hall, and chamber upon chamber, they decked with gold, and silver, and bronze. Hall upon hall, and chamber upon chamber, they carved in stone, in wood, and in amber. Hall upon hall, and chamber upon chamber, they set with jewels and adorned with tiles and paintings. At last the work was complete: they laid the last of the tomb's sunken ceilings, huge slabs of marble quarried far away, and allowed the sands to cover them. Then, one by one, collar chained to collar as they had arrived many long years before, they filed out of the desert, to inform the king that the palace of his eternal fame was now complete.

'"The king who received them in the city was not the king who had first put them to work. Then, he was young and victorious; now he was old and – still unable to find his heir – broken by sorrow. He received them with dignity, and rewarded them with fair conditions; but he instructed his chief counsellor, his wazir, his brother, to send them back into the desert, there to bury in his tomb not his body, but all of his worldly wealth, the spoils of his years of conquest and the riches of his kingdom.

'"The king's brother, who had never ceased scheming to dispossess the king, became frantic. What worth would the kingdom be to him, if his brother were to bury its treasury in the desert? By every persuasion of his art, he sought to move his brother's mind, and begged him to revoke his command. Even as the mules were harnessed, and guards posted to secure the loaded carts, the chief counsellor took to his knees before his brother's throne, imploring him to forgo this last madness. But all in vain; the king's heart was broken, and his broken heart would break his kingdom, too.

'"By certain spies whose credit he trusted, the wazir enquired of the boy whom he had sent into slavery, and learned that he was now a formidable man, known as 'the Giant', whose wisdom and good conscience had elevated him to the position of leader of all the slaves; moreover, the king's brother learned the secret of the Giant's ingenious instrument, which (after the manner of a riddle) men called the

*Almanac. By a dangerous agent whose secrecy he trusted, the king's* wazir *discovered the instrument, stole it, and – working in darkness and in haste – took a detailed wax impression of each of its four brass plates. He then returned it, the theft never known. These impressions he committed to a blacksmith, with instructions to create a replica of the original instrument. Meanwhile, with only hours before the king's slaves should depart for the desert again, there to bury the kingdom's entire treasury, with themselves, in perpetual obscurity, the king's brother sought out the man they called the Giant. He had only to take a single reading of the stars upon his head, and the key to unlock the treasure would belong to him – and to him alone – forever.*

'*"And so the* wazir *sent to the Giant, and arranged to meet him at the well that stood near to the slave camp, just outside the city walls – here at this place, brother merchant. They would meet at dawn on the morning of the slaves' departure. The* wazir *used fair words, but the Giant – remembering the cruelty of his torture when he was a boy – mistrusted the king's brother, and when the time came for the meeting, he slipped into the well, and waited for the other to arrive. The king's brother approached the well at dawn, accompanied by his trusted servant, who was his spy, his messenger and his assassin. To this man he confided all his counsels, and thought nothing of sharing with him – as he did now – his most inward plans.*

'*"'What a fool this Giant is,' said the* wazir *to his servant, 'ignorant as he is that he might have sat upon the king's own seat, and owned all of this wealth for himself! To think that he might have mounted in glory upon the city walls, rather than writhing in chains beneath them! Together you and I have ground down the man who might have been the* shāhanshāh, *the greatest king upon the face of the earth,* ground him into the very powder and scum that now stains his labourer's hands. My triumph is nearly complete. It remains only for us to copy the pattern of the stars upon his head. I will spin him some tale beside the well; you climb upon the roof of the well house, and as he stands beneath you, take a sighting of this famous constellation, this map of warts or tumours for which the king's slaves so revere him. When we have the map, I will promise some part of the treasure to certain armies in the north that wait upon my payment; with their aid, we will take the kingdom.'

'"The Giant heard every word. Clinging to the stones inside the well, his heart ran cold – for he understood at that moment that his years of toil and hardship, the king's years of sorrow and despair, were all the work of one, evil man. He knew then that he had but to escape the well, and present himself in the city, and he would be acknowledged the heir to the kingdom, perhaps even offered the throne outright. But he also knew that the king's brother would never give up scheming to take the kingdom, and that if he were dispatched, some other would take his place. Great virtue and courage create great wealth, but great wealth creates evil, or so he thought as he hung by his fingertips in the cool of the well's dark shaft. Perhaps because he had spent so many years constructing a magnificent underground tomb, a necropolis for the world's most famous warrior and king, the Giant had come to believe that riches belong buried in the earth. And so he remained in the well, clinging to his perch, until in despair the chief counsellor and his servant, long after dawn, departed empty-handed.

'"And the Giant took his place at the head of the slave army, and together they packed the mules and carts, the camels and the horses into the desert, watched helplessly from the walls by the king, his brother and the whole city. One by one the slaves disappeared over the horizon; one by one they unloaded the mules and carts and camels and horses into the vast, underground vault; one by one they themselves descended into their stone tomb. And the sands covered them, and they were no more."'

'And now, my eyes, I have again grown tired. But there is one further part of the story that my friend the merchant told me, on the last of the three days that I spent in that city. Come again to see me tomorrow, and I will try to finish it, for it is a thing of great importance to me that you should hear it.'

The old man's eyes were already closed by the time the boy had returned his stool to its place by the library door. He gathered the embers of the fire by the front of the hearth, so that they should stay warm a long while, and pushed the little table, bearing the board with its unfinished play, back into the corner. By the door to the library, for a beat of his heart, he lingered, looking as long as he dared at the thousands of books stacked upon their hundred shelves. The old man was not asleep, as he had thought, and observed his hesitation.

'My library is always open to you, my eyes. You must take whatever books you like, if you will only care for them, and return them. When I am dead, too, all this will be yours.'

He did not open the book he had taken until he had reached the grand staircase; but he stood there for a long time after, reading it.

8

*The case*

That night, Fitz had scarcely allowed his head to sink into his weary pillow before he felt someone shaking him by the shoulders. At first, clutching at the vanishing vision of a dream, he pulled himself into a tight ball, straining away from the rough hands that were reaching for him, pushing him, prodding him.

Stiff tips of fingers slid into the tender gristle beneath his shoulder blades, and pinched it. He writhed in a sudden, hot coil, and found himself panting in a squat. Eyes open, he was staring into Dina's startled but bemused face, dimly lit by light that floated through the court window.

'Wake up, little brother,' she said. 'We have a case.'

Fitz blinked hard, and a spasm screwed through his body from the bridge of his nose into the seat of his spine, making him shudder. For the first time in a week, he felt truly alert.

'A case?'

He was already taking her hands. She pulled him to his feet, and he skipped light from the bed.

'Your first.'

Fitz pulled on his long coat and stepped into his slippers while Dina explained. They were halfway down the tower stairs before the words began to make sense.

'Sometimes you wake up in the night,' she said. 'And you know something's wrong. Maybe you heard something – a footfall, one of those creaks on the stairs that isn't just the wood shrinking, or expanding, or whatever it does. Maybe it's that the temperature has changed. You don't know, but you know deep in your gut, or your heart, in the way that your pulse swells in your arteries, that whatever it is, it isn't just you. It's a feeling that comes from outside.'

They reached the foot of the tower stairs. In the sooty darkness just before she opened the door to the court, Fitz found himself very close to Dina – so close that her finger almost brushed his face as she held it up to her lips.

She whispered, 'It's a feeling that *does* come from outside. And it means you have a case.'

She pulled the door open. Fitz scanned the courtyard: still dark, cool but dry, the moon high, the windows on every face black as rotten teeth or empty sockets in the stone face of a corpse. It was late, but the hour nothing like near morning.

Dina nodded towards the centre of the court. Fitz had missed it: a little lacquered box, about a foot square and half as high, black but in the moonlight streaked and dully gleaming. Someone had set it on the ground exactly between his door and Dina's. Fitz started out of the tower, but Dina clamped her hand firmly in the crook of his arm, staying him.

'Not like that,' she said. Her voice was low and urgent. 'I'll get the box. You keep close to the near wall, and get to the Heresy Arch. I'll meet you there. Be ready to run.'

Using both hands and the full force of her shoulders, Dina nearly shoved Fitz out of the door and along the wall, crushing him against the wall's unrelenting stone. Her violence was emphatic, and he took the hint, keeping his body flat as he picked out a quiet footing to the arch that led to the Heresiarchy. He tried to avoid crunching the gravel underfoot. About halfway along the wall, he looked back. In the high, circular window of the Master's hall, the half-moon's reflection had slid into view, and the window showed it hanging brightly over the roof opposite.

And then, suddenly, it disappeared.

'Dina,' Fitz hissed. But it was too late. As she stepped from the doorway, he heard someone clamber into place on the leads of the roof just above him.

But Dina wasn't walking. She wasn't running. She cartwheeled: arms and legs extended, the tight plait of her hair lashing through the moonlight, she arced across the courtyard once, twice, and then – squaring her body against her direction of movement – flipped into a high somersault that laid her out, for the briefest interval, in a slide beside the lacquered box. Fitz, mesmerized, had come to a full halt against the cool and crumbling stone of the tower, now fully obscured in the moon's protecting shadow. From above he heard the quick thumping twang of a bowstring pulse through the cool air and rebound around the court. A trio of arrows clattered to this side and that, but Dina was faster than arrows, nimbler and better feathered. She swirled through the darkness, holding the box before her in a circle of arms that dizzied the night and made the heavy mass of the court's stone slabs seem to dance around her.

Fitz, finding his legs, scurried into the archway immediately behind her.

'Run,' she cried. She hadn't broken stride.

Through three courts he sprinted, trailing her, losing ground as she accelerated. As they rounded a corner into the Keeper's Yard, Fitz heard footsteps pounding on the hard earth behind him. Dina, too, had heard them, and changed direction abruptly, pulling up into a low alcove that led into a cellar store below the kitchens. If she hadn't put out her arm and grabbed him by the sleeve, Fitz would have overshot it. She yanked him violently, then drew him in.

For all the sprinting, Dina was hardly even winded. With one hand over his mouth, stifling him, she drew Fitz back into the deep shadow of the stairway. They pressed themselves side by side into the darkness, trying to squeeze their bodies into nooks that didn't exist, to wedge themselves, along with the box that Dina still clutched to her chest, into vanishing concealment. Fitz's mouth gaped as he breathed in silent, deep draughts that seemed to pinch his ears shut. Even above the strum of his racing heart, he was all too conscious of the Jack's slow progress through the yard outside. He was pacing it slowly, listening for them.

*Hunting us.* Fitz abruptly realized – as if he were only now waking from a sound sleep – that this was all some elaborate game of manhunt by moonlight.

*We're trying to capture the flag, and he's trying to capture – us.*

As the seconds ticked on, the heavy tread of their pursuer seemed to sniff at every crevice of the yard. Now and again he would stop, or seem to walk away, and for long stretches they would hear nothing at all, not even the swell or tumble of the sea on the wind, which often on silent nights seemed to find its way among the crags and wisp like scattered threads into their windows and dreams. Then Fitz felt his muscles slack, and his lungs their tight air expended – only for a sudden movement, something as small as the crunch of a foot on sticks impossibly near, to seize every one of his nerves and, in an instant, wring them tight as a tourniquet. By the time the Jack did finally give up, and the sound of his feet at last died away on the telltale flags of the Commissar's passage, every drop of blood in Fitz's body had cooled, congealed and clotted.

'He'll be watching still,' whispered Dina. Her voice was almost as dark as the darkness. 'We go down.'

She led the way, inching down the hidden steps. Fitz followed as closely as he dared, cleaving to her body's warmth and the rustle of her sleeve against the wall. His own finger he let trail the wall beside him as they descended, its tip gliding intermittently along the roughly mortared rocks. When they hit the bottom he crushed into Dina, slightly, and she steadied him before drawing him by the hand, through a low passage she must have known well. She knew it well enough, anyway, that after only a few steps, crouching to the floor, she drew from somewhere a little lantern and, striking a match, lit it.

'I keep this here for times like this,' she said, simply, and handed it to him.

Now it was Fitz's turn to check Dina. He took her by the arm, so hard she almost dropped the box.

'Why was the Jack shooting at us?'

Dina smiled. 'He wasn't. He'll be the guardian on this case. He set the task, and so it's his job to protect us.'

'Then on the roof –'

Dina snorted. 'Dolly with her crossbow. She always shoots in threes. So predictable.'

Fitz must have let his grip slip. Dina pulled away, walking a few steps further down the low-vaulted room, where she set the box on some large, flat-topped clay pots. They were huge, like urns, and Fitz decided they must contain kitchen stores. Apart from the little clump among which Dina had settled, beyond her in the gloom there were scores more.

'She wasn't trying to hurt me – just to slow me down. She wanted this.'

Indignant, Fitz had been determined to stand off, but he found his curiosity stronger than his resolve.

'What is it?' He had crossed the room with craven eagerness, and already found himself running his finger along the smooth lid.

'I don't know,' said Dina. 'The case always turns up somewhere in the Heresy, sometime in the night. It's usually pretty obvious – like this time. Finding it, and getting it, is the easy part.' She rolled her eyes, as if she considered the night's events so far a little disappointing. Fitz felt the indignation begin to rise again in his shoulders and throat.

'I guess Dolly isn't the only one trying to slow you down,' said Fitz.

'No. All the Prents will be out. Everybody wants to be the one to open the case.'

'Why?'

'It's always different. Sometimes it's a puzzle. Sometimes it's a prize. Sometimes it's just a test of strength or speed. You don't know till you open it. One of the Offs will make it up, and then act as guardian after the case has been laid. It's a little like a competition. All the Prents compete to take possession, and then to complete.'

'Complete?'

'Follow whatever's in the box.' Dina blinked. 'Read the clues. Take the plunge. Find the treasure. Work out the problem. Whatever. Keep going to the end.'

'And the winner –'

'Is me,' said Dina, flat and severe. Her voice rang dead in the air like iron clanging, like a gate shutting or a lock turning into place. 'I always win. I haven't lost, ever.'

They were standing immediately opposite one another, so close that their breaths mingled as they drew them, but Fitz thought in the silence following Dina's statement that a chasm as large as the world had cracked between them.

'And what are the rules of this competition?'

'There's only one rule,' answered Dina. Now her eyes shone brighter than the lantern in the dark. 'No one gets hurt. As you saw in the Master's court, that doesn't mean that everyone plays fair. Staying safe requires a kind of collaboration. I know what Dolly is going to do, Dolly knows what I am going to do, and we work with one another, trying to edge round one another's expectations tentatively enough that we're never in real danger. We're competing, but we're also collaborating. That's how games work, even when they're dangerous.'

'But if someone makes a mistake?'

'That's why the Jack is there. To protect us. And to clean up, if there's an accident.' Dina's eyes softened a fraction. 'I'll show you the ropes, little brother. Tonight you're my risk. Don't make a mistake.'

Her eyes dropped to the box. Planting the heels of her hands firmly at the base on each end, she pushed up the lid with her thumbs. Despite himself, despite his show of reticence, his fear, his annoyance and frustration, and above all his confusion, Fitz was hooked. His eyes worked themselves into the growing gap between the lid and the box as Dina began to run her prising fingers round its edge, seeking, exploiting every crevice. At last it came free and, in the light from the lantern, the contents were laid bare.

*Bare.*

The box was empty. An elaborate wooden setting, sanded and varnished, seemed as if it might once, at its centre, have held a jewel. Now it only stared at them like an empty eye, like a reproach.

Dina raised her eyebrows and set the box down. She tapped her forefinger hard, four times, against the box's edge.

A scuffing noise came from the stairs, as of a shoe slipping on a tread.

With a single motion of her hands, Dina indicated that Fitz should stay where he was, the box in his hands, with the lantern by his side. Moving like a cat, she seemed to flow through the darkness, utterly silently, and lodged herself in the alcove by the base of the stairs. When Dolly stepped through the doorway, Fitz met her eyes; they both knew at once that she didn't have a chance. Pouncing and subduing her in a single stroke, Dina leaped on her, at once both under her and over her, her arms circling her, her head craned back for balance as she dropped Dolly to the floor with a wrench of her whole weight. She hadn't hit the floor before Dina was on top of her, trussing her hands, then her feet. Fitz had never seen fingers work so fast, so dextrously; the lengths of cord drawn from a collar round her neck danced in the air as if the stunt had been choreographed, as if Dina were not a fighter but an artist, as if the neat twists that she bound round Dolly's ankles and wrists were not restraints, but sculptures worked from twine and motion. Dolly's face was a mask of resignation and discomfort. She grimaced as Dina drew a gag across her mouth and fastened it behind her right ear, cinching it tight.

'Wait here,' she said. She tossed Dolly's crossbow and quiver, still by the sounds of it full, into a stack of rags in the shadows, along with a loop of cable Dolly wore at her waist, then crossed the room back towards Fitz among the jars.

'That's one,' she said. 'I expect the others will be along directly.'

Fitz must have looked uncomprehending.

'I left prints,' said Dina, holding up one of her bare feet and wiggling her toes. 'On purpose. I'd rather they followed me, so I know where they are. It's much easier to beat them when you can lock them in a cellar first.'

Fitz might have smiled, but he didn't have the opportunity. Suddenly all around them the clay jars seemed to stand up, the lids rising through the air to reveal Padge, Fingal, Navy and Payne. From a standing start Dina tried to vault over their heads, but even she didn't have the power – and anyway the others had thrown a net across them both, and with practised determination, notwithstanding a quickfire barrage of contortions from Dina, they secured the net's corners to the floor, and then by means of a drawstring drew it close around them. Fitz found himself entwined with Dina, his arm round one of her legs, and his head bowed at an uncomfortable angle below her knee.

'Open, sesame,' said Navy, with satisfaction.

'Working together,' said Dina, in a low and steady voice. 'Cheating.' She paused. 'I like it.'

Padge was looking around while Fingal held the net closed. The tall boy's bitter lips smirked. He prodded Dina's nose with his boot. Navy had rushed to Dolly and was untying her.

'Where's Russ?' asked Padge. 'Did you see him?'

'No,' answered Dina. She sounded bored.

She always sounded bored when she wasn't in charge, Fitz thought.

'Try his bed,' she added. 'He always sleeps through cases.'

While Fingal was distracted with her nose, Dina had managed to get her other fingers far enough through the net to take hold of the laces of Fingal's other boot. With a sharp upward thrust that looked like it might have dislocated her own shoulder, she pulled his foot out from under him and knocked him to the floor. He landed heavily on Fitz's leg, but didn't drop the net.

Pain spiked through Fitz's thigh and up his back. He bit his tongue rather than cry out, hard enough that he tasted blood.

'Dina, let it go,' said Padge. He had been scraping at something on his leg, and now looked up at them in annoyance. 'You're out of the case. What was in the box?'

'Nothing,' Dina answered, from between her teeth. She had wrapped the lace round Fingal's boot and was now twisting his lower leg hard against his knee. He fought to get his balance, and kicked back at her hands, but the heavy cords of the net guarded her fingers and she wouldn't relinquish her advantage. No one else moved to help Fingal.

'Dina, come on –' began Padge.

'No,' said Fitz. 'She's telling the truth. There was nothing in the box. Just an empty niche, like it was made for a ring or something.'

'It was meant for this,' said Dolly. Finally on her feet, she crossed the room, wincing as she settled her weight on her bruised ankles, and drew from her pocket what looked, as it caught the light from the lantern, like a diamond. 'I found it in Russ's bed when I went to wake him. He wasn't there.' She set the diamond in the box's empty carved niche. It fitted perfectly.

'So,' said Payne.

'So,' said Navy, peering at the diamond in its wooden setting.

Fingal had unlaced his boot and pulled it off in order to free his foot. Now he was nursing it, with his back to one of the big clay jars. He was well aware of the indignity of his situation, Fitz thought, and he let his long hair cover his face from the others.

'What is that supposed to mean?' said the older boy, more as a petulant complaint than a question.

'It means we're looking for Russ, you oaf.' Dina had worked the net open with her foot while distracting Fingal with his boot. Now in a fluid motion she slipped out of the opening, sprang between two jars, and bent to a crouch as she backed towards the door. No one moved to catch her. Payne tossed Fingal his boot, as if to say, *Nice work. You let her go.*

'And the diamond signifies what?' Payne asked. She glanced once, furtively, at the open box where it lay again on one of the jars.

'I don't know,' Padge answered. He was standing near, and Fitz could see what he had been scraping on his leg. It was still there: a thick, black, sticky mess that must have been in the jar where he'd been hiding.

'It's the Jack,' said Dina. 'Don't be useless, rabble. I need competition.'

Something pushed at Fitz's memory, like a bulge beneath a heavy fabric. At first he couldn't make it out. His mind felt as black and tacky as the sludge on Padge's legs.

*No. I know.*

'The Helix,' he said, before he knew he was going to say it. 'It sits on a diamond. The Jack showed me. It turns on a huge diamond.' Only the day before, in the tall atrium at the centre of the Jackery, the Jack had shown Fitz how to turn the grand helical staircase that served his upper libraries. Rotating an ancient iron crank, he had laughed to see Fitz marvel as the huge machine slowly – by degrees infinitesimal – revolved the double strand of twining steps. And in the core of the machine, at the centre of it all, the gears had swivelled on the dull gleam of a perfectly spherical, giant diamond.

'The Jack's Blank Eye,' said Dina. 'It won't be in its socket.' She was almost at the stairs now, and put her hand out to the wall behind her. In the darkness, her head low, her eyes caverns, she looked dangerous. Leering at the other children, she suddenly shot her head forward on the stem of her neck, goggling with her eyes and lolling her tongue. The motion was deranged, sickening. 'A little jack-in-the-box for you, my slow-witted friends,' she said.

'Dina, don't –' began Navy. 'If Russ is missing, if he's locked up, he might need us, and we all –'

But Dina had already darted round the corner, and disappeared silently up the stairs.

'That girl,' Padge said. He helped Fitz out of the netting.

'You know, there's something else,' said Navy. She had removed the diamond, and was tracing her finger along the concavities of the box's interior. 'The setting – the way the wood is carved in the box – it's a perfect negative image of the fountain in the Commissary, isn't it?' She handed the box to Dolly. 'I mean, isn't it?'

Dolly scrutinized it, holding the box against the lantern and tilting it back and forth. 'Maybe,' she said.

Not one of them stopped to take the lantern as they ran from the cellar. As he brought up the rear, Fitz thought he was probably the only one who needed it; the rest of them seemed to know every inch of every room, every tread of every stair, every corner, every post and porch, every archway, every pebble and blade of grass in the Heresy. As he ran, the burn beginning to open and spread in his chest, the lantern clanking at the end of his wrist, Fitz yearned to know the place as they did, to be one of them and not merely the boy at the back – the boy at the back, struggling to keep up, struggling to imitate their movements, their familiarity with one another, struggling to penetrate the hidden language of understanding, habit and expectation that hung about and passed between them as quick as lightning. From court to court they raced in single file, each in her or his place – Navy at the front, as the cleverest and boldest; Padge behind, as the most senior; Fingal next, as the eldest; then Dolly, the most athletic and resourceful; and last of all Payne, brittle and disaffected, but shrewd and suspicious. She would want to keep the others in sight at all times, thought Fitz. She wouldn't trust them for a second.

Up ahead, something hard slammed into a piece of heavy oak. As Fitz approached with the lantern, he saw that the piece of heavy oak was a massive, solid door blocking the access to the Commissary, and the thing that had hit it was all of Navy. She was sprawled on the ground, her eyes squeezed shut, rubbing her left knee.

'It's locked,' said Fingal, flatly.

'We'll go round the other way,' said Padge.

'That will be locked, too,' said Navy through clenched teeth.

'I need hardly point out that, while we're stuck out here, Dina is certainly already inside,' Payne offered. Standing aside, she took the lantern from Fitz and held it up to peer at a downpipe that connected, four storeys above, to the lead guttering of the Registry.

'How –' Fitz began.

'She climbs the outsides of buildings,' observed Payne. 'It's uncanny. Not even monkeys move as fast as Dina. She's a real asset, when she's on your side.'

'Which is never,' said Dolly.

'Quite,' finished Payne.

'We'll go in through the Registry,' said Navy. Back on her feet, she had been testing her knee. Now she drew a huge key from her coat – iron, half a foot long, each of its teeth an ingot big enough to break a window – and held it out for all to see. 'Don't ask,' she said, almost forestalling their astonishment. 'I'm a sly one.'

The door to the Registry, heavy and solid, nonetheless opened easily. Navy had gone ahead while the others hid in the shadows, but as they darted through the court's lamplight, and scurried through the door – like rats down an alley in daylight, thought Fitz – the Jack was nowhere to be seen. Inside, the Registry lay in almost complete darkness, save for the luminous mystery of the half moon, sitting atop the building's glass dome, swirling down through the waters of its giant cylindrical tank. The curved crystal walls of the Registrar's pool were not so thick, not so opaque, that the moonlight did not filter through them; and as they passed round it, rising on the ramp that circled it, dark and menacing shadows kept pace with them, gaining speed as they veered away, then lunging back towards the perimeter of the tank. They moved with such purpose it seemed the fish might surge straight through the glass and sink their two-foot teeth into the children. Fitz shuddered at the thought of it, and kept his eyes on the lantern where it swung from Payne's limp hand.

When he finally reached the atrium at the top of the hall, he saw that Navy had already thrown open the balcony doors that overlooked the Commissary.

But that was all she had done. As she stood looking over the stone balustrade, something seemed to have rooted her to the spot.

'What is it?' said Padge, joining her. Navy didn't answer. Padge didn't ask again.

Fitz was the last to the balcony, but the first to say what they were all thinking.

'Are those *snakes*?'

The court had been closed off on all four sides, each of its gates firmly sealed. In its centre the fountain stood as usual, but around it the normal pattern of hexagonal paths lay in the high, bright light of the moon entirely invisible. Instead the ground seemed to heave with glistening black shapes; but these were far larger than any snakes Fitz had ever seen, or read about, or even heard about in stories. The slick bodies that writhed one over the other were thicker than ropes, thicker than cables, as brawny as a man's thigh; and in length – he squinted into the darkness, trying to follow the coil and tangle of just one of the bodies in that heaving twist of muscle and venom. They were ten or twelve feet apiece, if they were an inch.

'Those aren't snakes,' said Fingal. His tone was mocking, as if he thought them all credulous fools. Turning down the corners of his mouth in disdain, and looking away as if he almost couldn't bear the stupidity of his childish companions, he lifted the lantern where it sat before Payne on the balustrade, and tossed it down into the court below. It shattered on a bare patch of paving, and the oil in its reservoir – suddenly catching the flame as it exploded – spattered in sheets and tongues of fire across a wide area, then disappeared as quickly.

The burst of light from the lantern left them in greater darkness than before. But the flame had burned bright enough, and had spread far enough, to prove what Fingal had thought to dismiss. Twenty sleek heads or more had reared, hissing, as the burning oil had hit the ground; tongues had flickered against the fire; and now, in the moonlight that was left them, the gleam of their white fangs suspended on the air seemed to sear the children's eyes.

'Those are snakes all right,' said Padge. 'But the good news is that someone has dumped about half a ton of gigantic diamonds in the fountain. One of them is bound to be the Blank Eye.'

'If only we could get to them,' said Navy. Her eyes were on the left wall where, in the House of the Jack, down one of the long halls of his library, with a little help from the imagination one might almost make out the lofty screw of the helix rising. Her thoughts were with Russ.

'Give it a few minutes and we won't need to,' said Dolly. She pointed directly across the courtyard, where Dina was slipping with one leg extended down the steep pitched roof of the Commissary. She hit the iron guttering that ran across the outside of the building and carefully crouched atop one of the drains, craning her head round the eaves in order to take her bearings. Her plan was obvious; under one arm she carried what looked to be three or four makeshift torches – tightly wadded rolls of rags probably soaked in oil or fuel of some sort. Fitz remembered the matches she had earlier pulled from her pocket.

'Torches,' Padge whistled. '*That girl.*' He was impressed.

'She didn't see what they did – before – when Fingal threw the lantern,' said Navy. 'Whatever those things are, they didn't seem scared by fire. They'll gobble her up.'

'Good,' said Dolly.

'Not good,' said Padge. 'Dolly, give me your bow –'

'No.' Fitz cut him off. Even he was surprised. Everyone else turned as if they had seen a ghost. Fitz stammered for a moment, trying to frame his mouth to speak. The words hung on the air as Dina hung, now, from the gutter.

But when the lantern had hit the court, and the others had been watching the snakes, Fitz had been looking up. He had seen something else, something the others had overlooked.

*Friends.*

Mr Ahmadi's albatrosses – all seven of them – sat perched in a row along the topmost gable of the Registry. When the oil had exploded across the Commissary yard, the largest of them – the old one – had silently fanned his colossal wings.

'No,' said Fitz again. 'We won't be able to stop her. The only way to save her, is to beat her to it. Dolly, can you get me a fish? Or two? Meaty ones.' Dolly looked at Fitz and blinked twice, uncomprehendingly; then, like a fire catching, she saw Fitz's glance dart to the great birds sitting above them, and her eyes widened. Fitz motioned to the bow slung over her shoulder. Dolly never took asking twice. She disappeared inside, Navy close behind her.

'Padge,' said Fitz. 'I need your knife. And some of that revolting tar you have stuck to your leg.'

The older boy extended the knife, holding it out by the blade. As he took it, Fitz heard one of Dolly's arrows thud off the bowstring and into the water of the Registrar's tank. Navy came running as Dolly loosed a second. By the time she returned, holding a fat tuna with an arrow struck dead through its eye, Fitz had already split and gutted the first. He passed the knife to Dolly while he gathered into his fist as much of the fish's stomach, guts and blood as he could. The stench was almost overpowering.

'That's disgusting,' said Fingal.

'Shut up, Fingal,' cautioned Padge. He was scraping at his leg with the shaft of one of Dolly's arrows, peeling off thick, wet slabs of tar.

Fitz had turned to the roof above them. He took a deep breath, closed his eyes, and lifted the fish's innards over his head. With all his might, he hurled them at the king of the albatrosses.

His aim was good. The sticky pile of blood and guts landed close enough to the bird to catch its interest. With slow dignity, it inclined its head, then hopped along the slate ridge until it could reach the meat. Once it had sensed the nature of the offering, it lost no time in devouring it.

An electric current, passed through the roof, couldn't have startled the birds any more. They hopped and rustled their wings, raised their squat beaks against the moon, and began to dip their heads, as if to take off.

'Fitz.' It was Navy. She was pointing across the court. Dina was halfway down the side of the building, clinging precariously to the drainpipe with one hand, still holding the three unlit brands beneath her other arm, and fishing in her pocket for that match.

'Really quite extraordinary,' said Payne, who was studying her. For a moment Dina seemed to lose her grip on the drainpipe, and slid two or three feet before she caught herself with one of her legs, kicking it against the stone so stiffly that the drum of it echoed around the courtyard.

'That really must have hurt,' Payne commented. Dina was still barefoot. 'And yet, serene.'

Fitz wasn't watching. As the albatrosses leaped into the air behind him, he took the knife from Dolly and with three graceful slices sheared a slab of bloody meat from the first fish – as long and regular a steak as he could manage – then ripped it from the spine. Dipping the back of the knife in the tarry sludge that Padge had left for him on the balustrade, Fitz smeared it as thoroughly as he could across the fish, first one side, then the other. He passed the knife back to Dolly, who copied him precisely.

Fitz looked at the moon where it hung in the sky directly above the courtyard.

*If that much rock can hang in the sky and never fall down, then so can I.*

He planted his hands on the balustrade. He vaulted up to it. Heeding neither the cautions nor the cries of the other Prents, who stood back, he turned to the courtyard below, the slab of tarred fish in his hand, and sighted the fountain. This was a harder cast than his last: thirty or thirty-five feet away, it stood almost four storeys below, and Fitz didn't know if he could judge the height in the dark. Without taking his eye from the fountain, and with his forward foot firmly – rigidly – planted on the outer edge of the balustrade, he heaved the fish into the air.

It landed short by five feet, on a pile of twisting snakes. One of the albatrosses, seeing it, arced through the night and snatched it from the ground with breathtaking agility, then rose almost without exertion through the shadows, to disappear over the Jackery.

Fitz leaned down and took a second piece of fish meat from Dolly. As she turned back to the knife and tar, he took a deep breath and set his feet again. Ahead of him, Dina's first torch suddenly flared into a bright orange flame. She held it at the length of her arm and leaned down towards the ground, fanning the snakes with the heat and spark of it. Heads rose, hissing.

*There's no time.*

Fitz hardly looked. He hurled the fish as hard as the strained socket of his shoulder would let him. With agonizing slowness, circled by hunting birds, it dropped through the night against Dina's bright blaze. It hit the fountain's edge with a sickening slap, then slid into the heap of diamonds.

'Bullseye!' shouted Navy.

But it wasn't. As one of the albatrosses swooped and carried off the hunk of meat, it was obvious that only a few of the smallest diamonds had adhered to the sticky pitch coating the fish's skin. The bird rose on the wing, directly above them, and settled on the gable, tearing at the thick flesh. Diamonds – in which it took no interest – began to skitter down the steep roof towards the children.

'Genius,' whispered Fingal. With his hands outstretched, he caught at the little jewels as they skipped off the roof and on to the balcony.

But Fitz was already taking from Dolly the last of the fish. There was more meat – at least two or three more chunky slabs – but the pitch had run out. She had only been able to coat one side of this piece, and the stuff though sticky was thin, full of Padge's hair and even bits of skin. Fitz looked at it carefully, and tried to judge the weight, lifting it up and down. He would have to change his technique. He would have to be lucky.

Dina, surrounded by the reared heads of a score of enraged snakes, set fire to another of her torches, then a third. She was hanging from the drainpipe by her feet, nearly upside down, waving the fires at the enraged serpents – to no avail.

'Dina's in trouble,' Padge said.

It was essential that the piece of fish, once he had thrown it, not turn over in its flight: it had to hit the fountain square, with the tarred side down. He loosened his stance, leaned back, and tried to shove the sticky meat through the air, nearly throwing himself off the balcony with it.

Padge and Navy caught his legs as he teetered. He hardly noticed. His eyes were on the fish meat, willing it across the gap, willing it down, willing it to stay square. The birds screamed as it fell. They fell with it, swirling. The light of Dina's torches, across the courtyard, flared wildly as she swung them with frenzied violence.

Then the meat hit – slapping the shining stones, dead on target. This time his cast really had been a bullseye. As Fitz fell backwards, pulled into the arms of the other Prents, he saw the largest of the albatrosses, the king with his battered beak, diving towards his quarry. The other birds scattered before his prerogative. By the time Fitz had got his bearings again, the giant bird was already alighting on the highest pitch of the roof above them. The meat hung from his beak. He raised one foot, sank it into the flesh of the fish, and pulled it down with fierce hunger. From the bottom of the tarred skin, as it was torn away, the largest of the diamonds – a ball the size of a fist – dropped to the roof and began to roll downward.

Fingal, tall and sharp, caught it in his hand.

From across the courtyard, behind them, there came a scream – not of fear, nor of danger, but of rage. Her three torches had dropped to the ground, and Dina was already shimmying, fast, up the side of the far wall.

'Did anyone even see her go?' Padge was watching Dina with interest, or awe.

Adrenaline and pride surging through his body, Fitz turned to watch Dina. He didn't understand: of course they had all been watching Dina, watching her progress, all along.

Then he saw what Padge meant. He wasn't referring to Dina at all, but to Payne. She was kneeling at the top of the roof, directly above Dina, her hands on the drainpipe where it attached to the guttering.

*No. Where it used to attach to the guttering.*

Dina kept climbing. It was still her best move.

'Elegant,' said Navy, matter-of-fact. She turned to Fitz. 'You're probably not used to all this calculation – but there's only one way we're walking into the House of the Jack to get Russ, and that is if the Jack isn't there. Unless someone is in danger, he'll sit on the helix like a broody hen on her egg, and we won't get past him.

Payne, anticipating this, is going to put Dina where only the Jack can save her.'

'But that's awful,' Fitz protested. 'The snakes – they'll kill her –'

'Payne has done her maths,' said Navy. 'So has Dina. She wouldn't have screamed like that if she didn't know she'd lost.'

As Dina reached the top of the drainpipe, it seemed for a moment that she would make it, that she would leap free of the collapsing metal, that she would sink her grasp into Payne's wrists, grab her hair – something. But Payne chose her moment and pushed with all her strength, ripping the metal and its last bolts free of the stonework. Under Dina's weight it tottered for an instant, and leaned back, then – for agonies of long seconds – seemed to hang in the moonlight with Dina, helpless, flapping her arms around it. And then it began to fall backwards, ripping the rest of its bolts from the wall and collapsing in slow motion directly towards the fountain. Dina didn't pick up even a scratch; she landed standing on a pile of diamonds, a hefty sheared length of drainpipe in her furious hands.

She spread her stance and planted her feet on the fountain's rim. 'I concede,' she shouted, not bothering to look up. With wide sweeps of the iron pipe, held like a staff, she began to ward the snakes from the perimeter.

Navy smiled. 'She'll be fine, Fitz. Especially after the Jack has cleared the courtyard. Come on.'

Keeping low, they passed in single file back into the Registry, Padge in the lead, Fitz in the rear – carrying in his fist the big diamond, which Fingal had surrendered to him as his right. In the courtyard outside the Registry they met Payne, who had come down by a roof and a trellis, and was not – for once – sorry to receive the congratulations of the other Prents. Fitz noticed with satisfaction that, as they crossed the court to skirt the Commissary on their way round to the House of the Jack, Dolly allowed Payne to slip into the file ahead of her.

'It's not like the Jack to leave the doors open for us,' Padge said with surprise when they reached their destination.

'He doesn't want us to break anything,' said Dolly, gaily.

'Anything else,' Padge corrected her.

'Don't worry,' Navy said to Fitz, as she held open for him one of the big leaves of the Jack's great wooden doors; 'he'll be in the Commissary Yard now, plucking Dina to safety. I guarantee it. That's how these things always work.' Fitz nodded and passed in behind the other Prents. 'Only,' Navy added, confidentially, 'it's usually me he's saving.'

The Jack had lit the hall with candles, which still burned. The Prents swarmed over the complex illusory topography of the floor, making for the very centre of the Helix. There in the base of the mechanism, just as Dina had predicted, framed by its unlocked iron cage, the socket stood empty where the ball-diamond, the Blank Eye, took the weight of the turning staircases above. Padge held out his hand as Fitz approached, took from him the huge jewel, and crammed it into its place. He winched the mechanism back into gear, and then signalled to Navy to turn the wheel that drove the Helix. As she spun it, the two interlocked sets of stairs began to rotate on their pivot, swinging slowly free of the high rooms to which only moments before they had offered easy access. It was obvious, Fitz thought, where they would find Russ – the only alcove, at the highest elevation, in which candles had not been lit. Padge and Dolly joined him on the stairs that would, by the time they climbed them, lead them to this room; just to be sure, Fingal and Payne took the others, which would issue on the opposite side.

As they ascended, around them whirled and wheeled the great House of the Jack, its innumerable flames and rising threads of candle-smoke dazzling to the bleary eye, every wing and alcove stacked high with ancient bookcases, spheres and globes, armillary curiosities and geometrical puzzles, visual paradoxes and, on papers strewn everywhere across the whole of the library, endless and complex equations. Flushed with his success with the diamond, the hero of the night's work now set among new friends as an arrow nocked to a string, Fitz began to feel the place might actually be his – that, notwithstanding the calamity of his arrival, the anxieties of his enrolment, the terror and sorrow of the Black Wedding, like a pearl whorled from grit these halls of the Heresy might be a home for him, after all. Step after step he mounted, and his heart mounted with his steps, growing in assurance and satisfaction.

At every level they scanned the oak-panelled rooms as they passed, looking for signs of anything out of the ordinary. The Jack was never a tidy thinker, and they would have been surprised in this temple of disarray to discover neatness. Instead, in every direction they looked they saw comfortable confusion, the evidence of projects undertaken but never completed, thoughts half thought and truths only partly glimpsed, ideas and visions developed, broken and discarded, from desk to desk the signs of games in progress – games the Jack was playing with or against himself, whose winner as he left off, unsatisfied, he always was. Fitz thought as he climbed that the whole space was a monument to a mind that feared and expected nothing.

Round and round the spiral they climbed, taking the wide arcing treads of the staircase two, sometimes three at a time. The Helix had almost completed its turn, and as they cornered the last part of the highest curve, Fitz could see the end of the huge wooden structure, coming into line with the topmost of the hall's interminable landings: their destination.

And an arm – a brawny, lifeless arm that, as it came into view, they saw lay twisted against the Jack's massive, motionless torso. It had crumpled under him and lay extended at a sickening angle, radiating backwards from the shoulder from which it seemed completely torn. As they sprinted up the last twenty or thirty steps, they could see he must have broken a great fall by breaking his arm – comprehensively – beneath the crushing weight of his own heavy body.

The staircase slipped into its final position. Padge and Dolly flew up the steps before Fitz, and as they dropped to the Jack's side, checking his body for signs of life, Fitz took his bearings.

He had never been so high in the House of the Jack. In one way the room here was like any other that the hall contained: in all of them, the high ceiling accommodated on three sides a heavy oak case of twelve equal shelves, on which were ranged a densely crammed collection of books of all sorts – new volumes in bright and colourful cloth or paper covers, older books in bindings of leather and parchment, manuscripts, loose notebooks stacked in piles wherever the shelves afforded space. This room was no different, though all the books were of a uniform, tanned leather. Down the centre of the room, like all the others, ran a large, rectangular trestle table, on which two lanterns – dark – lay ready for lighting. At the far end, nestled among the shelves, windows looked out upon the black night – or, Fitz noticed, upon the advent of the dawn. On the tables scattered piles of books, along with a few papers, suggested the Jack's occasional, desultory study.

But something was wrong. Fitz knew that it was before he knew what it was. A chest – a locked trunk – stood at the near end of the table, and he knew that it didn't belong, that it must be opened. But there was something else, and as he kneeled and began to fumble with the locks, he couldn't take his eyes from the shelves around him, from their hundreds of volumes.

And then it hit him. It was the smell: a sweet, animal musk.

The lock with which he was fumbling popped open, then the next. From behind him he heard the Jack stir, grunt, and then moan in agonizing pain. He pushed up the lid of the trunk.

Within it lay curled Russ's body, folded and tucked neatly away as if he were a blanket that had been stored there against the winter. His skin, white as the dawn, felt cold to the touch. Fitz stared, for how long he wasn't sure. It was like seeing a snow scene in miniature, or the model made of a real building. It was like looking at a perfectly executed drawing, something lifelike that was not, for all its exactness, life.

*A little jack-in-the-box for you.*

The Jack, staggering to his feet, pushed Fitz aside. Had he cut out the lines on his face with a chisel, or etched them with acid on the plate of his cheeks, he could not have contrived a more complete mask of pain. With a terrible, bellowing roar that seemed to shake the whole of the hall, from its loftiest top, through the Helix to its core, he took up the space before the trunk and stared down at Russ's cold and folded body.

'Why?' asked Fitz. 'Why did you do this?' The nausea in his stomach had not yet risen, anguishing, to his voice.

The Jack just stared at Russ's body.

'Why?' he asked again, trembling now.

Slowly, like a balloon finding its level in the high atmosphere, the Jack's gaze rose from its abyssal anguish, travelling as if from another world, and with all the effort of the huge man's resolve settled on the near shape of Fitz's face. As his eyes found their focus, his understanding met the child's.

'This was not a case. I did not set you a case.'

'Then who did?' Fitz replied.

'I tried to get to him. Without the diamond – I could reach every other room but this – I couldn't – I fell from the roof –'

'Is he dead?'

The Jack turned back to the folded child. With his good arm he plucked Russ from the trunk and laid him, as delicately as if he were spun of silk, or gossamer, over his shoulder.

'This is what comes of helping that halfwit of a Master', he said. He didn't raise his voice, but his anger, sharp and drawn, might have cut stone. 'They're trying to get to me, to warn me. But they have gone too far. My apprentice cannot die. I will not allow it.'

And on those words, he turned from the children and stalked down the Helix and out of the Jackery, trailing his shattered arm behind him.

9

## *The Disillusioners*

In the end, Russ was fine. The Commissar put him on a strict
diet of broth, and kept him in the Commissary under
surveillance until his colour had returned. Each of the Prents,
including Fitz, stole in between their afternoon lessons, as by day
they passed around the courts of the Heresy, to bring him
diversions: jokes, news, and so many little objects that his window
sill in the Commissary's infirmary looked like a cabinet of curiosity:
pebbles, flowers and dried herbs, cheap gems, an arrow ('for luck,'
said Dolly, awkwardly), two lockets, a piece of narwhal tusk,
bones – the heap of plunder kept on growing till Russ insisted they
stop.

The Jack, by contrast, was never quite the same again. Fitz
noticed at Feeding how the big Off's eyes watched his colleagues
at every meal, from time to time scanning the hall, quick with a
new distrust. He was prone to anger, and, like the Master, seemed
to be growing ever more haggard. Fitz could see the evidence on
his face of the long vigils he must have been keeping – studying,
perhaps, or pacing the courts in the darkness. The other Offs all
sensed it, and the Prents; Fitz imagined that even the Fells and

220

Serfs, where they fed in the lower hall, seemed increasingly subdued, as if day by day a cloudy pall were settling on all of them.

And yet, at the same time, perhaps even because of that, he found his lessons enthralling, invigorating, like blissful dreams from which he cried to wake. He had come to the Heresy for Clare's sake. This was a certainty to which he clung like lichen to a rock. He pictured her back in the cottage by the Old Friary, at work in her garden, the trees blowing with their indistinct murmur beyond the defensive hedge, festooned with bindweed and blackberries. He longed for her to be able to return there, for things to go back to the way they were – before the letters, before loud voices in the night, before the fire. Before all this. The Heresy was always a means to an end, to that end; and he often – when no one was looking – took the little silver jay between his fingers, and reminded himself that he wanted to go home, that he wanted them both to go home. But new thoughts and new feelings, like weeds that will grow anywhere, seemed to take root in him and thrive. Although he couldn't say it – he wouldn't say it – nevertheless he felt that he loved this new place, its rituals and appointments and patterns and rules, its lessons and conversations. Every day the enchantment seemed more than the day before. Fitz couldn't make sense of it. He couldn't admit it. But he felt it. And then it took him over completely.

The enchantment. It stole on like a dream in sleep – from nowhere, out of time, disconnected to everything but itself. It encompassed him, swaddling him in a drowse, in a quiet, in a fullness. He forgot he had ever known anything else.

After three weeks of working in the Keep with Dina, during which time – judging from the position of the sun in the oriel window beside him – it was always early morning, Fitz put down his brush and placed his hand on his stomach. He felt well, healthy, as if he had just eaten, but he couldn't remember having stirred from his chair. Through the low arched doorway at the end of the library, he could see scores of his paintings hanging in the workshop; along the wall in the print bins, he knew, hundreds more – all now dry – were carefully filed in chronological sequence. He knew the subject of each of them, for it was the same subject he had painted again and again, and he recalled the exacting precision with which he had worked out these studies from memory, composing in green, in brown, in slate grey, examining the light as it drifted through the trees' canopy in the height of summer; the motion of the wind during fierce storms, which broke down the brittle growth and sometimes cleared large patches of the wood; the lives of the silent creatures that made their home in the forest, from the ants and beetles, the worms and lice to which the soil and leaf mould provided shelter, to the birds and squirrels, mice and in the ditches rats that picked, scratched and burrowed among the fallen and the live trees, to the occasional larger animals that passed through when he himself had grown silent and still enough to observe them – badgers and stoats, deer, and once a wild boar. Fitz had composed portraits of the Bellman's Wood in the night, studies of its trees in the rain, a series of small pictures of lichens, another of mosses, and innumerable vast canvases depicting one particular clearing, a glade over which presided an ancient oak, easily the oldest and most substantial tree in the wood, itself an abstract or epitome of every colour and quality that the wood at large contained.

'Aren't you forgetting something?' asked the Keeper, again and again, when she passed by, touching his brush lightly at its end, with just the right pressure to steer it to an unfinished corner, or to transfer a rich smudge of colour to the canvas below.

Fitz remembered learning to paint with oils, here in the Keep, sitting beside Dina and at times questioning, at times copying her. Under her patient instruction he had developed the ability to blend pigments, to compose and to layer them. From her he had learned brushwork, how to stroke and dab, how to stipple and fade in hue and in value. He had worked on figure, tone, shadow, and all the elements of composition, in work after work, exercise after exercise. No stroke or canvas was wasted; with each new attempt, he could both feel and see how his technique extended itself, how his capacity for representation grew, how he had come ever closer to a true account of the wood that he knew, in all its seasons and shapes, in all its hues and moods, in every last ridge of its bark and each of its countless sprays of ferns. He looked at the drops of rain that he was painting, proud on a leaf still unshaken after a sudden shower in May – and began to think they were in some sense truer, in some sense more substantial, than those he remembered seeing, or tasting with his finger, in the woods where he had in some other life, once, walked.

'Dina,' he said. 'Something strange is happening.'

'Yes, little brother, what is it?' She leaned over from her desk, where she was halfway through painting another seascape, dark, thunderous, and pregnant with violence. A solitary island of rock and moss reared in the distance from the inaccessible horizon towards which in canvas after canvas she laboured. She examined his painting – a detailed study of a fern, surrounded by half-rotten chunks of wood. She was troubleshooting, and her eyes moved methodically across the canvas.

'It's not the painting,' Fitz said. 'It's something about the morning.'

'Ah,' said Dina. 'You've noticed. It's been a while.'

'It's been morning for a long time. It's been morning almost as long as I can remember.'

'We've been painting together for weeks, little brother.'

'Why has the morning not ended?' Fitz asked her.

Dina settled back into her chair and returned to her painting. She might have painted for a long time.

'It's the stack,' she said without any hesitation. 'It's a root, ground up very fine. The Commissar adds it to our food at breakfast. The effects are a little different on everyone – some people don't experience much change, but for others it transforms everything. Its purpose is to enhance your concentration, so that you can focus with more intensity and productivity on whatever it is that you're doing. But a consequence of that concentration is that, whenever you are in a given situation, you tend to forget that you have ever done anything else. You haven't stopped living normally; if you think very hard about it, you will remember, even here, that we have been doing other things. You will recall our afternoons, and our nights. But when we go to them, later, you'll almost completely forget about this painting – until we come back tomorrow. And then it will feel as if we had never stopped, as if we had never left this place, as if brushes and colours and canvas are all that we have ever known.'

Fitz closed his eyes and tried to imagine his life outside the Keep, in a place where the Keeper didn't shuffle back and forth, absorbed in thought, between the tall shelves of her library and the bright, windowed tables of her workshop. No matter what he did, no matter how hard he tried to push his mind to think past his surroundings and the sensations present to him in his immediate experience, he couldn't conjure another space or action – at least, not one that felt to him like his own, like something he himself had been doing. He remembered hearing a story, or a collection of stories, over the last few days, or weeks, about another life that he might have lived. In these stories, he and Dina studied biology and medicine alongside the Commissar, and worked on engineering topics with the Sweeper. He had been told, he was sure, that he would be examining logic and paradoxes, mathematics and formulae with the Jack, and when he thought about it, he seemed to know exactly what they would be studying, not only the topics but the individual examples, and was able to run over in his mind the precise manner in which their conversations were going to turn – so much so, that he had the uncanny sensation that they had already talked about these topics and examples, that these conversations had already taken place. He could predict them all. And he knew that the other Prents were going to their lessons every day, each alone to quiet study and training; he remembered, as if long ago, passing them in the courts, and meeting them at Feeding, hearing their stories, receiving advice and guidance. But it was all so far away.

'So none of this – this feeling, what I'm feeling – is – real?' he asked.

'It's all real, little brother,' answered Dina. She sat back from her painting – a huge chalk cliff, seen in partial shadow from a dinghy at sea, swirling with seabirds, whose movements seemed to imply the complex currents of wind surging around the shore. Fitz found it completely engrossing. He looked at it for hours, and memorized every surface of the cliff, understood the paths taken by sea-surge and storm's rain, when they crashed and ran down its face, saw how the cliff's geology had exposed soft and porous rock to the elements, so that it broke and fell away over time, leaving the veins and shafts of harder, more durable stone to stand like pillars, or sinews, running up and binding the land together. He saw where at the summit of the cliff the topsoil had accumulated over a vulnerable spit of earth, a place that would soon collapse and thunder into the sea below, and be scattered on the low rocks and foam.

'The effect of the stack is to disorder your sense of narrative. Things that happen before other things instead seem later, as if they have happened after other things. The present appears to be one, an unbroken continuity that stretches impossibly far back into the past. This is what we call "stacking" – it's as if your brain gathers up all the different pieces of your life that form part of this logical or experiential "set" – all the things, say, that happen to you in this room with me – and treats them as if they are all happening in one, unbroken, coherent experience.'

Fitz took a deep breath. He knew he should be upset, that he should feel anxious or undermined. This was a terrible thing – wasn't it? But instead he felt a deep sense of peace, as if he were in an abundant and perfectly tranquil garden.

'Will it ever end?' he asked Dina.

'Yes, little brother,' she said. 'You metabolize the stack root during the course of the day, and as you digest it, it circulates in your bloodstream; by evening, when we sit down to dinner, it will have dissipated completely, and you will experience everything in the normal way.'

'And that's real?'

'It's all real – this is real, that's real – whatever "real" is. The Disillusioners give us stack not because they want us to under-stand that it – the stack – isn't real. It's because they want us to understand that everything is like the stack. Everything, stack or no stack, is equally illusory, equally real. You're always in the grip of something. Do you love me?'

Fitz realized that he loved Dina more than he loved the air he was breathing. He hadn't thought of it, until she asked him. Or maybe she didn't ask him until he thought of it.

'Yes,' he said. 'Can we stay like this forever?'

'I feel the same,' she answered. 'But it will wear off, mostly, by the time we finish lessons for the day.'

'I won't love you then?' Fitz began to cry. The tears, hot and sincere, fell like lumps from his cheeks, and fouled the corner of his painting – a huge canvas on which he had painted trunk after trunk of beech, lime, ash, hazel and oak. He felt like his body, everything that he was in heart and in soul, was a great trunk that had opened, splitting from its roots into a cleft that ran sap in torrents.

'Don't cry. You'll remember that you loved me, that you felt at peace and as if time spent with me was as long and as perfect as eternity, and – as difficult as that is to imagine now – you'll probably think it was all just an illusion.'

*Everything but this – the world and all it contains – is the illusion.*

Fitz carried on painting. That's all there was to do. He completed several more canvases before he dared to speak again; he was nervous that he might do something to upset the sun where it floated in the window.

'Dina, I have to leave this place. The Master will come for me.'

'I know, little brother,' she said. She was painting a gorgeously detailed vision of a low building perched on a cliff's edge. It had been constructed out of rough stones, without windows. The roof the cliff itself had provided; an overhanging crag dipping down to a point just at the right height, just in the right place, had offered shelter to which the builder had needed to supply only walls. Fitz watched Dina's hand and arm fly around the canvas, making minute adjustments to a scene almost entirely composed of grey, green and blue slashes, each one a stone, each one a glancing of the light against the eye, each one a piece of air between now and now. Fitz had the sense that this scene, this house, had been waiting in this place since the earth itself was, and the sea, and the sky.

'How do you make something so that it seems it has been there forever?' asked Fitz. His eyes were full of wonder.

'It's just an illusion,' Dina answered. 'You want to see something fixed, something eternal, and so you find that in the painting. Really it's the opposite.' And she showed him how she had painted the little precarious house in the moment before the cliff's collapse, how the whole structure of the land and sea was about to change, how everything she had pictured was on the verge of its own ruin. 'Nothing endures, little brother,' she said.

Fitz looked at the sun in the window, but it had not moved.

'Know this,' murmured the Keeper, who was passing. 'Every painting destroys the thing it shows you.'

Dina was telling him a story. The tall windows of the Registry, painted white and divided into twenty panes, had iron latches at the base. The Registrar had pushed them open, because in the late-morning sun the room could become hot, and heat wasn't good for the books and papers stored on the vast, open shelves that filled the archive. The breezes that swept through the windows ruffled the little hairs on the back of Dina's neck while she spoke. Fitz always liked to watch them while he listened to her.

'Do you know how mountains are made, little brother?'

He said he did not, even though he did.

'The earth beneath us shifts on huge plates. There are many of these plates, moving in different directions, sliding slowly on vast seas of molten metal and rock. At first these plates are flat. But when they collide, the stronger plate crushes the weaker plate, making it buckle and rear up into the sky – just as if you were to push your blankets from the foot of your bed up to the head, so they would fold and buckle, and rise up. This is how mountains are formed. But the wind and the rain, the ice and the sea crash and break and run upon the mountains, and after many, many centuries they are crumbled and washed again into the oceans from which they first rose. And then the mountains that seemed to pierce the stars are again flat. Many mountains have been valleys, and many valleys mountains. When you find the fossil of a fish upon a snow-covered peak, you must think that nothing is as it seems.'

Fitz where he was sitting at a long table had a book open before him. He was reading the names of plants and of constellations, not in one language only, but in many languages. He turned the names over on his tongue: Orion the Hunter, the Shepherd and the Deer, *Sah-Osiris*, the Fool, *al-Jabbar*, or the Giant. Under his finger was the picture of a slender reed crowned with a magnificent head of bloom, as red as blood and as fire.

'There is a secret to trees, little brother. If you were a giant to whom trees were as little weeds, so that you could pull them from the ground as you might a dandelion, you would notice a curious thing. Shaking the soil and rocks from the roots of the tree, and stripping the leaves and needles from all the branches, you would see that the tree is altogether symmetrical, that its lofty canopy in the sky looks no different from its spreading roots beneath the earth. And this is fitting, for a tree begins as a tiny seed, and then spends its entire life growing very large so that it may produce something no larger than the thought in your head or the dust in your eye – that is, another seed. And it lets this seed fall upon the earth, and at length, perhaps after thousands of years, it dies. When it dies, it does not disappear, or become a ghost and wander through the forest. Each twig, each scrap of bark, the heartwood and all that is in the tree very slowly break down into something smaller, into fine dust, into powder. Beetles and termites, worms and even other plants feed upon it, chewing and crumbling it into pieces so infinitesimally small that you cannot see them, so small that they are like the hairs upon your neck, that you know to be there only because you can feel that they must be. And the little seed, which the tree has long ago let fall, loves nothing better than this fine powder and loam from the tree that came before, and this and no other thing can make it grow.'

Fitz had turned over many pages that morning already. The breezes coming through the window, bearing birdsong from the court below, and from the trees that stood in it, ruffled in the pages before him. He always liked to watch the movement of the paper where it was stirred, intermittently, along its edges.

'Have you looked up at the stars in the dark sky, little brother? Have you seen the way they wheel in the night, turning round the brightest light in the north, that they call the Pole Star? There is a constellation among them which some call Orion, but a thousand years ago they knew it as *Giga*, the Giant, the constellation that in Arabic is called *al-Jabbar*. This giant is a great hunter, and carries a sword above his head called *al-Saif*, the knife with which he cuts the skins from the beasts he kills upon the mountains or in the forests. When this constellation appears in the sky in winter, it is a sign that men must go on the hunt, for the summer harvests have ended, the fields are bare, the fruit has fallen from the trees, the seas are wild and perilous, and there is no other sustenance upon the earth or in the waves. Do you think, little brother, that the ancient hunters saw the stars and named them for themselves? Or did they look upon the stars and see *al-Jabbar*, and from him come to understand that they must learn to hunt? Where does the wheel begin to turn?'

The words of the books that had been set before him by the Registrar appeared for a time to shimmer in the breeze, and Fitz liked to imagine that they were ruffled into voice by the air that stirred them. Dina always by his side, he sat through the interminable hours of the morning awash in her tales, and in the histories of the chroniclers, and in the poems of the bards, and in the catalogues of names recorded by the botanists, and in the myths that bound the gods and their constellations to the circle of the seasons, to the harvests, to the rites of priests, and to the prophecies that they revealed.

'My grandfather was very rich,' said Dina. 'He devoted his life to making miraculous and beautiful things, to buying and selling things, to discovering things throughout the world and in the quiet of his own contemplation. Over the years of his life he amassed a great fortune, not only in money but in objects, in rare and precious things of many kinds. He had many friends and associates. His name dropped from others' mouths as honey from the hive in autumn, and all the world knelt at his feet. But when he was old, my father, his son, spent his wealth, scattering it upon the winds and dropping it into the secret places of the earth. Where it came to rest, it was hidden, and a thousand thousand hands, taking and receiving it from him carelessly, like squirrels buried it where it could not be seen. My father turned his face against his father's friends, and made his way in his own life as a sailor upon a sea at night, alone amidst the black vast of a doubled deep. My father, born in riches, had no use for them; his life consumed them. But I, born in the long exhalation of my father's poverty, yearn to draw in the world again. I will become my grandfather, little brother, and my child will become my father.'

Fitz was always hungry in the Registry. It seemed always to be nearly time for his next meal, though that meal never seemed, quite, to come. Always Dina had another story before they should leave.

'I have been told a tale, little brother, of a king who was a great warrior, and conquered many lands. These lands were rich: from many mines lying deep in the mountains, from many fields and orchards thick with grain, and fruit, and timber, from many forests stored with beasts of all kinds, the people of these lands had gathered a harvest of gold and silver, bone and wood, of jewels and pelts, and from their plenty had risen works of rare and magnificent artistry. Nor did these peoples, in the luxury of their affluent peace, neglect to compose rousing and exquisite songs, poems extolling their gods and their heroes. Great gilt statues adorned their temples, and their cities sprawled without walls in towers and in tenements. When the conqueror came he gathered up the best of all of this spoil, as a farmer strips the grain from the husk, and he took it with him to his granary of war, home to his halls, there to store and revel in it – that the world might witness how triumphant was his hand, how glorious his battalions, keen and thirsty as the edge of their swords! But when this conqueror had lived out the length of his days, arriving at his last age he would not be parted from his wealth; and so he commanded his armies to march into the desert once more, there to construct for him a tomb as sumptuous as any of the cities he had in his youth subdued. Now under the ground, like a tree that sinks its strength into its roots, he built his last towers, and the craftsmen from exotic lands whom his armies had enslaved, whose unparalleled workmanship had once adorned the air and glittered in the skies, now carved and painted, tiled and enamelled, sang songs and wrote their epics down, down within the dark and airless bowels of the sands. And when the king died, his riches were buried with him, and the jewelled and metalled glories that had years before been fetched from foreign mines, and coaxed up to grow and flourish upon the earth, once more were laid abed in the thick womb of their mother and of time.'

'Dina,' said Fitz. 'I am hungry.'

'That is because it is time for us to leave,' said Dina, 'and join the others in the hall to eat.'

'Will you tell me another story?' asked Fitz.

'A time will come when you will understand that there is only one story, and that it has a beginning, and a middle, and an end,' she said.

'I will want to hear you tell it again and again,' said Fitz. He was ready to leave.

'Another time will come when you will see that the middle is not real, and that every story closes in its beginning.'

'Because the game is already ended,' said Fitz.

'The game is already ended,' Dina agreed.

At lunch, every day, the children of the Heresy greeted one another as if for the first time, or else as old friends with whom they were being reunited after a long journey into a forgotten distance. Their faces, fresh as if from sleep, wore none of the jaded fatigue with which they might be dressed by evening; even Fingal, who as a rule ended each day in despair, at the midday meal had not yet remembered his failures, and greeted the other Prents easily.

Navy was always the first to speak, and she always said the same thing.

'Fellow toilers in the great work of every day, let's eat! For the lunch is already ended!'

They took bread from the basket as if in a daze – a happy one – and while they chewed, the time seemed to dawn on them, as if the seconds were fragments, or shards, and they didn't manage to catch them all. Fitz became accustomed, as the days stretched into weeks, to the sense of embarrassment he often felt at lunch, a feeling that he had been sleepwalking and had both done and said things in a stupor. But mingled with this feeling of shame, he also noticed growing in himself a swelling emotion, something like pride, recalling over the brief flashes of lunch chatter the skills he had acquired and the perceptions he had begun to reach in his morning lessons. Nothing seemed to change; and yet he had a strong sense that he was changing very quickly, that he knew himself better every day, and that the self he knew was faster, more knowledgeable, less naïve than ever before.

'Be wary,' said the Jack when he met Fitz and Dina after lunch one day, 'of this pride of yours. It's an inevitable consequence of the stacking, a side effect of your training.'

Even after the midday meal, when the other Prents seemed to have recovered their composure and self-command, Fitz still felt the effects of his disordered morning.

'It's only because you're new,' said Dina, who seemed even in the afternoons to hear his thoughts before he put them into words.

Fitz decided she was right – and, anyway, he knew what Dina seemed always to forget, that soon they would come for him, that soon he would be leaving. But a niggling anxiety troubled him throughout his lessons with the Jack, and with the Sweeper, whom he often met in the afternoons, the thought that he had always felt something akin to stacking, even before he had arrived at the Heresy, and that he had always known that other feeling – the sense of coming down from the mountain, or out of the fog, the moment in the mind and heart that was like coming into shadow after glare, when nothing would focus and everything rushed. It felt like stepping inside, into the cool spareness of the cottage, after being in the riot of the wood. It felt like coming home.

'How is it a side effect?' Fitz asked the Jack. They were sitting under a large plane tree in the garden of the Jack's court. Dina was lying in the cool grass, reciting verses to herself in a low murmur. Verses, or formulae.

'The stack gives you a centred experience of place, time and your own attention,' said the Jack. 'You learn things very quickly, and very solidly, in that state. In a few weeks you have already mastered skills and knowledge that otherwise you might have required years to learn. I have seen your paintings. They are very good. Looking at them, I, too, hear the wind moving in the branches of the wood. Perhaps more importantly, you know more about your own mind than most people do; you have practised recollection, you have learned to look at yourself as if from the outside, and by repeatedly coming *out* of the experience of stacking, you have learned to question your sense of what your "self" is. Coming to know yourself is learning to know that there is no great self there to know. Perhaps there is nothing at all.'

The Jack sat still for several minutes, while Dina in the grass continued to murmur verses. Fitz realized at once that he was meditating, and he waited impatiently for the big man to finish. On it went. Fitz became restless, and several times he nearly got to his feet to go inside; at least there, he might find a book to work through.

'Let me tell you something that I find curious,' said the Jack abruptly, opening his eyes. Fitz was startled to see that, though they had been closed, they were already focused on him, as if the Jack had been watching him blindly all this time.

'There is a reason that my office is called the Jack. It is the word for a small bird, a bird of prey, a falcon more usually these days called the merlin. I wear its colours on my robe. This name was given to my office for a reason. The merlin is the nimblest of falcons. It can follow even the smallest prey, even on windy days, with relentless precision. In its flight it mimics the movements of other birds – pigeons, starlings, sparrows – so adeptly that they often don't recognize the danger until the jack is already among them.

'But in one ability it excels all other hunters. Its quarry when attacked is likely to circle, often in huge flocks; in starlings, we call these mass formations "murmurations". Higher and higher, in rings and gyres, the murmuration will ascend in the sky, moving in ever tighter circles, seeking to shake off the predator. The jack will hang on them as if by a string. He is relentless when on the ring, capable of withstanding impossible pressures, unimaginable contortions. And somehow, more often than not, by circling he comes away with a kill.

'It is this paradox that defines my office, which is itself the office of paradox. How to go round and round, and ever go round, and yet finish with the end.'

Under the plane tree they worked every day through this paradox in different ways – always the same problem emerged, but it was expressed in different forms. Fitz often saw the Master hurrying through the courts at this time, rushing from the Registry to the Keep, papers or a book under his arm. High above him, from time to time, wings circled in the sky. He was, Fitz knew, still looking for the answer that would enable him to escape, to leave this place and go home. But something about his gait and his posture, something about the way he looked up at the windows as he passed, something about those wings in the sky, made Fitz think that he was not just hunting, but that he was being hunted, too.

'What's that round your neck?' asked Dina on one of these afternoons. The Master had just appeared from under an arch, covered the length of the Jack's court in a distracted hurry, and disappeared into a staircase that led to the Keep. 'What's in your hand?'

Fitz realized that he had been holding the silver jay that Clare had given him, which he kept concealed beneath his shirt. It was too late, now, to pretend it was nothing.

'It's just a necklace,' he said, as if that might be enough for Dina.

It wasn't.

'Let me see it,' she said. She had been lying propped on her elbows on the grass. The Jack had disappeared inside, to rummage through one of his queer little libraries for a book. He had told them to use the time to recite some of the new formulae Fitz was learning. Dina sat up and held out her hand.

Fitz untied the necklace with reluctance, collected it in his hand, and held it out to her. She studied it for a few moments.

'Does it mean something to you?' she asked.

'It – somebody important gave it to me,' he answered. He found he couldn't say Clare's name.

Instead he thought it must be nearly time to go to the hall for dinner.

'I see,' she said. She was looking at the staircase where the Master had disappeared, moments before. 'You know, little brother,' she continued, 'the Jack lied to you about the stack.'

*So you* were *listening.*

'That is, he's right that it gives us a disordered sense of time. You learn faster. But you learn faster for a reason. You learn faster because you love what you are learning. You learn faster because you love the hand that feeds you, and the fellow mouths at the trough. You learn faster because you love the food, the air you breathe, because love is entwined with everything that you experience. By means of love, in love, people can accomplish almost impossible actions.'

'You told me that before,' said Fitz.

'But you don't seem to have heard me. If you eat stack every day, for years, and every day you live in the Heresy, and study its

239

teachings, and feed and sleep among your fellow apprentices, do you think you will still want to go home?'

'I'll always want to go home,' Fitz answered her, but he wasn't sure he meant it.

Dina turned the necklace over and over between her fingers.

'Stack will become your home. The Heresy, and all that is in it, everything that it is, will become your home.'

Fitz didn't look at her, but at his necklace.

She gave it back to him, saying only, 'Sometimes people keep the strangest things.'

That night, after dinner, Fitz went straight to his room and went to bed. The sun hadn't yet set, and the bell hadn't yet pealed nine. He had skipped Second and Third Feeding because he hadn't felt hungry; perhaps that was why his sleep was so broken. He woke several times in the night, and at one point – lying in the still moonlight – he began to hallucinate. He dreamed that he heard oars rowing on the river, which was absurd, because his tower room was much too far away from the river for that. But in this dream he knew that the boat carried his mother, and so he slipped out of bed and, without bothering to put on his shoes or change into his day clothes, he descended the stairs and walked quietly through the courts towards the river landing. He hadn't passed through the Heresy's gatehouse since the day he arrived; now he found it empty, and dark, but the door stood open and he quickly covered the distance between the lawns and the river stairs.

At the water's edge, a little wherry – it seemed that same little wherry that had first brought him to the Heresy – was pulling up to the bank. The rower stowed her oars and turned to grab the bank.

It was Clare.

They said nothing to one another, but Fitz took in the boat and ran its painter through the ring, just as the porter had done for him when he had first arrived. He offered Clare his hand, to help her ashore, and in silence they walked back into the Heresy through the avenue of still-blooming roses. Although the night was dark, the roses bloomed more darkly still, and in the cool air their perfume beat out from the buds in a rhythm as steady as the tide.

He showed her all the courts of the Heresy, and she seemed to know what they were, and what happened in each of them, without his having to say a word. Fitz marvelled at it, but said nothing until they arrived, last of all, at the Master's court, and, in its corner, the door to his tower room. Here he stopped at the foot of the stairs.

'How is it,' he asked her, 'that you know so much about the Heresy already, when I have lived here for months and get lost every day, and you arrived only tonight?'

Clare took his hands, and raised them a little, holding them out in the air between them. She looked at him; he felt her eyes on his, warm as daisies in the sun.

'I know a great many things that I did not know before, Jaybird. I have been to a place that you cannot imagine, and there seen things beyond the reach of fantasy.'

Longing tore through Fitz's stomach. It felt as if he were a boy of paper, and two hands ripped him. He wanted to ask Clare where she had been, what she had done without him, the dangers she had faced and the glories she had witnessed. He could see all of this in her eyes, that were fuller and wiser and brighter than ever they had been. But in the dream he could find no words.

'Jaybird, there is a place in this world – a place just beyond this world, but in it, too – of such goodness. A place where everyone dreams and tells of the best things, of love, and justice, of kindness and courage, a place where stories heal the heart's sorrows, and the mind's, a place where everything is possible. Come with me there, Jaybird – leave this Heresy, and come with me.'

'Is it over the green, green sea, Clare?' Fitz felt he could hear his mother's song, just beyond his hearing, or in the tips of his fingers. 'Will you be my Bibi there, and I a prince?'

'No, Jaybird, there are no princes there. There, everyone is equal, every voice part of the song, every thread a part of the same fabric.'

The blackness of the night seemed to deepen around them then, like the centre of a rose, lush and secret.

'Would you like to come up to my room, Clare?' he said. 'I would like you to see it. Except for the cells, it is the highest room in all of the Heresy.'

'I would rather you came with me,' she answered. She wasn't smiling, but her tone was so warm and so loving that he felt for a moment that he was returning through the Bellman's Wood at dinnertime, a book tucked under his arm, and Clare calling him from the kitchen.

'But I would like you to see my room here,' he said. 'It is the room I have always wanted.'

Just at that moment, lights simultaneously appeared in the three archways that joined the Master's court to the courts of the Registrar, the Commissar and the Heresiarch. Sharp footsteps, jumbled and echoing, tramped in the stillness.

Fitz took Clare by the hand and pulled her into the stairway. He began to run up the stairs, and she ran behind him. They took the steps two, sometimes three at a time, circling so fast that he grew dizzy. By the time they reached his room, they were both gasping for breath. In his chest Fitz's lungs burned as if they had been set on fire, or as if he were being smothered. Clare shut the door behind her, and dragged the desk in front of it.

'That won't hold the door against them,' Fitz said. 'They can get through anything. They are with me even in my dreams. They can make tomorrow come before today.'

'There isn't much time, then, dearest,' said Clare. 'I want you to understand something. Mr Ahmadi is not the man we think he is. He is using you. They are using you. They are using all the children. Come with me. We can get out of this place. There is somewhere safe we can go. We can go to the Mountain.'

The footsteps had reached the stairs, below. There was a sound of many people climbing. Whoever they were, they weren't speaking to one another, only climbing.

Above their heads, the trapdoor in the ceiling suddenly opened.

Ned More's head dropped into the room.

'Clare,' he said, 'we have to leave.' The urgency in his voice made Fitz very anxious to wake up. He tried to push himself from the dream, through the surface of it as one might push through the surface of a lake, up through the tangled water into the clear and untroubled air – but he wasn't able to remember how. Suddenly he wasn't sure he was in a dream at all. The steps on the stairs grew louder.

The people chasing him were getting very near.

Clare dragged the mattress off Fitz's bed, and with sudden and surprising strength upended the whole bed against the wall. Beneath the mattress, the bed's frame was fixed with wooden slats. She climbed them as if they were a ladder, so that she could almost reach the trapdoor in the ceiling above. She looked back down at Fitz.

'Now, Jaybird,' she said.

Fitz reached out his hand. Somehow he had managed to take off his necklace, and the silver jay was twined round his fingers. Instead of taking Clare's hand, he dropped the necklace into her outstretched palm.

'Clare,' said Ned.

From above, there were voices.

From below, there were voices.

*Everything is in my head. The mind is its own place.*

'Jaybird,' said Clare. But Fitz didn't climb.

Clare took Ned's hand, and he pulled her into the ceiling. The trapdoor fell shut behind her.

The steps had become very close, now, to the top of the stairs. Fitz could now make out what the voices were saying. They were saying, 'He is bound to wake up.'

He pulled the bed back down from the wall. It hit the floor with a crash. In his terrified state, he found it easy, somehow, to drag the mattress back into place. Its blankets were still on it. He pushed the desk away from the door and sat on the bed.

244

Through the window, a light flared in the sky. It took him a moment to make sense of it. It was a hot air balloon; he had seen the burner firing, and above it the looming darkness of the envelope. It fired again, and in the sudden illumination, he saw faces – Clare's, Ned's, and a third face – long, shadowed, beneath the hood of a cloak. Now the balloon, which was drifting in the sky, seemed to rise, and rising, to catch the wind.

The footsteps on the stairs stopped. In his dream there was whispering, but he couldn't understand it. He lay down on the bed, his body damp with sweat against the hot blankets. Then the footsteps died away again.

He fell back into a deep sleep, and didn't wake up until the next morning.

When he saw Dina at breakfast, he reached into his shirt for his silver jay, and found that it was missing.

10

# The Sensorium

Fitz took his place behind Payne as the others began to file through the low door into the hall. The bronze gong had sounded and the hundreds of feeders, already working their way through their first course, fell silent along the long benches that crowded the lower end of the hall. Fitz felt them staring up at the Prents as they walked in single file to their places at the table, fanning out to either side in the familiar motion that left him standing opposite Dina. For a few seconds they stood behind their chairs, and in the lofty cavity of the Lantern Hall not a muscle twitched within the skin. This was Fitz's favourite time of the day: an emptiness, almost like a moment forgotten between two others, between the arrival and the settling, the hunger and the satisfying.

'Don't eat too much tonight,' said Navy, from the other end of the table. Her eyes, merry, sat in her broad and freckled face like diamonds. Fitz had already started to reach for the bread, but the intensity of her expression brought him up short.

At this a few of the others turned their heads sharply – Dolly, above all Dina. Payne, the closest, reached out and took a piece of bread, then turned and offered the basket to Fitz.

'No, thanks,' he said. *It's some joke I don't get.*

Dina regarded him with settled power.

Fitz felt a tap on his shoulder. He looked up and was startled to find the Riddler standing very close to him, so close that Fitz had to crane his head awkwardly to see the Riddler's face.

'Aren't you forgetting something?' asked the Riddler. Fitz's stomach lurched. 'Which has the clearer sight,' the Riddler went on, 'the bat or the eagle?'

He was so close, Fitz could smell aniseed on his breath. He was stunned. He flailed, looked at Navy.

'The bat is blind, Fool,' said Dina. She poured half a glass of water. 'It sees nothing.'

'Yet that saw is sharpest that cuts without teeth,' said the Riddler.

'Go hawk your riddles at another table, Fool,' said Dina. She tore a chunk of bread with her teeth, and chewed it hard, as if she were trying to make a point. Fitz watched her, as they all did. She swallowed. 'We're eating,' she said.

'Not as well as I,' said the Riddler.

'Your reason, Fool?' demanded Dina.

'That maker makes best who makes without waste, and that artist who can coax a thing from nothing is nothing short of a god. Just so I, who eat nothing, eat best.'

'Every word you say is wasted, and you turn even things of importance into purest nothing,' said Dina. 'Which makes you a sad old man.' A smile was playing around her mouth, but her eyes remained cold.

'More generous I,' retorted the Riddler, 'to furnish so much nothing for others' crafty making. Read me therefore as you might a glass, and you may thereby make much of me. For my own part, being discontent, I find myself well contented with nothing. The man whom nothing satisfies feeds best, for he is past all waste.'

Dina seemed to be annoyed. She chewed fiercely.

'Am I not the light of truth, son of the king?' asked the Riddler. He had been walking slowly down the table, but now he came to stand behind Fitz again. 'Am I not past all waste?'

'This is the Riddler's way of telling you he expects you at the Sensorium after dinner,' said Navy, from the far end of the table. The Riddler squeezed Fitz's shoulders, one hand to either side of his neck, and withdrew. The pain lingered, and Fitz wasn't the first to speak – but the question must have been written large enough across his face. He had heard from the others about the Sensorium, of course: they seemed to spend half their free time complaining about it, in terms enigmatic enough that they both confused and fascinated Fitz. But he had assumed that training in the Sensorium – whatever it was – wouldn't be required of him. The Master had said to go to lessons; he hadn't mentioned anything about going down – down there.

'Like I said,' said Navy. 'Don't eat too much.'

'Everybody throws up, their first time in the Sensorium,' explained Dolly, sticking her finger in her mouth.

'Barforium, more like,' added Russ. Payne giggled, and was immediately embarrassed, putting her hand to cover her mouth while she frowned. This made Padge light up like one of the hall's myriad lanterns, and he elbowed Russ hard in the ribs. Fitz could see this was a form of congratulation for a bad joke well timed.

'You won't last five minutes,' said Fingal, without looking up from First Feeding. He was scooping rice with his spoon, a famished look on his face. But he laid his spoon down long enough to manufacture a taunting, hateful sneer.

'He won't be lasting any minutes,' said Dina. Her words, stern and curt, did not interrupt the circular motion of her spoon, which continued with mechanical regularity to deliver soup to her mouth. 'Fitz isn't going to the Sensorium.'

'Says who?' said Russ.

Dina held her spoon at her mouth while she swallowed her soup. She was staring at the metal in her hand, focused and intense. Just at the edge, in so minute a movement Fitz was hardly even sure he had seen it, her upper lip quivered. 'Says me, and I'm First Prent,' Dina said. 'When you're First Prent, which will be never, you can do what you like.'

At this the table, already quiet, fell still.

'Eat up, rabble,' said Dina. 'Feeding won't wait.'

It was an uncomfortable meal. Something had shifted, and no one – not Fitz, not the other Prents – was sure what it was. Dina didn't speak to anyone, but worked her way through First, Second and Third Feeding with a kind of professional efficiency that reminded Fitz of slaughter. After the meal he and Navy walked together back to the Master's tower, both of them silent and lost in their thoughts.

'You know who used to live here, before you?' said Navy, when they had arrived at the entrance to Fitz's staircase. The thought hadn't crossed his mind before – but of course someone else had lived here. He hadn't seen an empty room in all the buildings in the Heresy – the place was stuffed to bursting, teeming with children, adults, Officers, stores, archives, workshops, offices.

'Dina?' Fitz hadn't yet figured out exactly where her room was. It suddenly seemed strange to him that he didn't know.

It obviously seemed strange to Navy, too. She frowned at him. 'No,' she said. 'Not Dina. The Riddler.'

Fitz had been about to say goodnight, and had already put his hand on the carved frame of the tower door. Now he stopped, and squeezed his eyes shut.

*The Riddler?*

'The day before you came, he packed up his things and moved out. No one knew why, at the time. He took everything out to one of the sheds in the Sensory Garden, and set up there. Afterwards, Padge told us that the Master had arranged it with the Commissar, in advance, but I think he was making it up. Padge doesn't like it when things don't make sense.'

'Why doesn't Dina want me to go to the Sensorium?' asked Fitz.

'That doesn't make sense, either,' answered Navy, quickly, as if she had been dying to talk about it. 'You've been here *weeks*, and usually the Sensorium is the first place a new Prent goes. "Assessment," they call it. They sent me there even before they'd decided whether or not I could stay! Before I'd even unpacked!'

'When was that?' Fitz asked her. He realized with shock that he knew almost nothing about how the other Prents had ended up at the Heresy. 'How did you end up here?'

*Unpacked what?*

'I won a competition when I was little. Reciting the decimal places of pi. There are a lot of them. I could have gone on literally forever. The next day, the Registrar showed up at my house, and offered me a place at a school, fully funded. My parents sat down with me in the lounge, all of us in big chairs with tall backs, all at the table like we were having a very important meeting. They told me I would be a fool to turn down an offer like that. As if I had a choice.'

'Didn't you ever want to go home?'

'Every day, for a while. But now I'm not so sure there's a home left to go to. My parents wrote me a letter once – just news, you know – the dog, that kind of thing. But even that was a long time ago, and, to be honest, I've just told you pretty much everything I remember. I was only seven and a half when I left.'

'And now you're –'

'Fifteen tomorrow,' said Navy. She smiled, the kind of smile that pushes something away. 'What about you? Do you want to go home?'

Fitz thought about the cottage – the last time he had seen it, just before they had run across the road and into the Bellman's Wood, the smoke billowing in heavy clouds from the roof, then lifting lazily into the evening air. Surely there wouldn't be much left now.

'No,' he said, without meaning to. The word came out too fast for him to catch it, and he could see Navy was surprised. 'It burned down,' he explained. He hadn't convinced himself, much less Navy. This time her face didn't push anything away.

'I used to wish my house would burn down. I fantasized about it. But of course I didn't want to lose it. I'm really sorry. You must have lost everything.'

'I didn't lose anything,' Fitz said quickly. 'Nothing at all.'

Navy was silent. They had been standing by the door to the tower, but now she began to kick the little stones at her feet, and then, slowly, to walk towards the end of the grey court. Fitz kept her company. When they reached the end, they turned left and followed the court round.

'My house,' said Navy. 'My parents' house: it was called Roseland. That's a silly name, and it's silly for a house to have a name, but anyway that's what it was – full of roses. All kinds of roses – every colour, every size, some with endless pillows of petals, some with just a few, bushes, ramblers, big ones, little ones. Some of the stems seemed thick as my arm, with thorns like sharks' teeth. Others were tiny, spiny things. I remember my parents seemed to spend all their time on them. The summer I left, they were all in bloom.'

Fitz kicked a stone, himself.

'Clare used to paint me,' said Fitz. 'Paint pictures of me, I mean.'

'Clare is your mother?' Navy asked. 'So she's an artist?'

'She was going to be,' Fitz said. 'But then her mother died, and she found me, and so we just lived together at the cottage.' They had made a full circuit of the Master's court, and had almost reached the tower door again. Dusk while they were walking had given way to night, and the lamp by the passage cast a raking light over their features, so that they seemed sharp to one another. 'Our house didn't have a name,' he said. 'Clare just called it Mother's.'

Navy raised her hand, and Fitz thought for a second that she was going to touch his cheek. But she had seen something – a cord round his neck, caught for a moment on his shirt – and her precise fingers quickly set it right. She brightened.

'Birthday tomorrow. Better get some sleep before my big day. Betcha the Commissar gives me *extra stack*. Don't get too close to me at lunch,' she said, her eyes goggling – 'or I might fall hopelessly in love with you.' She stuck out her tongue, and disappeared into the passage beneath the shining lamp in the corner of the court. When she wanted, she could be even faster, and stealthier, than Dina.

At the top of the circular stairs, Fitz opened the door on the tower room with new caution. He tried to imagine the Riddler living in this space that he had come to think of as his own – no, more – this space that he had come to recognize was his, had always been his. He had fitted so naturally into its clean, square shape, its emptiness, its two windows that looked out on the morning and the evening. Surely no one else – and least of all that queer, enigmatic form, inscrutable and incapable – could have made this place their home. Moreover, why would the Riddler, of all people, have made room for him? He had had nothing to do with the Riddler. Fitz ran his fingertip along the lines he had scratched on the wall by the window, one for every night he had slept in the Heresy. In the three weeks and more that Fitz had been there, he and the Riddler had hardly interacted, not even to share a glance, until tonight.

*What if he wanted me to be here for a reason?*

Fitz sat on his bed. If Dina hadn't put her foot down, exercising all her authority as First Prent to keep him out of the Sensorium, he wouldn't have thought twice about it. But she had.

*And her lip twitched. She was angry.*

A sudden thought came into Fitz's head. He jumped up, took hold of his mattress, and dragged it off the wooden frame of the bed. On his hands and knees he inspected every surface of its slats, its posts, the headboard, the footboard. He had thought for a moment that the Riddler might have left him some sort of message. But there was nothing. Sluggish with defeat, Fitz laboured the mattress back into its frame. For a minute or two, while the sun dropped in the west window, he stared into the empty space of his room without thinking a single thought.

*What had the Riddler said at dinner?*

*Read me therefore as you might a glass, and you may thereby make much of me.*

Fitz leaped to the window. He crouched there, inspecting every millimetre of every pane in turn. At that angle, lit by the orange light of the setting sun, he saw the words that had been scratched lightly across four of the little panes of the window, as easily as if they had been written on paper.

'Come at nine bells.'

Two hours later, Fitz crept down the tower stairs and inched open the heavy door at its base. The night outside hung suspended, darkening against the wet, black stones of the Master's court, and – after some hesitation born partly from fear and partly from prudence – he slipped out into the open. Moving with that speed and glide that he had seen in Dina and Navy, he tried to cross the gravel of the court with hardly a noise. In the passage that connected to the Heresiarchy, he kept to the wall, avoiding the pools of light cast by the lamps fixed at intervals to the vaulted ceiling. He crouched in the corner of the passage for long enough to be sure he hadn't been seen, or followed.

Now, a few feet further on, he stood alone outside the carved stone porch of the Sensorium. The last light of the long evening was fading fast, and shadows clustered now like blotted ink, dark as old blood, in the deep-chiselled channels of the fluted grey stone. Fitz put his hand to the stone's heavy, cut corners, taking in its mottled texture. Five squared ridges ran immediately round the frame, conferring on the dark shadow within a strong sense of their order and regularity. But beyond that frontier, the stone seemed to erupt in a writhing mass, as if it were not stone at all – so tortured, so active that Fitz wouldn't have been surprised had the scaled torsos and feathered chests, the gripping fingers and scything teeth that thrust from and turned within the pillars and lintel suddenly given way into real motion. His eyes coursed over the bulging and unsocketed eyes, glaring in terror; the lizard tongues that flicked across the surface, here and there curling to a point in air; coarse bristles of great shagged paws, concealing in the gathering gloom curled claws embedded in the stone like flesh; and countless wings, legs, mouths, snouts, ears quivering with sense, fins, teeth, muscles, talons, jointed haunches, tails, and, everywhere, everywhere eyes that peered, burned, gazed, watched, and killed with basilisk cruelty. With indifference.

The porch stood eight or nine feet high, and about five feet wide. Within, the air lay darkly draped, as if gathered in shrouds of shadow. Alone of all the major houses of the Heresy, only the Sensorium remained to Fitz entirely an unknown. As he peered into the darkness, and down the stone steps that descended as if to a tomb, Fitz realized that he couldn't even place it; while he knew that it lay underground, and that its entrance stood here, beneath the Master's library, beyond that he couldn't say a thing about it. Did it all lie underground? How far did it reach? How was it organized? What did it contain? From the others he had gathered only fragments, odd phrases that suggested its size, its mystery, something about it that set it apart from the rest of the busy and sociable halls, libraries and workshops of the Heresy, from its quiet studies and snug-eaved lofts. One evening, on their way to the hall for dinner, Padge had told him it was the oldest of the Heresy's buildings, by centuries, a structure so ancient that the earth had silted and settled upon its walls until, today, it lay sunken in the ground like a huge buried palace. Gazing into the shadow of the staircase, his heart still resisting his eyes' curiosity, Fitz thought it might be so – like a gouge in the earth and time, a void of night concealed in the night, black within black, it lay waiting for him.

He took a deep breath, inhaling the cold, wet night air, fortifying himself against the shadows below.

A hand took him by the shoulder. He hadn't heard her. He never did.

'No, little brother,' whispered Dina. 'I said no.'

She released his shoulder, and he turned. Her face against the shadow told him nothing. Implacable, stern and commanding, she watched him not with concern but with the indifference of a power that foreknew his every move.

'Do you know why this place, why everything that we do here, everything that we are, is called the Heresy?'

Fitz shook his head. He need not have bothered.

*Third lesson.*

'It's an old word. All words are old, but some feel their age more than others. This one feels it the most. Thousands of years ago, when the game first was played, before all this, it meant a simple thing. *Hairesis* – it was just the taking of a move. That's all it is – a choice, a decision, a single play in the game. All these towers and cellars, these halls and houses, all the people here, from the Offs and Prents to the Fells and Serfs – they're all part of this one move, this one choice. They – we – don't act outside it. There is no *outside* it. I'm First Prent. I told you that you don't go to the Sensorium. So you don't go.'

Dina watched him as he crossed the court and slipped round the lights through the archway. She stood motionless, seeing him off. She had been standing guard, he knew, and would stand guard still; there was no way he would be able to slip past her down the stairs of the Sensorium – not tonight, probably not any night. It made him feel so frustrated.

*Because I'm forgetting something.*

What it was he had no idea. But those words, the Riddler's words, for some reason, in a way that he couldn't understand, had punched the breath out of him. He knew in his stomach he needed to find a way into the Sensorium.

Only, not tonight. Fitz came to the door of his tower and put his hand to the handle. The whole evening, from the moment the Riddler had stood behind him and summoned him to the Sensorium, had been a waste.

*Waste.*

Fitz dropped the handle, and instead of entering the tower, turned away, already walking briskly and – if anything – more silently even than before.

*Waste, he said. He said waste. He said he was beyond all waste.*

It was a simple thing to slip through the great oak doors at the long end of the Lantern Hall; they were never locked. Outside he had taken up two full fists of gravel; now, standing beside the well of the Sad King, he emptied them into the big pockets of his coat. The weight pulled down at him. He hoped it would be enough.

This time, when he stepped into the air, there was no great, glowing light by which to see the shaft of the well as he fell. But no sooner had he dropped through the well head, no sooner had the sickening void opened in his stomach, than the arms, hundreds of arms, broke his fall, cradling and supporting him, allowing his hunched and cowering body to tumble, gently, downward, ever downward, waved on the way as he passed through the warm salt stench of the Sad King.

When he hit the water, he didn't struggle. He let his body straighten like a wand, and the pebbles in his coat pockets – just a little added weight, but enough – pulled him swiftly down. He blew air through his nostrils, holding his breath, and held his hands protectively around his face. Squeezed shut, his eyes had they opened would have seen only darkness, only salt, only the lightless pools of their own tears. He dropped ever down through the warm brine.

It seemed a long time that he sank through the well, and yet he had counted only eight beats of his heart by the time his feet hit the bottom. He made sure of them, made sure that he was standing, before he dared look. In his chest his lungs began to tighten.

*I don't have long.*

He opened his eyes; they were full of panic and water. To his immediate left, through the murk of the water, he could make out light. He pushed towards it, down an open tunnel, swimming, pulling himself along with one hand as with the other he drew stones from his pocket and let them tumble into the water. Stroke by stroke he shifted along the close and rounded passage, shedding pebbles into the murky water, until he came to a submerged stair. Here the light was stronger. He turned his head to look up. A dazzling brightness shed through the long water above him, culminating in a gleaming pool at the top of the stairs.

He hardly needed to climb the steps, but one by one he pushed off them as he rose, increasingly desperate for breath. By the time his head broke through the surface, his lungs were already convulsing; a moment later, and he wouldn't have been able to stop himself from sucking in the warm, salty water. He would have drowned.

Instead he was standing in it, his feet still immersed. Fitz rubbed the stinging water from his eyes, gasping. A few steps further on, the staircase ended in a low, domed room of white stone.

In its centre stood the Riddler. Lighted lamps lay on the floor all around him.

'I thought I heard you,' said the Riddler.

'You couldn't have,' Fitz wheezed. The walls around him were of brilliant white stone, of a strange translucence that seemed to blush with violet wherever the light hit it. Squinting and reluctant, Fitz let his hands drop from his eyes. 'I haven't made a sound.'

'Silence sometimes tells a tale. Come in,' said the Riddler. 'If you can find your way in all this light.'

The long and loping man disappeared through a passage carved in the wall behind him.

On the floor of roughly quarried quartz, the water poured from Fitz and collected into shallow puddles. His body flushed with exhilaration and pain: exhilaration to think that he had been right, that the well of the Sad King was more than that, was more than a place where they dumped the waste after feeding, that it was a passage; and pain where his muscles, starved of oxygen during his long groping in the flooded tunnels, now cramped with fatigue.

*I was right. Let her watch all she wants; I made my own choice.*

Fitz drew deep breaths, trying to steady himself, and as far as he was able he wrung the water from his clothes. He tried to take his bearings. Around him the walls, where they caught the direct light of the lamps, glowed faintly pink as if bruised by the exposure. The floor beneath was set in huge, irregular slabs that gleamed dully in the light, like sheets of poured glass that had hardened here and there upon and within the rock. When he felt ready, calmer, Fitz stepped across the uneven surface, took up a lamp, and passed through the low arch of the door, and then a short passage.

The room he entered seemed entirely made of light. The walls here, like the floor, the ceiling – every surface – had been carved from the smooth, even, brilliant white stone. Round, twenty or thirty metres in diameter, with a gently domed ceiling, the chamber was lit by a hundred lamps standing in a ring round its perimeter; the purple flush where the lamplight struck the walls beaded or threaded the colour in a ring that put Fitz in mind of a necklace, and of coral. In the centre of the room, beneath the soft peak of the dome, the Riddler stood by a kind of table or – as Fitz studied it from this doorway – a high bed, like an altar, all of white stone. He was sorting through what looked like a tangle of leather belts. As Fitz stepped into the room, he set his lantern down by the others on the floor, hard enough to clatter, slightly, against the cave stone. The Riddler paid him no notice.

The table before which he stood was two metres long, or a little longer – the length of a man. It was obviously a kind of bed. *A hard bed*, Fitz thought. On the long side facing him, within a rectangular panel, the figure of a snake had been carved in relief, at one end coiled, at the other reaching with its slender head poised as if to strike. Fitz circled the room quietly, studying the table. On its end the head of a dog stood proud of the stone, its snout lifted, scenting the air. Fitz continued to round the perimeter of the room. Here, opposite the Riddler, he faced an owl, its eyes like blank orbs, each one the shield of some hero, and every feather carved like the plate of an armoured coat thick and impenetrable. It stood on a branch, one set of talons curled tightly on the wood, but the other, detached, slowly opening in a gesture of menacing, imminent attack. Behind Fitz where he paused, another door led from the chamber, down a passage into darkness. He hardly thought of it, so intent was he on the short, last side at the table's head, where the panelled tablet showed the fat head of a toad, its lips slightly parted, and from them a swollen tongue beginning to force its way, in disgust, into the rank air of its breath.

'Delicious are the poisons that destroy us,' said the Riddler. Fitz startled, suddenly shaken from his reverie.

The Riddler held out one of the belts.

It was too short to be a belt.

Fitz approached the table cautiously, keeping his eyes on the leather strap the Riddler had extended, the full length of his arm, for him to inspect. It was broad, five or six centimetres wide, and at one of its ends hung a thick steel buckle, burnished and softly gleaming in the lamplight.

He knew what it was. Padge and Fingal had tried often enough to scare him with stories about the Gyves, the Manacles and the Collar – the Five Fetters of the Sensorium over which the Riddler presided. Each one, when strapped to and tightened round the appropriate place on the body, interrupted and suspended one of the senses. As he took the short strap from the Riddler, holding it by its buckle, he drew a full breath, and as he exhaled tried to steady his busy heart. He laid the strap across his left hand. Black and stiff, it had a surprising weight for a piece of material so short. Then he turned it over.

There they were: small, slender, gleaming faintly in the lamplight, two spikes sharper than thorns, riveted or embedded in the leather strap so that, when it had been properly fitted, their points would slide into his skin and, by the Riddler's dexterity, disrupt the operation of his nerves. The sight of the little spikes, combined with the knowledge of their function, made Fitz's skin shiver, as if a current or a ripple had passed through it. Goosebumps fleshed across his arms and thighs. He handed the strap back and held out his wrist. He wasn't about to falter where the others hadn't.

*First lesson. Your eyes don't need to follow your body.*

The Riddler fitted the strap round Fitz's wrist with nimble and practised speed. His eyes found Fitz's, and when he nodded, once, the Riddler pulled the strap tight, drawing the leather against the steel of the buckle. Fitz thought he felt the tiny pricks in his skin as the thorns pierced his wrist. His whole body arched with tension, as if bracing for an explosion.

Instead, he felt almost nothing. A dead sensation pooled in his face, which at first he couldn't describe, or make sense of. It was as if the lights had been dimmed or the temperature had changed.

But that wasn't it.

It was only as the Riddler knelt beside him, already at work fitting the second of the Fetters to his left ankle, that Fitz was able to put a name to the sensation – or, rather, to the lack of it. His smell – the sense of the coolness, the slight dank of the basement room, its stone walls, its oil lamps, the fragrance sweet and acrid that had shaped his experience of the Sensorium – had faded and then gone out.

The Riddler drew the second strap tight, so quickly that Fitz hardly felt it coming.

Now the dead feeling spread in his face like a banner, taking in his mouth, and throat. He swallowed hard; and, where the familiar clarity ought to have settled in his palate, that awareness of the flavour of his own saliva and the fragrance of his breath, that background hum or metal of the self that he had never lacked – where that ought to have settled on him like silt in a pool disturbed, instead he tasted nothing. He tried to speak, but just at the moment when he thought to form words, they grated like straw or sand on his tongue, and he faltered, blabbing. At these infant murmurs the Riddler paused a moment, his hand firm round Fitz's right ankle, as if to steady him.

He breathed. Air filled his lungs.

*I'm fine.*

'Go on,' he said.

The Riddler set the third of the Fetters in place on his right ankle. Fitz felt his skilled fingers searching out the dimples between his bones and sinews, feeling for the place where the thorns should pierce. The fingers stilled. The strap tightened.

When he next spoke, he couldn't hear the sound of his own voice. Not even those low reverberations and deep notes that normally resonated in the diaphragm, not those underwater bells and drones of the voice in the body, the inward voice, the fingerprint of sound that was his alone – nothing. Fitz pushed his hands to his ears, clumsily covering and compressing them while he howled in painless, silent agony. His vision swam, and the lantern lights with their threaded coral shadows seemed to dance and weave before him. He was only dimly aware that the Riddler now stood before him, gripping his shoulders, holding him still.

He could feel that. He could see that, and feel it. Despite the warm circulation of air in the room, he could feel, too, somewhere hanging above his own tension and his puckering, unyielding skin the cold wrap of his clothes. He shivered once, and was glad.

A tight shock of panic had clutched at him; now that tightness started to drain away, slowly, like water subsiding in an agitated vessel. It sank through his chest, then dropped to his waist; he tightened the muscles in his hips and thighs, then loosened them, and the panic flowed into his knees, his calves, and at last sped through the floor. The Riddler still gripped him. Fitz tried to smile.

He felt he had come over a pass, taking a buffet of wind and storm at its height, and that he was now beginning to descend into the safety of the further valley. It would be dark, and quiet, but it would be safe. He had done the hard part.

Fitz looked at the Riddler's shock of white hair, thick and bristled, where it stood on his head. He was busy at Fitz's right wrist. Thick wiry tufts sprouted from his ears, and his neck seemed to bubble with moles and growths that might have been warts. Fitz might have laughed had that very head, that very neck, not been so intensely focused at just that moment on the process of blinding him.

The Riddler looked up. The strap of the fourth Fetter he held loose in his hand. His eyes seemed to ask permission. Fitz took a deep breath.

*Yes.*

He felt the pressure strap and bind on his wrist as the room went dark.

The black was blacker than anything he had known – blacker than a moonless night, blacker than the mute terror of his most sudden nightmares. Black he had known against the light – the black of lines, of voids, the black of an after-image or of char, that which was left behind after brilliance, or that which lay against the light. Soot-black, coal-black, the black of midnight: these he was familiar with. Here there was neither contrast nor story, no sense of border or definition. The black that encompassed him seemed as bright as day, a black milk, an ivory opacity that shone out with radiant beams of emptiness, and negation.

Fitz felt himself falling into it.

The Riddler caught him. His long arms encompassed him like wooden limbs, like boughs into which he slumped hard. His core, limp and slack, crumpled; even had he meant to stand, for the space of his long fall Fitz couldn't find his bearings, and when he pushed with his feet against the floor, his toes seemed to flex wildly in air. Dull, mute, deaf and blind, the movement of his body against the air, against the Riddler's arms, seemed like a subsiding in the earth, as if clods and stones, dirt and gravel were tumbling around and upon him. He gasped for air and reached, scrabbling, towards a dark light.

The Riddler held him, not just with his arms, but close, embracing him. Fitz couldn't taste the air; he couldn't hear the breath flooding in and ebbing from his spasming lungs; but as the Riddler grounded him, he felt his body settling again, felt the intermittent surge of his pulse and breath receding, until at last the Riddler laid him slowly on the stone table. Fitz felt his body uncurl against the stone from the extremities inward: first his wrists and elbows seemed to lie heavy on the platform, then his shoulder blades, then at last – as he pressed himself into the cool, ridged surface – each articulation of his spine, like a word, sounded.

Fitz pressed the back of his head hard into the stone, crushing his skin into the bone until it hurt. As he felt the last of the Fetters slide beneath his neck, he pressed ever harder, concentrating all his resolve into that one point of contact, skin on stone, summing himself up, tethering himself to the world by a single point of pain.

*Hold on.*

*Third lesson: never forget to forget yourself.*

He had seen the Collar, the longest of the Fetters, out of the corner of his eye. He had tried not to look at it, or notice its three longer spikes, those gleaming thorns that were now poised above the tender flesh of his neck, two pricking on opposite sides of his spine, the third against the Riddler's finger, ready to thrust lightly up towards his gullet. Quick things fluttered in Fitz's abdomen. Tremors lanced through his legs. He could still feel them.

*Go ahead.*

The Riddler felt his acquiescence. As the strap tightened, the numbness that had earlier stripped him of his tongue, then even of his breath, now dropped like a plummet through his neck and detonated in his chest. It rolled through him like silent thunder, rose in him as a still and obsidian dawn. For a long time – it might have been forever, or an instant, but it seemed to him as long as anything he had ever experienced – he flew in a void. Time, space, and all sensation had like a flower in the night closed, and the bud of all that was, was hidden.

He knew nothing at all.

'Fitz.'

The voice came to him from within himself.

*Who's there?*

He hardly needed to ask. He couldn't ask anyway. He couldn't hear a thing. He knew that. But through the bark of the trunks of trees he saw the motley flit, vibrant and elusive.

'Fitz,' said the Riddler again, in his ear. 'Come on.'

*I'm dreaming.*

Fitz pushed hard on his legs, breaking into a run, leaping between trunks and threading the trees as if he were a shuttle working in the weft. Bars of light, green light, the rich living hue of moss and leaf, of springing stems and the weed that grows on still water, jagged between the tall masts of the trees. He chased it as a parched traveller might run down water in the desert. Above him butterflies and moths beat their noisy wings, scattering like timbrels into a swelling and operatic movement themed with green. He tasted soil in his nose and on his tongue, the sweet, wet flavour of earth that worms and beetles, stirred by vernal rains, put out as vines do flowers. Still the motley eluded him; still he darted, flying in the green air.

'Fitz,' said the Riddler again.

He stopped. He was in the wood – the Bellman's Wood. Away to his left an old stump he knew, the shell of some towering hulk of oak, stood broken and blackened with rot, big breads of fungus tabling from its sides. He had always liked to think of it as a wrecked and capsized boat, the rot its tarred and barnacled hull, the fungus its keel and fins. Behind the Wreck, he knew, lay a clearing, and beyond that the stone outcrop and gully that marked the near boundary of the wood by the cottage and chapel. He had lost the Riddler. All around him the green light seemed to sift in the air, rising and falling between the trees as clouds of syrup swirl in water. All around him the wings of moths like sails batted the breeze.

He looked up. Between the flapping cloths of wings the green sun poured down like syrup, sweet and stifling. In among the streams of light thick as ink he saw the Riddler's motley, still.

Fitz climbed, hand over hand, feeling the tough knobs of the ancient oaks solid beneath his hands, solid against his feet as the rungs of a ladder. He climbed hundreds of feet, sure with every handhold that it would be his last, that he would reach the Riddler, that he was almost there. Again and again the boughs above receded into the green light, pouring. Around him the air was thick with wings. They rustled in the air as worms might in soil, and flew in ranks rife as angels.

At last he broke free of them as if from the canopy of the wood. Before him the Riddler sat on a sturdy limb. He was smiling.

'Fitzroy,' he said.

'You know my name,' said Fitz, surprised.

'I know many things,' answered the Riddler. He held to the bough with his hands. His feet dangled into the green.

'Where are we?'

'We're in a wood,' said the Riddler. 'You climbed this tree yourself.'

'But how did we get here?' Fitz felt as if he had to brush the huge canvas wings of angels from his eyes, just to keep the Riddler's motley from subsiding into the green density. 'I thought I was in the Sensorium.'

'This is the Sensorium,' said the Riddler. 'Everyone reacts differently to the loss of sensation. Some people go catatonic, collapsing into themselves as if into a deep sleep. Some people find their minds pulse with images, lights and sounds, neither more nor less ordered than a kaleidoscope or a carousel. Others seem to dream. You are doing yet another thing.'

Something was niggling Fitz. He looked at his hands. He half expected to find his right hand at the end of his left arm, or something even more bizarre. But they seemed normal. He held his face.

It was his face.

Then it hit him.

'You aren't speaking in riddles,' he said. 'You're making perfect sense.'

'Yes,' said the Riddler, 'I noticed that, too. It's a new experience for me.'

Fitz sat on the branch next to the Riddler. They perched there together, swinging their legs against the clouds of moths and butterflies, for a few minutes.

'Well,' said Fitz. 'What am I supposed to be learning in the Sensorium?'

'That's up to you,' answered the Riddler.

'Doesn't everyone train in the same way?'

'Hardly,' said the Riddler. 'For one thing, no one else talks to me like this.'

'Why me?'

'I don't know.'

'Why did you ask me to come here?'

'I didn't,' said the Riddler.

Fitz almost fell out of his tree. 'But the writing on the window –'

– 'was written almost fifty years ago,' said the Riddler.

Fitz pondered this time for a space.

'Why then did you expect me?'

'Because,' said the Riddler, 'I remembered the writing on the window.'

'Whose life am I living?' asked Fitz.

'That is a very good question,' answered the Riddler. Suddenly his face was very close, and Fitz could see in the Riddler's eyes his own eyes. 'But it is time for you to leave the Sensorium.'

'Why?' asked Fitz. He kicked a cloud of moths with his foot, and their huge canvas wings flapped hard in the green wind, like sails on the sea.

'It's not a good idea to stay under for too long,' said the Riddler.

'Why?' Fitz found himself on the ground again, darting through the trees, the Riddler just ahead of him, his motley weaving between the trunks.

'Because if you spend too much time in the air,' answered the Riddler – and now he was holding him by the shoulders, hard, and staring deep into his eyes – 'you might find you can't come back down.'

As the Riddler stripped off the Collar, Fitz felt his body convulse. Reality intruded on him like the clutch of talons, like still pictures – at intervals, in spasms between bouts of darkness. He was on his side weeping; he thrashed for a moment wildly; he grasped his foot in his hands, howling to extend his leg. At length he found himself hunched on the table, panting, with his arms round his knees. His body spasmed. Again. Again.

He held himself, and the hold held.

'Sometimes it takes a man until the day of his death to live his own life,' said the Riddler. He held the Collar in his hand. He turned away, and left the room through its far door.

Shivering, his stomach churning, Fitz crawled off the stone table and let himself out of the Sensorium. He climbed the stairs in darkness, threaded his way quietly through the courts, and – somehow, dragging his body behind him – subsided into the safety of his bed.

That was only the first time. The next night, the Riddler called him at ten bells; Fitz stole to the Lantern Hall, slipped between the huge wooden leaves of the carved door, and dropped himself into the well of the Sad King. Another night, he was called at eleven; days passed, and then the Riddler summoned him at nine. Each time he had loaded his pockets with stones; each time he fell through the forest of arms, knifed deep into the warm brine of the well, and then shed pebbles as he pushed down the underwater well passage and bounded up towards the light. Whatever the hour, always the Riddler stood there, in the hush of the deep-hewn antechamber, regarding Fitz with curiosity as the water drained from his clothes; sometimes he spoke in his inscrutable way, other times he didn't, but always he ushered him into the white chamber, strapped the Fetters to his wrists and ankles, and while Fitz lay upon the stone table set the Collar in place. It became easier. In his dreams in the Sensorium, in the freedom of his imagination, he only ever went to one place, and the story always seemed to be similar – the Riddler would run through the wood, and Fitz would chase him, eventually cornering or catching him, sometimes among the branches, sometimes upon the ground, occasionally in a gully or by the railway line, or in one of the wood's several clearings.

Always in the green light among the wide sailing wings of the moths and butterflies they talked; and from the Riddler Fitz learned a great deal. One evening, as Fitz hunted the motley through the trunks of the forest floor, the Riddler jeered at him from behind a great beech, saying, 'It seems you aren't very good at being alone.'

'I am, too,' Fitz retorted. He surprised himself with his vehemence.

'I think you will find,' said the Riddler in his ear, 'that *you* are the one chasing *me*.'

Later, sitting on a yardarm above the forest floor, Fitz turned this over in his mind.

'I like being on my own in the tower room,' Fitz said.

'And what do you do when you are there alone, at night?' the Riddler asked him.

'I look out of the window,' Fitz said. 'Both windows. I can see over all the rooftops to the west and to the north. I can see into the Lantern Hall, and across to the Jackery, and the room where –'

The Riddler was very close to his face, peering into his eye with his eye.

'Aren't you forgetting something?' he asked him.

The words lashed through him like a streak of lightning. In a flash of sudden brilliance Fitz pictured the room at the cottage, the room that looked out over the wood and, to the west, the corner of the Old Friary and Mr Ahmadi's study. And the library. The room with all his words –

'What do you think of, when you don't think of anything?' asked the Riddler. As he spoke, butterflies poured from his mouth.

Fitz would have answered, but too much crowded into his thoughts at once.

'You remind me of someone,' said the Riddler. He told him of a pupil he had once taught in the Sensorium, who had at length proved so adept at imaginings that he no longer required the Five Fetters, but could slip into the suspension of the dream state entirely of his own volition – and out of it, too.

'Like you,' said the Riddler, 'he could communicate with me in his dreams, though not in language. But he showed me many things, and in the end he uncovered much about me that even I did not know. He became gifted in these illusions far beyond the course normal even for those special minds who are selected to train at the Heresy; the Officers called him "Dreamsnatcher" for, not content with our explorations here, he began to adventure into the minds and thoughts of those who, in everyday life, for a moment or for many moments made themselves vulnerable to his observations, intuitions and musings. He could slide by night into a bedchamber and, sitting by the side of a sleeper, from his unconscious respirations draw his character and person almost complete. If a woman were to pause on a street corner, and for a moment dissolve herself in any light or temporary abstraction, in that moment the Dreamsnatcher might pounce, and from her worm and pilfer the innermost secret fancy of her heart, a fancy so precious, perhaps, it was locked where even she had no key to redeem it. From his subjects in sleep and wake the Dreamsnatcher harvested much: their hidden thoughts and desires, their regrets and wishes, those secret parts of ourselves from which most of us are permanently exiled.'

Fitz had pondered this for some time.

'How can we be unknown to ourselves?' he asked the Riddler.

'Oh, child,' answered the long man, and shook the bough on which they were seated, so violently that Fitz feared it might break, tumbling them into the thick green light, 'how can we not? The greater part of our lives we shall never live: the choices we do not make, the paths we do not take, the wishes that remain unfulfilled, the guilt and sorrow that we bear with us for that which we have done and is lost, and that which we never did and so never had even the fortune to lose. The painful renunciation of that which is not yet ours, or which – oh misery – we have forfeited, and shall never enjoy. All this is not ours – the things we have lost, those that we have not yet, and those that we shall never have – but we bear its absence with us all the same. It is so very, very hard to come home.'

'And so,' asked Fitz, 'the Dreamsnatcher took from others what they didn't know they were?'

'And more,' said the Riddler. 'He was the greatest student ever to pass through the Sensorium. So great an adept he became that, it is said – at the least, it is suspected – he travelled to the Mountain, and was received there not as a Disillusioner, but as an Imaginer.'

'What's the difference?' Fitz asked.

'You may well ask. The purpose of your work in the Sensorium is to teach you how much of what we accept as reality is merely illusion. Even that concrete-seeming certainty, the self, is little more than a tissue of hypotheses, approximations and lies. Once you accept this, you may approach the world around you as if with new eyes, understanding it as it truly is – that is, understanding it as a pageant of appearances, like a series of pictures projected upon a wall, no more.

'But there is another way of seeing things. As I have just described it to you, the goal of your work in the Sensorium is to understand that every sensation you will ever have – every taste, every smell or touch, every sight and sound – is no more than an illusion. But if instead of understanding every perception as an illusion, you were to understand all perceptions – even fictions, even stories, even lies and the contrivances of your imagination – as *true* – what then? What if you began to see dreams as not *unreal*, but *another kind of reality*? These things are not so different, perhaps. But the imaginer who believes stories are real – this belief weakens him. In his tenderness for others' unlived lives, their dreams and hopes, their regrets and losses, he surrenders up the Kingdom. For him, the game never ends.'

'What is the Mountain?'

'The seat of our ancient enemies, the Honourable Society of Wraiths and Phantasms,' answered the Riddler. 'A benighted and disorderly assembly of charlatans and idiots, poets and fantasists. Their scouts, called Wispers, flit across the world sowing and gathering lies, but it is to the Mountain that they retreat, like dogs to a kennel, when they are whipped.'

Something stirred in Fitz's memory – the image of slender, loping forms hastening towards him down a long tunnel, the light behind them, and the roaring wind.

'Who was this student of yours?' asked Fitz. 'Where is he now?'

'I believe at this moment he is in the Keep,' said the Riddler. 'He is called Habi Gablani Ahmadi, and, like his father before him, he is the Master of the Heresy.'

That night, as he stepped from the long stairs of the Sensorium, Fitz sensed something was wrong. The air was heavy, pregnant with something – lightning, maybe, or at least a heavy rain. But that wasn't what had alarmed him; it took him a few moments, paused on the path, before he recognized that all the lamps between the Sensorium and the Master's court had been extinguished. At first he was relieved – it would make his surreptitious dash back to his room that much easier – but then he heard the footsteps racing towards him down the passage.

So thick was the ink of night that their arms fell on him before he saw their faces; it was only after they had pulled him back against the wall that he saw it was Navy and Russ. The Master was right behind them, carrying a long, heavy staff in his hands.

He wasn't just carrying it, either. He was brandishing it.

'All of you with me,' he said. 'Russ, Navy, keep him close.'

As they ran from the Heresiarch's into the Jack's court, then through an archway into the gardens by the lawns, Russ and Navy explained as much as they could.

'An attack – Wispers – we thought they had you – the Offs are all on the lawns by the river – there are hundreds of them –'

Lights moved on the dark lawns, dancing like intermittent flames here, then there, as the Officers dealt heavy knocks to the tall, slender forms that seemed to melt away before them, regroup, then attack again. The Master had drawn the children on to the lawns behind the attackers, so that as he joined the battle – swinging and beating with his oaken staff – he seemed to be fighting not only against the cloaked and shadowy Wispers, but against the other Officers, too, who were pushing towards him, shedding blows. Fitz hung back with Navy, frightened, above all by the disconcerting sense that some of the Officers – some at least – but which ones? – wouldn't hesitate to crack their staves over his own head; and among the hooded, fleeting forms of the raiders, he seemed to see eyes, flashing, turned on him, seeking him, hunting him. Breath, arms, teeth, hands, feet planted in the muddied grass, thuds and cracks, a flash of red, eyes, swings, turns, dodges, feints, redoublings: through it all, through the roaring in his ears and the thuds of his heart against his neck, Fitz watched the hooded forms, evading them; but more, he watched for the eyes that sought him, knowing that that siege was the greater, that fight the deadlier. *Zenith*, he said to himself, forcing the breath steady in his ribs, *nadir*. And then at last the lines began to give way, and as he dodged the humming cudgels, pivoting and diving beneath last and desperate sallies as the fight broke up, Fitz for the first time felt certain, in the pit of his stomach, that the Heresy was for him no refuge, but a trap.

*Algorithm. Albatross.*

*Albatross.*

From somewhere, Russ had reappeared, breathless and triumphant, and now he flung his arms round Fitz's and Navy's shoulders, binding them. To the north and west, where the high stone walls defended the last lawns from the river meadows beyond, Fitz could see climbers leaping and bounding over the perimeter with unlikely agility. To the south, others had launched on to the river in flat rafts and barges, and were with light rods and poles pushing themselves out of range. Only one figure, alone in the centre of the lawn, seemed willing now to stand his ground, and to him Arwan had turned his attention and his intimidating pier-like bulk. They all broke into a run. As Fitz ran up with the others, the first thing he noticed was the handle of the man's long cane, which he had raised and squared to his chest, ready to meet his opponent.

*You.*

Sassani was tougher, older, and more imposing than Fitz had remembered. Grizzled, a little haggard, nonetheless he looked like a man with sinew. Even Arwan was weighing him carefully, and eyeing his cane with distrust as he approached him. But there was no need. The moment Sassani saw Fitz, he abandoned the fight. Straightening, he turned towards the Prents. He laughed to himself, and with a flourish planted his cane in the turf.

'They haven't told you,' he called to Fitz across the lawn, through air imminent with rain. 'They haven't told you who you really are. Who you could be.'

With a sickening thud, Arwan's staff on a wide swing crashed into Professor Sassani's ribs. He didn't double over. His body simply folded, fell and lay still on the grass. Arwan gathered it up, slung him over his shoulder and set off back to the Heresy.

'Put him in the thresher,' said the Rack, as the Jack passed him. 'I'll get the chaff out of him tomorrow.' Fingal smiled.

The lawns were clear.

'Go back to your rooms and get to sleep,' said the Master to the six of them. Only Payne and Padge weren't there. For a moment Fitz hesitated; the Master looked at him, narrowing his eyes.

Navy dragged at his arm, and he turned. And that's when he saw it.

The Commissar, staff in hand, was walking beside the Sweeper down towards the riverbank. She was wearing over her blue felt coat an unmistakable red cloak.

*The train. That night. She was driving the train. The one that tried to kill us. She was smiling. Those eyes.*

The Master saw him stop on the grass, and followed his gaze.

'I said I'd keep you safe,' he said. 'And I will. Come to my study the day after tomorrow, after you are finished with the Jack. Bring Dina.'

Navy drew on Fitz's arm, and as a shower of rain began to fall they ran for shelter, leaving the Master alone on the wide lawns.

II

*Nightwalking*

The next morning, Fitz stopped Dina outside the hall before porridge, and told her what the Master had said. It was the first time he'd seen even the slightest flicker of surprise in her level, distant eyes.

'He wants us to come to the Mastery? For a lesson?'

She pursed her lips, and went into the hall without a word.

By the time they began their lessons at nine bells, Dina had regained her composure. Fitz slipped easily into the warmth and focus of stack, the happy hours painting in the Keep and studying in the Registry, and then, as easily, into the waking camaraderie of lunch. Whatever anxiety Dina had raised in him, the morning's efforts had dispelled, and he found himself hungry for both food and conversation as never before. Russ passed the whole meal pressing Payne for information about a complex series of calculations she had worked out on the Model, which described the propagation of a virus according to certain constraints and variables that only they understood. Over their heads, Dolly, Navy and Fitz compared notes on a book of poems from which the Keeper had read aloud, in their individual lessons, to all three of them. Fitz had never heard such beautiful language, sonorous and patterned, but had no idea what the poems meant. Much to Navy's feigned disgust, Dolly agreed with him. Only Navy had had ears for the hidden connections, interpretations and arguments that the poems presented, and she marshalled them methodically to howls of dismissive protest from her friends.

'But, Navy,' said Dolly, 'it's so obvious. Even if the poems *do* mean those – those complicated things you're saying, whatever they are – we're never going to know anything about it. They're so much fun just to hear, it's as if the poet didn't want us to press any further.'

'You need to go easy on the stack, Doll,' answered Navy. 'It's possible to enjoy something and understand it at the same time.'

'Like you did,' said Fitz, grinning.

'Yes, like I did,' answered Navy, pretending to frown at his sarcasm.

'I don't think you enjoyed the poems at all,' riposted Dolly. 'I think you enjoyed your own feeling of cleverness.'

'So?' Navy protested. 'Fitz, back me up. My pleasure in understanding is also part of the poem. Surely.'

'Of course it is,' said Fitz. 'Naturally. You are in everything, Navy. All art and music is just a series of pictures of you, and the way you think and feel.'

Navy threw some bread at him. Fitz looked up sharply, even before it hit him, knowing that Dina would have words. But she wasn't there.

'Where did Dina go?' he asked, of everyone and no one.

But no one had seen her leave. It wasn't like her to miss feeding of any kind, even when she was plainly in a temper, or so preoccupied that she hardly said a word.

'She's probably cross that you got summoned to the Sensorium,' Padge said. 'She thinks of the Riddler as her own personal creature.'

'Yeah, the way a cat thinks of a mouse,' said Russ, joining in. 'Mine for playing, mine for – eating!' He stabbed the chicken on his plate with a sharp thrust of his knife. His miming was so exaggerated that they all laughed, even Fingal.

That afternoon, Dina didn't show up at any of their usual joint lessons. Fitz enjoyed having the Officers to himself, and felt he learned two or three times what he normally did.

No one mentioned the events of the night before, the fight on the lawns, or the prisoner in the tower. That is, no one mentioned it until he got to the Jackery, late in the afternoon, and he found the Jack sitting under his plane tree, his eyes closed, with his hands on his crossed legs.

'Do you know that man, Sassani?' asked the Jack. He hadn't opened his eyes, and Fitz hadn't even yet sat down. 'The one with the cane.' The ground was cold beneath his legs as Fitz settled on the grass, and he wrapped himself in his arms while he thought about what to say.

'No,' he answered at last. He knew he could trust the Jack – Arwan Abramanian, the big man who had held the dying Aslan in his arms. The Jack was a friend. It wasn't that. He just didn't want to talk about Sassani – not now, not ever. 'I don't know him. Not really. He came to my house once, in the night, and

283

scared us. But Mr Ahmadi – the Master, I mean – helped drive him off.'

'Do you know what he meant, when he asked you if you knew who you are, who you could be?'

In the pleasure of the morning's lessons, Fitz had forgotten it completely. Now it rushed back to him, so suddenly and fully that he felt overwhelmed. He didn't answer.

'What he knows, what you know, what each of us knows – we must be careful. Sometimes knowing too much is dangerous.'

*Ignorantia sapientia. There is wisdom in ignorance.*

'I know he thinks I am the answer to some sort of prophecy, that I look like someone that the Heresy wants very much. He knows that I am about to come of age. I think he didn't want me to come here, because of that, and I think now that I'm here he wants me to leave.'

'And do you want to leave?' asked the Jack. Now he opened his eyes, and, as always, they were already focused directly on Fitz's own.

'No,' Fitz answered. 'I'm happy here. I'm safe here.' The fear he had felt the night before, during the fighting, rushed back through his veins, hollowing them. *Don't tell me I'm not safe here.*

'For now,' said the Jack. 'But remember that, while one is often safest in the eye of a storm, still, one is surrounded by a storm.'

That night, after Fitz had gone to bed, he was woken from a light sleep by the sound of stones hitting the west window. His first thought, as he came to, was that only Russ could throw so far, and so he was surprised, on lifting the window latch and looking out, to see Payne in the courtyard below. She lifted her face to him – for a moment, catching the light of a nearby lantern – and then turned away, walking fast into the shadows towards the Jackery.

At first Fitz assumed it was a case. Accordingly, he dressed fast, slid down the stairs hardly touching his feet to the steps, and threw open the tower door a full five seconds before he dared – as it closed – to flit through it. But no one shot at him, not Dolly with her crossbow, not Padge with his unerring sling. He half expected Payne to ambush him, but as he circled north and then by the lower Commissary back towards the Jack's upper court, he saw exactly nothing out of the ordinary: no Offs lingering, no Prents stalking the gables, no Serfs standing sentry outside forbidden entries. By the time he'd reached the Jackery, a chill had started to tingle on the back of Fitz's neck. Something had to be wrong.

Then a voice hissed him from the west range, just under Russ's window. Fitz dropped to a crouch, keeping his head low.

'Get over here, newbie.'

It was Padge. He was waving his arm in exaggerated but almost invisible strokes of welcome, in the darkest shadow of the court's south corner.

Fitz scanned behind him, guessing it was a trap, but found nothing.

'It's not a case,' Padge whispered. 'Don't make me call you again!'

Staying low, Fitz scurried over. Padge pointed up, where Russ's window was edged with soft light. Someone had blacked it out with a blanket. 'It's Russ's birthday,' he whispered. Fitz ducked into the staircase, climbed to the first floor, and pushed through the open door.

The little room – no more than a closet with a bed, really – was almost full of Prents. Only Fingal was still missing – and Dina, of course – and when Padge pushed in behind Fitz, he realized he'd been the last to arrive. The room was softly lit by an oil lamp sitting on the desk, which burned unevenly, creating sudden and spectacular flares, and at other times almost sputtering them into darkness. The conversation, by contrast, though barely audible seemed to be moving in a pretty good flow, everyone jumping in on everyone. And conversation imitated life: there was so little space in the room that they were all essentially draped on one another. Fitz took a place in the hollow of Navy's arm, and listened.

'Is Fingal coming?' whispered Dolly to Payne.

Payne shook her head. 'He said he'd rather sleep.'

'Good,' said Dolly, who looked relieved.

'Look, Navy, you can scoff, but I'm only telling you what I heard,' Russ was saying. 'I was right round the corner for ten minutes at least. They had no idea I was there, so there's no way they were making it up.'

'Well, I still don't believe it,' said Dolly, joining in again.

'What's all this?' asked Padge. He was pouring a little more oil into the lantern, and seemed fixed on it, determined not to spill a drop.

'Right,' said Navy, sitting up, 'if I've understood correctly, it goes something like this. Russ has been spying on the Offs after Feeding, because he is by nature devious.' Russ rolled his eyes and Payne picked delicately at one of her nails, a smile on her face.

'And during one of these sessions, he happened to catch the Sweeper and the Commissar discussing arrangements for the election of a new Heresiarch.'

'Only it's not an election,' spluttered Russ.

'Only,' affirmed Navy, 'according to Russ, it's not an election. Because the Offs don't get together and agree on the appointment of a Heresiarch. That would be too sensible. Apparently the Riddler gets to choose.'

'That's not what I said!' said Russ, hotly. He had raised his voice, and the others quickly hushed him. Padge picked up a thick red blanket and offered to throw it over his head, if he didn't keep it down. Fitz looked from one face to another, not yet aware just how much he was enjoying this fracas.

'I don't know, Russ,' retorted Dolly. 'That's what I heard.'

'And I,' agreed Payne, still smiling, still looking at her nails.

'It's what half the Heresy heard,' said Padge. 'It's past eleven bells, Russ. Keep your voice down, or the Jack will be in here like a flash, and we'll be flushing out the sewers till dawn.'

Russ was quieter now, but he remained uncowed. 'The Riddler doesn't get to choose. It's a lot worse than that. We all know the Riddler's clever. He'd probably choose a good Heresiarch, even if he couldn't talk about it in any kind of sensible way. But that's not what the Commissar said. She said –' Russ stopped, climbed to his feet, and stood in the centre of the little room. 'Look, Padge, hand me that blanket.'

Padge gave him the woollen blanket, and Russ wrapped it round his body, securing it with a length of sash that looked like it normally held up the curtains.

'There,' he announced, pleased with his costume. 'I'm the Commissar, okay?' The red blanket shared with the Commissar's famous cloak only one feature – colour – but Russ immediately threw his head back in a posture of airy disdain that all the children knew only too well. Giggles and even outright laughs erupted from around the room.

'She's not that bad!' protested Dolly, laughing.

Navy raised her eyebrows and commented in an even tone, 'She's pretty bad, Doll.'

'I never saw it till now, Russ, but one day, when you're older, you'll make an excellent . . . Cossack bandit,' said Padge. He turned the wick up so high that the room suddenly flooded with light just at the moment that Russ began to strut back and forth in the narrow strip of open floor.

'Right,' said Russ, finishing with his parades. 'Just for that, you can be the Sweeper. Role play.'

Padge stuffed a couple of pillows under his shirt and began to twitch his nose, as if he smelled something unpleasant. Unable to control her laughter, Dolly buried her face in Navy's armpit and wept tears of mean delight. The others, including Fitz, watched with interest.

Russ struck his condescending pose. 'You were asking me just now,' he said, 'about the next Heresiarch.'

'I wasn't,' said Padge.

Russ dropped the act and remonstrated with him. 'In character!' he hissed.

'Sorry –' a twitch of the nose from Padge – 'of course I was, yes, yes.'

'As you *well* know,' said Russ, 'no one can claim the place who can't open the Heresiarchy.'

'Yes, I *well* know that,' answered Padge. His hands mimed the scrabbling of a rat in the soil.

'And there is but one way, and but one way only, into the Heresiarchy.'

'And what is that?' asked Padge, in a tone of great servility.

'By the door, *obviously*,' said Russ. He scowled, as if to say, 'try harder.' Padge stood up straight. 'And thus one has need of the *key*.'

'Quite so,' answered Padge.

'Now, there are but two people on this earth who know the location of the key to the Heresiarchy,' continued the Commissar. She began to strut back and forth, very briefly, from side to side, and the Sweeper hung like a toy dog on her elbow, snivelling at every stride. 'And one of them is dead.'

'Quite so, your Commissariness,' said the Sweeper. Padge was embellishing the role now, but they all loved it. Even Dolly, holding her sides, was drinking it up. 'But to whom did the Heresiarch commit his secret, before he passed from this world?'

'To the Riddler, naturally,' answered the Commissar. 'Always the location of the key is known to two people, and two people only: the Heresiarch, and his fool.'

'This I did not know! This I had never imagined! Then surely,' said the Sweeper with excitement, 'if I wanted to be the Heresiarch myself –' here Padge turned to his audience and flicked his eyebrows, miming the words 'and I *do*' – 'all I need to do is apply myself to the Riddler, get the key, and let myself in!'

'Fool!' cried the Commissar, and whipped him with her sash. The Sweeper cried out, and put his tail between his legs. 'Of course that is the one thing that the Riddler cannot tell you!'

'Cannot?' asked the Sweeper, rubbing his chin and looking up in wonder. 'Or will not?'

'He *cannot*,' affirmed the Commissar. She was now at her most imperious. 'When they addled – interfered with – when they did to him whatever they did to the Riddler to make him the Riddler, they made it impossible for him to reveal the location of the key. At least, not willingly.'

'Then how can anyone discover its location?'

'Trickery. Torture. Ingenuity. Indirection. Means fair. Means foul. Hook and crook!' cried the Commissar, and now she did look at her minion, and her minion grovelled.

Navy had sat up. The expression on her face was anything but merry.

'Did you really hear the Commissar say this?'

Russ's face dropped out of character, and he turned to the others where they sat watching from the bed.

'Not exactly in those words, but that's more or less the gist of it.'

While Padge got up from the floor, pulling the pillows from his shirt, and Russ unwound the thick, red blanket and put it back on the bed, a heated argument started between the six of them, over which of the Officers stood the best chance of beating, worming or beguiling the secret out of the Riddler; and, therefore, which of them was most likely to prevail as Heresiarch. Dolly, who was terrified of the Rack, thought for sure he had already put the screws on the fool, and was now only holding back for the most opportune moment in which to reveal himself. Padge favoured the Jack, whom he admired before any of the other Officers, and Navy reckoned that it was bound to be the Sweeper. 'It's always, always, *always* the one everyone is ignoring,' she said, and held her finger to her nose.

All the while, Russ tried to intervene, but got nowhere, so heated had the others become in advancing conspiracies, motives, theories, evidence and deductions. Fitz watched him with intense interest, knowing that when the conversation finally receded enough for him to make himself heard, he was going to resolve everything.

Suddenly Russ stood up on the bed, knocking Dolly into Payne and shocking the rest into silence.

'It's none of them,' he hissed, with a face screwed up with exasperation. Everyone looked at him, and he suddenly realized how silly he must seem, towering over the lumpy huddle of his friends in the middle of a dark room, whispering. He sank to a crouch and wrapped his arms round his knees. 'The last thing I heard the Sweeper say last night – to the Commissar, I mean – was, "Is there any way we can stop her?" And then the Jack grabbed me from behind, with one of those grips you don't argue with, and sent me to bed.'

'The Keeper!' said Navy. Her eyes were boggling almost out of her head.

'Dark horse,' offered Padge.

'Well, Dolly,' said Payne, 'you've got it made.'

Dolly snorted. 'If the Keeper becomes Heresiarch, the first thing she's likely to do is send me home. I must be the worst painter in the history of the Heresy.'

'Yes, you are,' said Dina. She was standing in the doorway. No one had seen or heard her come in, yet there she was. 'But you're not bad with that crossbow. Now, Rabble, you have about half a minute to get to your rooms. I don't know where the Offs have been, but they must be on their way back – I've just seen about twenty Serfs leave the kitchens with firewood, heading off in different directions. Ten to one they're laying fires to warm up the Officers' rooms. So, scram. And Russ, put out that lamp and take that stupid blanket out of the window. It's not fooling anybody.'

Before they could react, she was gone.

'That girl is a lot faster than a cat,' said Dolly.

'And sneakier,' said Padge.

'And meaner,' said Russ.

'Happy birthday, Russ,' said Fitz.

Chastened and silent, they said their goodbyes at the foot of Russ's stairs with nothing more than a wave, and vanished into the darkness on their separate ways: Navy with Dolly, Padge at a run, and Payne, by her own offer, leading Fitz.

'Put your feet where mine go, and you won't make a sound,' she whispered. 'I'll get you back all right.'

She was as good as her word. Five minutes later, Fitz was climbing the blind turns of the Mastery tower, shuffling out of his clothes, and falling asleep – just before his head hit the pillow.

The next afternoon at five bells, his thoughts heavy with a long day of study, Fitz made his way, as instructed, to the Master's tower. To his afternoon lesson with the Jack he had gone alone; the Jack had told him that Dina had long before exhausted all that he could teach her, and when she did condescend to join him at the Jackery, her contributions were generally either enigmatic or idle.

But Fitz had told her about their appointment with the Master, and while he was used to her absences, he had never known her to be late. Today she was late; what is more, the door to the tower was locked. Fitz stood outside in the sharp wind and kicked the ground. When it began to rain, he crossed the court and went up to his room.

It was the same at Feeding a few hours later. Dina arrived ten or fifteen minutes after they had begun, swirling her black gown with an aggressive flick before sliding her feet over the bench to claim her usual seat. She was barely in time for Third Feeding, but managed, before the Serfs came to clear, to eat more than the rest of the table combined. The Master was nowhere to be seen. Fitz thought to ask about his absence, but Dina's manner stopped him – as it did the rest of the Prents. If they talked at all – Fitz hardly noticed – it was by hushes and hand signals, among themselves.

Fitz was the last to leave the hall that night, the last to hang up his gown, and the last to slip out of the Porch door and make his way back to his room. The night lay still and quiet over the courts; even the bats, who still sometimes haunted the warm autumn evenings, had retired. For no reason at all, Fitz turned left when he ought to have turned right, and made his way through the Jackery towards the Registry. Through its high windows, even at night, he could sometimes catch the gleam and flash of the huge sharks circling in the Registry's massive, central aquarium. Towering in the Registry's atrium, the tank held every kind of fish he could imagine; and somehow, by feeding them – and who knows, perhaps by training them – the Registrar contrived to keep them all alive.

Passing the Registry, the streaks of night-blue still fresh in his eyes, Fitz bumped into Dolly and Navy, holding hands as they took the long way round to Dolly's room in the Keep. Dolly ran in just as Fitz caught up, and Navy greeted him with bright, generous eyes.

'It's almost nine bells,' she said. 'Don't let the Rack catch you out here or he'll make pasta out of you, or something.'

'Don't you have curfew, too?' Fitz asked her.

'No,' Navy said. 'I have to lock up the aviary most nights, and then give the nocturnals their grub; so I'm allowed to be out till whenever it's done. Nightwalking. It's one of the perks of training under the Registrar. I guess it sort of balances out all the hours I have to spend mucking out the cages.'

A breeze stirred in the darkness, and Fitz shivered. Above them a light was shining in one of the Keep's high windows. Fitz wasn't sure if it was Dolly, or the Keeper.

'Shall I walk you back to the Mastery?' asked Navy.

They took their time: nine bells wasn't quite as near as Navy had thought. As they went along, she asked him about his lessons with Dina, and whether he was enjoying them. He nodded.

'And you're still feeling all right – about being here? On your own and everything?'

Fitz nodded again. He hadn't looked up, all this way.

'Dolly's been here two years, and she still cries about home most nights. You'll never meet anyone more enthusiastic – about everything – than Dolly. She can do just about anything, and do

294

it well: sports, maths, computers, music, whatever. She throws herself into everything as if it were the only thing. But she cries nearly every night, on the way back to her bed after Feeding, because she's going to her room, and it's not a home.'

Fitz said nothing. He was thinking about Mr Ahmadi's library, back in the Old Friary. A world away.

'You don't ever cry, do you?' asked Navy. She put her finger on the inside of Fitz's elbow, and he stopped. 'Not even that first night?'

Now he looked at her. 'Why would I cry?'

'Have you always been like this?' Navy asked him. 'So – I don't know – easy about things? So able? Do you remember ever being upset? I mean, really upset?'

Fitz shook his head heavily. He knew he was avoiding Navy's eyes, and that the heaviness in his head was in part a kind of guilt, because he was conscious even as he shook his head that he was lying. Of course he had been upset.

*Once. The day I learned my words.*

The darkness grew heavier as they left the Keep behind, but even in the darkness Navy had seen through him.

'Tell me,' she said, and kept walking. Fitz hurried to catch her, and they passed into the Heresiarch's court together.

'There are some words – this will probably sound stupid,' he said – 'but there are some words I learned once, in – my neighbour's house, when I was small. He has – had – the most amazing library, full of ancient books, tall books, leather books, dark and huge and heavy, covered in dust. They were filled with stories and histories, with every kind of tale and life you can imagine. He used to let me borrow them. One day I was angry – or sad – I don't remember which, or why – but I came to his house, to the Old Friary where he lived, and he showed me the library, and he gave me a book to read. I'd only just learned to read, I think. And I found these words. It took me hours to get my mouth round them, saying them over and over. They became special for me, sacred. Like a spell, maybe. And whenever I went to the library afterwards, I always said them – aloud, or in my head. And they always made me feel happy – happy and calm.'

They had reached the Mastery, and were standing outside Fitz's tower. Navy made no move to go, so they just stood there, alone, together.

At last she said, 'And you still say them?'

He nodded. 'Sometimes.'

'I don't think that sounds stupid. I think that sounds brilliant.' Navy drew her coat round her neck, and looked away, into the darkness. 'Tell me the words?'

Fitz hesitated. 'I feel silly.'

'Don't,' she said.

'All right, then. *Algorithm*.' He took a deep breath.

'And?'

'And *zenith*.'

'That's a pretty one,' said Navy.

'*Nadir*.' He paused. His heart was racing. '*Albatross*, the diver.'

His voice had risen at the end. She looked at him, full in the face. She was expecting one more. Maybe he was, too.

'*Almanac*,' he lied.

'Those are beautiful words,' Navy said.

They stood awkwardly for a few heartbeats.

'It's my birthday in a couple of weeks,' said Fitz.

From somewhere across the court, maybe in one of the passages, came the sudden report of a sharp crack, as of wood landing on wood, or a person stumbling into something in the dark. Fitz and Navy both snapped their heads at the sound, alert to the possibility of an Off catching them outside after nine bells.

'I'd better go,' Navy offered. 'I don't want to get you into trouble.'

'Do you think someone is watching us?' Fitz asked her. 'What was that noise?'

'It's a strange night,' Navy answered, diplomatically. 'It could have been anything. Tell you what, though – keep your words handy.'

And with that, Navy melted into the darkness the way they had come, slipping in absolute silence through the passage to the Heresiarchy, wrapped in her dark coat against the lonely night.

Fitz took no lantern up to his room. He wanted quiet. More: after talking with Navy, he craved concealment. The Master was his teacher, and he had missed their lesson; but he was also Fitz's protector, and when he hadn't shown up to Feeding, Fitz had felt the floor slip a little from beneath his feet. Shifting out of his clothes, he folded them neatly and placed them as usual in a square pile on the ledge of his casement, next to the pitcher and laver. At first he climbed into bed, huddled in the corner, and drew the blankets as close about his neck as he was able. The world was closing in around him.

*The game is already ended.*

Fitz listened with his skin to the pulse that his heart made in it. *They will come for me. Of course they will. They will come for me.*

The words knelled in his head like five bells pealing. He almost desired it. He wondered if he would hear steps on the stairs, and he felt his ears straining to discern the least creak in the door below, or the slightest of treads on the stone. All he heard was wind – not the kind involving hands that rushed along the boughs and made them sway and tremble, not the sort of breeze that ruffled gables and nooked nimbly between the tiles, but a spare wind and a steady, a low drone that threatened howling. It was the sound of emptiness sweeping across nothing but bare stone.

The hour was late, but in the voids between rushing clouds off the sea the moon was full, and silvered the far air. Fitz kicked down the covers from his bed and swung his legs to the floor. From the window he could make out the headlands that rose from the Heresy's little valley towards the sea: a darkness that hunched before a greater darkness, an emptiness standing between them and another emptiness more vast. In the near scape of roofs and chimneys, of towers and walls, lamps and windows lighted seemed to disperse the darkness and spell out the void beyond; but it was always there, and Fitz ran his eyes along its long contours of spike and fell, crag and gully, the little peaks that sprawled low towards the cliffs beyond.

What he couldn't see in the dark was the path that by daylight a keen eye could almost pick out from the moss and grass and loose stones, the thrift and vetch, gorse and heather and lichens abounding, the path that led from the walls of the Heresy through the meadow and up to the quiet caves where the Master had said the Heresiarchs laid themselves to rest.

He remembered a thing the Riddler had told him, one night as they sat upon their limb in the Bellman's Wood.

*When his time is ended a Heresiarch makes a choice. The choice. He puts down all that has belonged to him in this life, and without farewell takes the way out of the valley. Very often he goes at night; seldom is he seen. In a cave that leads deep into the headlands, there is a place he knows, for he has seen it once before, sometimes many years before. There he lays his body, upon a stone carved centuries past to receive it. He lays his body in its best hour upon the bed that has been prepared for it. And then he is free; and there he sleeps.*

Fitz thought of the old bones of scores of Heresiarchs, crumbling to yellow dust in their common tomb beneath the cliffs. As his breath stirred mist on the panes before him, he wondered if any live thing ever entered that catacomb. Gulls, perhaps.

The clouds now scudding over the hills seemed to huddle and curdle on them. They were low, and being low, where they shadowed the land beneath they plunged it into darkness. As Fitz watched them sweep across the moonlight, almost in time, as if in a dance, a light seemed to gleam on the cliffs. Unlike the diffuse and glowing light of the moon, this beam was focused, sharply defined, and small. It shone clear and straight. Fitz scowled, and with the edge of his coat that lay folded beside him, rubbed at the mist his breath had made on the glass.

The light went out.

For a minute, then two, then five, he stared at the hillside while the clouds, ever darker, ever thicker, drove off the sea. Now the steep side of the valley lay so thickly blanketed in shadow that he wasn't sure, any longer, where the cliffs ended and the sky began; stuttering here and there with his eye, he couldn't even be certain he was looking in the right direction. He wanted to tear at the glass before him, tear at the air, tear up the distance between his room and that cliffside as if it were so much netting, so much gauze of a veil that lay between him and the catacombs.

And then the light gleamed again – this time, nestled like a shining pearl in the deep folds of an inaccessible fabric, the only bright thing in a world of blindness. It glimmered, and while he held his breath he thought it might go out again. It didn't. He bore in on it, stared at it, drilled through the darkness trying to make it out; as if a pole star the earth turned like the heavens around it. The whole field of his vision swayed.

The light was moving. Fitz felt himself lurching and he grabbed the window ledge beneath him, but as he steadied himself, driving his feet like jambs into the floor below, he could see its long arcs describing distances of night between that place and this, between the cliffs and the Heresy, as through the valley by throws and volleys it swept the night and space towards him.

With eager arms, straining against the casement, Fitz twisted the iron handle until it hung free. He pushed the heavy window out in the night air. The wind rushed against it, throwing it back. Iron groaned on iron, then clanged as the window slammed into its frame. Fitz climbed on to the ledge and hurtled at the window, throwing it open as wide as he dared; this time, the wind caught it and threw it swinging in a long and sickening crunch against the stone of the tower. The air rushed in on him, swirling leaves and dirt against his face, all the detritus that it had scoured from the courts below, from the gables and slopes of tiles and towers and miles of running gutters that surrounded him in the insane stir of this tempestuous night. This heaving darkness. And still the light, on which his eye was fixed, which he drew towards him as a fisherman his line, reeling and reeling it in, advanced. One hand to either side of the frame, kneeling before the night and the clouds and the air and the advancing sea, he waited.

The albatross shrieked like a horse on a high gale as it dropped from the clouds towards him. Ten or twelve metres from his window, descending all the time on the impossible, gliding sails of its wings, it seemed to pull up, and from beneath its feet where the crescent light trailed on its long cord, the weight of it slung forward like a shot. In a self-preserving reflex, Fitz's arms flew to his face, and it was only thus, shielding himself with his hands almost together, collapsed almost in a gesture of prayer, that he managed to catch the heavy weight of the light when it nearly struck him, slicing through the near air into which the bird had released it. The cord lashed him in the face, and his hands, knocking against his cheek, knocking his teeth against his cheek, might have bruised it.

Fitz hardly noticed it. He hardly noticed anything but it.

He dressed quickly. He didn't bother pulling the tower door shut behind him. Taking the long way through the Commissary and the Keep, he entered the Heresiarchy from the side, almost crawling along the narrow shadows that clung to the west wall. A simple passage led out on to the west lawns.

*When one of the Officers has stood and been acclaimed as Heresiarch, he passes through the Door of Humility and on to the west lawns. It is a long walk across level ground to the walls. That is his first place of*

301

*challenge, for anyone can strike him there – there, between the Door of*
*Humility and the Gate of Resignation.*

Fitz stood before the heavy oak door. So thick ran the blood through his veins that he had only intermittently been aware of his movements. He flashed before himself like moonlight through shifting clouds. It seemed as if he were being drawn by some hidden thread or by a song that only he could hear, which was plunging him head first into a deep swell of doing. He put his hand to the wicket that opened through one side of the Door of Humility. At first he thought it was locked, but its weight was only that of the wind, which gave way unwillingly as he pushed against it and stepped through.

The path wouldn't have been visible even by moonlight, and there was none. For the first hundred feet, or less, scattered lights still shining in high windows of the Heresy picked out the blades of grass over which in long and silent strides he ran towards the Gate of Resignation. After the light failed, and darkness alone surrounded him, Fitz ran onwards only by the light of his own trust and determination. With each extension of his limbs into the nothingness that surrounded him, his blood skimmed a little the beats that it normally would have struck; but on every stride, his foot hit the earth, pressed it, and rebounded again. He ran. Into the darkness he ran. Towards the cliffs he ran. Against all sense and with no plan at all, he ran.

When he reached the gate – astonished that he should have come so far, but unconscious of his own astonishment – he didn't bother trying the iron handle. He knew it would be locked. Instead, he tried the mortared stones of the wall to the left side.

Where he pulled at the pliant vines, their stiff roots drew the mortar with them, and he found he was able to dig his fingers securely into the rock, and by their purchase, lost, to climb with ease. He ascended by heaves, kicking his throbbing toes into the stone crevices as he climbed, taking what support he could and, where he couldn't, fumbling higher for safety. When his reaching hand found the top of the wall, he dragged himself level and swung his leg over. If it had been light, if the moon, clearing the clouds, had revealed even the least detail of the terrain that awaited him on the wall's far side, he might have drawn breath at the top. He might have paused. He might have felt fear. But he was passing by shallow fingerholds from one shadow to the next; he rolled on to his back, sat up, and without a thought sprang for the far soil.

Fitz landed on his feet, then toppled to his hands. The ground beneath him sloped upward, and his face hit a stony earth that seemed to rear to receive it. His skull clanged, and he thought – hearing a deep crack somewhere in the confusion of that impact – that he had torn the cartilage in his nose. He felt for blood on his face, and found his hands were covered in something wet. It was only after he had climbed the ravine, after he had begun to run across the low expanse of heather and could again feel the salt wind whipping his ears, that he smelled the stench. Tumbling from the west wall of the Heresy, he had landed in a sewer.

Fitz didn't know for how long he ran, climbed, crawled and staggered across the wide meadow that separated the Heresy walls from the rising ground of the sea cliffs to the west. It might have been an hour; it might have been two. By the time the ground began to rise, and he found himself pushing up against the slope, now in the lee of the scouring winds, he felt exhausted. He didn't know which direction he had taken, whether he was on the right path or not; only he knew that somehow he had threaded the sprawling carpets of thorny gorse and rough heather, that his ankles had not twisted in the treacherous voids between slippery stones, that though he had fallen – often – among the meadow's trickling streams, he had not dashed out his teeth or gouged his unseeing eyes.

*That's not bad for a path, then.*

Now he found himself stretched on drier stone, pulling raw-skinned fingers across rough surfaces that sometimes held, sometimes crumbled beneath his talon grip. He drew his breath steadily, pacing himself, never pausing to try to gauge the way but always taking the vertical, moving ever up. He was conscious that his trousers had torn and that his knees, where they knocked and pivoted against the jagged and pebbled surfaces of unyielding boulders, left little prints of blood among the moss and lichen. Still he climbed.

After a long time, when he had long since ceased to hear the wind rushing overhead into the valley, when he had long since ceased to notice the cold that was hardening off the long tautness of his brittle sinews, the cloud above him broke and moonlight like a dazzling angel floated on the air. Fitz had come to rest on a slab of something that seemed like granite, as cold as the bottom of the sea and harder than he had thought possible. His bones where they ground on the rock through his skin seemed to burn, and he had laid his cheek as if to sleep on the stone's stippled and unyielding pillow. He had only meant to pause for a moment. In the moonlight that startled him, falling from above, he stared stupidly to the side, at first seeing only a near foreground of rock after rock, their edges serrated in a sharp relief of sudden silver. He thought as his eyes began to close that the ridges of stone lay like the crests tipped with white that swelled over the sea, and he wondered in an abstraction as heavy as sleep why the waves were still, and how he had fallen among them.

Then something moved.

Fitz felt adrenaline spear through him as violently as if it had been fisted through his guts. He pushed himself to his knees, following the thrashing form with his eyes. It lay at a distance of a hundred metres, on higher ground than his. He found himself running, tripping over the rocks.

The Master recognized him long before Fitz's muddled eyes could recall the man before him.

'Child.'

Fitz stopped. His right hand grasped a stone before him; his left foot lay pinched in a crevice between two boulders. He had been about to gasp with pain. Now it hung suspended, exquisite, both in his foot and out of the gap of it, while he stared at the supine form shackled to the rock beneath a splash of moonlight, swept with rain and bloodied.

'You came.' The Master's voice vied with the wind and surfed on its low rush, hitting Fitz's ear in a turbulent crush of sound from which he felt he had to disentangle before he could understand it. 'I wasn't sure you would come. I didn't think you would find me.'

Fitz pulled his foot free. Even in the moonlight it was hard to make sense of what he was seeing. The Master was dressed, wearing the same clothes as ever – the black suit, the white shirt stiff beneath his jacket. His polished black shoes were laced on his feet. But in places his clothes had been torn open, and his skin seemed to extrude through the gashes in the cloth. One of the soles of his shoes hung, limp, from the bottom of his foot. His familiar hat, his sign and the soul of him, was nowhere to be seen. But stranger than all this, he lay bound to the rock, riveted to its flat face, by five hooped rings that contained his ankles, his wrists, and his neck.

'Who did this to you?'

Fitz stood over the Master. Blood crusted on his temple. There was none in his skin. His body, paler than his shirt, looked like it had been cast up from the sea and washed over the cliffs.

'I don't know,' answered the Master. 'Whoever it was knocked me over the head, first. I woke up here like this.'

Something stirred at the side of his vision. Fitz immediately crouched, defensive. He brushed the rock beneath him with one hand, sweeping for loose stones.

It was only another albatross. In fact there were four or five of them, standing sentinel almost in a row, on a near stone.

No sooner had Fitz relaxed than he was forced to spring backwards. With balletic precision, folding its broad wings as it set its body down, another bird dropped through the darkness and landed inches from the Master's head. It hopped slightly towards him as Fitz stumbled away, inclining its head. Water gushed briefly from its bill, landing on the Master's cheek. He turned his mouth to it as well as he could, pushing his lax pale flesh against the iron ring that bound his neck. Some of the liquid dribbled between his lips, and he drank it down.

Thought and feeling drained from Fitz's body while he looked on in simple amazement. Having emptied its bill, the bird with a brief expression of its wings hopped to join the others, ten feet away. The Master swallowed, in pain.

'How long have you been here,' asked Fitz, 'like this?'

'All day. Since last night,' the Master answered. 'These birds have been good to me. The king even pulled some pieces of stone from the wound in my head. At least I think that's what it was. I'm hoping it wasn't bone.'

Keeping one eye on the restive birds, Fitz circled around to the Master's head. The wound above his temple wasn't deep, though the swelling was still high; he touched it, lightly. It seemed clean.

'Not bone,' he said. 'There's a bad bump, but whatever it was that cut you, it didn't cut deep.'

The Master sighed and his body stretched into the shackles. Fitz realized that anxiety about his head had been giving the Master strength.

'You're going to have to get help,' said the Master.

For the first time, Fitz turned his gaze back down the slope and across the valley towards the Heresy. Only a few lights glowed from its hundreds of windows. In the courts, lanterns, still burning, gave a sense of the place's size; but, though the slope to the valley floor seemed from this height much shallower than his knees and shoulders remembered, Fitz shivered when he saw how far across the valley he had come, how much open ground now separated him from the warmth of his bed, from the safety of the walls, from the company of – of his friends.

'You're cold,' the Master said, 'but you can't possibly get down the slope safely. Not in the dark.'

'I can –'

'No,' said the Master. A spasm seemed to be running through his body. Fitz realized that he, too, was shaking against the breezes. 'Whoever did this – is still down there. We'll need help by daylight. It's two or three hours to dawn. We'll make it.' Fitz felt he could hear in the Master's voice the dull metal pain the words made in his aching head.

'Hold your hand out to the birds. As if you're inviting them.'

Fitz stepped around to the far side of the Master's trembling torso, and did as instructed. Almost immediately, as if waiting for the summons, all six of them began to stir. By a series of little hops they crossed the ground between the rock and the Master's body, and, without any further invitation, all in a neat row nestled into the crack between his body and the stone on which it lay. The wind at this elevation wasn't high – it was much less than in the exposed flat of the valley – but what chill it carried the birds, like a living blanket, sealed and excluded. The Master stopped shivering almost immediately.

'What were you doing up here?' Fitz asked him. He feared the answer. At the back of his thought, just beyond his awareness, a part of him thought the Master might have given up, might have come to seal himself in the tombs.

The Master took a deep breath, as if about to speak. Then he sighed.

'Have you finished my book, my child?' The question was asked with such tenderness, with so much patience and love that it shamed Fitz to shake his head.

'No,' he said. 'Not yet.'

'You remember the night we left your cottage.'

Fitz said nothing. A little howl or moan rose from the caves above them, where the wind had snagged in a hollow. The Master took this for his assent.

'You noticed, I think, that my attempt to get you to the Heresy did not go unopposed.'

Again Fitz was silent.

'Outside the walls of the Heresy, an Officer is not safe from the other Officers. Perhaps one will have reason for opposing another. Perhaps that reason will be serious. Perhaps it will be mortal.

'We are locked in a game. There are rules, but the game is a grave thing. On the death of the Heresiarch, an Officer who would take his place must do one thing and one thing only. It is a very difficult thing. He must find the key to the Heresiarchy. Once he has found the key, he must summon the other Officers to the Palace of the Heresiarch. They will come if he is ready. By oath they must come. And there – and only there – they will acknowledge him. But here is a thing I think you have not imagined: the Heresiarch's key, which opens the door to the palace – you don't need it to get in. The door always stands open to those who would enter.'

'Then why –'

'It locks instead from the inside. You can't get out without the key. So an Officer who wishes to become Heresiarch summons the other Officers to the Heresiarchy. One by one they enter the palace, allowing the door to close behind them. There they wait, as the new Heresiarch retrieves the key, and returns. The new Heresiarch then enters the palace, and takes the Officers' new oaths of obedience. Only then can they be dismissed. That's one possibility, anyway.'

Fitz shuddered again against the cold, but the shaking of his body did nothing to warm him. It seemed, rather, to let the cold fix its teeth more firmly, more deeply, into his flesh, that prickled where it bit.

'But it's not the only move. The new Heresiarch has a choice. He is not obliged to go to the Heresiarchy and swear the Officers to him. He can, instead, pursue another way. He can swear the Apprentices to loyalty in their place, and build the Heresy anew.'

'But,' Fitz protested, 'then there would be two of everyone – two Masters, two Commissars –'

'No,' said the Master. He spoke very gently.

'What happens to the old Officers?' Fitz asked. Immediately after speaking, he wished he hadn't asked the question.

'The new Heresiarch passes by the Heresiarchy, but does not go in. Instead he goes to the Apprentices, room by room, each in turn, and invites them to join him. There is a term for it. It is called the Nightwalk. If the new Heresiarch chooses this path, he leaves the old Officers to die. The palace becomes their grave.'

Fitz said nothing. There was nothing to say. In some way, somehow, he had always known – all the Prents had always known – that their place at the Heresy was some sort of curse. Till now, it had been inexplicable, a riddle. It would have been better had it remained that way.

'I knew where the key was. For many years, since long before the Heresiarch died, I have known exactly where it was waiting. Three times over the past few weeks I have summoned the Officers. Three times I have waited patiently. Three times no one has answered the call. I think, when I summoned them, that the other Officers feared I would abandon them. But I would never have done that, child.'

'I know,' said Fitz.

'The other night, after the fight on the lawns, I decided I would take my chances in the darkness, and climb for the key without the call. This would be a dangerous journey, because outside the walls the rules of the game are not secure. Outside the walls I am not safe.'

'The key was here, in the catacombs?'

'Yes.'

'But someone attacked you before you could get to the tomb?'

'No, I got to the tomb. I looked upon the Heresiarchs of old.'

Fitz shuddered, but this time not with the cold.

'The key wasn't there.'

A cloud crossed before the moon.

'One of the other Officers is playing a dark game. A game within the game. I thought – bringing you here to the Heresy – they would be sure to answer my call. Once I was in the palace, you would have nothing to fear, you would come of age, and I could –'

The Master broke off as the moon swept back into a clear expanse of the night sky. Fitz had been seeking for the light with keen, tenacious eyes. Now it blinded him, and he looked away.

The Master was unable to look away. Two moons in his two eyes burned like silver flames.

'Fitz, my father was the Heresiarch, like his father before him.'

'I know,' said Fitz. He turned towards the valley, and tried to judge the distance across it, back to the Gate of Resignation.

*Downhill. Two hours.*

'What you don't know is that I hated him.' Fitz looked at the Master. With his arms spread wide, and his ankles bolted to the rock, he looked as if he were being crucified. It was horrible. It was torture. But it looked, too, somehow comical. Two of the albatrosses, sitting face to face, parleyed with their bills and stuttered staccato clicks, as if they were tap-dancing in an old film.

'I hated him,' said the Master again. 'And on the day when he summoned the Officers to the Heresiarchy, to take up the office for which he had been born, on that day I left this place – as I thought – forever. I turned my back on my apprenticeship to my father, the Master. I turned my back on everything I had known, on all my friends, on my own – on everyone.'

The Master's breath came in short, shallow draughts. Every sentence dropped from him as water drops down a pane of glass, discontinuously and in runs.

'I lived for a while. I lived, I loved, I made discoveries. I became another man. I became something other than a man. I learned things about the world, and about the Heresy too, that I cannot unlearn. But I was never at peace. Eventually I went to the sea. Maybe I thought I would die there, swallowed in a storm. Perhaps I thought the opposite; perhaps I thought it would be the making of me. The sea is like that – a place where your purpose steals over you, belatedly, as a sun that rises only after the dawn. I had a little boat – two sails, a simple cabin – and I lost myself in the gorgeous whelming swells of the southern oceans. Swells like houses, swells like . . . like mountains. You cannot – imagine them. What could my little boat do against seas like that? For days I had tried sailing athwart them, tacking up and down their endless slopes while the gales shredded the canvas on the mast. It was no use. I took in my sails, and let the sea push me where it would. I watched from the deck till I was weary. Till I dreamed. Till I raved. Till I collapsed.

'These birds found me, then. I don't know how close I was to death. I still had a little water. I had a little food. What I didn't have was the least will to carry on. And then one day that great king of albatrosses – that one, there –' the Master would have gestured with his hand, if he could have, but the flick of his eyes in the moonlight was enough, and Fitz saw a few metres away, huddled in the dark, the eyes of the great bird, watching him – 'he was hanging in the wind off my wrecked bows.'

Fitz watched the eyes that were watching him. They were old eyes, and sharp, eyes that could thread winds in a storm, and pick out a fish from the deep a mile off. He wondered what they were seeing in him. He wondered if there were anything in him to be seen, at all.

'He was still hanging there, hovering on the winds, two days later when the swells deposited me into a flat sea. Do you know,' said the Master, as he watched the silent clouds racing over him, as deep as the sea and as swollen, 'that an albatross's wings are relaxed when they are open, and not when they are closed?' He was silent a while. 'It's a strain on them, not to be flying. It's difficult for them to be still.'

'They've been sitting on the roofs of the Heresy for months,' said Fitz. Now that he wasn't climbing, and his limbs were still, the cold had begun to soak into his body. Water from somewhere – from mud that had splashed him, or maybe it was his own sweat, cooling – touched his skin with damp and set it shivering.

'I know,' said the Master. 'That day, years ago, when the seas calmed, I had what sailors called a sea dream – a vision, an experience, as real to me as this rock is now. Maybe it was real. Who can say, after all, what is seen on the wide ocean? Who can say what things are known over the deep? I woke to a blistering sun. My eyes burned, and my lips were parched, scaled. I drank the last of my fresh water. I covered myself; but I knew I had to get ashore, anywhere, and soon. As if in answer to my prayer, as if in response to my need, almost immediately I sighted an island. I supposed it was an illusion, that I had been staring too long astern or that, dazzled by the boundless volume of the still-swelling water on every side, I had conjured its necessary complement. It seemed a small, a lonely, a lovely and a simple place, rock and sand standing not more than twenty metres proud of the waves. There were trees, and in the island's centre a little pool of fresh water. I intended to pull up my boat, and set myself in the warm sand, to rest in the shade, to drink my fill, rest again. I never reached the island. I was luckier than I knew.'

Fitz thought beneath the moonlight that the skin of his hands was changing colour. It seemed paler than it should, almost blue. The shiver that had started in his wrists and armpits had now settled, digging in, to a deep throb turning over in his chest. While the Master was talking, the last of the albatrosses, the great one that the Master called the king, had been stepping towards him. Now Fitz realized with alarm that the bird was very close, and while the blood knocked in his veins against the shivering in his bones, the white wings lifted as the bird advanced on him. Its eyes were on his.

Fitz backed up, towards the Master. The bird came closer again, fanning his wings into a kind of broad dome, keeping its head down, staring, always staring. Fitz shuffled back again, and again, till he was almost standing on the Master's hand, till he almost tripped on the rivet by which his wrist was stapled to the rock. Still the great bird advanced. Only when Fitz had backed all the way to the Master's very side, so that his heels nearly touched his torso, did the bird fold its wings and raise its head. It emitted a low trill of clicks. Fitz, startled, sat on the ground – and realized that in the near shadow of the Master's side, not far from the other, huddling birds, the air was warmer and more human.

*He saw that I was cold. He's herding me.*

While the Master went on with his story, Fitz put out his hand. The great bird eyed him for a minute or two, then slowly drew up alongside him, settling against the Master's waist. It hunkered down on to its legs, as if rocking back and forth with loving delicateness on an egg that lay beneath.

'A brisk breeze was blowing. I had only just trimmed the sail when, looking ahead, I saw the whole of the island buckle. The ridge of rock at its centre rose into the air even as the beach before me slid under the waves. It was no island at all, child, but the back of a gigantic sea creature, a monster larger than anything that has ever moved on land. My eyes couldn't take in the size of the thing, but my little boat felt the force of its dive. The creature's tail, broad as a city, reared out of the surf. The eddies and curls that it made in the sea's surface would have capsized a craft far larger than mine – and wrecked it, too, had I not foreseen the danger and tacked, at the first moment, into a better course. And it dived – the monster dived – so slowly, lumbering in the sea the way a cloud, when you see it from a great distance, fleets by inches across the sky. And I reached into its colossal shadow, so that when at last with a mighty flick it sank beneath the waves, that rushing swell it made, half a mile high, caught me square on the stern and drove me ever before it – out of control, but so long as I held the place, as safe as anywhere on the face of the sea.

'By the time that swell gave out, I found myself again in the cold seas of the north. These birds – all of them – they had followed along with me as the swell pushed ever on, throwing up whole shoals of fish that made their pickings easy. And they haven't left me since.'

The breeze was flickering across them, tasting them with its cold tongue. Squeezed against the Master's side, Fitz had drawn up his legs and sat hugging his knees, face to face with the albatross. Its eyes where they caught the light of the moon – dark, glinting, alien – seemed as deep as any sea. Fitz hadn't even noticed when the great bird slowly lifted, then extended its wings over both boy and man.

'Imagine,' said the Master. 'Imagine being able to look into the air, to see its flows and currents. Imagine the ability to unthread its tumbling turbulence. Imagine that. Imagine bending the eye on vacancy. Wind, my apprentice, is the roaring voice of nothing at all, the song of wild visions and of sleep, the sliding and the friction of non-being across being. These birds have eyes so fine, so sharp, so old that they can pick out those hidden flows of nothing that current all around us. They are the riders on dreams. There is hope yet, child.'

When the dawn came, and the air around them had begun to furze and felt with tiny dew, when the heather and grass of the meadow below them cupped its wide, grey hands like a prayer offered to the paling sky, then Fitz stood and shook off the pain and cold that had pinned him, as it had the Master, all night to the rock. He dropped down the hillside, boulder by boulder, and ran across the faint trail that divided the valley. With the last strength of his arms he pulled himself over the Gate of Resignation, stumbled over the lawns, and tripped through the wicket into the Heresiarch's court.

The Jack, passing in the dawn like a monk meditating his own mysteries, did not recognize him. But the great albatross had coursed the meadow beside Fitz, feathering the wind rising at his back; and now it landed on his shoulder, and – broad, regal, intelligent – it spoke in a single shriek the whole history of the night the boy had passed beneath the cliffs, the horror of the man shackled to the rock, and the long suffering of his ordeal by the tombs. Then the Jack collected the crumbling child in his arms, and Fitz – passing almost out of this world – lay swaddled in his tower bed, and dreamed of nothing for days but of a rising white wing, spreading in pale air.

## shāh māt

*A*s he pushed open the door to the library, the boy noticed that he had dirt on the sleeve of his cotton shirt – a little clod and an autumn burr that had attached themselves to him while he was playing in the wood beyond the garden outside. He was embarrassed to have brought dirt into this open, clean and silent house, and hesitated to carry it into the room. Picking it from his sleeve, he put it into his pocket.

'Come in, my eyes, come in,' the old man called from his chair. He was not alone. A long figure with a white beard sat at his side. Though he was the taller of the two, the low stool on which he lightly perched made him seem small, humble, as if he were a supplicant. Beneath a light grey, hooded cloak, he was impossibly gaunt, weathered as a saddle ridden many years beneath the sun. His eyes moved to the boy's face as a cat might pounce on a bird.

'This is the boy I was telling you about,' said the old man to his guest. His voice had grown even feebler since they last met, when the boy had sat by his side to study mansūbat on the board, and to listen to his tale. Perhaps he had already been speaking for some time.

319

'My friend Hožir is just leaving, child,' said the old man. 'Pour me a glass of water, and come, and take his place.'

The visitor stood up. He still had not let the boy slip from his gaze, but watched him intently. The boy was reluctant to turn aside and go to the table, where the pitcher stood, until the eyes had released him. In a few strides, these eyes had crossed the room: blue, and of an exhausting depth, they lay stirred before him like an evening sea. The visitor had clasped his hands before him as a monk might, or a solemn teacher, but now he took the boy's chin between his thumb and forefinger, and raised it, so that he could search his eyes. What he sought in his eyes the boy didn't know.

'We will meet again, child,' said the man, 'but you will know me then by another name.' The corners of his mouth, beneath the wisps of white beard, turned slightly as his eyes kindled with kindness. 'Meanwhile, do not allow yourself to forget what you have seen.'

And then he slipped from the room. He had offered the old man no goodbye, and he made no sound on the stairs.

The boy poured water from the pitcher into a glass and brought it to the old man, who thanked him and drank. For several hours they sat together in silence before the ornate shatranj board, the old man laying out problems, and the boy first considering them, then proposing solutions with deft turns of his wrist and decisive twitches of his fingers.

At length the old man sat back and closed his eyes.

'You see many things, my child. Never have I known a child to notice so much, so readily.'

The boy pulled the table into the corner of the room, moving slowly and with precision so as not to disturb the pieces in their arrangement on the board; their long game remained in play, and many days might yet pass before they should finish it. He retook his seat on the stool before the old man, and waited for him to continue his story. The old man seemed to doze for some time.

'The playing of shatranj,' he said very suddenly, his eyes still closed, 'is nothing but the telling of a story. I have told you, my eyes, how many years ago I travelled to a far country to buy and sell merchandise, how I set up my wares in a certain city at the bazaar there and, as was my custom at that time, traded my store in three parts over three days. I told you also how I befriended a merchant in the bazaar, and how this merchant invited me to his house on the first night of our acquaintance, and told me the tale of a king and his brother, of a conspiracy, and of a great treasure. Lastly – it has not been many days – I told you how on the second day I spent in that city, my friend the merchant took a walk with me after our evening meal, and outside the city walls showed me a well where the king's heir had escaped the wazir's plot to murder him, and steal the king's treasure. On the third day, I went again to the market, but my mind was not at all fixed on my custom, but on the end of my friend's story, which he had promised to tell me that night. During the day I made many false bargains, and traded away much of my wealth. I was not myself. It seemed to me that I had become this other man, this king, this sorrowful master betrayed by his wicked brother, and I lived only to hear the end of his tale.

'That evening my friend came to my table when all my wares had gone. He had had a very successful day's trading, but even in the midst of his own affairs he had been mindful of my fortunes, and had seen how I had given away so much in exchange for so little.

'"Brother merchant," he said, "the day has been unkind, but I fear the conclusion of my story will be harder still. Perhaps it is better that you should not learn what remains of this tale."

'With all the strength of my eloquence, to which I conjoined not a few oaths, I implored my friend the merchant to finish his story. I felt I could not be master of myself until I had heard and knew the end of this king's life.

'"So be it," said he, and together we left the bazaar and wandered through the streets of the city. On this evening we had neither mules to pack for the next day's business nor wares to stow, for my friend had been shrewd and had sold all that he possessed, in exchange for a great fortune that he had sent before, with cunning and prudence, by a trusted servant to his home; and I, as you have already heard – if truth be told, I had little at the end of that third day, for my bargains had been poor, my credit unworthily extended, and my poor eyes easily swindled. Like two beggars, then, we went through the ways of the city, until we came to the great gate by which all who came or went from that place, whatever their business, had to pass.

'Here we sat upon a piece of old stone, a slab that had once, perhaps, formed part of the city walls, but had long since fallen from its place and been by winds and rain worn smooth. And then we seemed to ourselves beggars indeed, for that was the place where the poor and houseless of that city, at the end of every day, gathered to receive alms. For an hour as the sun dropped behind the city walls, we watched these men, women and children accept their charity: soup, and bread, a little money, clothing and necessaries of that kind. This was, my eyes, a spectacle of misery, as all spectacles of compassion always are; for what is compassion but the insufficient human gesture called forth by irremediable suffering? There was not bread and soup enough to fill those hungry bellies; there were not smocks and blankets enough to shield those helpless bodies from the cold winds of the desert nights. Many went hungry, or knew that they would do so another time. Watching their suffering, many times I stirred myself and made as if to stand, to go to these people, to give them what I had, whatever I could to alleviate their suffering and privation; but my companion stopped me, his hand light upon my knee, with these words.

'"Brother merchant, humour me. This time, sit here, sit here upon this stone, and hear what I have to say to you. I brought you to this place to show you these miserable people, their starving bodies, their terrible and consuming need. The heart goes out to them – your heart, my heart, the hearts of those at whose hands they have taken some little food, clothing, the little things that will sustain them tonight and tomorrow night, from night to night as they scrape their survival from the raw face of the rock and from the sand that blows upon the wind. But ask yourself, why does your heart go out to them? Ask yourself, is it not because they are miserable?"

'Here he took me by the shoulder, and pointed my gaze to two men standing by the gate, not far, but far enough that they stood out of our earshot. Though we could not hear the substance of their conversation, it was plain that they were engrossed, even then, in a terrible argument. One of them, a rich man, had come to the gate that evening to dispense charity to the poor; we had already seen him, many times, with his hand extended, a beneficent smile expressing on his face the deep love that was in his heart. Now, instead, he held his arms crossed upon his chest, and his chin tucked against his neck. His eyes blazed

323

with fury while the second man beseeched him, harangued him, chivvied and worried him.

'"Do you understand the argument between these two men?" my friend asked of me.

'I told him I did not.

'"I do," he said. "I have seen both these men here, many times. The rich man is a philanthropist, a man whose heart, like yours perhaps, is full of love and generosity. Every evening he comes to this place, to share his wealth with those less fortunate than he is. The other man is a beggar – indeed he is – though by his sumptuous clothes and the lustre of his skin you may suspect he has done rather better for himself than many who seek charity at the city gates. I can say more, indeed – so rich has he grown, by feeding on the charity of those wealthier than himself, that he has become, himself, a man of substance. Now, seeing him so fat, seeing him so well provided, his former benefactors spurn him. They give him stones instead of bread, cruel words instead of compassion. He has no right to their goodwill, and now when these two men encounter one another, they do not part friends. The rich man goes home not with love and satisfaction in his thought; his heart is troubled, and he sleeps poorly. The poor man – he has enough, perhaps, for now, but – one cannot say.

'"Two nights I have told you the story of the king of this place. Once the greatest conqueror the world has ever seen, once the richest man in a thousand kingdoms, to the sands and the hope of his heir he committed everything he had – to a little beggar boy, to a child who came across the sands, and disappeared, at last, back into them. This king gave all, and in giving all, became at once a beggar himself, and the subject of our story. Now, ask yourself, brother merchant," he said

324

to me, "would you be half so moved by his story, half so eager to hear its conclusion, if I told you that this king had yet another treasury, as large as the first that he buried in the sands? If I told you that he married a new wife, that she bore him a new heir, and that he bequeathed this heir the greater part of his kingdom, which passed by a long dynasty in unbroken succession through many ages, would you have come with me tonight, eager, concerned, engaged, and – my friend – full of compassion?"

'I pondered this while I watched the beggars before me supping their thin broth. At last I admitted to him what I wished I could forget – what I wish, my eyes, I could forget even now – that I had heard his story with compassion because it was a terrible story, because I had assumed it would have a terrible end.

'"And so it does, brother merchant," he told me. "And this is why we listen to all stories, both those that end well, and those that end badly – because no matter what we do, we cannot change them, cannot reach through the wide abyss of time, or the impassable void that stands between what is real, and what is not. And indeed, in this respect, no story ends well, but it asks our compassion, and receives it, because it must forever fall short of that fullness of truth and fulfilment that even these beggars, starving as they are, enjoy. How much happier to be a beggar, living forever on the very walls of survival, than to be nothing but the subject of a tale!

'"The sad king, poor and joyless, grew weak and unable to govern. His riches he had buried in the sands, and with his riches his power, his influence and his security. One by one, then by tens, and scores, his vassal kingdoms revolted. One by one, then by tens, and scores, his liege lords and his captains abandoned him. In the end, only his council remained, along with the eight generals who had from the first directed his campaigns. He became a prisoner in his own palace.

'"One solace was afforded him in those, almost the last of his days. Every afternoon as the desert's heat relented, and the cool scent of well water, infused with the fragrance of jasmine blooms, spread in his private courts, his brother the former wazir came to him to play shatranj. This one game had occupied them for many years, ever since the day that his brother had become the king's wazir – that is, ever since the day that the little beggar boy had saved the king's life. They were locked in a mansūba which has become since their time very famous, and is known as the Sad King. It has only one solution, a solution which neither of these players – dedicated and not unskilful, but neither of them great masters – had yet discovered. Day by day they sat opposite one another, and regarded the board between them. Birds sang among the flowers in the courtyard gardens, and lesser lives came and went, much like the birds, much like their song, passing around the two ageing men as they confronted one another over the board. From time to time, sometimes after many months of quiet, one of them would move a piece from one square to another; in some years, one or the other of them would capture one of his opponent's pieces. But these moments were rare, and growing rarer. It was not clear to either of them whether the game would ever end.

'"One afternoon the old wazir, who had long since given up his post, came to the terrace outside the king's chambers, where the great board lay spread beneath the tamarisk trees, in the scent of cinnamon and cloves, ready for the continuation of their game. He looked at it, at its alternating squares of black obsidian and beaten gold foil, latticed with miniature sapphires and carved with verses of love, and war, and contemplation. Its pieces to one side were cut from whole rubies, to the other from whole emeralds, dazzling in their size and purity, some of the most valuable gems ever to have been mined in the dark bowels of the grudging earth. They were things of great rarity and, if it was possible, of greater beauty; to touch them, which a few times he had, was to the old *wazir* an exquisite pleasure. As he stood waiting for his brother, he regarded them with unalloyed pleasure.

' "But of late, whether by accident or some unconscious design of his own, the pieces on the board had become configured in a shape that seemed to him a great reproach. His brother had shown him how the pieces on the board seemed to mirror the king's own sagging eyes, his melancholy frown, the heaviness of his cheeks; and now the *wazir* could not help but see it himself. Moreover, he still saw no way out of this problem, for the solution still lay beyond his power. Therefore it was his intention to leave the game, to leave the king his brother, to leave his city and his kingdom, and to go into a far country and never be seen again. He had in his hand the copy of the *Giant's Almanac*, its plates cast in bronze, and when his brother appeared on the terrace, and had taken his seat on the verandah, the old *wazir* gave him the instrument, confessing his evil and all the history of the beggar boy who had become the man known as *al*-Jabbar, *the Giant*. He asked his brother his forgiveness, and with a heavy feeling of his guilt, he went away.

' "But the king would grant no forgiveness. His heart, broken once before, and then again, was broken afresh, and this time it would admit neither forgiveness nor healing of any kind. The old *wazir* departed from the city and from the kingdom, and was never seen again; but the king swore his revenge, kindling in his heart so great a hatred and so hard a resolve that it was said his eyes bled fire. Kneeling in his chamber, he called upon the gods, on time, on every power of the earth, to give him back the heir to his kingdom, for he plainly declared he would not die, nor his kingdom should not end, until the heir was found. Having gathered his council and his generals, they took to their horses and – aged as they were – set out on campaign. For the king had seen the solution to the problem called the Sad King, and he trusted in his heart that the game was already ended."

'"What happened to this king?" I asked my friend the merchant.

'"He scoured the kingdom, gathering men to his banners. From realm to realm he rode, razing cities to the ground, searching for his brother, searching for his heir – but to no avail, for he found neither the one nor the other, neither dead nor alive. At last he arrived at the coast of a vast sea and, having no more lands left to search, he seized a ship and set sail for the end of the world. Some say he made landfall on a deserted island, and died there, that he is buried for eternity in an empty tomb; but others say he sails the seas still, or walks the earth, or flies through the air, still searching."

'I told my friend this was a sad tale, the saddest I had ever heard. I told him that my heart suffered for this broken but undefeated king. He answered that that was as it should be, for my heart could afford a sorrow for one so lost, who should never be redeemed. We were then to part, for it was my intention to leave that city on the morning after, and never to return.

'"My friend merchant," I said, "I thank you for your tale, and for the nights that you have spent in my company, telling it. What is your name, so that later in my life, as I travel through the world, when I recount your story to others I may say I learned it of you?"

'"When I was a young man," he said, "I was called Hožir; but you may know me hereafter as Phantastes."

'"Perhaps we will meet again, Hožir," I answered him, "in another place, when we are other men."

'And now, my eyes, you have heard the end of my story, and learned how I first met my friend Hožir, who as you have seen, has indeed met me in another place, and learned that I am another man.'

The old man's words had, while he told his story, been growing ever slower and fainter, and now they ceased altogether. His eyes, nodding against the light of the weak fire, closed, and the boy thought he had fallen asleep. With a light and a nimble movement, he rose from the little stool where he had been sitting, and edged towards the door of the library.

'My eyes,' said the old man from his chair by the fire. 'Dear child, soon you must leave this house, and go to the Heresy. There you will complete your education, so that you may go in search of the Kingdom. It was not in my power to finish the game, but it will be in yours.'

The boy crossed the room again, and stood before the old man. He looked down at him, at his tired face, the neatly folded blanket that covered his lap, at his hands that lay folded over the blanket. Quickly, he leaned to the old man's face, and kissed him on the cheek. Then he crossed the room again, pushed the heavy wooden shutters across the daylight in the window, and put his hand to the library door.

'Habi,' said the old man. 'Habi Gablani Ahmadi, son of my son, you are a good boy, and dear to me.'

## 12

## *The blank eye*

Several anxious days passed, each more exhausted and feverish than the last. Fitz was aware of others coming and going from his bedside: Navy, Dolly, and on one occasion Padge and Russ. Each of them sat on the little wooden stool by the window, and from time to time they took his hand in their cold hands, and from time to time they said words that, like far waters, ran into secret places and were hidden from him. They told him about the Master, and about the Jack, how he had cut the Master free from his shackles on the cliff, and carried him across the valley and through the Gate of Resignation. They told him how the Master had appeared, bruised and frail, at Feeding, and had been greeted in silence by the other Officers, how they had risen as one from the table and left the hall. They told him how the Master now kept to his study, how he feared a conspiracy against him. But all the words passed over Fitz, leaving no impression at all. He couldn't hold them.

When he was strong enough, Fitz passed hours reading over his book, and after a few days began again to attend lessons; but though his body moved from place to place, keeping its appointments and making its appearances, his mind sluggish and inert could not help but tarry – in his room, at the tombs, atop a wall in the dark. Fitz moved through his days as if in a trance, even in the afternoons when usually his thoughts were clear; it was as if words, sights, sounds, even smells came into him and passed through his body without his knowledge, as if the shell of him but not the soul remained. Bright sudden things, loud noises, extremities of any kind made him not flinch, but ever more retract; one evening, climbing the stairs to his room after lessons, he had to pause before the top, unable for the present to lift his legs again.

Dina was in his room. Fitz was surprised; he had only just left her, on the stairs outside the House of the Jack. Somehow she had contrived to slip back to his room before him, so quickly and silently that he had had no inkling of her presence.

'We have another lesson today,' she said. She was agitated, and her voice seemed to strain tight from between her teeth, like the thin, high note scraped from a string, a string that was about to snap.

Fitz's eyes looked at her. He could feel them hanging heavy like lead balls in his cheeks. He couldn't think what to say.

Dina ground her right heel into the floor. She never wore shoes, and her soles ought to have been calloused and tough, but they seemed instead supple, soft as the inside of her arm. Fitz could hear that delicate skin chafing against the stone floor of the tower room.

'The Master,' she said, answering the question he hadn't asked. 'The Master has summoned us to a lesson.' Her voice was flat as her foot ought to have been. Fitz sought out her eyes. Whatever the tension in her heel, in her voice, her eyes were serene as ever. The long ice would never melt, there, no matter what heat or frenzy raged in her heart. That ice was equal to anything.

*I know*, Fitz tried to say. *He called us to a lesson, but you never came.*

He followed her down to the court, across the flags, and up the stairs to the Master's own tower. It was a tall tower, and as they climbed Fitz matched his pace, the lifting of his exhausted legs, to Dina's own. Or anyway he tried, lagging. When he finally caught up with her, at the heavy wooden door to the Master's study, he found it standing open. Dina put her palm flat on one of its dark, carved panels, looked at Fitz with an inscrutable challenge, and pushed it wide.

The Master sat slumped behind his desk. A grey pallor draped his face, as his crumpled body, though suited in stiff black, draped the heavy oak chair – almost a throne – in which he sat. His eyes followed them with minute precision as they crossed the twelve-sided tower room, walled on every side with bookcases, and took the two chairs set before the desk. Fitz sat on the right, Dina on the left. However difficult the last week had been for him, Fitz thought, it had been harder for the Master.

He looked at them for a long time. On any other day, in any other company, Fitz would have fidgeted. But at last, here, in this study, at the very heart of the Heresy and in the Master's presence, with Dina at his side – after all the uncertainty and exhaustion, the sickness and confusion of the last week – he felt an overwhelming sense of safety. If he'd told her, he knew what Dina would have said: it's just the lingering effect of the stack, she'd have said, her lip tending towards the curl of a supercilious sneer. But it was more than that. He knew the feeling, recognized it. After all that Dina had said and done – from the day of his enrolment, to his first case, to that night outside the Sensorium – he couldn't explain it. Despite that mockery on her cheeks, despite the distance in her eyes, despite her imperious commands, her ridicule, here in the Mastery with Dina at his side, he still knew what he felt.

It was the feeling of home.

'My two apprentices,' said the Master.

'I didn't think you were well enough to see us for lessons,' said Dina.

'But you see that I am,' answered the Master.

'What will you teach us?' she fired back.

The Master regarded her.

'When I was young,' the Master said, 'I lived my life as if in a dream.' He spoke slowly, and with effort. 'From place to place I walked as if on air. I breathed light. The ground was not yet hard to me. The cold did not yet sound like a cracked bell in my joints. In those days, my eyes were not yet draped with shadows.'

The Master had pushed himself up, straightening his folded spine, and sat now with his arms flat on the arms of his broad oak chair. Its tall carved back towered above his head. From one of the finials that crowned it, his hat hung askew. He looked at them with intensity, first one, then the other, then back again, his dark eyes boring into them, tight and insistent as an awl.

'You have read books. Perhaps you have read of that hunter Death, and of his scouts and skirmish parties, the little infirmities

333

that surprise the body, and the mind, too, as a man makes his way towards his end. Perhaps you can imagine them: a weariness that saps the muscles and dries out the bones; a sluggish drag on every action and on every thought; the dimming, the little crazing of the eyes; the long and restless nights; the tattering of recall. But what you don't know, what you cannot know, is death's *dearness*. The full day of youth shines with only a brittle and a skimming light. The afternoon, much more than the morning, lies deep and lush among the encroaching veils of night. Here cool quiet steals along the nerves like sugar on the tongue, that pleases even as it sickens. Here darkness huddles at the edge of every vision, every memory and idea, by contrast brightening it, conferring on it a lustre that the object, in itself, never had nor could ever have.'

They watched him. His body seemed so weak, but his voice, for all that, sounded so strong.

'You see me cast low. I have suffered since the night I passed at the tombs. Illness, weakness and fear have been constant visitors to my bedside – more constant, even, than the Commissar, and she has watched the dreary and the tedious nights with me, and kept my body whole.' He paused, gathering his breath. 'But you find me in the tower of my strength. Do not be deceived by appearances. For now, when Death is nearest, I feel most keenly my lingering powers. Every word I choose in pain, like jewels prised from the rock with hammers. Every word is a jewel, every thought a hoard. Each moment that passes is for me an eternity. Death greens the world, and I find myself besotted with it.'

Moving slowly, as if his bones were brittle glass, the Master pushed himself to his feet, turned, and stepped to a tall wooden cupboard built into the wall behind his desk. He opened it, and from it withdrew a large wooden case. It seemed impossible that he should hold it, but he turned, and set it on the empty desk before them.

Fitz had to stifle the gasp that very nearly burst from him.

It was the *shatranj* case that Mr Ahmadi Senior had given him, that he had given to Ned More, that had to be –

It lay on the table before them. The Master opened it, and Fitz felt with his gaze the cool lustre of the emerald and the ruby pieces, of the gold tooling that ran between the chequered wooden panels. It was like a drink after thirst, a breeze on his cheek at noon in summer.

'In the lessons to come, I will teach you the secrets of this game,' he said, looking with even detachment at Fitz. He knew what the look meant: that he should say nothing about the days he had passed in the Old Friary, sitting before the fire with the board laid out on the little table. He should say nothing about the winter afternoon when Mr Ahmadi Senior closed it for the last time, and committed it to Fitz's keeping, telling him to use it well. He should say nothing about the fact that the board must have gone to the Mountain, that it must have returned to the Heresy with his mother, in the night, in a dream –

'It is the ancestor of chess. It is like chess. And like chess it is a game played between two opponents, the object of which is to capture the opponent's king, his *shāh* –'

'What's the purpose of this?' said Dina, sharply. Fitz could read the suspicion and impatience clearly on her face. She didn't try to conceal it.

The Master didn't answer. With quick, trembling fingers, he retrieved from the case the emerald and the ruby pieces, and set them in their arrays on the board. Once they were in place, with a further series of quick, judicious motions he manoeuvred them into a new configuration. 'You see,' he said to them both, looking up and taking their eyes with neither embarrassment, nor anxiety, 'the dilemma I have laid out for you.' Fitz glanced at the board, and understood at once how every one of the ruby pieces stood in danger of capture, whereas every emerald piece was perfectly defended by a network of further moves. Dina didn't deign to scrutinize the problem.

'You have been unwise,' he said, sweeping his hand over the board to indicate that Fitz and Dina should understand the ruby pieces as their own. 'You have left yourself exposed almost everywhere. But see how wise my own play has been. Every one of my active pieces threatens one of your own, some more than one. With precision and with foresight I have put you under enormous strain, for I know each of your vulnerabilities, and they lie open to me as leaves on the trees in summer.'

Dina snorted.

'But I have also defended myself. You cannot capture any of my pieces without yourself suffering a loss – a series of losses. I will win this game, for it is already ended. But I will win it because I have treated each of my own pieces in exactly the same way I have treated each of yours.' Fitz fumbled after his meaning, and the Master saw from the concentration in his brow that he would have to explain himself. 'I make myself safe by defending my own pieces exactly in the same manner that I threaten yours. What makes it defence, in one situation, and attack in the other, is only a matter of colour. Change the pieces, and change the operation. The play is the same.'

Fitz sat back in his chair.

'You have been awakened in the night for cases.' He had turned towards Fitz, and was addressing him directly. 'By day you attend your lessons. But you are tested by night. The call comes suddenly, and the rules are unclear. But the case set for you to solve always requires the same skills: the merciless ferocity of the Rack, the organization of the Sweeper, the knowledge of the Registrar, the resources of the Commissar, the creativity of the Keeper, the cunning of the Jack. But above all you require this knowledge of the game, the play of the Master.'

Fitz was almost surprised that Dina didn't snort again.

'A problem. A challenge. A riddle. An adventure. The case takes many forms, but it always has this quality, that all the Apprentices must compete with one another, and yet no one can reach the prize alone.' The Master pulled the board towards him, and replaced the pieces in their felted nests. 'We must work together, against one another. That is the essence of play,' he said, closing the case. 'And the nature of any game.'

'The game is already ended,' said Dina, almost to herself, with satisfaction.

'And so is Feeding, unless you're quick about it,' said the Master. The clock struck then, and Dina jumped to her feet as if a cat, and startled. 'Go.'

Walking outside, on their way to dinner, Dina put her hand to Fitz's arm and stopped him.

'You know that there is disagreement among the Officers,' she said. It wasn't a question.

'What sort of disagreement?' Fitz asked.

'Some of the Officers don't think the Master should have brought you here in the first place, or that he should have a second Apprentice. You can see why.'

Out of the corner of his eye, Fitz saw swifts in the sky, combining long arcs of graceful soaring with fast bursts of manic fluttering.

'No,' he said.

'It sets us against one another,' Dina said. 'We can't both train to become the Master. There is only one Office.'

Fitz looked at Dina full in the face. She still appeared to be upset about something. She had begun this conversation; he knew he should wait for her to end it.

'That's why we haven't met with the Master until today. Ever since you arrived. The other Officers wouldn't allow it.'

'The Jack doesn't seem to mind,' said Fitz. He was thinking of the little toilet in the leafy square outside the British Museum, in another world, where Arwan had covered the walls with equations. It was a rash thing of him to say, and he regretted it the moment that he said it – regretted that he had mixed that other world with this one. Into his mind, very suddenly, flashed the image of Mr Ahmadi on that night, hurrying through the square beneath the trees, watching in every direction, as if – as if he were being hunted.

Dina smiled a cold smile that had no kindness in it. 'You're right,' she said. 'Now that I think of it, the Jack doesn't seem to mind.'

Dina said nothing further to him while they walked together to Feeding, nothing in the Porch while they gathered with the other Prents, and nothing, almost, in the hall. The conversation among the others started out entirely a Navy affair, good-natured and erratic, and Dina had no trouble withdrawing into her own private thoughts, chewing her way with muscle through First and Second Feeding without missing a scrap. But her tension like stench in the room affected them all, and as the meal wore on they all, finally, succumbed to it. Fingal was the first to break.

'So,' he said, taking up one of the increasingly protracted silences, and addressing Fitz from across the table, 'how are you two getting on? Which one of you will be the Master, and which one of you is going to get posted to the bottom of the sea?'

Everyone looked at Fitz, except Dina.

'It's not a competition,' she said, as she wiped her plate with a crust. She didn't look up.

'Of course it's a competition,' said Fingal. 'Everything's a competition in this place. Only the strongest will survive, eh, Dolly?'

Whatever this barb meant to Dolly, and to the others, Fitz could see right away that it had stuck fast, and rankled. She put down her fork, and looked at her plate as if she had forgotten why she was eating.

'Oh, come on,' said Fingal. 'This is not news. We all know they're watching us all the time, testing us every day in ways we haven't even imagined. Dolly's been given a second chance; good for her. Whatever. But there's no way this runt is going to stack up to Dina.' He looked around. 'Don't even pretend you haven't all been thinking it.'

*Runt.*

'What's your *game*, *Fitzroy*?' sneered Fingal, turning to Fitz again. 'What do you actually think you're doing here?'

'Enough, Fingal,' said Dina. Again she didn't look up, just helping herself to more bread as the Serfs began to lay Third Feeding.

'Come on, out with it. What special plan have you and the Master cooked up for the rest of us? What are you *really* doing here? You go to lessons, sure, wander about looking dreamy and never asking any questions. You act like you own the place, and you've only been here a month. What do you know that we don't?'

'I said *enough*,' repeated Dina. She glared at Fingal, and for a second – but only a second – his face fell.

'You know you're only picking on him because you're still sore about your Black Wedding,' said Navy. 'He has every right to be here. He was enrolled same as the rest of us.'

Padge, Russ and the others were watching carefully, none of them bold enough to take on Fingal in one of his moods, or Dina at any time.

Fingal blew air through his lips. 'Maybe he enrolled. But what is he good for? What can he do? Did you know, newbie, that Padge has just published two papers on seismology, dealing with complex fluids in unstable topographies? And Russ, he doesn't look like much, but he's doing mathematics I don't even understand. Have you seen his proofs? I see them, sometimes, when the Jack leaves them out on the desks in the afternoon. He leaves them out because he is *studying* them. Dolly, fine, she's had some ups and downs, maybe she's not Leonardo, but I doubt there are better sculptors working in clay right now, *anywhere*. And Payne – we all know Payne can design simulations in the Model that would make Harvard blush. And Navy, you're a dab hand at cleaning up horse manure. So what can *you* do, newbie? Anything? Or are you just good at keeping your mouth shut? Is that a talent?'

Fitz wanted to cry. He wanted to tell Navy that he wanted to cry.

'And what can you do, Fingal, if you're so smart?' said Navy. Her lips were set like stone. Dolly could have carved them. 'What can you do, apart from fail your examinations?'

Fingal's eyes hardened.

'You know,' he answered, cold, almost whispering, 'there's a reason why the rest of you don't have lessons with the Rack. He trusts me. Me. I didn't *fail* my examinations. He didn't tell me *I* wasn't ready to move on. He told me *he* wasn't ready for me to move on. Whatever the rest of you are doing, it's *nothing* compared to what we're doing in the cells and in –'

'Stop it,' said Dina. The rebuke was sharp and final.

'No,' said Padge. 'I want to know what you're doing with the Rack, Fingal, that's so important.'

'Torturing bunnies, most likely,' said Navy.

'Why do you all look down on me?' said Fingal. 'I'm proud of what I do. The rest of you pretend you're doing noble things, beautiful things. Fine. But this place wasn't built with maths and paintings. It was built with *power*. With *money*. With *force*. Beautiful things won't grow unless you spread manure on them – isn't that right, Navy? Have a look in the Armoury. Have a look in the Commissar's closets. The locked ones. Stack isn't all she hides in there. She has a thousand poisons. Padge will tell you. You think she doesn't use them? You think the Rack doesn't use them? If it weren't for the Rack, there wouldn't *be* a Heresy.'

'We're done with this conversation,' said Dina.

'No, Fingal is done,' said Navy. 'With this conversation, and with everything. You should go home, Fingal,' said Navy.

'At least I came from a home,' he shot back. 'A real one. With real parents. Not some hostel cottage for foundlings with some fake do-gooder and five magic words. Right, newbie? At least I had a home to leave.'

Fitz dropped his fork. It clattered on his plate, and fell to the floor.

*How –*

But it was obvious. By their faces, downcast, ashamed, Fitz could see at once that they all knew everything. Navy, humiliated by her indiscretion, turned bright red, red as the Commissar's cloak. Without pausing to think, Fitz rose and walked out of the hall, through the Porch, and into the night. He didn't bother to close the door behind him.

He might have walked for hours. For a while he walked in circles around the gardens: the herb garden, the poison garden, and among the locked greenhouses where the Commissar grew her tropical, man-eating flowers. He walked the circuit of the walls, taking the path that ran down to the river and back up, through the Sweep, to the steps at the foot of the Heresiarchy. He hardly noticed where he was. In his mind, over and over, were Fingal's words. It didn't matter that he had said them in anger. They were true. Fitz had nothing to contribute. He wasn't distinctive. He didn't have a real mother. There was nothing in him that he could trust. There was nothing out there that he could ever go back to. He came from nowhere. He was going nowhere. And he was going there with nothing.

At last he found himself sitting at the top of the Heresiarchy steps. He wasn't sure how long he had been there. He wasn't sure of anything. In his thoughts and feelings, two equal forces wrestled: an irresistible urge to get out of this place, and an irrefutable conviction that he had nowhere else to go. As he looked out upon the dark courts of the Heresy, for some reason he could not name he thought of the beggar boy, from Mr Ahmadi's book, the one they called *al-Jabbar*, the Giant. He thought of him at the moment that he descended for the last time into the treasury beneath the sands, out of love with the world and caught forever in the struggle between two brothers whose hatred would destroy them, and him, and everything that was beautiful. And he envied the Giant, that for him there had at last been a place to go, albeit one he had built with his own hands, anonymous and lost, a place of oblivion. He envied him that he had fashioned for himself an instrument, the Almanac, that could guide him unerringly to this place. He envied him that, even in the ruins of everything, even in the shadowy, swirling mists of the myth he had become, he had claimed a true place in someone's heart. He'd been good for something.

'Fitz.'

His stomach tightened. Nine bells had rung, or maybe ten – he hadn't counted and he hardly cared – and he had thought he would be alone. After what had happened, Navy was nearly the last person he wanted to talk to.

'I'm sorry,' she said.

She had stolen silently up the steps, a black silhouette against a night-black void, and Fitz hadn't seen her.

'I know,' he answered. 'It isn't your fault.'

'I did tell them what you said. And I'm sorry. I really am. But the hatred – the insults – all that was a twist of Fingal's own making.'

'It's all right,' he said after a moment. 'He's right, anyway.'

Navy sat down next to him. Fitz's arms were crossed against his chest. Where his left hand hung under his right elbow, Navy touched him, then held him, fast. He let her.

'Yes, he is,' she said. 'You did come from nowhere. You don't have a mother, not a real one. You're clever – I'll never forget your first case, the one with the snakes – but no, you're not brilliant. Not like Russ. And you're not good with your hands, like Dolly, or able to see twenty-five moves ahead, like Payne. You don't have my memory. And you'll never work as hard as Padge, not at anything. So, yes, he's right.'

'Did you come looking for me, just to tell me that?' said Fitz. He pulled on his hand, but Navy held it.

'No, I came to tell you this. You're not those things. But nor are you as evil as Fingal is. And you don't have one ounce of the devious, manipulative selfishness with which Dina does absolutely everything. In fact, I'd say the opposite. I'd say you have something that none of us has, and I think that's why you're here.'

Fitz began to cry. At first the tears gathered silently in his eyes, and overran his cheeks like small rain on thick, snug panes of glass. But it wasn't long before a sob shook him, and then another, and Navy wrapped her arm round him and held him tight for a long while, as long as he needed. She didn't tell him to stop, or tell him that he was wrong. She just let him cry. It was all he had ever wanted to do, and she shook with him as the heaves came rushing out of nothing, out of the nothing that was in him.

'You don't belong here,' she said at last. 'And that's exactly why we need you.'

When he had finished crying, the night and the air, the space around him – everything – seemed clearer. He took a deep and unbroken breath.

'You know, there's more.'

'More what?' Fitz asked her.

'More to the Heresy. When I first got here, when I was little, I was pretty messed up. I mean, I liked it – the lessons every day, all the new information. You know how I am with facts and figures. In one way, I couldn't get enough of it. But it was exhausting, too. We work all the time, seven days a week, and with the stables and the cages and the aviary . . . after a while the novelty wore off. I started to feel like I was falling apart: lonely, tired. But above all, I felt so *enclosed*. Porridge in the morning. Stack for four hours. Lunch. Lessons. Feeding. Nine bells. Repeat. I was like a zombie. But one person noticed, and he said something important to me.'

Fitz waited.

'It was the Master. He took me aside one night after Feeding, and he said, "Navy, you know, there's more." I had no idea what he meant. He said, "You seem like a girl who likes to go for a walk. Would you like to go for a walk?" I said yes. And he brought me here, to the very door of the Heresiarchy where it's nestled under the mountain, and he showed me the whole of the Heresy, laid out at our feet, just like this, at night, with the moon shining all over the lead roofs and the glass atrium down there to the west, and the weathervanes turning in the sea breeze, and the smoke curling out of the chimneys. All as it is now. And he asked me if I thought it was beautiful. I said it was, but he knew, I knew, that that wasn't it. And he said, again, "You know, there's more."'

Navy was still holding his hand. She squeezed it.

'Did you notice that the steps continue around the Heresiarchy, on both sides?'

Fitz turned round. In the darkness he could hardly see anything, but he could see – or maybe he could remember having seen, and only believed he could see – that she was right. Two narrow stairways, one on each side, curved round the round curve of the building, leading up and away.

'He told me that night he had arranged with the other Officers that, on account of all my duties in the stables and the cages and the aviary, and everything, I should be allowed to stay out at nights as late as I liked. I didn't have to observe curfew like everyone else, even Dina. From that night on, he said, I could go for walks whenever I wanted. And so, together, we climbed up those steps – those ones, behind us – and he showed me that there is more.'

'What's up there?' Fitz asked her. He had forgotten, now, all about the argument in the Lantern Hall. He knew he had forgotten.

Navy took him by the hand and they climbed the steps. The stairs passed behind the palace, and rose, circling, in the mountain, by spirals through steep and narrow arches. It was an arduous climb. They took it in silence, trusting their feet to find the stone, step after step. But as they rose, the air lightened, and Fitz realized that he could see over the valley, over the cliffs, out to sea. And at last, before them, there was a tall building.

'That's the Heresiarch's personal library,' said Navy. 'Supposedly only the Heresiarch comes up here. I mean, the Heresiarch, and me.'

A light flashed suddenly over them, and then disappeared. Fitz instinctively pulled back, into the shadow of the last arch they had passed through. Navy, still holding him by the hand, hunkered with him in safety against the wall.

'And that's what he showed me,' she said.

She pointed out to sea. Fitz didn't see anything.

'Wait,' she told him.

Sure enough, a few moments later, the light flashed over them again.

'What is it?' he asked her, his voice hardly more than a murmur.

'It's a lighthouse. I don't know if anyone is in it. Maybe it's mechanical. But at least once, someone must have gone out there, on to a rock in the middle of nothing, and built that thing. Someone must look after it. And its only purpose is to warn people. To take care of them. To help them keep an eye out.'

Fitz waited for the light to come round again. It was exciting, mesmerizing, reassuring to find that in all that nothingness, there was such a light.

'I used to come here most nights. Now I come only once in a while. But I think about it every night, before going to sleep, and it helps to remind me, you know, that there's more.'

Above them, on the top of the cliff, someone opened the door of the Heresiarch's library, shut it, and started to walk towards them. The top hat was unmistakable. Navy pulled Fitz further off the path, on to the edge of the cliff, dragging him down to the ground. He knew to be silent. Only when the Master had passed them, and gone on down the steps, and disappeared below, did he dare to breathe.

'That's the other reason I brought you up here. He's been coming up here almost every night since you came to the Heresy. These days, he comes during Feeding, when everyone else is in the Lantern Hall. He doesn't eat. I doubt he sleeps. He's looking for something, isn't he?'

Fitz nodded. Navy felt it.

'Something to help you. Fitz,' she said, 'something awful is happening in the Heresy. I know it is. And when the Master left, last year, it got worse. Fingal, Dina, the Rack, the Commissar, the Registrar – they're all in on it. So many secrets. They're never around. They're always looking at one another, looking like they know something. Whatever it is, I know the Master must be against it. And that's all I need to know. I'd follow him anywhere. And he brought you here, and he looks out for you, so I think you must, somehow, be important. I think I know why you are here.'

'Why?' Fitz asked her.

'Everyone feels it, even if they react in different ways. Even if they react in terrible ways. We all know it. You're here because, unlike the rest of us, even me, even Dolly, and I love Dolly – I don't know exactly how to put it – you're here because, wherever you go, whoever you are with, love – happens. That's a gift that's greater than any of ours.'

They walked back in silence, down the thousand steps, through the Heresiarch's court, and into the Mastery. Navy dropped Fitz's hand at his tower door.

'It may not make any sense,' she said. 'But you belong here because you don't fit.'

Then she was gone.

13

## The Incoherentists

The next morning, four weeks to the day after Fitz had first arrived at the Heresy, everything changed.

For one thing, he stopped eating the stack. It was a simple thing to do. Once he had learned about it from Dina, he had noticed it on the porridge that was served them each morning, sprinkled on the surface of every bowl set before the children. It smelled sweet and earthy, a little like nutmeg, and was russet brown in colour. At first he hadn't minded it much; eager for the concentration it allowed him, the sense of unity, the quick gains in understanding and in feeling, he ate it almost greedily. But now, since Russ became ill, and after the Master was attacked, with Dina – stung and surly – absent from half their lessons, and given all that Navy had said, Fitz wasn't so eager. So when the bowl was set in front of him – and always without looking, especially if he were in the middle of a conversation with Dina – he dragged his spoon lightly across the surface of his porridge, scraping up the stack, and folded it over on the inside lip of his bowl. It was a technique adapted from his new practice in oil painting. That bit he left in his bowl, when he was finished; and if he ate a few grains of the stuff on this or that morning, it didn't seem to have anything like the effect it had had before.

It didn't go unnoticed. One of the Serfs brought a fresh laver and pitcher to Fitz's room every morning, setting it outside his door. The jug of water was for washing; but next to it there was always a glass of cool water for drinking – and the first thing Fitz usually did, on waking, was to take it down by gulps. Sure enough, not two days after he started avoiding the stack at porridge, the daily glass of water had an unmistakable new smell to it. So, he was being watched, and closely. That morning, he contrived to climb from his bed, using the window frame as a step, just high enough to push open the trap in the ceiling. He poured the water on the roof, and with satisfaction heard it trickle into the gutter and down the leads.

After that, Fitz had to simulate the effects of the stack, so that Dina would remain convinced, so that the Officers would remain convinced, that nothing had changed for him. He enjoyed this, and was surprised at how easy he found it to concentrate entirely on whatever he was doing, to let himself go, to become absorbed in it, as if it were the only thing he had ever known. He was surprised at how easy it was – despite everything – to dote on Dina completely. All things considered, the simulation wasn't so different from the real experience of stack, save that a little part of him, something like an eye or a little window on himself, remained open and conscious of the passage of time, of the existence and importance of other ideas, other people and other actions. He came to feel that he wasn't faking anything at all, but rather that he was in two states at once: entirely submerged in the present, and all that he was doing in his morning lessons in the Keep, in the Registry, in the Sweep, but also, somehow, somewhere else, quiet and dormant, but expectant, biding time. He was in the Heresy, and he was also at sea, behind a light.

Fitz's days at the Heresy thus passed differently. But they changed in another way, too. Where before he and Dina had gone to lessons with the Keeper, the Registrar and the Sweeper each morning, and with the Commissar and the Jack each afternoon, now they were summoned to the Master's study at the end of each day, for an hour before the evening meal. Each time they climbed to the Master's study, Fitz felt tense with excitement; surely these lessons would be different from the others, a chance – finally – to work alongside the Master to end the long game they had begun at the Heresy. Surely, as with all their other afternoon lessons, Dina would lose interest, and stop attending; and Fitz craved the opportunity to sit with the Master, alone, and talk through everything that had happened, everything that would happen next. But their afternoon tutorials offered him no such opportunity; Dina walked to the Master's tower with him, they climbed the stairs together, in the dark study they sat side by side for the whole of the hour, and at the meeting's close Dina held the door for him while Fitz left the room before her. Through it all, her presence lay on him like an exquisite weight.

But despite Dina's dampening influence, something strange *did* begin to happen at their evening lessons, and every step Fitz took, as he left the study by its circular stair, felt to him like a surge of power, as if electricity were coursing through the floors of the

Master's tower, and he had but to place his foot upon the tower step to set his hair on end.

Their first meeting had gone badly. But their second was better. It turned on the experience of eating stack. The Master told them of another part of the same tree – not the root, but the leaf – which, when chewed, caused the person chewing it to slip into a hallucinatory rapture. The white milk in the veins of this leaf had its devotees, he said, who had once gathered the tree's leaves by the cartload. The priests of this religion believed that the hallucinations they experienced gave them special insight, for in their ecstatic visions they were conscious of themselves as two distinct selves, at once both fully immersed in an experience, and conscious of themselves in that immersion. Dina laughed at this, and said that they were probably poets. 'Indeed,' the Master answered her, his dark eyes burning a dark fire in the shadows of the shuttered study, 'indeed they were.' This discomfited Dina; her eyes narrowed, and her distraction gave Fitz a moment to enjoy what happened next, without fear of betraying himself.

'Today,' said the Master, producing a key from a cord hung round his neck, and using it to open the cupboard behind his desk where the *shatranj* case was stored, 'we will begin to study some well-known problems, which the masters of this game call *mansūbat*. The play of the game will be our only focus now, until you have both become masters.'

The next few days passed without event: in the mornings, Fitz feigned the absorption of the stack, and despite himself, enjoyed it. In the Keep they had moved on from oil painting to sculpture in terra cotta, and Fitz found that he had good hands for this, too.

The Keeper showed them a great number of examples, both in the gallery and from books in her library, and instructed them to start with the human shape. 'This,' she said, 'is the most familiar and therefore the most difficult.' Within days Fitz was making complex figures, and beginning to experiment with distended human forms, accentuating the length of their limbs, or drawing them to an almost wraith-like abstraction. Dina told him that they didn't look like people at all.

'They're the thoughts of people,' Fitz answered. 'What people would be, maybe, if they gave up their bodies for ideas.'

Dina scoffed, and left him.

True to his word, in the late afternoons the Master played *shatranj* with them. He treated Fitz and Dina as beginners, teaching them the names and meanings of the eight pieces in the back row, and then describing in detail how each of the pieces was able to move on the board, and what strengths and weaknesses these limitations conferred on them, both alone and in combination with the other pieces. Dina watched all this with detached interest, perhaps the effect of the loosening grip of stack, late in the afternoon each day, but perhaps too because she still retained some suspicion or reserve about the Master's tuition. Fitz concealed his knowledge of the game, and his knowledge of the beautiful board that was already, truly, his. As the Master began to work his way through the set problems of the ancient masters, Dina hardly said a word, and it was up to Fitz to respond to every new fact, to every question and invitation that the Master offered. This wasn't a burden; Fitz found the game engrossing, even when he was merely pretending the instruction was novel, the more so because it connected him to those long spring afternoons the year before, to Mr Ahmadi Senior and his gentle, quiet manner, to his home, to the smell of the wood and earth as he leaped from the roof of the well house and darted through the trees to reach the gate to his back garden.

The Master covered many *mansūbat* in their afternoon sessions. Always he would begin these sessions by reminding the children that, for a true *shatranj* master, the game is over before it begins. 'For a master, the possible moves are so well understood that the first motion implies the last. The master knows how the adversary will respond. Nothing is left to chance, and in this way the game has no true middle. The purpose of learning this *mansūba*, you who would be Master in my place, the purpose of learning all *mansūbat*, is to control the middle. The master who understands the middle, destroys it. And then the game is already ended.'

The Master began with Dilaram, but he taught many other problems as well. Each, like Dilaram, was not just a configuration of pieces on the board, not just a set of strategies for ending the game, but a story, too, by which the problem and its associated moves could be understood. In *ad-Dulabiya*, the waterwheel, two emerald horsemen chased the ruby *shāh* around the board in two or even three large circles, before capturing him on his own home square; this, said the Master, recalled the history of the campaigns of Tamburlaine, whose armies circled the world like a great scythe, reaping men, until the day that Tamburlaine himself died of a fever not far from his home. Or, again, he showed them the Arrow, a problem in which the ruby *rokh*, the chariot, struck across the length of the whole board, removing a single emerald *sarbaz*, or foot soldier, and so set the stage for the conclusion of the game. This problem the Master illustrated with the story of a strange coincidence, in which a man crushed with debt fired a single arrow into the clouds, which, carried by the winds across his city, over many houses and across the river, struck the malicious creditor who was bent on ruining him, and so saved both him and his family from destruction. Day after day, problem after problem, the Master unfolded the predicament on the board, narrated the story that lay behind it, and explained its meaning before showing his two pupils how to bring the game to a close.

Given the origins of *shatranj* in warfare, it was not surprising to Fitz that these problems – many of which he already knew – should recall famous battles or bear the name of the kings who had fought them. One, which the Master called *al-Nadirah*, described a situation where one player – unable to penetrate the defences of the other, and locked into repetitive and circular play – at last seemed to relent in the attack, giving up his *wazir*, or counsellor. The purpose of this sacrifice was only to open the second player's fortified defence, after which, despite the loss of his *wazir*, the first player was able quickly to pick off his opponent's pieces and force his *shāh* to his knees. The Master told them how Shapur, crown prince of Persia, had been playing *shatranj* outside the gates of the city of Hatra during a long siege. Able neither to win the game nor to penetrate the city, but advised that the daughter of the city's king, known as al-Nadirah, had fallen passionately in love with him, he sent her a messenger promising to marry her if she should defy her father and open the gates. When later that night the gates were opened, Shapur stood up

356

from his game, saying that he had seen how both the game and the city could be won, and that the tale of both was ended. He destroyed the city of Hatra and executed its king; but the daughter he married, as he had promised, before he executed her, too, as a punishment for betraying her father.

On other afternoons, the Master showed them *mansūbat* of a less bloody character. One problem that Fitz particularly loved was the story of the wren's love for her mate. The Master began with a *tabiyya* in which one player had layered the *shāh* with two perimeters of defensive protection. 'This,' said the Master, 'is the nest of the wren.' The pieces were so configured that no side could attack the other without sustaining unacceptable losses, but the Master showed Fitz and Dina how the first player, safe in the 'nest', could exploit the mobility of the *wazir* to lure the other player to launch feeble attacks with petty pieces, trifles the loss of which appeared to pose no risk. Again and again these pawns were sent forward, and again and again the first player nibbled them up with little twitches of the *shāh*. Eventually the *wazir* had fed its mate so many of these little pieces that the *shāh* was able to fly from the nest, attack the second player, and end the game.

Fitz delighted in these afternoon sessions with the Master. He forgot that he was not at home; or, he felt that he was again at home. He committed to memory every one of the hundreds of problems – those that he knew already, and those that he did not – and by night he rehearsed them in his head, lying in his bed in the dark tower with the pieces arranged on an imaginary board. Quite naturally, the problems presented on the board began to stand as symbols not only for the stories that the Master told to explain them, but also for all the other things he had encountered in the day, in each of his lessons. The movement of the tides and the currents of the world's oceans, the circulation of populations within the walls of a city, the spread of a virus throughout the human body, the charging and discharging of a battery, the flow of green in a painting or the gesture of the body in a model he had worked from clay – no matter what it was, it began to meld with the structure and the strategies of the problems that the Master presented each afternoon, in the quiet withdrawal of his study in the north tower of the Mastery. This, *this* was the master language that controlled and explained all the other languages, the world of pure symbols that offered a key to all other knowledge. Fitz began to think that, if he but understood these problems and memorized them, he would know everything that he needed to know about the world, and how to act within it. Any new discovery, thereafter, would be nothing more than a recognition, like saluting a trusted friend.

The Master's study was a round room, the top storey of a round tower that rose from the north-east corner of his court. This turret was taller than the court's other tower, the square tower in which Fitz's room was located, and it was also a great deal more substantial. Four round windows, set high in the high walls, allowed very little light to the large space; the Master worked, instead, by the glow of a small gas lamp, and – Fitz supposed – in the winter by the light of a fire. The room was lined with bookshelves, which transformed the large circular space, at least at eye level, into a twelve-sided, wooden frame; the bays, each containing eight shelves, were numbered on plaques at each head, giving almost the impression that the room was a large clock. The bookshelves themselves appeared to be largely filled with manuscripts; the Master waved to them carelessly at one of their meetings, in answer to a query of Fitz's, saying only, 'the works of my predecessors in the Office of Master'. Fitz wondered if the Master had read them. His desk he always kept bare, anyway when the children were there, nor did Fitz ever see him open one of the many drawers that, on his side, made up the desk's pedestals. In short, unlike the other Officers of the Heresy, who seemed to thrive on presenting the children with art, instruments, books, manuscripts, designs, models, visual puzzles, even weapons – the Master appeared to be much happier working with words, ideas, and the sorts of questions that Fitz and Dina could conjure in their own imaginations.

Except for the board – the gilt and silvered, jewelled, and finely carved board, over-written with ancient verses and set with pieces each one of which might have purchased a kingdom. But what made it more precious, by far, was that Fitz knew that it was his, that in taking it from the cupboard on that first afternoon, and setting it on the table before them, the only object of any interest to the Master in the whole room, the Master was making a gesture to Fitz not only clear, but secret. In the simple laying of the board on the table, it was as if he told him, 'You and I will communicate, now, silently, in this language, and everything that we say to one another on this board will be significant.' In that single moment and in that simple gesture, he laid the foundations for a poetry of understanding with which Fitz could struggle each night, running over the individual moves and the patterns that they created as if they were so many verses, so many lines or stanzas, the constituent coordinates of a complex song that spoke to him of fate, of love, of war, of hope, of patience, of ambition, of daring, of understanding. He saw that the board was an endlessly capacious and precise instrument for thinking, on which one could calculate and conclude solutions for every problem faced by the human mind or heart; moreover, if the board was an instrument in that sense, in another sense, too, it worked like an instrument – that is, like a violin, or a harp, some rhapsodic medium through which the most beautiful music could be created and enjoyed.

Fitz was thus not surprised when, one afternoon about a fortnight after the afternoon sessions with the Master had begun, he interrupted their discussion of *mansūbat* somewhat early, with a strange question.

'Why, my Apprentices, do masters sit down opposite one another at the board to play?'

'To win,' said Dina, immediately.

'But if the *tabiyya* is as we have shown it to be, and if each of the players knows the skill and knowledge of the other, then the game is already ended before it can begin.'

'That is correct,' said Dina.

'So why bother playing at all?'

'To prove that the game is as it should be. To prove that one is the best.'

'There are *mansūbat* that I have not yet shown you. These are intractable and insoluble problems. They lead to situations in which neither player can win the game. The Spider's Web, the Whirlpool, the Desolation – these problems describe situations where the play cannot continue because it must always continue. Would two masters sit down opposite one another, if they believed that the game would end in this way?'

'Never. No general would lead an army into a field where neither side could claim the victory. Even a poet would not begin to tell a story that had no end. The general would choose another field. The poet would choose another story.'

The Master sat back in his tall chair. He took off his tall hat and set it on the desk by his side. Fitz had rarely seen him without his hat. For the first time, he noticed that the Master's thick, black hair had a streak of grey growing through its centre. He regarded the children quietly for a few moments.

'And you, little brother?' he asked, a wry smile on his face as he called Fitz by Dina's preferred epithet. 'What do you think?'

'A true master loves the game for its own sake. To the true master,' said Fitz, 'the movements of the pieces on the board speak the language of birds in flight, or the stars in motion. Like the constellations they whisper the secrets of things that grow and die and grow again. A true master longs to hear this language, and if the true master wins at a game, it will not be long before the game begins again. A true master is always playing, and cannot help but play.'

'No,' said Dina, sitting forward. She was agitated.

'I will tell you a story that my grandfather told me,' said the Master. 'For this board belonged to him before it was – before this time. The wood from which this board was made was cut from a tree in a very distant place, in a city that is as old as any city on the earth. At the same time that this board was made, from the same wood another beautiful thing was made – a machine of unimaginable intricacy and wonder. Every piece of that machine was crafted from the wood of this tree; some pegs and joints from the hardest parts of the heartwood, other more flexible working arms from the pliant boughs and the new growth that the tree, when cut, wore as it were upon its waist. This wondrous machine was called the Great Loom, and upon it stories were made by an artist whose hands were equal to its potential, whose vision was equal to the instrument he wielded. Ordinary weavers work at looms of ingenious construction, and they, too, can produce beautiful work – carpets, tapestries, cloths of different kinds. But their work is slow, and the constraints on their creativity, labouring with an everyday instrument, are many. Sitting at the Great Loom, a true master can weave a story that – believe me, for my grandfather who was very wise said so to me – a story that you would not wish to end. Do you think a weaver would sit at such a loom, if there were a risk that the work could never be completed?'

Dina was silent. She was furious.

'Yes,' said Fitz. 'But I think more than this. I think the true weaver, like the true master of this game here on the desk before us, always hopes to begin a story that will not end.'

'What could be more satisfying than the end?' said Dina, sharply.

'Let me show you a *mansūba* of this kind,' said the Master. 'It is called the Giant's Almanac.' He began to rearrange the pieces on the board in front of him. 'You will see an image of the Great Loom of which I spoke before. I need but to set this piece –'

'No!' cried Dina. She reached forward and with the whole of her forearm swept the pieces from the board. They clattered on the table. The Master and Fitz were both shocked; although the Master didn't move, Fitz, startled, sat back in his chair, which scraped against the floor. Dina was evidently embarrassed by what she had done.

She stood. She seemed about to say something. Instead she left the room. They heard her feet on the stairs, and then – nothing.

The moment the sound of Dina's footsteps had died away, everything about the Master changed. His brows clamped and furrowed, his eyes narrowed, and he appeared to be grinding his teeth. His hands began to shake, and Fitz feared that he might be about to have some sort of seizure. Fitz sat up, as if he might stand and offer the Master his arm, or get him a drink. But the Master motioned for him to be still. His hands danced in the air, as if he were planning or projecting something. They made sharp and jerky movements, the stutterings of ideas or actions undertaken in contrary minds, the lunges of a man at war with himself and with the world.

'We haven't got long,' he said at last, gasping out the words. Fitz hadn't realized that he had been holding his breath all the while. 'They'll come for me in a few – minutes, at the most. The Heresy has plenty of prisons – no end of prisons – but there's only one cell, here, where they can hope to hold me. It's in the high tower in the south-west corner of the House of the Rack. Unlike your room, unlike this room, it has no hatch in the ceiling – of course. And the windows are barred – there's no way in except by the key. But it has another door, to the north, one that opens on the air;

the drop to the court below is more than two hundred feet, and prisoners usually don't exit that way by choice. When the time comes, you'll have to get me out that door. I don't know how; you'll have to dream up something.' While he was talking, the Master had collected the pieces Dina had scattered on the table, and had begun to rearrange them on the board. With a few focused adjustments, he finished.

'This teaching, child – it has kept you safe. Meanwhile, I have made my preparations. The time will come very soon when this game – all of this – can be ended.'

Fitz was dazed. Outside, at the bottom of the tower stairs, there was shouting.

'For now, child, I am sorry, that while I am locked in the Rack's prison, I cannot protect you. Trust the Jack, trust the Keeper; since we have returned to the Heresy, they have been my friends. They'll be yours. Which of the Apprentices will help you?'

'Navy. Dolly.' He hesitated. He wanted to say Dina's name.

'No,' said the Master, reading his thoughts, 'not Dina. She is – too angry. Call on the others for help, then, if you need them. You *must* manage until a week from tonight. Until your birthday.'

*My birthday.* He had forgotten. *When I come of age. They will come for me.*

'Just a week,' said the Master. 'Whatever you do, don't eat the stack – you'll need –'

'I haven't been eating it for the last few weeks,' said Fitz.

The Master was stunned. For a few moments he was silent. Footsteps sounded on the stairs. It reminded Fitz of his dream.

The Master held his hands out over the board. 'Do you see this? This *mansūba* – the last one I wanted to show you?'

Fitz nodded, staring hard at the pieces, noting them.

The Master moved one of the ruby pawns, and with emphasis placed it in its correct spot. 'Here,' he said. 'This is it. Remember it. It is the key that unlocks everything.'

The door burst open. The Registrar led the way, accompanied by the Rack and the Sweeper.

'My Apprentice will be expected at dinner,' said the Master, with sudden and elegant composure, as he rose behind the desk. His agitation was gone. He had put on his hat.

The Sweeper made way for Fitz to go. He was halfway to the door when the Master called him.

'Fitzroy.' He turned. The Sweeper, the Rack and the Registrar looked from Fitz to the Master, with suspicion. 'Aren't you forgetting something?' the Master asked.

For an instant Fitz was at a loss. And then he noticed his lamp in the Master's hand, its leather covers bound tight with cord. He had forgotten it on the rocks, amid the rising of the dawn, after that long night passed shivering at the tombs. He had forgotten it, but the Master had not. Now he tossed it across the desk in a low arc; Fitz caught it in the pit of his stomach, with both hands.

'My lamp,' he said, for the Rack's frowning benefit. 'Thanks.'

He passed out of the door and down the stairs, straining to hear what was going on in the room behind him – but there was nothing. At the bottom of the stairs he passed others – Fellows of the Heresy – going up. They were carrying large canvas bags.

Fitz crossed the empty court to his staircase, and on shaking legs climbed the steps to his room. He opened the door and stood in the doorway. It had never seemed so empty; its emptiness had never seemed so much like emptiness.

A change had happened in him, without his noticing. Playing every afternoon on the *shatranj* board, he had begun to feel at home in the Heresy; but not because he *was* at home, rather because it *reminded* him of home. It was all as Navy had said. He didn't fit here, any more than the Master did; and that's what he could do for them, for all of them. He could remind them of the thing that they had lost, the place that they had left, the home that they were missing.

He sat at the little desk. No books were piled at its edge. He opened the drawer that lay in front of him. No papers, no pens were stored inside it. He had no drawings, no stories, no keepsakes. At home he had preferred this, had begged Clare to take the furniture out of his room and allow him to keep as little as possible in his few drawers and his cupboard. At the end of the day he took pleasure in the quiet and simplicity of his meagre living. He could fall asleep happily, knowing that he shared his little room with two books, eight articles of clothing, a pen and notebook, and a pair of binoculars. His little lamp. Now, sitting alone in his tower room, waiting for the bell to peal six, for the first time he knew why.

*I didn't need anything else, because I had Clare. I didn't want anything else.*

The less clutter had lain in the way, the more easily he had heard her stories. He had seen other children's bedrooms: piles of clothes, and toys, and even litter on the floors, old ramshackle shelves loaded with unnecessary, sometimes unwanted stuff, their chests of drawers and wardrobes and cupboards and closets crammed with clothes, some of which they had outgrown but couldn't quite surrender, some of which they had never liked, and wouldn't even try on. Other children had hand-me-downs and souvenirs, tat from flea markets and pound shops, old schoolwork they hadn't enjoyed and weren't proud of, the packaging from birthday presents, pieces of lives they hardly cared for or had forgotten – if they ever lived them at all. Fitz had never wanted any of it, because he had had Clare, and her songs, and her stories, and her pictures. Her endless capacity for making. Everything she had ever said, or sung, every odd noise she had made in her workshop or in the garden, the least tread of her careful slippers on the squeaking floorboards of the downstairs hallway, had had its own space in his notice. Each one of these sensations now hung, framed, on the clean walls of his memory.

Now the clean, clean walls of his memory were all he had left.

*I don't even have the silver jay.*

The bell pealed six.

*Clare. Clare. Clare. Clare. Clare. Clare.* How would he make it a week. *I won't even make it a day.*

Fitz pulled himself to his feet, and took up the jug of fresh water that had been left for him on the window sill. He poured some water into the laver, and dipped the edge of a cloth in it. Slowly, as if he were wiping away a stain, or clearing a canvas, he began to wash his face. He scrubbed every part of it with an even, methodical motion. In his head he heard the music of oars on the river, the over-arcing swirls of unfurled petals in the close buds of roses; like them his hand turned, holding the cloth, wiping the dirt from his face and clearing a day's grime from his neck. After, he cleaned his hands, first the backs, then the palms, and his forearms. He poured the excess water from the laver back into the pitcher, wiped out the bowl with his cloth, and set them together back on the sill.

He knew he didn't have long until the meal would begin, but something in the air, or in the light, held him in a kind of suspension, as if he were a fly trapped in amber, or a fish snagged in a net. His hands moved over the buttons of his felt coat like priests at their libations; he adjusted his belt, drew down and smoothed the long drop of his coat to his knees. He brushed his trousers. His slippers had on them the dust of one or another of the courts; with deliberate strokes, he swept it away. There was no mirror in his room, but he hardly needed one anyway; he saw himself in his mind, and with careful fingers he picked a parting in his hair, and smoothed each strand so that it lay evenly over his forehead, and upon his ears.

At last he was ready. He pulled the door of his room shut behind him, and paused on the top step of the tower stairs. The stairs had a sound like the inside of a shell, the sound of the sea as if heard from a great distance. He walked down into it.

Fitz arrived in the hall and took his place just as the other Prents were sitting. Already the gong had sounded, and the Officers – all save the Master – had begun First Feeding. It was obvious that the others, too, knew something was wrong, that they sensed in the air that same thickening, that same congestion full of omen that Fitz had felt. On his approach to the table, he had seen them whispering, heard them sharing rumours – that the Officers had imprisoned the Master, that the Master had tried to eject the Rack from his office, that the Heresy was under fresh attack. Fitz hadn't heard every syllable of the fevered, half-voiced words. But now, the meal begun, no one spoke at all, not even Navy. Across from him, Dina's face showed no trace of the anger in which she had left the Master's study, but her eyes never met Fitz's; they seemed to be still, fixed on her plate. After a few minutes, she set down her fork and put her fingertips to the table on either side of her plate.

'Eat up, rabble,' she said, her words like metal in a mouth of metal. 'I'm tired.'

She pushed herself to her feet, stepped out of her place, and disappeared from the hall. The moment her back was turned, from the opposite end of the table Navy rose and scurried to her place.

'First Prent,' she said, quietly, but firmly, while she sat. No one demurred.

Second followed First Feeding. The Servers danced their complex dance, delivering platters and tureens, taking away plates and cutlery, each spinning round the other, fleets of them coming and going from the hall. Out of the corner of his eye, while he ate and did not eat, Fitz monitored their regular motion. Every hair on his neck stood at attention; no spoon touched a bowl at his table, no hand reached into a basket for a crust of bread, no cup met a lip but he marked it, and noted it down. From the Officers' table he caught occasional words where they rode high on the flood of ambient noise and bustle: 'never again' he heard the Commissar say, 'too lenient' in the big voice of the Jack, 'I'll know soon' in the thin rasp of the Rack. Fitz gathered all this motion and noise, every discrete observation, and parsed it all.

When the attack finally came, he was ready for it. From the far end of the hall, two Serfs began to cross the long floor. The line they took between two of the long benches was unlike the motion of every other Serf. In their hands they carried no platters. Their feet did not dance quick steps between feeders. On and on, inexorably, they came. Beyond Navy's bowed head, though without looking directly at them, Fitz could sense with perfect clarity their meaning and their aim. He breathed, and straightened. The others at his table sensed it. The Officers had turned, and broken off their conversations. By the time the first Serf struck the gong, the hall was already hushed. The second Serf stood by Fitz's side.

'No,' whispered Fingal with ferocious intensity. 'No.'

The Serf standing next to Fitz was a tall man with a face that looked as if it had been hacked out of stone. Even his beard, grey and square, gave nothing away. His eyes were sand. In his hand he grasped a large handbell, brass with a thick oak handle. To the astonishment of the entire hall, he held it up and rang it – three sharp, sacred peals.

Fingal stood up.

'Sit down, boy,' said the Rack in a withering hiss. Fingal sat.

The Bellman waited for the last peal to cease shuddering in the brass of the bell. When the sound had died fully away, he turned to the table and set the bell directly in front of Fitz. Hundreds of eyes watched his face. His own, he thought, were among them.

'Fitzroy Worth, Apprentice to the Master, you are called to your Black Wedding. Do you accept?'

'He can't do it,' bellowed the Jack. 'He won't even survive the preparations.'

No one answered him.

Fitz had been staring at his plate. Now he drew his head up, level, and looked directly before him. Everything in Navy's eyes, in the round turn of her lips, in the white tips of her fingers where they pressed the table's oak top told him no, told him to resist, told him to fight, to run, to hide.

'Yes,' he said. 'Yes, I accept.'

*Let it be next week.*

'What must I do?'

'The wedding party will assemble at daybreak at the Palace of the Heresiarch. Mark well the hour, for the game is already ended.'

The Bellman turned again and – joined by his fellow – strode the length of the silent hall. They departed through the far door.

Uproar followed: benches were overturned, plates and glasses dashed heedlessly to the floor, Serfs sent sprawling as hundreds of Fells, Offs and Prents rose as one to their feet. Fitz had just time to grab the wedding bell by the handle, and clutch it to his chest, before the Jack lifted him from his place and carried him from the hall.

# 14

# *The Black Wedding*

'Twice twenty curses on that stupid halfwit of a Master!' shouted the Jack. He was pacing, then ranting, then pacing and ranting in the upper gallery of the Jackery. The Keeper slouched in a low armchair before a stifled fire, her legs splayed out before her. She had only just shuffled into the room, silent and dejected, and was still dressed in her black gown from Feeding. Fitz sat on the stool by the door, where the Jack had deposited him after carrying him up the steep staircase, slung over his shoulder.

He didn't dare move. He didn't want to move.

'I still think he can succeed,' said the Keeper. 'The Heresy needs a new Master, and this boy already has ability.'

'No,' said Arwan, turning, and lunging with his eyes. 'He can't succeed. Even if he were to spend all night in the Sensorium rehearsing the forty temptations, even if he had mastered the Ten Modes of Agrippa, even if he had logged a thousand hours of mimesis practice, even then – he simply isn't *old* enough to withstand it. The others want him to fail, and Habi let it happen. We'll never know – *he* will never know – what this boy might have been.'

The Jack paced the long wooden boards of the attic. He could only stand upright in the very centre of the room, where the pitch of the roof was highest, and it was in this space that he turned and turned, shaking the rafters with every step of his hulking frame. As Fitz watched him pacing, his own heart rising and falling as the Jack and the Keeper debated his future, he wished there was somewhere in the Heresy – even just one place – where he felt *he* could stand up.

'Why does it matter to you,' said Fitz, 'if I fail?'

The Jack wheeled on his heel, and stared at him.

'I mean,' said Fitz, unsure of himself, 'what happens then? What happens to me? What happens to you? Why does it matter?'

The Jack was at a loss for words. The Keeper answered for him. 'You picked Dina, child. She will be at the Wedding, there at the end; if you are not able to sustain yourself in the face of temptation, if you are not able to preserve yourself when confronted with doubt, if you cannot withstand the onslaughts of illusion and of paradox, then it will be a mercy for her to cut the cords.'

'To cut the cords that bind me to the mast?' Fitz asked.

'To cut the cords that bind you to this world,' answered the Keeper. 'If you succumb to temptation, to doubt, to confusion – then you will lose your grip on your mind, and you will not regain it after. It has happened before.'

'The Riddler?' asked Fitz.

'Among others.'

'And why should it matter to you, if I fail?' Fitz had been biting his lip so hard it bled.

'Because we have staked everything on your success,' said the Jack. 'Not just our position among the Officers. As if *that's* worth anything. Half the Officers think you're some kind of messiah, a redeemer come to save the Heresy from itself, restore the Kingdom, and usher us into a new golden age. Some of the Officers are so overdosed on their own stack they actually believe that cult stuff. Some of them want you to succeed; some of them clearly want you to fail. It was all we could do to get you here alive. But Habi, Habi had a better story. Habi convinced me, gave me some of that dust he peddles, *hope*. Habi said maybe there was a chance, if you came here, if you worked with him, that through you we could *change* the Heresy. Maybe we could heal that which was broken. Maybe we could look at ourselves in the mirror again.'

Fitz looked from the Keeper to the Jack, and back again, blinking.

'Broken?' he asked.

'He hasn't told you,' said Arwan. A new rage seemed to kindle in his thought, and his eyes burned with it.

'Ignorance is wisdom, Arwan,' said the Keeper. 'Whatever we don't tell him tonight, the Rack can't use to torture him tomorrow.'

'That's the way farmers treat their lambs, Agatha,' the Jack spat. 'That's abattoir talk. He has a right to know.'

*A right to know what?*

'What do you think the Heresy is?' asked the Jack. 'What do you think we *do* here?'

Fitz sat up on the stool. He looked around. It seemed a trick question. Even here in the attic gallery of the Jack's House, the room was packed with books and papers. The Jack had been using them, surely – his pen lay on the desk. Fitz had seen his writings on the wall. He was a mathematician. He was doing research, or –

'You teach,' Fitz said. 'You are teachers. You are training children. The Apprentices.'

'Yes, that's what we tell you,' said the Jack. 'But think about it. What are we teaching you to do?'

'To take your places. To become Officers. To lead the Heresy, if it comes to that.'

'And which one of the Apprentices has become an Officer? Was I an Apprentice? Was Agatha, here, apprenticed to the Keeper, back in the day? Where are all the other Apprentices whom you suppose we trained, over the years? Where have they all gone?'

Fitz moved his mouth. He didn't know what to say.

'And all the Fellows who sit in the hall at breakfast, at lunch and at dinner each day – where do you suppose they *work* when they're not chomping their way through First, and Second, and Third Feeding? Where do you suppose they go? What do you suppose they do? What do you suppose they are *for*?'

'Arwan,' said the Keeper, quietly. 'You're not helping him.'

'No, Agatha, I'm not,' said the Jack. 'But I'm treating him like a *person*.' He stared hard at Fitz. Fitz wasn't sure he wanted to be treated like a person. 'Anyway, they mixed so much raw stack in his plate tonight he'll be lucky if he remembers his own name tomorrow night, much less our conversation. Lucky fool.'

*Ignorantia sapientia.*

'The thing that makes the Heresy the Heresy is that we who run it, we who teach in it, we who are its Officers, we take an unflinching view of what is real. We hold no illusions about the

375

world, or about ourselves. Nor do we ever tickle your senses with magic, or strain your credulity with deceptions, sleights, feints, phantasms. We have tried and tested every possible representation there is, and practise constantly the refutation of illusions and false coherence. You know this much from the time you have spent here. Our goal is simple: to put this clarity of vision and understanding to work in the world, for our own benefit. We own many corporations – some legally vested in the Heresy by name, others operated through the hands of our members. Governments come to us for advice; and if they don't, we remind them – by toppling them – that they must. But this is straightforward; these are the clumsy levers of power that any fool, that the Riddler himself, could operate.'

Fitz sat on his hands, unsure where the Jack was going.

'We control society around us a little more thoroughly than that. Tell me,' said the Jack, 'if you wanted to change a river – change the nature of its flow, the kind of water that ran in it, the sort of life that lived in it, everything about it – would you start upstream, at its source, or downstream, at its mouth?'

Fitz imagined a river and the water flowing through it.

'Upstream,' he said. 'Anything you do at the source will be carried down to the rest of the river.'

'Imagine a tree is a river, except that its course lies not across the land, but in time. It starts as a seed, a shoot, a sapling; but over time it flows into itself, reaching its sea at the moment that it pours its last burst of vital force into the ripening of its last fruit. That piece of fruit, at the moment it drops from the tree, is the latest mouth of the river of that tree, spreading from its whole life's course into the ocean of its end. If you wanted to shape the course of that tree, where would you intervene? When would you intervene?'

'At the beginning,' said Fitz. 'At the root. At the seed.'

'So it is with society. So it is with the Heresy. If you want to control the man, teach the boy. Raise the girl, and you will own the woman she becomes. If you want power among any people, understand its children. Shape the seed, and the fruit is yours; mould the children, train them, and they will grow into the adults you require.

'We're not training Apprentices, boy. We're running experiments on you. We don't teach; we test. Do you want to know what the Heresy really is? We are in the business of power. We want it, so we create it. We create it by finding out how children work, so that we can use that knowledge to control them. We feed you stack and set you tasks, and then we study you to find out how you complete them, and what sort of person you become. When we have stripped you of every last shred of imagination, when we have scoured and sanded you down, blasting away your ideals, your principles, your passions, your sentiments, when we have robbed you of your creativity and walked off with it, when we have wrecked and wasted the last of your dreams, then – *then* – we send you to a Black Wedding. If you survive it, we give you a job, and we use you for the rest of your life, because like a knife that has been forged in the heart of some black sun, then – when the forging is at last complete, and you are hard, when you are *hard* – and not until then – then you can be trusted. Trusted not to think for yourself, trusted not to resist. Trusted not to believe in anything, to stand up for anything. And if you don't survive – and you *won't* survive, you *can't* – then at least we don't have to clean up the mess.'

Fitz felt like he was going to throw up.

The Jack was staring at him with pure and consuming rage. '*That* is the Heresy,' he said.

'Stop,' said the Keeper.

*Stop*, Fitz didn't say.

Fitz knew he had begun to tremble, then shake, but he was aware of it in the way he might be aware of a storm on a dark night, when he was lying safe in his bed. The shaking wasn't him; his body wasn't his. All he knew of himself was the sense that he was far away. The nausea, the slack and listless paralysis that had crept over him while the Jack was ranting – this couldn't reach him. He was somewhere else.

'But you Apprentices – you're the tip of the iceberg. You have no real idea what we *really* do. Beneath the Heresy lies a network of dungeons, prisons, laboratories the likes of which you wouldn't believe. You kids, you know about the Offs, the Fells, the Serfs. You think you know everything. But you don't know about the Subjects. You never *think* of the Subs. We keep them like cattle – not the kind you see pastured on hills, but the kind you *don't* see, the kind farmers lock in cages so tight they have to be cut free when they're slaughtered. Down below, in the rock, in the cellars, a dedicated army of Fells tests them morning, noon and night. We feed them strange things, things that aren't even food; we starve them of sleep; we needle and tempt and distract them, we wreck their concentration; we show them visions; we addict them to everything you can imagine; and all the time we watch them, measure them, score them, then rack and poison them again. And why? Because we want to know how children *work*. We don't just want to know who they are; we want to know everything it is possible to know about what they *might be*. We want to know *what we can turn them into*. And in the dark, in the cellars of the Heresy – oh, in the Hell of the Heresy, *it is possible to know it all*. We want to be able to control every last thing about a child, down to the least wish, the tiniest scrap of a fear, the shred of a half-dreamed dream. And we're *winning*. Give us ten more years, twenty, and there will be no possibility, no eventuality in the whole freedom of a child's life or imagination that we have not strapped, shocked, strobed, strafed, stripped and stifled. And *sold*. We will *own* the children. We will *own* the human race.'

*Those arms. Those reaching arms in the well of the Sad King. How did I forget those arms?*

'What does any of this have to do with me?'

The Jack rounded on him, stared at him. His eyes, boiling with fury, spat fire.

'Are you serious? Are you asking me that?' he bellowed.

'Arwan,' said the Keeper, 'please.'

'Yes, I am,' said Fitz. 'I can't save these children. I can't save my friends. I can't save any of you. I can't even save my mother. Or myself.'

'*Everything* depends on you. You are the Heresy's most important experiment, its greatest test in a thousand years.'

'Why?'

'Because, child, we are in the business of breaking souls, crushing hearts, grinding the imagination into powder. We anaesthetize. We stupefy. We stultify. We enervate. We drain and we burn. Some children take to it very readily indeed. Try Fingal; he craves brutality, sucks it down like milk. And he's a lovely boy, but don't ask Russ to take a stand on a principle; he'd sooner prove a theorem than lay down his life for his friend. Other children are harder to tame, harder to break. We have to try. You think it's been easy testing Padge? Cracking through the thick, lustrous glaze of Payne's love for herself? Do you honestly think Dolly will ever be dead behind the eyes? That quick, indomitable, self-doubting, but ultimately dauntless girl? And don't even get me started on Navy. These children have colossal spirits. They're titans. They're magnificent. The best there is.'

'Then why – why do you bring them to the heart of – why try to train them? –' Fitz was at a loss.

'The taller the tree, the harder it falls.'

'I don't understand,' said Fitz.

'What the Jack is trying to explain,' said the Keeper, 'is that often it is the noblest and most heroic spirits who, when they are broken, become the greatest villains. And if you can turn *them*, you can turn anyone.'

*And I –*

'And you are the best of all, child.' The Keeper was almost whispering.

'I'm nobody,' said Fitz. *I'm not smart, or knowledgeable, quick, musical. I'm not Dolly, or Russ. I'm not Navy, or even Payne.*

'You are the heir to the Kingdom,' said the Jack, 'who could not be found. You, who walked into the trap, *knowing* it was a trap, without a second thought. At the Sad King you could have betrayed anyone, anything. Everyone – everyone – protects themselves at the Sad King. Not you. Instead you gave yourself.'

*She told you that. But it's not true. I betrayed Clare in the end. I stayed. I felt something. I felt at home.*

'You, boy, are the lamp in the night. If we break you, we have fulfilled everything. *Everything.*'

'And if you don't?'

'Then maybe there's hope for us after all,' the big man answered. He laughed. It was a curt, dry laugh, with no feeling in it. 'But we will not fail.'

Fitz sat, stunned, crowded, unable to think or to feel, unable to move.

'I'm not telling you this to scare you,' said the Jack.

The Keeper snorted.

'I'm telling you this to save you.' The loft gallery was lit by two blazing lanterns, hung from old hooks in the rafters, one to either side. Their light glowed like rich, rotten yolks against the white walls. Till now the Jack's face, in this light, had seemed menacing, twisted tight as a rope, but now the light appeared to soften him. He had come to stand over his desk, hands tightened into fists and his broad, muscular knuckles ledged on its polished wood surface, each plane of contact a confrontation. He stared at them, breathing slowly, measuring gulps of air as he drew his lungs in, and out.

He didn't look up. 'Run,' said the Jack quietly. 'Run if you can.'

Fitz hardly got to his feet. He pivoted on the tips of his toes, and without lifting his head or straightening his back, ducked into the stairwell that led down by many turnings to the Jack's court below. Where it thudded in his chest like the slap of surf on stone, his heart seemed at once engorged and empty, a voracious mouth biting out big chunks of air. Every cell in his body, from his marrowless bones and muscles flimsy and loose as shrunken petals, to his skin that yawned with hurt and fear, seemed to gape for substance, for some sort of certitude. He had felt more stable falling through the sky above London, more stable crashing from track to track on the hopper. Fitz ran his hand on the bannister, and squared his feet with the treads as he went down. The dark wood of the stairwell, unlit and stained with the traffic of centuries, seemed for a moment reassuring. How many had passed this way!

*How many had passed this way, up and down this staircase, up and down every staircase in the Heresy, as if on tracks leading – where? To one place, to the one thing, to this simple recognition, that the track is all there is.*

At the base of the stairs Fitz laid his palm flat on the door frame and stood, breathing, trying to hold the world in one place. His chest, his head swam. Thoughts shouldered into his head.

*They're using me. They're using all of us. They're even using themselves.*

Fitz ran into the dark. He didn't care where he was going, and gave it no thought. If his eyes saw the ground before him, they committed the benefit of that sensation to his feet and not to his understanding. If his ears heard the report of his feet on stone, or if his jangled nerves registered the shudder of his staggering steps, he knew nothing of it – only that his body continued to stagger in a kind of sustained fall through court after court, past the dizzying pillars and buttresses and beams and arches and sills and cornerstones and bricks and posts and lamps and copings and every hard and solid thing from which the buildings of the Heresy had been fashioned, on which they had been founded and from which they were raised. The concrete reality of them, irrefutable and inexorable as the end that lay before him, threatened to grind him like a mill, and he knew only that he wanted, as the Jack had said, to run.

*To run, but not like a river – like the wind, that is its own master.*

The further he went, the darker the courts became. At first lighted windows and the lamps slung on posts had illuminated every paved stone of every court; now in the outer courts, and then among the outbuildings within the inner skirtings of the grounds, Fitz found himself on gravelled paths among shrubs and trees, winding through paths where he had to feel and hear, rather than see, his way. As he slowed, and pushed against the growth, the darkness, and the thick pungency of musk rose and lilac, lavender, honeysuckle and mint, he came gradually back to himself. Turn by turn, his senses settled, and he touched with his hands, and saw with his eyes, and smelled and tasted and heard that which was before him and around him on every side.

He found himself standing beside a dark path outside the walls of the Registry. His gown like the night had slipped off his shoulders and was trailing in long grass; above the tall stems where they wafted in the light of a new moon swayed stiff heads of seed.

A slight chill of damp brushed his ankles where the morning's rain, collected in the roots and thick stems of the grass below, had begun to seep into his socks. In the night air he heard the last of the autumn caterpillars moving through nearby leaves, their mouths rustling like another breeze within the breeze. On his lips the taste of mint, especially, gathered as he breathed. Everything in the near-stillness collected into itself. Everything seemed an arrow striking home.

A hand fell on his shoulder: twisted, tense and tight, its grasp was as sudden as it was final. At another moment he might have screamed with the jolt and shock of it; but now and in this place, his skin seemed to welcome the pain of the arrest as if it had expected it.

'Running away,' said the thin rasp of the Rack.

Fitz stood still, and said nothing. He concentrated on the pressure of the Rack's second, third and fourth fingers, which were digging into the soft flesh beneath his collarbone. The bruises that were forming beneath each of these fingers, like lamps in the night, both darkened and lightened the touch.

'You've been conspiring with the Master all along,' said the Rack. His thumb turned in Fitz's back with the motion of a slow screw, grinding its thread.

'No,' Fitz whispered.

'No,' the Rack answered. 'You're too weak for that. No, you're not worthy even of his conspiracy. You're a drone in the hive. He has been manipulating you.'

'No,' Fitz whispered again.

'Did you ever stop to wonder who your real parents are?'

Fitz was silent. The Rack's fingers kneaded his skin now, as if he were massaging Fitz's shoulder.

'Did you ever wonder how it was that Habi Ahmadi, of all people, came to be your neighbour in a tiny village in the middle of nowhere? Did you ever wonder whether those books you took from the library in the big house – perhaps, just maybe – they weren't just *your* choices? Maybe the books you thought you were choosing were set out for you, by someone else? Maybe you took one, now and again, that had been left on a table? Maybe the books to which you set your hand had been pulled out, just a little, from the shelf? Maybe the windows had been opened to let the light fall on particular titles?'

'No,' Fitz whispered. He thought of the shutters in Mr Ahmadi's library, of the drift of the sunlight as it moved across the shelves through the afternoon. It wasn't possible. The Rack put his other hand on Fitz's left shoulder. He ground his fingers into the bones and muscles around Fitz's neck, the grip so tight that he didn't try to pull away.

*A wrong move and he'll break my neck.*

'What were you learning from all those books?' asked the Rack. His voice was thin, a drill that cut into Fitz's ears the way a saw cuts into stone, with a piercing whine. 'What did they teach you? That you were special? That some extraordinary fate was waiting for you?'

Fitz's mind raced over the books he had borrowed from Mr Ahmadi's library: stories of adventure and ambition, stories of cunning, achievement and courage, of resolute determination in the face of adversity, of perseverance and endurance. Stories that taught him –

'Did you think your life was like a life in a story? Did you think some sort of magic would send you where you needed to go? That the author might intervene to save the main character? Did you feel the guiding hand of providence on your shoulder? You didn't even think you needed to try. You didn't even think you needed to care. You just *knew* in your heart that he would come for you.'

Fitz fought to keep his face still, to keep his cheeks, his lips, from quivering, and betraying him.

'Those stories taught you how to be a hero, didn't they?' The Rack was pushing harder again, on the nerves that ran along Fitz's collarbone and collected in his spine. The Rack needled and twisted them, prodded and rolled them beneath his fingertips, as if to say, 'Your pain is mine.'

'Didn't you ever want to ask yourself, who wants you to be a hero? Who benefits from these delusions you have about yourself?'

'No,' Fitz said. 'It isn't like that.' Every word he squeezed out between the bursts of pain that the Rack was inflicting on him. The relentless rolling of his tendons, of his nerves between thumb and forefinger was becoming excruciating. It reminded Fitz of children at school scraping knives against their teeth.

'Who benefits?'

'I don't want anything,' said Fitz. 'I just want to go home.'

'Of course you do,' hissed the Rack in his ear. 'That's why you pushed your mother away when she came to rescue you. Because you wanted so very much to go home. Because you wanted to go back to your quiet, ordinary, uneventful life, back to your lonely cottage with beetles and ferns and stones for friends.'

*But that wasn't real. She wasn't here.*

'Who benefits from your pathetic, self-loving ambitions?'

'I don't know,' Fitz answered.

'The Master benefits, or maybe his little girl – the one you sit in windows with, the one who tells you stories and holds your hand at Feeding.'

Fitz tensed. *His little girl.*

He knew before the Rack spoke that his shoulders had given him away.

'Oh, but didn't you realize that the Master was her father? That daddy and his daughter have been working on you, day and night? What else haven't you realized? What else don't you understand? Do you know what the word "grooming" means? Don't you understand that they have been *using* you? Don't you understand that you are just an *instrument*?'

'An instrument for what?' In the pain of the Rack's pressure on his tendons, on the back of his shoulder joints, Fitz was murmuring almost at random. The pain blazed in his awareness like a fire, blotting out everything else. He might have said anything; he wouldn't know.

'Don't you know that the Master is trying to destroy the Heresy? Do you pretend that this isn't what you discuss in your meetings? Do you dare? The Officers know that the Master frequently mentions our enemies, that he wants to set you up against the Heresy and undermine everything that it stands for.'

Now the Rack took between his thumbs and forefingers the ridge of muscle that ran along Fitz's shoulders, and pinched it.

Slowly, he tightened the pressure. Fitz had long since closed his eyes; in the darkness of his blindness, lights began to bloom, then to explode: pink, then red, then blue, pulsing and detonating with electric clarity.

'We'll talk further about this tomorrow, don't you think? When the Commissar is there with her syringes of stack, to focus your mind and your concentration; when the Registrar is there to make careful records of all your answers; when the Sweeper can join me, to piece it all together. We'll get to the bottom of the Master's plot. We'll scrape out of your greasy little shell every last scrap of meat, until there is nothing left.'

And then, as suddenly as he had taken hold of him, the Rack let him go. The pain in Fitz's shoulders still screamed and burned; the rest of his cramped muscles, contorted in his effort to shore up and support the violent tearing in his shoulders, he didn't dare try to move. Instead, paralysed and sweating, Fitz stood in the long grass beside the path and waited for the night to settle again like a blanket on his shivering body.

Slowly, like blood leaking from beneath a nail, night returned and the darkness reasserted itself. Where the drone of his own pain died away, the hum of the wind and the rustle of the grasses revived. Fitz tried a step, didn't fall, and tried another. He took to the path and followed it, slowly at first until he reached the high stone wall that ran round the whole of the grounds of the Heresy: rough, mortared and uneven, it had the look of immense depth, like a pier or a bulwark, and it extended in both directions long into the night, reaching as he knew a formidable compass. There would be no way out, here: he could neither climb over it, nor dig under it, tonight – not without being seen and stopped. And he was sure, too, that if the Rack had seen him in the garden, other eyes would be tracing his movements, even here, even in the dark. He reached out and touched the cool stones, and the grainy cast of the mortar that had oozed from between them. Walls were so final.

'Sssssssssss.'

Fitz's first thought was that he had stumbled on or disturbed a snake. For the second time since running from the Jack's gallery, he froze, his right palm still flat on the stone wall before him.

Again the low susurration, almost inaudible, cut through the yielding night. Fitz turned his head to the right, then slowly to the left. Before him the gravel path stretched along the wall as far as he could see, running a few metres beyond him behind a screen of dense shrubs. Nothing moved there. Between him and the courts of the Heresy lay nothing but open lawns; these were silent, too, and still. The long grass and the densely planted orchards through which he had earlier passed now lay far behind him, too far to carry so subtle a sound.

And then he saw it: the motley of the Riddler darkly shimmering in the grass before him, as if Fitz could somehow see him standing below the ground. He shook his head, trying to clear his eyes.

'Sssssssssss.'

A long rectangular patch of the grass seemed to lift slightly, then to open, and Fitz saw that it wasn't grass at all, but the illusion of grass; beneath the glass panel that he had taken for the lawn, the Riddler was beckoning to him, from only a metre or two away.

'Quickly,' whispered the Riddler. 'Wolves hunt in packs.'

Fitz ran towards the gap that the Riddler had opened in the lawn, fell to his side, and rolled into the void, twisting his torso so that his feet would drop into the hole before his body. He pushed against the soft turf edge with his stomach, controlling the short drop into the tunnel with his arms. Behind him, the Riddler let the glass pane fall noiselessly to.

'What is this place?' said Fitz, looking around. They seemed to be in a low sort of tunnel, the walls constructed of stone slabs not dissimilar to those of the perimeter wall of the Heresy, the floor gravel like the path outside. 'Is this part of the Sensorium?'

'Every artery runs with blood – not just the heart,' answered the Riddler.

Fitz nodded. It made a kind of sense.

The Riddler was unslinging his pack. With a single fluid gesture, he took it from his shoulder and scattered its contents on the floor of the tunnel. Fitz wasn't surprised to see the Five Fetters, each of the leather straps with its iron buckle and its burnished steel spikes. He might not have been surprised, but his chest constricted anyway.

'Why this, now? It's hardly the right time for a lesson,' he said.

'A bird cannot *fly* the nest until it *sees* the nest,' said the Riddler.

'Is the Heresy the nest?'

The Riddler spat on the gravel. He picked up one of the Gyves, and held it out. Fitz took it, still hesitating. Dark and mortared though they were, the walls around them glowed faintly with that luminescence that he had come to associate with the Sensorium.

He knew if he pressed his hands to the stones he would feel nothing but cool glass.

'They smell blood miles off,' said the Riddler. He tried to hand Fitz the second Gyve. 'Close the wound.'

*Wolves. Arteries. Blood.* Fitz stared at the Riddler, turning the words over in his head. The Officers would be coming for him – he knew that much. They would be looking for his weakness.

*Nest.*

'Are you talking about my mother?'

The Riddler raised his eyebrows, pursed his mouth, and tilted his head, as if in derision. 'As if boys had mothers,' he said.

Fitz threaded the strap of the first Gyve to his left ankle, and drew it tight, driving the spikes into the inner base of his leg. He had gritted his teeth, but he felt little – only a tiny prick, followed by the familiar dead weight in his mouth. His taste was gone. He took the other Gyve and the two Manacles from the Riddler. Each of them he strapped on and tightened, finding the points with ease, dreading the moment of loss but hardly noticing it when it finally arrived. The Riddler held the Collar. He didn't speak, but waited until Fitz was ready, then placed it with care round his neck, fitting it so that the central spike sat directly over his spine, the buckle lying to Fitz's right. He nodded with his eyes, and the Riddler began to draw it tight.

The explosions of thought torrented into his mind like ever, like breathing honey, like the thick slip of eternity into moment. He was growing accustomed to it, to the veering, blazing disorientation of it; he had even begun to like it, and thought of it as the fast rush of sense that a jumper might feel before the wings of the parachute opened, or a diver the moment before the plunge hit, and the water slugged the leap in its cocoon of deceleration and clarity. Fitz watched the rush wash over his mind as a storm rips across a flat and ready landscape, savouring the rip and slash of it that meant the eye was near.

'Fitz,' said the Riddler, 'Fitz, wake up.'

His face was there. Fitz held it for a moment, and smiled.

'Thanks,' he said.

'Guess where,' said the Riddler.

'Always here,' said Fitz, putting out his arms to grasp two soaring trunks, beeches by the look of them, standing close. Around him the Bellman's Wood lay still and quiet, muted in the moments before evening. It would soon be dark.

The Riddler was a long way off. Fitz could see his motley shuttling between trees as he sprinted away.

'Come on,' he said, into Fitz's ear. 'You don't have two seconds to rub together, not tonight.'

Fitz chased after him. He tried to shout to him, to ask where they were going, but there were leaves stuffed in his mouth and in his nose a terrible stench, so terrible that he could hardly breathe, much less speak. And he was running, his body jolting like a dead thing at every step, every step like a stumble. Always the light was falling, and he was finding it harder to pick out the Riddler's coat among the trees, to sight him as he vanished like the glow between the still trunks. The woods were growing so thick. There was dirt under his nails; his nails ached with it, as if he had been scraping the ground, clawing at the earth and the roots, at the clay beneath the soil. The woods were growing so thick. His skin was clammy, moist and cold; he could feel it shrivelling as he ran, slowly puckering as the water leached from his body into the night. The woods were growing so thick that he couldn't get through them. He stopped, tangled in roots.

'We're here,' said the Riddler.

Fitz had closed his eyes. This time, there was no cascade, no carousel, no pageant of bright images. He saw only darkness.

'I said we're here,' said the Riddler. 'You have to look, or you won't survive what's coming.'

Fitz heard a train whistle. He could feel the steel of the track running beneath him as he sped down it, bearing down on himself, bearing down on the place where he would open his eyes and see. The track went through him like a spear, over and over continuously.

'Look,' urged the Riddler.

'I can't,' Fitz answered him. He was gasping, leaves caught between his tongue and his teeth, dirt caked in his eyes, the plugs of it wormed far into his nose. He tried to cough but there was dirt running in his veins, and it crumbled by clods into his lungs every time he moved. Everywhere was wet, and cold. He heard the silence of it lapping at the shore of him, little vacancies between his bouts of struggle. They were getting longer.

'You can,' said the Riddler. 'Open your eyes to it.'

Fitz opened his mouth. The further he stretched it, trying to yawn and swallow in the air, the more dirt seemed to clog it. He made incoherent noises, straining to draw tiny breaths of air through the fissures between the muddy clumps wedged in his teeth, jammed hard against his tongue.

'What are you most afraid of?' asked the Riddler.

393

'Smothering,' said Fitz. 'Obviously.'

'No,' said the Riddler. 'More than that.'

'Dying,' tried Fitz.

'More than that. More than that. More than that.'

He opened his eyes.

The light had not faded completely. He was still in the wood. He knew the place well, a little thicket bordering a glade, a place where robins and wrens spatted at midday not far from the porch stone. Unlike the wood, in which the trees rustled with life, and moaned or creaked in the heavy southerly winds, this place was silent, a kind of dead centre at the eye of the wood's wild whirl, an island of gold in its green, green sea. Owls stood sentry in the branches nearby, and kites coasted the skies above; no little bird, no mouse dared venture on the short grass of the glade. But he had eaten there, once, with Clare, a picnic of chicken and toast.

Now the sun didn't fall on the wide gold grass. Instead, a mist clung to the ground, little wisps of it threading from the trees, and gathering around the short, slender spring blades. The leaves in the trees had only just begun to uncurl from their winter buds, and in this weak light they seemed sickly and abortive, what was at morning vital now at evening shadowed and deformed.

He heard a noise. It was a noise he remembered – the sound of a knife scraping on toast. He looked at the trees. Clare was speaking.

'Don't run away,' said the Riddler. 'You are always running away from this place.'

394

Fitz looked at the trees. Clare was speaking. There was the sound of a knife scraping on toast.

'Don't look away,' said the Riddler.

Clare was telling him she loved him very much. He was looking at the trees and their thousands of shades of green – so much life, so many different sorts of lights –

'You're looking away,' said the Riddler. 'They will find you there if you don't find yourself first. This is what they will use against you.'

There was the sound of a knife scraping on toast, dragging across the surface of the bread. Then there was a new sound, which he knew was the sound of the knife digging into the chicken liver. The jar of it. It went on and on. Through the trees.

'Stop looking away,' said the Riddler.

The trees he thought full of eyes, the eyes of owls and finches and tits and robins, wrens and martins, wood pigeons and woodpeckers. How many eyes did he see, unseen, at that very moment? They were watching him; he didn't dare to go out on the grass.

Digging, the sound of digging reached him, and Clare was talking, telling him how she came to be his Bibi.

'Why were you not always my Bibi?' he asked her.

And the knife scraped on the toast once more, and was silent.

'Look,' said the Riddler. And he took Fitz's head, and turned it to the grass, so quickly that he didn't have time to shut his eyes.

It was a memory he could not recall. The mist had covered it almost completely. But there were two figures there in the glade, at evening, moving darkly in the dark. One held a shovel. He was tall, and wore a top hat. He drove the shovel into the broken earth. Leaning down, he took hold of something and dragged it, scraping, along the earth. It was the corner of a sheet, or a blanket. Fitz peered at it through the gloom, and saw in its corner, where the man gripped it in a tight twist, chequered squares of red and green. And then the scraping of the shovel on the earth had ended, and Fitz saw a body tumble out of the blanket into the hole that the man had dug.

Fitz saw a body tumble into the hole that Mr Ahmadi had dug in the glade in the Bellman's Wood. And the girl turned and looked at him and it was Dina.

Fitz said, 'I don't really like chicken.'

Clare said, 'I will always love you anyway.'

Dina said, 'The eyes don't always have to follow the body.'

The Master said, 'The wind never breaks faith.'

And the body was the body of Mr Ahmadi Senior.

Fitz looked down at his hands and arms where they were tangled in the thicket, but they were not in the thicket at all. Instead they were twisted and wrapped in the light blanket Clare had embroidered for him, covered with wagtails. He was lying in his bed, at home.

*Home.*

'What are you most afraid of,' asked the Riddler. He was sitting by Fitz's bed.

'Death.'

'No,' said the Riddler. 'That is not dirt in your mouth. You always say that it is dirt in your mouth, but you are wrong. Don't you understand that there are some holes much deeper than those in the earth. You still are seeing lies, lies, lies.'

Fitz felt with his tongue and realized that the Riddler was right. There had never been dirt in his mouth. He was choking on something else.

*The words are sticking in my throat.*

*The blood is sticking in my veins.*

*The love is sticking in my heart.*

'How did you get here?'

Fitz looked at the trees, at the tall, straight trunks in the liquid green light. The butterflies and moths poured through the trees like a wave, their canvas wings flapping hard in the air, snapping against the gales of green. He was lying.

'What do you see?' asked the Riddler. 'Talk, talk, talk, talk, talk.'

Fitz saw the white chamber of the Sensorium, with its beaded ring of purple. He saw the green liquid light, the trees straight and tall as masts, the moths and butterflies with their angel faces and their huge wings like sails. He was lying.

'Mother,' he said.

'Yes,' said the Riddler. 'Aren't you forgetting something?'

*I have forgotten everything.*

He saw it then, a sight he could not remember, could not bear to remember, a thing he knew before he had words to know it with: the white sky, the green sea, the vast blue distance of the sky, the little boat with its tall mast, now wrecked, its hull scraping with every swell across the rock, and in the heavy wind the scrap of dry canvas, still like a joke flapping and filling with air. And there, on his mother's lifeless body, his real mother's lifeless body, at the edge of the shore, the little rings of purple bruises, like coral – on her bleached arms, on her thighs, on her face. Lying. She was just lying there.

'How can I love another mother in the place of my mother?' he asked. 'How can I have a home that is not my home?'

*Clare.*

'You have been here too long,' said the Riddler. 'It is right before your very eyes, as plain as day. And still you cannot see it. Remember this, heir to the Kingdom, when the time comes, that there are holes worlds deeper than those dug in the earth. Remember this. But you have been here too long.'

Sobs began to course through Fitz's chest, pushing towards his throat. They were his sobs, a long and retching music that sucked his breath away, that was his breathless breath. His body shook, rattling his hands where they gripped the tartan blanket like dead seed pods shuddering in a wind. Snot and saliva, tears and sweat soaked his pillow and matted his thick hair as he moaned, as blood surged in his hot, tight temples. The rhythm of his sobs shook him and grounded him, like chanting, like swells passing on a high sea, turning and turning in circles through his body. His body pushed against the measures of it, pushed against the Gyves and the Manacles where they bound him, against the Collar that ran about his throat. He felt that his sorrow might burst through the leather straps, as if they were paper.

But the Riddler stripped them off. Sight, sound, smell, taste – and pain, the searing pain of his touch – fell on him like an avalanche.

Fitz was not on the High Table in the Sensorium. He was not in a passage beneath the lawns. He was hanging from the mast in the Great Hall. The Black Wedding had begun without him. The Officers circled him, chanting; beyond them, a ring of black-liveried Servers revolved, their voices joined in a low and modulating humming. Fitz's eyes widened. He tried to shake his head, to make sense of the order of events, to understand how he had come here.

*I have been asleep. I haven't been myself. I have been lying –*

His heart stuttered, and the dirt of his own tongue choked in his throat.

The Riddler was nowhere to be seen; instead, the face that bent over his was the huge, masked visage of the Heresiarch, wielding his ornate, bowed knife. Below him, on the floor, Fitz could see the Five Fetters where the Heresiarch had cut them away, leaving them to fall where they would. Now the Heresiarch danced like a mesmer around him, the knife hovering in the air before those socketed eyes, catching the light of a hundred lanterns that hung from the ceiling.

The Riddler must have given him up to the Officers. They must have carried him from the Sensorium, strapped him to the mast, and begun the wedding while he lay still in a dream. Somewhere in his guts, Fitz was screaming.

*Maybe.*

*I am here. I am myself. Whatever I am, I am myself.*

The knife danced up and Fitz felt his legs come free, then his hands. He arched his feet, standing into his toes, then stretched his arms out at his sides like wings, like victory in an agony. The

Officers circled in their hook-beaked masks. The Servers circled in their funereal pall. Every syllable they chanted was a knife. Fitz's ears throbbed with time as the Heresiarch rounded before him, boring with the dead and hollow socket of the bulging mask into his own eyes. Around them the circles turned, the chanting rose and fell wordless and traumatic; around them light shifted like a carousel, a thousand or ten thousand figures revolving in the paintings that covered the walls, in the mosaics that tiled the floors, in the carving that crawled everywhere upon the benches, tables and woodwork like a live thing; around them the air seemed pregnant with motion, as if it might spasm in a cataract at any moment. But the Heresiarch now still as a spider in a web with a simple motion drew Fitz into the centre of that stillness, the pivot of all the dance.

He stepped close, very close, looking up as his hands held out the knife, so that Fitz should take it.

Fitz knew that this, this honed and deadly edge, was his temptation, the last question. He took the knife.

'I will always love her anyway,' he said, forcing the words out through the swollen exhaustion of his throat.

Both hands to the handle he raised the knife, and with its point sliced at the mask in front of him. With a neat motion, as if he had practised it, he sheared its surface in a long line from crown to chin. For a second nothing happened; but then, like a tower falling, the sundered sides of the mask began to cleave and fall away, heavy and ponderous off the back of the Heresiarch's shoulders.

The Officers and Servers fell silent then, standing struck dumb where they were.

The Heresiarch shook out her long hair, so that it fell black over her black gown. She smiled, never taking her eyes from Fitz's. Around her neck hung the key to the palace.

*How.*

She stepped on to the plinth to join Fitz. Every eye stared at them. The Officers, one by one, ripped off their masks. The dance was ended. The still point, the one against one, detonated across the hall.

She took his hands. And then she kissed him, once, as gentle as a breath on his lips.

'Little brother,' said Dina, 'welcome to the Heresy.'

15

## The Kingdom of Bones

There was a knock at the door.

'Fitz,' said a voice, high and tentative. 'Can I come in? Fitz? It's me, Navy.'

She didn't wait for an answer. The door pushed open and she stepped into the room, in her hands a candle. She looked around her, studying every corner and surface. She caught her breath and the candle began to gutter.

'There's nothing here at all,' she whispered, as if in awe. 'Nothing.'

Apart from the pitcher and the laver, which stood fresh on the window for morning, she was right.

She crossed to the window and stood quietly, looking down at the hall below, where the Sweepers and the Commissaries were still scouring the space after the Black Wedding. Fitz could from time to time hear the sharp squeals of wood on stone as they dragged tables and benches back into place. These noises of pain carried on the air.

Navy turned back into the room. Her candle, sputtering now, gave almost no light. She blew it out.

'Oh, Fitz,' she said, 'where are you?'

'Up here,' he answered.

Navy seemed to know instantly. She craned her neck to peer at him where he sat in the trapdoor in the ceiling. He waved between his dangling legs. The rest of him was already in the sky.

'What are you doing up there?' she asked. Her voice rose soft upon the air.

'Waiting for something to happen to me.'

'What?'

'I haven't thought that far ahead,' he said.

'Come down.'

Fitz lowered himself through the gap, kicking out his feet to stand on the carved stone cornice that framed the room's heavy, peaked window. He had climbed the cornice, wedging himself against the adjacent wall, to get up; the same method would get him down.

He hit the floor softly, landing on his toes.

'The Rack sent me to the Master,' said Navy.

'How does he look?'

'I haven't been yet. I came here first. I want to ask you something.'

They sat on the bed.

'The Rack gave me something to bring to the Master, but I don't want to do it.'

Navy set down the dark candle. There was something else in her hand. She opened her palm and in the darkness Fitz could see it was full of seeds.

'*Conium maculatum*,' Navy said. 'Poison hemlock. We studied its uses and effects with the Rack last winter, and grew some over the summer in the Herbarium. A small amount will give you vertigo, shorten the breath. It could knock you out, or put you in a coma.' She began to number off the seeds in her palm. 'But this much – ten seed heads – will kill you. Fast.'

'It's just a message,' said Fitz. 'This place. Everyone is always reminding everyone else to be ready for death.'

'I don't think so,' Navy answered. She was silent for a few breaths. Her palm tightened round the seeds. 'His exact words were, "Take these to the Master, or take them yourself."'

'Maybe tonight is your Black Wedding, too,' said Fitz.

Navy threw her arms round him, suddenly sobbing. Her head she pushed into his shoulder, and he held the thick nutty fragrance of her hair close to him as she squeezed his arms to his side, rocking and crying.

'We saw, we saw,' she said. She sobbed the words in thick gushes of mucus and emotion. 'We were all there. It was horrible. Dolly threw up after.'

Fitz felt cold as she rocked him, as if he were standing across a water from Navy, driven by a pelting wind. Her cries reached him as if from a distance, and only the smell of her hair bound him to her presence. He was grateful for it, and his shoulders slumped.

'What do you want from me?' he asked.

Navy let him go, sat up, and rubbed the tears from her eyes with her free hand. The other, still clutching the seeds, she had pressed to her chest.

'It's late. Maybe I'm not thinking straight. But I didn't want to do this, go to the Master, I mean, with *this* –' she held up the seeds – 'unless you said it was okay.'

Fitz felt his blood rising again, as if the Officers had begun to circle around him, as if his arms were being slowly twisted behind his back.

'It has nothing to do with me,' he said. The chill in his voice was like the ice in Dina's eyes: blue, far and hard. *Like the air on the sea over her body.*

'But it's like – he's your – *family*!' exclaimed Navy.

Fitz stood up. He wanted more: to stand up to the size of a giant, to pierce the ceiling of the tower, to stand up into the sky and never stop standing up until his standing up encompassed everything that was. His indignation, this colossus, demanded it.

'No,' he said. His voice was flat and final. 'No, no, no.'

Without meaning to do it, he had rounded on Navy. He hated her. She stood up from the bed, bewildered.

'Maybe I don't know how you fit in, but you do. And anyway Dina said –' Navy stopped.

'Dina said what?' Fitz demanded.

'The Heresy is a family business, Fitz.'

'If the Rack gave you hemlock, and told you to take it to the Master, then I think you have no choice but to take it to the Master,' said Fitz. 'Now I'd like you to leave.'

'But –' She had more to say.

Navy stood before him, close. She was just his height, and her eyes – catching the weak light from the window – looked right into his like all the windows in the world. They didn't bore into him; they didn't pierce; nor did they rebuff, or refuse him. They invited him, as if Navy had thrown open every sash of her soul, as far as the eye could see, or the heart could know.

'Leave.'

She put her hand to his elbow, and touched it lightly, once.

'I'm sorry, Fitz,' she said. She turned, and was gone.

Fitz stared at the wall in front of him.

*Little brother.*

He put his fingers to his eyes. He rubbed his eyelids gently with the backs of his knuckles. Then he rubbed them harder, increasing the pressure until it began to hurt, to ache where he was pressing into the sockets, pushing the tender balls of his eyes into his skull.

*Her love for you is just a story that she tells herself. Love is not a work of the hands, little brother. It's a fact in the blood.*

*How could I not have seen this.*

Fitz turned his hands and began to probe his eyes with his fingers. His eyelids still closed, he felt for the firm but delicate curve of his eyes beneath the skin. He squeezed a little, taking the meat of them between his thumbs and forefingers. He didn't want these eyes, this blood.

*My hands before my eyes.*

His eyes ached in his head. He saw pools of red so deep that they were black. Still he pushed into the corners of his sockets; still he squeezed with the tips of his fingers, pinching the balls of his eyes, imagining them as grapes ready for plucking, as little purses of jelly, as ink, as melting ice. He pressed them, willing them to break.

'Stop it.'

*No.*

'I said, stop it.'

It wasn't a voice in his head, and the bright light in his eyes came, instead, from the doorway. Someone was standing before him, but – his eyes throbbing from the pain he had caused them, and from the brightness of the light shining on them – he couldn't see who. He held up his hand against the flickering candle.

'Whatever you're going through,' Navy said, 'I won't leave you like this. You don't have to do it by yourself.'

Fitz almost laughed.

'There is only myself.'

'No, that's not right.'

'Navy,' Fitz snapped. He tried to control his voice. 'I don't know what's real and what's not. Not now. Last night – the Jack and the Keeper – they said a lot of crazy things. Terrible things. I spent the whole night and day in the Sensorium, seeing things that – half of them I remember, and half of them I'm sure never happened. I can't tell a dream from my hand in front of my face any more. And they gave me so much stack at Feeding last night – well, for all I know you and everything about you is a figment of my imagination, a delusion as flimsy as a will-o'-the-wisp, as fleeting as that candle.'

The candle was flickering wildly in the draught that ran up the tower stairs.

'It's not the stack, Fitz. I'm here,' she said. Her voice was quiet, hushed, like a bruise.

'How do you know,' he spat.

'Because when I saw the Bellman in the hall, at Second Feeding, I switched your plate with Russ's. He's been raving ever since. He asked me to marry him forty times, and that was only on the first night.'

Fitz felt a peal of laughter spasm out of his throat, but not in happiness. It was followed by a warm gurgle, a choking pain, a listlessness or numbness that stroked through him like an electric charge.

*It was true. There was no stack. Everything the Jack said, everything I remembered him saying, all of it. And the Rack, and the Sensorium, and the Riddler, and –*

'Wait,' said Fitz. 'You said, "the first night". What do you mean, the first night?'

Navy sighed.

'You weren't in the Sensorium, if that's where you were, for only a night. You've been gone for a week. We were frantic. Until the Black Wedding finally began, well, we thought maybe that you –'

*A week.*

'Fitz,' said Navy. Her arms were on him. Round him. They were under him, and he was on the bed and the bed was falling through the air.

'Fitz.'

Navy had him.

'You're safe.'

*I'm cold.*

'I remembered my mother,' Fitz said.

'What is she like?' asked Navy.

'She isn't like anything. She died. She died bringing me to this place.'

'To the Heresy?'

'No,' he said. 'Much further back. My real mother. She – I don't know. No place. She didn't bring me anywhere. We were trying to

408

find a new home. I just remembered that she is gone. I let her go. I remembered the white of her arms.'

Now they were standing in front of the window. Navy's candle stood in its stick disregarded near the door. One hand on his near shoulder, the other on his back, she stood beside him as they looked out at the dark landscape that lay, lit with fires, beyond the Heresy walls.

*Fires.*

'There's more, Fitz,' said Navy, quietly. 'Some of the Offs – they're gone. Nobody knows where. And Dina has tapped four Prents to fill their places. Dolly is the new Keeper, Payne is the Sweeper, Padge is the Commissar, and Russ – little Russ, as if he could ever be anything but himself – he's the Jack.'

A vision of the Officers in their masks, dancing round him, lit by a thousand lanterns, weaving, drunk with murderous cruelty, swam before his eyes. *Dolly. Russ.* Fitz fought it off, trying to get back to what was in front of him – to the fires –

'Navy,' he said.

The fires were moving, coming down the hillside, crossing the valley.

*Fires. Moving in the valley. A week has passed. Behold me, that I am alive, and have come of age. They will come for me.*

'Navy, they're coming for me again. Wispers from the Mountain. Now. Tonight. Just like before – but more, many, many more. You can see them in the valley. The Master has called them, and they're coming.'

Fitz pulled himself on to the window ledge, turned the handle of the window, and threw it open in the cold, quiet air. Even from so far, the sound of whispering on the night, floating as if on a mist – vaporous, uncohering – reached them with unmistakable clarity.

Navy leaned forward over the ledge, her face warm against his side, her eagerness warm beside his fear. 'How long do you think, before they're here?' Navy asked, her voice caught up in the wonder that shortened her breath.

'Half an hour,' Fitz answered. He turned to her, and took her by the hands. 'Navy, you were right. Something awful *is* happening in the Heresy. It starts with us, but it's much bigger than us. It's unspeakable. It's unspeakable, so I'll show you.'

'Fitz, you're talking like the Riddler.'

'Trust me. You said you'd follow the Master anywhere. Now's your chance. Follow him. You said I belonged here. Maybe you were right. But I only belong here because, like the Master, I have the courage to leave, the courage to pay the price of my own freedom. We're leaving, Navy, and we're going to do whatever we have to, to leave for good. We have half an hour – half an hour to break the Master from the tower.'

'The Master from – how?'

Fitz watched the fires bobbing on the darkness of the valley, a line of torches advancing, trailing flames. He thought there were hundreds of them. A rescue party. An attack. A rescue attack. They weren't coming stealthily, but openly, drawing every eye in the Heresy. He thought of Clare and Ned among them, in each of their hands aloft a burning brand, trailing smoke and purpose as they wove pathless across the valley floor, trampling the heather and gorse.

*Drawing every eye.*

'No one will see us.'

*It's a diversion.*

Fitz pulled free of Navy's arms that still gripped him by the shoulders.

'Can you get into his cell?'

Navy held out her hand. The little seeds still lay in it.

'By order of the Rack,' she said, 'Warden of the high tower.'

'Take this,' Fitz told her. From his bed he had retrieved the lamp, and wound round it its little cord. 'When you're in the tower, open the north door, and show the light. That will be my target.'

Navy had been watching the roofs of the Heresy while Fitz spoke. Now she turned to him, taking him full in the face. 'Target for what?'

'Dolly's crossbow. Can you get it for me?'

'Yes, but Fitz, from where's – there's no way you can make that shot from the ground. That angle – even Dolly couldn't.'

'From there.' Fitz pointed in the darkness, to the little cupola on the top of the Palace of the Heresiarch. It would be almost a straight shot from the top of the Heresiarchy into the door of the tower.

They didn't speak. Skipping as many steps as they could, they ran out of the tower and into the court of the Master. From the pen where Dolly slept in the Keep, Navy fetched the crossbow and twenty metres of the cable. Together they doubled back to the Heresiarchy, through courts beginning to stream with Serfs and Fells. The Door of Humility had been thrown wide, and tides

411

swept from the Rack's arsenal on to the lawns, wielding staves, knives, bows, spears, even swords – whatever the ancient weapon store would yield. Alone beside the rush, unnoticed, Navy put her hand once more to Fitz's elbow.

'Do you think you can do it?'

He looked at her.

'Go – in there? The *Heresiarchy*?'

'It's not locked,' he answered.

'But Dina –'

'I can do it.'

'Give me ten minutes,' Navy said. 'I'll open the north door of the tower.'

Navy slipped into the darkness, weaving between the unseeing eyes of the men and women pouring in the opposite direction, heading for the tower cell. Fitz watched her go, unwilling for a moment to open the Heresiarch's door. He took a deep breath, stood, strapped the bow to his back, and looped the cable over his head so that it sat snugly round his chest.

He had to push the door with all his force, grinding his heels into the stone paving for pressure. When it was open just enough, he sliced through the gap, then pushed it closed behind him until he felt the bolt make contact with the latch – and there he left it, in case he needed to get out. Then he turned on his heel, lifted his head, and surveyed the interior of the Palace of the Heresiarch.

It took his breath away.

*It's empty.*

The whole hall, the dome, everything – nothing – it was all a huge void. Around him, grey stone walls rose vast and dark on every side, brooding, silent and hollow, a towering shell of stone as still and as secret as the air that filled it. He had expected rooms, stairs, an orderly progression of levels, even locked doors. He had expected impediments. Instead, there was nothing at all.

There was one exception. A hundred exceptions. The walls rose in a broad ring to the dome above, unadorned but for scores of stone ledges that protruded from them, spaced at regular intervals in an ascending spiral that wrapped the hall with its coil. On each of these ledges stood a bust or statue, the faces of Heresiarchs, Masters and Officers of ages past, staring into the centre of the palace's wide void. Fitz felt the seconds spooling away from him, the moments ticking away like Navy's steady tread up the tower stairs.

'Boy.'

The word punctured Fitz's resolve like a knife in flesh: sudden, painless, chilling. He searched the dim light of the vast interior space, backing towards the door.

'Here,' said the voice. Weak and frail though it was, it echoed against the dome. By the time he saw the Jack's huge form, slumped to his right, his hand was already on the edge of the door.

'Wedge the door. Then help me up.'

In only a few minutes he heard it all. The Officers had been summoned to the Heresiarchy. Some had come: the faithful, the dupes. The Jack showed him the bodies, lying close to the wall and stretched out beneath their robes: the Sweeper, his hands folded across his sagging chest; the Keeper, pale and tiny, with her long hair no longer plaited but carefully arranged around her head like a radiant fan, as if she were floating away; the Commissar, slack, but still imperious. The stench around them was so strong Fitz gagged.

'We've been here for a week,' said the Jack, as Fitz pulled him, with all his strength, to his feet. 'A Nightwalk. The Sweeper – Adrian – was the first to go. Diabetes. He had no insulin. The others – Ludmilla, Agatha – maybe dehydration, maybe hypothermia. I did what I could.'

'How –' tried Fitz.

'By drinking my own piss, boy,' barked the Jack. His anger hardly seemed frightening now. 'I expect the girl went through with the Black Wedding after all. I see you survived it.'

Fitz nodded.

'Don't hold it against Dolly and Russ. Don't hold it against Payne. They didn't know what they were doing. That girl will have made sure they were out of their minds on stack.'

'But the Commissar –'

And then Fitz realized why the Commissar lay dead in the Heresiarchy.

'She wanted her out of the way. Stack is a weapon; Ludmilla wouldn't have given it up without a fight. Let's just say –' the Jack paused to catch his breath, unsteady on his feet – 'Dina is not her father's daughter. It was a putsch, a coup, a revolution; and she planned it perfectly.'

*Almost perfectly.*

'Can you walk?' asked Fitz.

'I'll be all right. Just get me out of the door.'

Fitz helped him to the entrance, which he had blocked with a shoe. The Jack hobbled through, then turned, waiting for Fitz's arm to guide him down the steps.

'I'm staying here,' he said.

'Don't be a fool,' growled the Jack. 'You don't want to end up like them.' He nodded to the bodies.

Fitz grimaced, pointed up.

'Be careful,' said the big man. He was already turning away. Fitz watched him take the steps one by one. Something inside him had collapsed, and every step he took seemed a kind of descent within himself.

Fitz shoved the door closed, and heaved on it until he heard the heavy bolt shoot with a thud into place. Once it was closed, he breathed more easily. Now there was no going back.

*I have to climb.*

There was nothing else for it.

Fitz crossed the hall, put his hand to the grave marble face of the Heresiarch who confronted him, and pulled. The stone hit the floor with a crunch, a single fracture running along the back of its head, and lay still. Fitz leaped on to the ledge. From there it was a metre, maybe a little more, to the next, the slope just shallow enough that he could make the leap. He made it; and as his foot reached the ledge, he swept the next bust from its place with a precise, coordinated swing of his arms. It hit the floor below with a harder crash, skidded, and stopped. He was already in its place. Again he leaped, knocking the marble face from its perch. And again. He didn't dare look down, but followed the gentle curve of the wall, the slight slope of his ascent, almost running from ledge

415

to ledge, hurling the marbles down as he went: faces, statues, some white, others veined with blue or pink, some painted, some rough, some fine, faces bearded, some with tresses pinned or braided, whole bodies standing broad like conquerors, or hunched like sages at their desks. As he rose against the walls, gaining height against the dome, the stone images fell further, crashed and splintered with ever more spectacular and deafening noise, and Fitz knew now the floor below him was littered with fragments like the white bleached bones of the Heresy's history, exhumed and spread beneath its temple like a carpet of sharded sorrow and loss. Again he leaped. Again he dashed the idol down. Again, again, again. All the while he circled the vast space, racing along the wall, rising from ledge to ledge towards the dome, throwing himself up and the marbles down, rising ever towards the lofty arc of the palace's dome. Anger drove him on, and resistance, refusal, rejection. Horror.

At last he stood before the final ledge. Before him lay the last of the plinths, perhaps the first of them, on it a face so fresh and full of its sadness it might then, through the ages and the hard case of stone in which it stood, imprisoned, have shed a tear. Beyond it, above it, the ceiling of the dome rose in a shallow curve towards the little stone cupola at its centre – where, open to the skies, the Master's albatrosses perched, restive and expectant. The roof of the dome was supported by eight massive oak beams that lifted like bent bows, like the heavy bent stems of roses towards one another, to flower in the dark night that bound them. The underside of the beams had been carved with a simple repeating pattern that from the side Fitz recognized at once: the blank eye, its lids drawn on emptiness. From one wooden loop to the next, along the length and height of the dome, he might lift himself as if by handles.

He steadied himself. He looked down. The floor, far below and in shadow, lay littered with broken stone. Near the door, the bodies. *But not mine.* Fitz closed his eyes, and opened them again on the Sad King. He sprang; but this time, hurling a shout from his throat as he stepped to the far ledge, he pushed against it even as he reached it, propelling himself arms forward towards the beam and the first of his handholds. His fingers slapped against it and he clutched them tight against the wood, seating his palms snug against the dark oak eye.

Above the floor, catching his breath, he dangled. Beneath him, the bust of the Sad King rocked on its plinth, and was still.

Fitz reached for the next handhold. His arms tore with pain. He tightened his grip, pulled into his shoulders, and swung for the next. And the next. Lifting himself across the ceiling by swings he raced to the centre. The albatrosses, clucking, parted above him as, from the last of the beam's looped eyes, he swung his feet on to a ledge, writhed into a flip, and pushed himself up. One of the birds clicked at him, and from its turned head – at once both facing and ignoring him – it watched him breathe.

Fitz looked towards the tower. Already the north door had swung open, and in the rectangular void it made, his little lamp glowed with a fierce and unbreakable constancy.

*It's too far.*

The cable would cover the distance, but he would miss the target. It was smaller than he had imagined, and tighter. He climbed into the cupola, and stood against one of the stone columns that supported its little roof.

*I can't make it.*

Navy's face appeared, for an instant, in the black void of the door. Her gaze seemed to dart past the Heresiarchy towards the lawns, then return to the dome, scanning it, searching for him. He looked down at the roof of the tiled dome. From this side, from the outside, it seemed to slope away precipitously. He imagined jumping down on to it, trying to get closer to the Rack's tower, closing the distance; but it was impossible. Slick and steep, he would fall before he took two steps. He looked again at the crescent light where it glowed with serene intensity in the tower door.

And then the albatross, the nearest of them, still watching him, trilled another barrage of little clicks, opened its wings, and sprang into the darkness. Its flight was true and even, its bright white wings against the dark of the night as clear as a beacon at sea. It hardly moved its wings at all, but rose in a single, steady arc from the dome of the palace towards the north door of the Rack's tower, settling as lightly as Fitz's own eye, and as silently, beside the light that lay there. A plumb line could not have described the space more truly, the required arc of the arrow's flight with more precision. Etched on his gaze like a searing white trail in the night, the path lay clear for Fitz to follow. He unslung the coils of cable from his shoulder, laid them neatly on the wall beside him, and drew out the free end. With quick, delicate fingers he paid out an ample length, drew it round the column, and hitched it firm to the stone. He took the crossbow from his back, fitted the single bolt, and winched it tight against the coil.

The albatross had hopped away from the door. The trail it had made, remained. Fitz snugged the wood in his shoulder as he had seen Dolly do, sighted along the bolt, and closed his eye. He pulled the catch.

The bolt, a slug of iron, disappeared in the darkness. Fitz, recoiling from the discharge, struggled to retain his balance on the narrow inner ledge of the cupola. But the cable paid out freely, and he knew his shot had hit home. He watched the spent cable, willing it to go taut, willing it to rise into the position that would mean Navy, or the Master, stood at its other end, and had lashed it down for the crossing.

He waited.

At long, agonizing, last, it rose, snapping taut. Five albatrosses huddling on the opposite side of the cupola stood.

Beyond the tower, the first of the torches were crossing the last stretches of the valley. They were almost at the walls, almost at the lawns – the dark lawns, heaving with dark forms. Fitz thought of Clare and Ned, surely at the front of the tide as it swept towards the walls, thought of the clubs and fires, the staves and knife-edges that awaited them.

*No.*

One of the albatrosses shrieked. Fitz looked to the tower, and saw the Master sliding along the cable, head first like a piece of meat trussed and strung over a fire, breaking his speed by dragging on the cable with his crossed legs. Slowly, excruciatingly slowly, he began to slide across the void between the tower and the cupola.

*Let it hold.*

It held. No sooner had the Master touched the stone arch of the cupola than he unhooked his legs, suspended for a moment from the hook by which he had crossed, and then swung his body safely on to the wall.

'Well sprung, child,' he said – but his eyes were already on the cable, on the tower, on Navy, who was sliding at speed out of the door of the tower. Halfway between the tower and the cupola, she threw her legs over the cable, crossed her shoes on it, and bore down, hard, to brake her slide. The tension in the cable sang.

'She'll fray it,' cried the Master.

The albatrosses, frighted by the whining cable, scattered into the air.

*Let it hold.*

It held.

But Navy wasn't the last person in the tower. As they drew her over the wall, Fitz and the Master each with an arm round her body, he saw over his shoulder the movement of a face in the shadow.

'There's someone there,' he said. 'There's someone else in the tower.'

'Sassani,' said the Master, and spat with disgust into the great abyss of the dome beneath them.

'No,' said Fitz, the cords of his voice breaking before his thoughts had overtaken them. His eye had seen something else, but his mind refused it. He couldn't think. His world whirled. He clutched the pillar.

And then she was out on the wire, inching towards them, then sliding.

*Clare.*

The cable lurched, then held. She slid faster. The cable sang again, louder, and deeper.

'It's breaking,' said the Master. 'It won't hold her.'

From below, within the dome, inside the palace, came a scream: long, sustained, a peal not of fear but of anger, of terrible fury, of a passion that destroys, wastes and desolates.

'Dina,' said the Master. 'She'll try to stop us.' He turned to Fitz. 'How long?'

Fitz knew she would move at twice his speed: faster, and with nothing in her way, she could climb the ledges in . . . 'Five minutes. No more.'

Clare swung her legs over the wall, and slung her arms round Fitz.

'We saw the light in the tower,' she said. She was breathing hard. 'We came up from the shore alone – there are two boats moored – Ned –'

She turned back the way she had come, where Ned was already on the cable. He never bothered with his legs, but slid the whole of the long distance between the tower and the cupola at speed, slamming into the stone so hard that it shuddered around them. With a single hand he gripped the cable itself as he lifted his legs over the wall to join them. The metal bar with which he had crossed clattered against the tiles of the dome and slid out of sight.

'You tore one of the bars – out of the window?' said the Master. He was plainly amazed.

'Not me,' said Ned. 'Him.'

Professor Farzan was on the cable already, sliding freely along it as Ned had done, but with his legs up behind him, dragging against the free whine of metal on metal. Now the cable groaned, and it seemed as he reached the centre of his passage that it would snap. The albatrosses wheeled around the cupola in scything rings, their white bodies a dance of anguish. Fitz, from the rough nest of Clare's embrace, counted down the seconds, wishing that he could squeeze his eyes shut, not daring to, and wishing it all the same.

Clare turned to take hold of the Professor's body as he reached the cupola; as she turned, turning Fitz's face as her coat turned, he saw the fires on the valley floor. They were streaming towards the wall. As he watched, the first of them disappeared from sight beneath its shadow. They would be climbing.

*Dina.*

There was hardly room left in the little space above the dome, but Fitz pulled away from Clare and leaped lightly across the void to the other side. There, from the north rim, he scanned the tiles of the dome where they fell towards the corner of the Lantern Hall. One of the finials that spiked up from the edge of its gable would, by means of a drainpipe, allow them to climb to the broad roof, and from there to the first of the two lanterns that crowned the hall's long nave.

'Down,' Fitz said to Navy, gesturing with his finger, 'and up.' She hurdled the wall and jumped down on to the steep tiled slope of the dome. Knocking herself into a crouch, she kicked out her legs and began to spider down the slope, arching her back and scurrying as low as her arms could bend. Ned ruffled Fitz's hair as he passed, following her. Next went Clare, then the Professor.

By the time Fitz was ready to leap over the wall, last of all and hard on the Master's heels, he knew Dina couldn't be far. He didn't dare look. On the northern wall of the Heresy fires briefly blazed; some toppled forward, others back. One or two stayed. The Wispers were not advancing; and Fitz could feel the pressure of them, the hot and smoky torchlight mass of their arrival, huddling just out of sight at the outer base of the wall. There was a sense of imminence everywhere in the night around the Heresy, the sense that a tide was poised on its turn.

*The tide.*

His thoughts swept across the roof and through the lantern, to plummet through the hall to the well of the Sad King.

*It's not a well at all.*

In a sudden concussion of understanding that seemed to detonate across his whole body, Fitz grasped for the first time the true nature of the well of the Sad King, the way the Serfs used it as a scullery, the briny, cold taste of its waters, the odd hours at which the Riddler had called him down to the Sensorium. It wasn't a well. It was the tide that filled the shaft, washing in at the flood, washing out at the ebb. The Riddler had appointed him hours when the tide was high, so that he might splash safely into the waters beneath the hall, then drift through the still point of the water at its height to emerge dripping from the stairs in the Sensorium. But if he had ever leaped into the well at low tide . . . Fitz's shoulders slumped, and rattled violently.

'Little brother,' Dina hissed from below. 'I'm coming for you.'

A crash came from the palace beneath him, and Fitz realized with a shock that Dina must have thrown down the last of the busts – the baleful, empty portrait of the Sad King himself. She had so little left to climb. He hurdled the wall, fell on his back, and slid down the roof so fast it ripped gashes in his long coat. At the bottom he tore his coat open, put his arms round the drainpipe, and hauled himself up with the last strength in his arms. The Master pulled him on to the roof by his collar, and together the two of them ran, keeping low, across the slates towards the high lantern above the hall. Ned and Navy had already kicked in one of the broad windows, and the Professor, more agile and nimble than Fitz had realized, had climbed across the array of ropes and hooks that covered the ceiling inside and was sliding, hand over hand, down the great eastern wall.

The lanterns blanketing the ceiling of the hall, swinging in an undulating canopy of amber effulgence, still glowed from the wedding earlier.

*The Serfs must have been interrupted by the attack.*

Navy handed Fitz the Professor's long knife, and the Master took Fitz's legs. He hung down over the distant floor. Three lanterns he cut free, dropping each of them, still burning, to the stone below, where they smashed, throwing out oil in long arcs that, only partly by design, pooled in a ring round the open black hole, swirling with mist, of the well head. The limp lengths of rope Fitz tossed down, away from the burning oil; they hit the floor in thudding, loose coils. Then he clutched at three adjacent lanterns and, with a length of cord he had saved before, bound them together.

Fitz drew the braided rope up towards the ceiling as the Master pulled him back.

'You first,' he said to Navy. She clutched the three bound ropes, then pinched them between her knees, clamped her feet together on the lanterns beneath, stood up, and smiled. The Master joined her, and they spun slowly under their own weight, first this way, then that, as they caught their balance. Below, the Professor – who had watched Fitz's every move – uncleated the three ropes and began to pay them out. They dropped into the glowing air of the hall. Ned, then Clare, caught a loop of one of the ropes as it went down, and fell with it, hanging. At last Fitz followed, praying that the thick iron hooks in the hall's ceiling would bear their weight. All the while the Professor paid out the ropes steadily, leaning back against the three staples through which they passed, bracing his foot on the wall before him. Fitz handed himself down the length as he approached the floor, securing himself with his knees and taking the burn of the cord across his thighs. When he finally hit the floor, the last of the little group to alight in the empty chamber, they found themselves standing in a ring of flame, directly beside the Sad King.

Professor Farzan bounded over the flames, swirling his long travelling cloak about him to ward the fire away. In one hand he carried the ends of the three thick cords. In another he dragged a length of one of the other ropes Fitz had cut down. He bound them together with a braid, pulled on it to tighten it, and handed it to Fitz.

'Twelve bells has struck, and the tide is out,' Fitz said. 'The well of the Sad King is empty. It will take us to the sea. The walls are under attack. It's our only way out of the Heresy.'

The Master only smiled.

Somehow, they all managed to get a foot into the tangled knot of cords that bound the lanterns, even as it spun over the mist rising from the well below. With several hands on the long length of rope, they dropped into the floor, paying out the cable as they went.

For the first time, as they fell through the floor, Fitz could see the sides of the well shaft. Built entirely of stone, it was nonetheless studded everywhere with holes, from which, even now, tentative hands extended, reaching towards the light as if for food, then pulling back. The sides of the well were near enough that the six of them, falling slowly through the centre, could reach easily to the walls.

It was studded everywhere with holes. But it was studded, too, with doors.

There were no handles on the doors. There were no locks.

*They're devoted to their own captivity. They don't even know they are free to escape.*

Fitz reached out as the lanterns drifted past, and thrust a hand into one of the holes. He pulled. As they fell past it, the wooden door yawned slowly ajar on its hinge. A terrified, pale body, dressed in rags, stood behind it.

'Go!' shouted Fitz. 'Get out!'

The lanterns fell further. Another door was in his reach, another bar, which he lifted. Opposite him Navy did the same on the other side, then Clare. As they passed, again and again they pulled open the doors – five, then ten, and as they fell, ten more, then twenty. Behind every door the forms crowded – pale, ragged, frightened. Cold and shivering. Boys and girls.

*The real children of the Heresy.*

'You're free! Go!' he shouted, his voice rising with confidence.

The lanterns began to fall faster, now lurching along as the rope dragged above them on its hook, the three men straining to hoist against the weight of their bodies. As he watched above through the swirls and curls and eddies of the mist, through the rays cast by the lanterns slicing through the gloom, a few arms, then faces, here and there pushed into the well shaft.

'Tear it down!' shouted Fitz. They were almost at the base of the well, almost at the place where soon the tide would flow anew. There wasn't long to go. He looked down. He looked up.

'Tear it down! Tear the whole thing down!' he screamed. 'Every stone! Take it apart and throw it into the sea!'

Then the silent forms began to swarm through the open doors, body upon body, crawling and climbing up the shaft, the holes through which they had once extended their arms, hoping for food, craning for scraps, now serving them for steps and for handholds as they tumbled up and over one another, climbing towards the light of the lanterned heavens above. Ten, then twenty, then fifty took to the walls, and then they poured out of the doors by their hundreds, moving silently, their long and emaciated limbs writhing one over the other like worms squirming beneath a flat stone lifted.

Tears were streaming from Navy's eyes, from the Master's, from Fitz's own. The Professor and Ned, holding to the ropes, swore grim oaths as the lanterns still dropped, lurching and swinging dangerously from the tumult of bodies that blocked and blacked out the passage above.

'Tear it down!' Fitz cried, his voice cracking like glass, his voice shattering against the bodies that climbed away, and up, that erupted above him from the floor of the Lantern Hall. 'Tear it down! Tear it down! Burn it all to the ground!'

When the lanterns touched the ground, they all leaped instinctively to the floor. The rope slacked above them, but danced wildly from side to side as above, out of sight, it was caught in the surge of bodies climbing through the well.

*Let them go. Let them burn the Heresy to the ground.*

'Follow me,' said Fitz, and he set off running down the wide tunnel through which – swimming – he had so often passed before. Light behind from the lanterns, and ahead from the Sensorium, showed the way, and they made quick time down the sandy, soggy floor of the passage. At the stairs, Fitz didn't look up to acknowledge the Riddler, who stood above them, watching them go; he kept running, this time into darkness, holding before him the crescent lamp that Navy had brought with her from the Rack's tower. On and on down the straight tunnel they went, Fitz first, then Navy, and behind her Clare and Ned, the Professor, the Master. Still the tunnel dropped, and the thin trickle of water at their feet, sandy and crusted with grit and sludge, began to thicken and deepen, until they were running through half an inch, then an inch, then a shallow pool of cold and stinking seawater.

'Fitz,' yelled Navy. 'Stop.'

He splashed to a halt, and the others behind him. Navy took the light and held it up, over their heads.

They were passing beneath an arch in the tunnel. It was framed and adorned with beautiful white carving, in the most intricate patterns.

'It's beautiful,' said Fitz. 'But down here –'

'Those are bones,' said Navy, and Fitz saw that she was right – bone after bone set together with geometrical regularity, creating regular geometrical patterns against the dark stone surface beneath.

'Those are human bones,' she said.

They advanced more slowly after that, beyond the arch and into a tunnel lined ever more thickly with the same terrifying geometries. At last, less than twenty metres on, the tunnel opened on a broad, low cave, at its centre a pool of water, but on its sloping sides, where they rose to the ceiling, dry. The walls and ceiling of the cave as far as their eyes could pierce through the gloom had been entirely covered in bones – stacks and ranks of them, here clustering in fans, there forming circles and grids and spirals, bones of every shape and size, from the neat slender arcs of ribs, and the tiny lumps of knuckles and vertebrae, to the long, thick staves of the femur and tibia, the humerus, the ulna and radius.

Clare gasped.

'It's disgusting,' she said.

'It's the Ossarium,' said the Master. 'In days gone by, the Masters of the Heresy called it the Kingdom of Bones. It was built as a place of pilgrimage and meditation. I don't think anyone has been here for centuries. Meanwhile, the sea has been washing the bones twice a day.'

'How do we get out of here?' asked Clare. 'It must open on to the beach – if the tide –'

'It does,' called Ned, from the darkness ten metres further down the dry shore of the cave. 'But there's no way we can climb through that until the dawn comes.'

He pointed into the gloom where in a symphony of bleached bones the walls of the cave fluted into dark and forbidding water. There was an inlet down there somewhere, beneath the cold and swirling ebb, but it was far too dark to make it out.

'Then we wait for the dawn to save us,' said Professor Farzan.

'Or for the high tide to drown us,' said the Master.

'Either way, we wait,' said Navy. She climbed to the highest ledge on the cave's near inner slope, and sat down.

# THE KINGDOM

16

# The Game of Kings

The Riddler's Song

The king sat at his supper
  and chewed upon a bone;
the worm sat next beside him,
  dining upon his own.

The king called for his servants
  to cast the vermin thence;
the worm cried, 'Man! Attend me!
  Dispatch his eminence!'

The king, in stupefaction
  at so unusual terms,
demanded satisfaction
  in the quarrel of *Men v Worms*.

Said the worm, 'Your vermin's dainty,
  nicer than men on thrones,
for though he eat much putrid meat,
  he reverences the bones.'

'No worm,' the king insisted,
  'beside a king is aught.'
'And yet by supper's end,' he said,
    mark well my words,
    by supper's end
I'll gnaw your flesh to naught.'

I n the end, the tide came in well before the dawn.

Clare and Ned set their backs to the water, where the little group cowered on the top of the innermost slope of the cave, and the others sat around them, nervous, tired.

'Will they follow us here?' Fitz asked.

'We'll know if they do, when they do,' said Mr Ahmadi. 'But there is one thing of which you can be sure. The Heresy will follow you every moment of your life, across the world if it must, as it did me, until it has taken from you what it wants.'

'And what is that?' asked Fitz.

'The Kingdom.'

Mr Ahmadi took the tall hat from his head, and set it on the cave floor between them. He put his fingers to the hat's rim, and seemed to snap them, and the hat broke apart – sprang apart – into a long coiled band of black cloth. He took this between his fingers, turned it over, and laid it flat, then reached for the lantern, opened its glass window, and touched the corner of the cloth to the still burning wick.

The whole black and silken band burst into blue flame. All of them lurched back – Navy a good deal closer than she would have liked to the skulls on the wall behind her.

'The Officers seized and examined everything I owned,' said Mr Ahmadi, 'except the clothes off my back.' The blue fire began to subside; as it did, within the black silk silver traces began to appear, coalescing into gleaming, pen-like strokes that ran across the fabric, each channel running into the next in a cursive illumination that gleamed in the void of the cave.

'And the hat off my head.' He looked up and smiled at Fitz. 'Obviously.'

Fitz stared at Mr Ahmadi with a tangled knot of emotions: caution, fear, loyalty, pride, excitement – even love. He looked down at the bright map lying on the cave floor. It had clearly been traced from some sort of sea chart; in its corner lay a finely drawn compass rose, along its lower edge ran the crenellated line of a rugged, probably rocky coast, the place names tricked out in an elegant, ancient-looking silver hand, and, in the wide emptiness of its central void, a small cluster of blobs and dots, the smallest of which – a pinprick of light in the wide draught of dark ruffled silk – was annotated with a star, and a single word.

*Kingdom.*

Mr Ahmadi's finger dropped on this silver speck in the ocean like an eagle diving out of the sun.

'The Kingdom,' he said. 'It has gone by many names. Navy?'

'The Joy of the Heart', she whispered, as if her mouth were as dry as sand. 'The Great Hoard. The Treasure of Incoherence. The Tamarisk. It has a hundred names. But it's been lost for a thousand years. More.'

'Correct. Even with the aid of a full set of notes, which I confess I stole from the British Museum and do not intend to return – it took me three weeks of searching through the Keep, then the Registry, to find the manuscript containing this map. And that still wasn't enough.'

'But that doesn't make any sense,' said Navy. 'The whole purpose of the Heresy is to recover the Kingdom. How could there be a map in the Keep showing exactly where it is, and we not know it?'

'There wasn't,' said Mr Ahmadi. 'I found many maps, but every one of them was imperfect or incomplete. The more I searched, the further I seemed to fall from the truth I sought. I was as blind, stumbling around in the dark, as all the Masters who have come before me. But last night those fools my fellow Officers put me in a cell with Professor Sassani.'

'The manuscript,' said Ned.

'Indeed,' said Mr Ahmadi. 'Sassani is another kind of fool, but he had seen your manuscript, Ned, and while he was determined not to reveal the least scrap of information to the Rack, not even in the throes of the thresher – which is impressive – he was no match for a snatcher of dreams. I waited until he had fallen asleep, and then I whispered into his ear, such things that could not but provoke him to gabble everything he knew. I had gathered much information from my research, but from Sassani I discovered that which I still lacked. And then I finished drawing my map.'

'And the Kingdom?' asked the Professor.

'If the winds are favourable, half a day's sail,' said Mr Ahmadi.

'But the Kingdom is in the desert,' said Navy.

'It was buried in sand,' said Fitz. 'In *The Giant's Almanac* –'

'You think a king delights in *treasure*?' shouted Mr Ahmadi. The noise of it, the shock of it, startled them. No one moved. 'You think a king buries his heart for two thousand years for the sake of *gold*? No,' he said, his voice falling again, until it was little more than a spent whisper, a broken reed. 'A king's delight is not in jewels, not in gold, not in all the riches of his kingdom, not in the wealth of the wide world. A king's delight lies in *bestowing* it. Tell them, Hožir.'

The water, now, was rising, and beyond the light cast by the fluttering lantern, and by Fitz's little lamp, the wet darkness of the cave had begun to feel threatening, as if it might overwhelm them at any moment. The Professor, who sat cross-legged beside Ned, with his long cloak draped for warmth round his ankles, had been watching the water as it gathered in the shadows; and Fitz knew that he spoke, now, in large part to distract them. He spoke directly to Navy and Fitz.

'I once knew a man, my children, not much older than you,' he said, 'who made a terrible mistake. He was young, passionate, impetuous – as perhaps the two of you are. He had a gift for telling tales, imaginative stories of all kinds. He could picture with absolute clarity anything he had ever encountered, as if it stood before his eyes whenever he but summoned the thought of it; more, he could dream and conjure forms never known in nature – great monstrous and colourful beasts of all kinds, winged, scaled, furred, the most exotic and wonderful creatures and plants, fields of grass that seeded themselves in the clouds, snakes of gleaming white stone that tunnelled in the desert sands, whole cities of living coral that rose out of the midst of the sea. From imaginations of this kind he wove complicated and engrossing tales, fictions and entertainments that delighted his family and friends. When he grew a little older, he had greater ambitions, and studied to become a poet, one of the priesthood of men and women who made it their life's work and end to see the nature of things in stories, and to travel the world telling tales. In those days poets were judges and they were teachers; they conserved the chronicles of time, and the mysteries of religions. Wise women and holy men, the greatest of them were – he thought – those whose visions were sharpest, most inventive, most fantastic. This man considered the good that he might do, and believed that he could become the most accomplished poet his people had ever known.

'His elder brother was very different. Where the young man loved to join people together by the telling of some tale, or bring reconciliation through the citation of some ancient precedent, where he loved to conserve the old rites and joyed to teach children by fables how to be just, generous, fair and modest, his brother instead seemed to love only himself. He inherited their family's petty kingdom; within a few years, he had purchased a better one, trading blood – his own, and those of his soldiers – for gold, land and crowns. Abroad, on foot, haunting markets and shady groves, the young man gathered stories; at home, in the saddle, thundering in the plains and on the mountains, his brother collected kingdoms. His conquests staggered his treasurers, who were forced to construct new vaults to house his gold, while the storyteller gladly and freely surrendered every dream of his heart or eye to any peasant who would share his crust of bread. In all of this he considered his rich brother the poorer for his insatiable greed, and himself the richer for what he considered his endless – boundless – generosity.

'The two brothers could not have been more different, my children –'

Just at that moment, they were all startled to hear, from the darkness beyond the Ossarium, back down the tunnel through which they had walked, the sound of singing. The voice was high and strained, and the pitching of the song erratic, unstable, as if sliding in drunkenness across the notes and words – in drunkenness, or madness.

It was the Riddler.

The tunnel, much lower than the slope on which they now sat, had flooded. All of them – save for the Professor, whose back was square to the Ossarium's entrance – turned towards the sound and peered into the deep shadow hanging over the porch of bones through which they had, themselves, earlier come. The song was nearing, always nearing, lapping on the water. Fitz wasn't sure at which moment he first became aware that the Riddler was swimming, bellowing out verses between wide, extended strokes. All the while the Professor continued his story, his back to the porch of the Ossarium, as if he were completely oblivious to the splash of the Riddler's arms, to the echo of his song in the tunnel.

'But the two brothers were not so different, after all,' said Farzan. 'In those days the younger son gave up his house, and his name, and travelled into the north to join an ancient society of those who, like him, had no need for the things of this world, but lived only for the love of stories. You cannot, I think, imagine the peace and tranquillity in which that society lived. In the feasts of their great temple, together they told tales that broke upon the ear and eye like a dawn upon the mountains, glancing with light and colour, full with the promise of life and power. In their communal life they enriched one another's art, refining their practice through the study of language and music, voice and gesture, passing stories between them in great rounds and cycles that could stretch not just for days, but for weeks, months, even years. Their art seemed to promise health and order, civility and peace. It was the expression of all that was best in human virtue, love, order and achievement, the flower of mind and heart. Its highest form and the vehicle of its performance was a great instrument on which their music was played – not by one of them alone, but by them all at once and together, an instrument which threaded and wove together the voices of a thousand singers, speaking in unison. Just so, many runnels, flowing together, may make a river; just so, many currents, combining, grow to a wave or swell.'

'He reverences the bones!' sang the Riddler – very near now, so near that Fitz thought he could discern in the darkness behind Farzan the flash of motley upon the water. 'The bones, the bones – he reverences the bones!'

'This instrument,' Farzan said – and his forehead where he leaned over the lantern was a study in concentration, furrowed and etched with deep lines – 'this instrument was known as the Great Loom. In the high assemblies of the society, one of their number, the first among them, sat before the Loom, and as they spoke and sang, a thousand voices blending in a feast of hymn and harmony, this Weaver wove their song together into a single piece or work, at once both tale and picture, story and image. The means by which he worked, as he sat before the Great Loom, partook of the human, but also of the divine, for it was said – and believed – that the Loom had been a gift of the gods and not the manufacture of human hands at all; that to sit before it was at once to fulfil the greatest promise of humanity, and to commune with something beyond our world. The secret of the Loom's design was to the society as precious as the instrument itself, a precise set of proportions and a geometry that they guarded closely – for in the wrong hands, what could the power of such an instrument not accomplish? This machine, whence song issued from silence as light from the darkness, as the world itself once sprang out of eternal nothing – the members of the Honourable Society guarded its power jealously, even as they took pride in their possession of it.

'They never saw the snake among the leaves.'

Now the Riddler was among them. His motley dripping with the rank brine of the tunnel, he crawled from the water, still singing under his breath the final refrain of his song, almost chanting it, over and over.

'Mark well my words, by supper's end, mark well my words, by supper's end, mark well, mark well –'

The Professor's chin dropped to his chest. He seemed for a time lost in his tale, disordered by his own memory. Black water began to lick the slope of stone on which the little group was sitting, rising ever nearer. It pooled around the Riddler's feet where he stood, hunched, behind the Professor, his white hair slick and flat against the taut line of his skull, his waterlogged motley sagging under its own weight, and only the hairy crests of his brows truly visible. His gaunt form seemed to partake of the bones around him, and Fitz had for a moment the impression that the Riddler was nothing but bones and skin, only the mummy of a man – and he shivered.

'One summer, my children, the conqueror rode north with his armies. He had heard of his brother's famous society, of this instrument of theirs, and came to satisfy his curiosity. Perhaps he was jealous of his brother. Perhaps he was spoiling for more worlds to conquer. The Society sat in congress before his embassy, he throned amongst them, and sang a great song of their fellowship, a hymn of the creation of the world. Gardens seemed that afternoon to grow out of the air; rivers while they sang poured through their halls, and life grew spontaneous in the fatty waves; silver and gold, mined from the light that swept across the storeyed hall, dropped in ingots to the floor and strewed the company with dazzling. The conqueror, if he had not been jealous already, conceived in his heart a violent appetite for the jewel of the Society, for the Great Loom on which they wove their thread of heaven. It seemed to him a prize greater than any plunder or spoil he had ever desired, or got, and he would not rest until it lay within his grasp – or, at least, until he had wrested it from his brother. Before the evening fell upon that evil day, he wrecked the Society's temple, soiled the great library, ripped down and trampled its gardens, and drove every member of the fellowship into exile. They fled to a mountain wasteland, while the conqueror – abetted by certain traitors in his brother's company – seized the Loom, along with the Society's only record of the principles of its construction.'

'I'll gnaw your flesh to naught, to naught, to naught, I'll gnaw your flesh to naught,' sang the Riddler quietly, and he danced to his music in the water, causing little ripples to splash on the stone. The water reached almost to the Professor's cloak.

'The younger brother, the storyteller, knew that this calamity was in some sense his own fault. The rest of the Society had hidden themselves in the Mountain, but he alone came down and rejoined the world, determined to bring his brother to his senses, or to account. He hoped to repossess the Loom, to refound the paradise his brother's greed had destroyed.

'His pilgrimage was long and arduous. On foot he journeyed through his brother's kingdoms, as wide almost as the world was wide, seeking audience with his brother's captains, his governors, the members of his council, and the great families joined to him by treaty, by alliance and by marriage. Using his voice to plead and persuade, and spinning music of such melody that even the deaf delighted to share his table, he gathered to his cause a thousand captains and princes. When he reached his brother's capital, a city he had never known, so opulent in its luxury and power that he doubted whether he still walked the earth, he carried his petition to the king and humbly supplicated him to return what he had stolen, or else to face the displeasure and – he did not doubt – the judgement of the gods.'

'To naught, to naught, to naught, to naught, to naught,' the Riddler chanted and sang, on and on as the Professor told his tale, all the while his voice lilting and falling, crazed, musical, like bells and glass and water.

'The conqueror laughed. Listen to the wind and the water, my children, moving in the dark caves, rolling down the tunnels around us, and you may hear the song of his laughter even now. It is the laughter of the void, of emptiness, of an insatiable hunger. Before his brother's eyes he commanded the Great Loom to be carried into his judgement chamber, and there broken up with axes. His servant and a man of his inner council set it ablaze, the fire filling the whole of the palace with smoke and horror. Through it all, he laughed. The storyteller had thought himself prepared for the worst, and in his hubris, then, he sought to call to his aid the thousand captains and princes who, in their wisdom and judgement, had subscribed to his petition. But the king his brother was informed of this conspiracy and – calling for his personal guard – he dispatched orders for the arrest of every one of the conspirators. Still he laughed. Only his brother, among all those, he permitted to go free, so that he might both see and be powerless to contain the horror that he had unleashed – not just the destruction of the beauty of his art, with all its sacred mysteries and traditions, but the final dissolution of his sacred order and the enslavement of all who had once believed in it. Indeed, the king was not content merely to make him free; he created the storyteller his *wazir* – his chief counsellor – and forced him to complete the work of his own destruction. By his own hand the thousand conspirators should be punished; by his own hand the secrets of the Great Loom should be lost.'

Now the Riddler approached them where they huddled on the slope, and stood just behind the Professor. He drew himself to his full height, and shook his motley free of seawater. His thin hair he drew back from his face, and with an elaborate flourish he extended his arms, level from his shoulders, so that his body made a kind of cross behind Farzan. And he hung there, his eyes closed as if in sleep, listening.

'If there was evil in the *wazir*'s heart, he told himself it was a righteous anger. He could not touch his rich and powerful brother, but the informer – a little child who had betrayed his confederacy and caused the ruin of his hopes, an innocent, and a bystander – this child he could punish. He was a little beggar boy, who had overheard some embassy or message, and by pulling on this thread had unclued the great knot of the conspiracy's design. The *wazir* thought it was a small matter to ruin him, and, without his brother's knowledge he caused him to be enslaved alongside the thousand captains the king had ordered to be sent into the desert. Little did he know his brother had fixed his twisted heart on the love and service of this child; in the deformity of his greed and self-love, in his paranoia and derangement, he had concluded that only this child among all his many millions of subjects was his true and loyal friend; no family, no servant could be closer nor more trusted, and this urchin – wherever he could be found – the conqueror declared his prince and his heir. At first the *wazir* clapped his hands at his good fortune; at the very least, he thought, he had hurt the king where he should suffer most, for this child would never be found.

'This man was sick with grief and horror,' said the Professor. 'He did not know what he did. In your hearts, forgive him.'

'To naught, to naught, to naught, to naught, to naught,' whispered the Riddler. Fitz couldn't take his eyes from the rough terrain of his ancient face, every crack and crease and fold of which the lantern crusted with shadows.

'By the evil of his hand, this man had put the beggar boy where he should never again be found. And he never was. But it was a strange and a just twist of fortune, a justice truly fashioned by the gods, that with this beggar child perished too the *wazir*'s hopes of recovering the Great Loom. For the child knew of his desperate desire to recover the tablet on which the sacred proportions, and their exact geometry, were enrolled, and this tablet – heaped among the king's spoils – had been delivered to the king's slave army to be buried amongst his most splendid treasures in his desert tomb. The beggar child himself had become the keeper of the secret of the Great Loom; and yet neither of the brothers could reach him, for the slave army had disappeared into the salt waste to build in a secret location, and no man – on pain of death – no, not even the *wazir* – was permitted to go in search of them. The king himself did not know the location of the great tomb his slaves were constructing for him.'

'Gnaw to naught to gnaw to naught to gnaw to naught to gnaw to naught to gnaw to –'

'How the *wazir* raged, and ground his teeth in despair! How he paced! What oaths he muttered at his own stupidity! And yet, even then, after so much, the gods were not finished with the *wazir*. For, after many years – during which time he had left no means untried to find the child, to recover the tablet, and to revive his ruined and dispersed Society – the slave army appeared again out of the desert. The tomb was complete, and the king – broken by years of slowly encroaching despair – ordered the contents of his palace to be buried in his place, and the slaves with them. In the meanwhile, as spies informed his brother, the beggar child had become the leader of the slave army, a quick-witted man known to all as *al-Jabbar*, the Giant; moreover, this Giant had constructed an ingenious device, a kind of map or compass, which when correctly calibrated provided the location of the king's tomb and, by certain secret markings on its reverse face, the very secrets of the Loom that more than life itself the *wazir* still sought. The *wazir* contrived to have this compass stolen and copied, but learned to his dismay that it could not be calibrated by any man but *al-Jabbar* himself. How the *wazir* wept with distracted fury, when he discovered how powers beyond this world had put the compass into his hands precisely to taunt him, to knock the cherry against his hungry lips, and then leave him with nothing but ash for his sustenance!'

By now the Riddler, still standing behind the Professor, had begun to weave from side to side, as if in abstraction, or meditation, as if possessed. Still the story went on, as if the Riddler weren't there; and yet it seemed to acquire by his presence the features of his song, and of his movement: an overwhelming bleakness, a despair, emptied of all meaning, a mere wagging and swaying of the organs of sense, without sense. Listening to the Professor, watching the Riddler, feeling the cold water begin to lick at his fingertips where he braced himself on the rocky slope, Fitz fell into a kind of trance or reverie in which each element was implicated in the other, in which they all told the same story, and the tale was of nothing but death. He could feel them all, huddled in the darkness, possessed by this story and its dance, by this dance and its story: two faces of the same coin.

'The *wazir* tried to meet this Giant. He would have done anything – he would have imprisoned him, killed him – whatever it took. He was delirious with his frustration, insane with his desperation. He failed. The Giant disappeared, and the *wazir* was left with only the bronze copy of his compass, a complex system of circular metal discs intricately cast and minutely inscribed – as beautiful and as ingenious an instrument as the Great Loom itself, but useless without its creator. The *wazir* understood the futility of

447

his situation, and accepted at last the punishment for his own greed and error. He went to the king his brother, and confessed all that he had done. To him he surrendered the copy of the Giant's ingenious instrument, which in after-times we have come to call *al-manac*, "the end of the journey". After this, having given up the Almanac, he passed out of his brother's kingdom into exile. He learned many years later that the king himself, impoverished and isolated, had at last been beaten from his own palace and, with the seven officers of his council and the eight generals of his army, had been sent into exile. They sailed far from their country, across a sea as vast as was then known, and came to land on a wild island at the farthest end of the world. There, the king dying, his officers buried him with his Almanac – the very last of all his treasure – in a secret tomb.

From the Riddler a low murmur had been building, and growing in intensity, at first no more than the vibrations a gnat might make with its wings, but after a time more, stronger, insistent, the humming of a reed, the insistent, angry, nasal drone of an engine.

'But even this was not the end,' said the Professor. 'For the officers and generals of the king's court, beleaguered and dispossessed as they were, believed in a prophecy that had been given them, that the heir to his kingdom should be born again, once in every generation; and if only they should find this child, he – and only he – would be able to regain and rebuild the Kingdom, the greatest empire ever known to the world. To this end, though surrounded by barbarians and in a remote country, the fifteen of them founded a society they called the Heresy, whose purpose was to prepare for the coming of the heir, and the recovery of the kingdom they had lost.

'Their hope was a hope born out of vengeance. They could not be content with their defeat. For them, the great game of power, the struggle between two brothers, the fate of an empire, would one day be resolved; more – when the game was finally ended, they were determined they should be its victors.'

*The game is already ended.*

Suddenly the Riddler's arms – muscular, deliberate, ruthlessly efficient – flashed into motion. So abrupt was the action, after so much stillness, that it was over before anyone could react. In his hands he had brandished the Collar, and with practised, unerring precision slipped it round the Professor's neck. With a deft turn to his wrist he had cinched it tight, cutting off – as Fitz well knew – the old man's sense of feeling. And then, with another flash of his arm, hoisting the whole of the Professor's body with the full strength of his legs, the Riddler had toppled him into the silent, black, rising pool. Together, thrashing, they sank below the surface of the water, which churned and bubbled for almost a minute after. Fitz and Navy, alone, knew what the Riddler had done, how thickly numb and disorientating the Collar could be, how impossible the Professor would find it to defend himself, to fight free of the Riddler's hold, to escape the dark engulfing water. They watched the edge of the water helplessly.

And then it was still. The cave subsided again into darkness and silence.

They had been forced to compress themselves into the farthest, sharpest angle where the wall of bones met the side of the sloping floor. Wherever they stood against the wall, sharp bones tore into their clothing, and around them over the flat expanse of the rising seawater they could make out nothing more than the vanishing dome, festooned with swirls and shoals of skeletal geometry.

The stillness was absolute. Seconds ached by.

'And what happened to the *wazir*,' asked Navy. She was grasping timidly at the story. 'Did he ever give up his search? Did he ever succumb? Did he ever lose faith?'

'Never,' answered Mr Ahmadi, quietly. He paced from them, and crouched in a far corner, his head nestled among skulls. 'He returned to his great guild of plotters and imaginers, and continued to do the work of story. From generation to generation, he has sought the heir to the Kingdom, searching for the child who should bear the mark of the Giant, never giving up hope, never surrendering to despair. From generation to generation, he has sought the lost secret of the Great Loom. He is one of the immortals now, the last of the great Imaginers, and lives in this world almost as a shadow – a bright and vital shadow, the very stuff of magic.'

With no warning, like a strike of lightning lashing up from the depths, a huge showering form shot from the surface of the water, almost breaching the surface entirely. His cloak as he rose billowed from the water, and as he landed on the rock it settled around him like the petals of a dark flower. He crouched on his hands and knees, breathing like a man in love with air, for whom every deep draught was a romance. His neck, strong and bare, bore the red welt of the strap he had torn from it.

Navy stood before him, plainly awed – but not so awed that she hesitated to hold out her hand. He took it, and stood.

'If Fitz is really the heir to the Heresy,' said Navy, to all of them, but holding the Professor's eye, as metal metal, socketed, 'the

Kingdom is all but at hand. We should find this exile, this other brother, this immortal, this *wazir*, and take him with us to find it.'

Holding her hand as in the old tales a knight might the hand of his lady, the Professor, though already standing, seemed – impossibly – to stand yet taller, yet further, to stand with his head through the roof of the cave. Then he turned, strode past the Master to the far end of the cave, and set his hands to the wall. Bones rained into the water as he tore them down before him, and dawn light flooded into the cave, glittering on the water and setting fire to their weary faces.

'But there is no need to look for me,' said the Professor, turning again to face them, 'for I myself was this *wazir*. And I am now Phantastes, High Imaginer of the Honourable Society of Wraiths and Phantasms. I have found you, and been with you all this long night.'

# 17

# *Navy*

By the time they came out on to the sand beneath the cliffs, the tide had risen far enough to drown all but the highest part of the beach. Skirting the rocks, they headed north towards the little cove where, the afternoon before, Ned, Clare and Phantastes had moored their boats. They were two small, light hulls, each of two sails and with a shallow keel. 'Fast,' said Phantastes. 'Dangerous,' said Clare.

Mr Ahmadi drew them in through the shallow water of the cove, and put the children aboard.

'No,' said Clare. 'I want him with us.' She and Ned had already begun to raise the sails on the other boat.

'There is no question,' said Phantastes. 'Habi is the best sailor among us, the most experienced, and he knows these waters. The children will be safest in his care. They go with him, and you with me.'

Clare fumed, but Fitz was pleased. Ever since the night they had passed by the tombs, he had wanted to see Mr Ahmadi at the tiller. This was a chance he hadn't dreamed might be his.

They set out a few minutes later. Mr Ahmadi and Ned pushed the hulls through the surf during a dull spell in the breaking waves, while Fitz and Clare in their boats, side by side, began to draw on the mainsheets, pulling wind into the cloth. For the first ten minutes, their progress was rocky. Every time they surged forward, the wind locking for a moment in the suddenly stiffening sails and driving the boom forward against the mast with a jolt, the whole boat seemed to hover on its purpose – only to subside, dropping with a change of the swell back into a listless clamour of sheets and shrouds, rattling and knocking in the wind. Staring behind them as they failed to make real progress from the beach, Fitz wondered if they would be driven back on to the shore, into the streaks and ridges of rock that rode into the sea from the cliffs like rails, like the spines of some prehistoric sea-lumbering animal that hadn't yet quite retired into the sands beneath. But as the tide began to change in earnest, and Mr Ahmadi pulled himself over the side, the wind began to stick in the jib, and Navy called out with delight as she managed to hold it, straining, in the fore blocks.

For the better part of an hour they pushed into ever colder waters. On the sea everything was motion; there was no air, only a shifting tumult of movement across their faces and hands as they reached against the sails; there was no water, only a billowing pulse of swells swinging into them like a pendulum from the south-west, skimming them on, then dropping them, then skimming them on again; but above all, the sky declined to vault over their heads, but rather ledged like a hard and implacable shelf of blue, unbroken by clouds, glaring and glazed as if it were clay still firing in the cracking heat of a colossal oven. Mr Ahmadi sat with the tiller in his hand, guiding the boat expertly across the surges as they swept forward and across their bow, trimming the mainsail to catch every curl that fringed and purfled the sheets of wind that drove them steadily north. In the other boat, now and then dropping behind, Fitz could just make out Phantastes' white beard flowing towards the sailcloth, his eyes fixed intently on the shape and profile of Mr Ahmadi's bearing, and always Clare's hands, steady on the jibsheet, willing their journey over and the children safely on the shore again.

Behind them as the dawn spread above the cliffs, they had seen the smoke rising from between the headlands. The Heresy itself lay beyond their view, but the night's events were written on the sky, and Fitz felt with fear, and pride, and sorrow the fury that must have driven those unfed and unclothed bodies, hungry and destructive, wielding fists and fire, through the Heresy's dark and quiet courts. What the Wispers had done, what the Subs, what had become of the Fells and Offs in their hundreds, armed, they couldn't know; but they did, with grim resignation, note on the cliffs, about half an hour after setting out, a little knot of figures standing together, figures that perhaps were watching them. The Master said nothing about it, and Navy and Fitz followed his example. But they all saw it.

Soon that was the least of their worries. Fitz first realized that something was wrong when he heard thunder roll in the long recess of the sky behind them. Mr Ahmadi didn't look back as Fitz had, but his face set at the sound – close, too close, and meaty, like a thick throat gargling blood. Behind them a rack of black clouds, chasing the sun, advanced over the rocky promontory of the coast, and Fitz could almost taste on the forward sweep of its violence the salt spittle of a ranting, gasping, torrenting storm.

He didn't dare mention what Mr Ahmadi clearly didn't want to see, but Navy did.

'That doesn't look good,' she said. 'Electrical storms on the water can be dangerous, and that one is bringing high windspeeds in a direction orthogonal to the prevailing oceanic swell.'

Fitz stole a glance back at Clare. She had turned to watch the big black thunder cresting the cliffs.

'It will get dark and wet very fast,' said Mr Ahmadi. His voice barked with authority against the rising drone of the wind. 'I'm going to tack back into the wind, to see if we can't get into the lee of the shore again. Watch your heads.' For the first time since they had set off, Fitz and Navy had to duck as the boom swung across the boat and the mainsail filled on the port side. Phantastes followed suit, coming inside them as they tacked back towards the storm and the hope of lighter winds towards the cliffs. Fitz noticed he had set his teeth, and was grinding them at the back, working his lower jaw hard against his back molars. He wished that he had something to do besides grip the wales and try to help his stomach to rise and fall with the swells – swells that were now rolling straight into their stern and tipping them, repeatedly, into yawning troughs. The air thickened, stinging them with salt spray, and as the clouds rolled forward, unfurling their huge inky banners, the light began to constrict around them, to tighten and to pale, so that the sea itself seemed to shrink and all that they did within it. No longer did the mast yearn for the far distances of the horizon, or the jib pregnant with the wind's pressure for the north that had lain before them like a gauntlet to be seized; now they saw only as far as from one surge to another, darkly, and when the rain began to lash down and the first of the squalls struck them like a flat palm, the salt in his eyes seemed to collapse Fitz's world still further, until everything he knew and could understand lay in the two hands – still gripping the sides and stays – immediately before his own face.

'I have to try to reef the sails!' shouted Mr Ahmadi. Fitz could barely hear him over the slap of the swell and the roar of the wind, but he could see that Mr Ahmadi was right – if the gusts intensified any further, this sudden autumn storm might tear the sailcloth, or worse. At first Fitz tried to stay out of the way as Mr Ahmadi clawed a route forward, but then he took the tiller, and held it jammed to the left as the sails started to inch down and Mr Ahmadi went to work gathering them along the length of the boom. Crouching in the jerking boat, Navy helped Mr Ahmadi to gather and roll the cloth from luff to leech. It was all they could do to keep their feet against the spray and sudden, strong shifts in the wind, the unpredictable lurches of the foaming swells, and the constant threat of the heavy boom; Fitz had to wedge his feet hard under the deck, trying to maintain purchase through the tough soles of his stiff shoes by cramming his toes beneath a strut. From breath to breath and task to task, they were surviving the storm by inches.

When Mr Ahmadi took his seat again at the stern, and shifted them back into the wind, he pointed them higher, and closer to the coast. Fitz climbed forward and joined Navy again on the starboard side, where they used their weight to balance the boat against the lean of the ripping wind. With his hand firmly gripping the side stay, Fitz craned his head round to catch sight of the other boat.

It was gone.

His heart staggered, and as he tried to swivel and catch Mr Ahmadi's eye, to shout, to point, he let his hand slip from the stay. If the boat at that moment hadn't crashed off the crest of one of the larger rollers still sweeping into its transom, he might have caught himself. Instead, feet splaying in the air, he tipped backwards in the beginning of what seemed the longest, most perfect reverse somersault he had ever executed. To slip into the surging water, and knife down inside its parting and soundless deep, would have been the work of a second, a story told in a breath or a blink; but the process of it seemed to unfold into chapters, sections and subsections, each minute element of the experience a discrete compound of sensation and observation.

*I am going to die.*

His hand waved in the air, as if he were conducting a furious passage in some titanic overture. It looked to him very small against the grey sheets of flying rain that stacked one on another above the mast.

Mr Ahmadi rammed the tiller to port, sending the boat into a windward spin. As it came round beneath his tumbling back, Fitz saw the side stay dip back towards him, a dancer bowing at the conclusion of a gavotte.

No one seemed to make any noise as he fell. It seemed to him strange that so consequential a thing should take place, so little remarked. He tried to shout, but his voice was too slow in coming.

And so little thing as a voice would never make it out of him, anyway, with all that grey and silver water rushing around his face, filling his nose, stoppering his ears.

Navy's reflexes must have been very fast, or perhaps time really had slowed in those few beats between turning, falling and entering the water; because as Fitz passed through the shocking membrane of current froth, then felt the cold, numb quietness close around his ears, he felt also a sharper, harder pain closing around his ankle – and knew at once that it was Navy's hand, grasping and clutching him, retaining him, dragging him hard through the raking water as the boat still pitched forward on the swell, so that first one shin, then the other slammed against the wooden deck. A cracking spasm coursed through his body from his knee through to his throat. Every muscle in Fitz's frame contracted against the pain, trying to pull through the flow of the water through which his body was dragging, and he realized that in his disorientation he had swerved, writhed and turned, and that his head was now curling up towards the hull of the boat. He reached for it, not sure whether he was trying to grapple it or to shield his head from knocking against it; but he never reached it. A hand had hooked into the tail of his heavy woollen coat, and in a single, heaving motion he found himself lifted clear of the water and dragged, not without scuffle and knocking, back into the boat.

By the time Fitz had recovered his bearings, Mr Ahmadi was already back at the tiller, steering the bow back out of the wind. He didn't say a word, but was watching the sails and peering anxiously beyond them into the shifting depths of the storm as it blew through them. Navy sat above Fitz, more solicitous; she had taken his place, and with her free hand clutched the side stay with white knuckles. The skin of her hand was torn and bleeding. The blood was running pink down the shroud.

'You're supposed to stay in the boat,' she said, and notwithstanding all the blood she smiled.

Fitz spluttered; too much water spurted from his nose as he laughed and coughed. Clearing his lungs and wiping down his face gave him relief, but the real cold was within, and he didn't laugh long.

'Have we lost them?' he asked.

Navy didn't answer; she turned her head out to starboard, and watched for a time, while in the boat's bottom, his feet jammed against the hull, Fitz tried to wring brine from his cuffs and hems.

'They'll be along,' she said, turning back to him so that she could be heard over the wind, and giving each word a lot of space. 'There's only one real bearing in this wind.'

Maybe it was the shock of going overboard, or the cold that now clung to him and seemed to pass through his skin to his joints and bones, but the next twenty or thirty minutes – it must have been that long – passed in a blink. Fitz didn't dare lift himself out of the boat's bottom, even when the wind quickened and they began to heel; without complaint, Navy tried to compensate for his injured courage by hiking out further, herself, so that at times only her legs remained within reach. Between holding himself against the shivering cold and hovering over Navy's legs in case she should lose her balance and need rescuing, Fitz passed the rest of the storm as quickly as it passed over them.

No sooner did the cloud and murk begin to clear than it raced off, as if scrubbed away by some scouring hand. The change struck so suddenly and with such completeness, at a stroke wiping away not only the impenetrable and pelting rain, the thick, low cloud, and the battering squalls, but the heavy swells and its curdling caps, too. Behind the cloud as it cleared to the north before them, the pristine and glittering air scattered bright on the waves, and the boat seemed to respond by dipping and darting over the swells with a new lightness. Mr Ahmadi didn't go so far as to unreef the sail, but he did let the sheet out and guided the boat into a wide reach. As the bow turned downwind, Fitz saw the island for the first time, a little hub of rock, gold in the afternoon sun over the green, green sea.

'That's it,' said Mr Ahmadi. His mouth was set tight as a knife, but his eyes smiled.

The storm was still rolling over the little island's high ground. It stood out of the sea like the arched back of a roused cat, its upper ridges spined with jagged striations of bare, weathered rock. Below, patches of grass and moss clung to steep slopes that ended in crumbling cliffs, and those cliffs in the sea. It was difficult to judge scale from their position and perspective, but Fitz thought the island fairly small – only a few hundred metres across at its longest. He supposed it was just visible, most days, from the coast, which lay twelve or fifteen miles away.

'That?' he asked. His voice carried easily in the muted air.

'Look at the peak of the dome,' answered Mr Ahmadi. He cleated the mainsheet against the block and pointed to the highest point on the island's summit. 'Do you see that jagged rock?'

Mr Ahmadi brought them into a dead run, so that the island would swerve more easily into view beyond the bow. Fitz and Navy studied it carefully. At the place where Mr Ahmadi had pointed, a huge menhir had been planted, isolated from the rest of the stone outcrop on the hill's height. It seemed a kind of statement, aggressively confronting the eye as it came up the slopes from the sea, on a line from the coast. It might have been five or even ten metres tall, the sort of stone over which archaeologists would shake their heads in puzzlement.

Fitz wished he could shake his own head in puzzlement. Instead it shook with cold.

'What about it?' he asked.

'The stone that couldn't be moved,' said Navy.

'At least someone pays attention in lessons,' said Mr Ahmadi, drawing in the sheet again, and shifting the tiller hard to port, in order to put them back on a bearing that would come just short of the island.

'It's an important idea in the sorts of work we do – we used to do – with the Sweeper,' said Navy. 'Payne never stops going on about it. The basic point is that sometimes when you're solving a problem you have freedom to change your parameters, your materials, your methods, or the outcome. But, more often, you don't. Most of the time, there is some aspect of the situation that has to be accepted and incorporated, somehow, into your solution, whatever the problem is and whatever the solution. In a way, then, your response to the stone that can't be moved is always *really* the problem, the one at the centre of all the other problems. And in some sense, that problem, and the stone itself, is symbolic of –'

'Let me guess,' said Fitz. 'The stone that can't be moved represents your own death.'

'Well, yes,' said Navy. 'Obviously. Because your inability to do something, or change it, the necessity of accepting the world the way it is and recognizing, and acknowledging, your powerlessness within it – that's just a version of your own death, isn't it?'

Fitz thought about this for a minute as the water slipped past his hand.

'What does the stone that can't be moved have to do with the Kingdom?' he asked.

'It's the foundation of the Heresy,' said Mr Ahmadi. 'Obviously. At the centre of any life is death, the stone that can't be moved. We build our existence like a tomb around it, and when we die it becomes the door through which we pass.'

'So that stone, up there – is that an entrance to a tomb?'

'I certainly hope so,' answered Mr Ahmadi. He hauled on the mainsheet, pointing their course higher into the wind.

He steered for a point just to windward of the tip of the island. From about half a kilometre they could see the swells crashing against broken rocks at the foot of sheer cliffs. Letting out the sails again, they ran round the island's north side before jibing and drawing again to windward – now knifing directly into the current – to draw along the island's west coast. Here the landing was more straightforward, beyond a small breakwater against a low shore. They tacked, turning, and rode in on the swell.

Leaving the boat tied loosely to a spur of rock, the three of them climbed on to a low shelf of slick wet stone that rose gradually towards the north of the island. Mr Ahmadi tried to find footholds to climb across it, on to the higher ledges above, but it was too steep and the face of it too slippery.

'We'll have to go round,' said Navy's eyes. She and Fitz set out.

He was eager to get to the high ground as quickly as possible, and from there to search the water on every side. Had Phantastes seen them, when they hadn't seen him? Did he hold his bearings well enough in the murk of the storm, to be able to find the island when it had cleared? Mr Ahmadi seemed almost frighteningly single-minded, focused on locating the Kingdom, and on that alone; the loss – the death? – of Clare, of Ned, of Phantastes, meant nothing to him.

Almost running, Fitz came round a narrow part of the ledge to a vantage from which he could see the sea stretching north from the island. It lay empty, calm and blue under the late afternoon sunlight. Fitz's heart sank.

Here the ledge crumbled away, and they would have no choice but to climb. He and Navy were scrutinizing it when Mr Ahmadi finally caught up with them. He spent a few seconds looking down at the sheer drop where the ledge tumbled into the sea, and kicked a few loose stones over the side. They made no sound as they fell through the uninterrupted air, straight into the churning water below.

'That's a strong tidal current,' he said, and looked up.

There were footholds, and he found them.

Navy studied him carefully as he ascended, then turned to Fitz.

'I'll follow him. I'm better at this than you. Watch where I put my hands and feet, and do exactly what I do. You're stronger than I am, so you can definitely do whatever I show you.'

She climbed slowly, adjusting Mr Ahmadi's route for her smaller frame. Fitz studied her movements carefully, and memorized the places where she jammed her feet, the angles at which she held her legs, the curl of her fingers on the stone's jagged protrusions, and the places where the footholds were stable, as well as those where they were loose.

When she was safely out of the way, Fitz followed the others. He climbed easily and securely, and covered the distance in half the time it had taken Navy. As he reached the next ledge, she put out her hand and hauled him effortlessly up the last few feet, to stand beside her. Fitz hadn't expected her grip to be so firm, or her arm to lift him so easily.

'I'm not stronger than you,' he said.

'I know,' said Navy. 'But saying so got you up the wall. Fast, too.' She smiled, but she was already moving on, back towards the east face of the cliffs, where Mr Ahmadi had already disappeared. The dark shadows on this side of the island gave the cool sea wind a bitter edge, so much so that beneath his sodden wool coat Fitz shivered. He scanned the water below as they continued to come round the ledge, bearing ever right, but here, too – between the island and the mainland – the seas were resolutely empty.

Mr Ahmadi had stopped in a narrow place. Pushing fast past a spine of rock that jutted from the wall, they almost collided with him. He didn't seem to notice. His eyes were fixed on the water below.

'That's where I would have liked to have moored, if we could,' he said. 'If the wind had allowed it.'

They followed his gaze. Below them the water appeared to be swirling, heaving, turning in a massive frothing spiral that seemed to flush the sea much as water swirls round the bowl of a basin when you pull out the plug.

'Is that a whirlpool?' asked Navy. It was clearly a whirlpool, and a powerful one. Fitz could see that Navy was already scanning the local area for clues as to what had caused it, and was no doubt formulating in her imagination a complete map of the probable bed of the ocean lying beneath.

'Anyone coming from the coast, from the mainland –' Mr Ahmadi was gesturing back into the evening, towards the coast from which they had sailed – 'say, two hundred or three hundred years ago – would have rowed, or sailed. And anyone rowing would have tried to put in just here, the nearest approach, the easiest foothold on the island. They never would have seen this tidal run. That must be why –'

'Why no one has ever discovered the Kingdom?'

Mr Ahmadi didn't answer. Like Fitz, he was scanning the seas. His thoughts had turned somewhere else.

They carried on round the east side of the island. Here the rocky ledges opened up into a broader, scalable face, and one by one, Mr Ahmadi first and Navy bringing up the rear, they picked their way across its loose strew of shale and moss. The slope was just steep enough that a fall could be awkward, or in places dangerous, and Fitz was conscious of Navy's hands behind his feet, of the quick reflexes she had shown on the sea, of that hidden power in her shoulders – and grateful for it all. For what seemed an hour they made slow progress up the inclined face of the cliff, skirting patches of crumbling stone, but reaching for handholds among the rough tufts of thrift and samphire that seemed to grow from every crack and crevice in the rock. In the island's wind shadow they found themselves shielded from the worst of the gusts, but while Fitz was grateful for a respite from the wind's prising fingers, he was – equally – impatient to get back into the open, to a vantage from which he could once more scan shorewards for any sight of the other boat.

When they reached the standing stone, Fitz's first thought was that it seemed taller than he had expected. Seven or eight feet across, and wider at the base than at its top, it carried no mark of hammer or chisel – scoured by the sea and the rain, buffeted by winds and baked by the sun, broken here and there by ice and stained by lichen and moss and birds, it stood bare and honest, a simple table of all that had befallen the island in the years since the stone had first crowned it. Fitz had expected to find it before some ancient cave or temple, like a door that had been rolled or lifted into place, guarding the entrance; but instead the stone appeared to stand free and president, on its own, a simple and ambiguous monument to the ingenuity and strength of those who had raised it. Like a stalwart sentry or a faithful dog, notwithstanding its isolation and remoteness, it had endured.

*It hasn't been moved.*

Mr Ahmadi had stopped several feet behind them. He stared at the stone, judging it, trying to make sense of the scene in front of them.

'This isn't right,' he said. 'There's nothing here. It doesn't mean anything.'

Fitz felt a weight turn over in his chest, as if his blood, for some battle roused, had surrendered. He knew exactly what Mr Ahmadi meant. The stone, so visible from the sea, ought to have stood for something, or pointed their way to somewhere. It ought to have led them to something, or revealed the secret of the Kingdom. Why else was it so visible from so far?

'Maybe it's just a stone,' Fitz said. 'Maybe it's just part of the island.'

Navy was running her hand along its surface. 'No,' she said. 'Look at it. It's obvious. The island stone is basalt, tuff, the sort of aerated igneous formation that was coughed up by volcanoes in the Ordovician. It's everywhere on the coast around the Heresy. This is different – sandstone – and much older. It might have been deposited here during the last ice age, sure – there was a massive fast-moving ice sheet running south all along this seaboard, and it left chunks and boulders as big as this all over the place. But a glacier wouldn't have left a menhir this size standing in this orientation. And it wouldn't have carved it, either.'

With the sun starting to drop to the horizon behind them, Fitz could hardly make out the contours that Navy was tracing with her fingers.

'These markings must have been deep, and they're old. Hardly anything's left,' she said. 'But if you run your fingers in it, you can feel how extensive it must have been. I think it's writing.'

Mr Ahmadi paced from side to side of the narrow summit.

'If the writing is illegible, it won't be any help,' he said. 'We're going to have to find the tomb the old-fashioned way.'

'I don't think so,' said Navy. Her hands were still on the stone, but now they were moving both deliberately and urgently from one place to another. Straining on to her toes, she reached for something high on the shadowed side of the standing stone.

'Can you make out the words?' asked Fitz.

'No,' she said. 'The words are gone. But there's more to this stone than that. Put your finger here.'

Taking his hand, then his finger, Navy guided it to a place about five feet off the ground where Fitz felt something that his eyes hadn't seen – not a groove or the trace of an old cut, but a dimple that, when he probed it, he found to be a hole. It was a little narrower than his finger, but seemed to run very deep.

He bent a little, and put his eye to the hole. It did go very deep; in fact, it went all the way through the four or five feet to the far side of the stone, where its surface was still bathed in evening light from the declining sun.

'What's the date?' asked Navy. 'The twentieth? The twenty-first?'

Mr Ahmadi had joined them and, reaching high against the stone, was using a pebble to scrape lichen from another hole that lay further up the face.

'Hurry,' he said.

While Fitz and Navy scraped at the holes, on both sides, with his foot Mr Ahmadi swept the ground obscured in the shadow of the tall stone. It was a rough job, but it was obvious what he was doing, and to Fitz's surprise, it worked.

'There,' said Mr Ahmadi. The light from the sun as it settled towards evening fell broad and warm on the south-west face of the menhir. On the north-east face, though, the shadows of night already clung to the stone, and a kind of gloom or pall hung over the tough brown rock on which they stood. But now, in the darkest fold of that evening veil, lights like blurred and gauzy diamonds began to glimmer and appear, some brighter than others, projected upon the dark flat of the ground. At first Fitz fought the urge to rub his eyes: so soft and astray these little lights lay, lingering day in among the pockets of evening, their luminous shells like shades as indistinct as water is in water. But as the sun fell, far away, into the horizon, so instant by instant their edges sharpened, hardening and focusing on the ground like small rips tearing in old cloth, and every filament and shred of light resolved its threaded border, so that as he squinted at these little suns, these spots of day reserved for evening as tight harmonies survive in the subsiding lines of some still candescent polyphonic vesper hymn, Fitz sensed a dawn breaking even in the accumulations of the shroudy files of evening – and he caught at his breath.

'At first,' said Navy – she had stood aside, like the others, to let the lights fall – 'I thought maybe the shadow of the stone at evening might point us back to something.' She levelled her arm to the east along the axis of its needle-pointed shadow. 'It's as if the island were a giant sundial, and this stone were its gnomon.'

No sooner had Navy finished speaking these words than Mr Ahmadi turned and strode along the length of the menhir's long shadow to the edge of the flat ground cleared at the summit of the island, where the dark border hemmed against the light tumbled on to the rocks falling away towards the sea. He was scanning them, and the sea, the horizon – anything that might give him some purchase on this riddle of space and stone and light – when Navy called after him.

'But the shadow is a misdirection,' she said, throwing her voice along the length of its cast. Mr Ahmadi turned.

'Look at the line of the lights,' she said, sweeping her extended finger as the little lights also swept, towards the south.

Fitz could see what she meant. Against the line of the shadow's sharply pointed needle, the lights projected by the stone upon the ground defined a clear line lying thirty or forty degrees to the south. Almost unconsciously – merely aware of his own involuntary motion – Fitz found himself turning to align himself with this line, even as Mr Ahmadi strode along the uneven perimeter of the summit to the place where the line of lights, extended, would direct them downslope.

Fitz regarded him as he stood at the border of the slope. The wind moved in his hair, and ruffled with impatience the base of the black cape he still wore, draped like night round his shoulders. Time and care had scooped at the sockets of his eyes, and in profile his face disclosed dramatic promontories, from the high scarp of his forehead to the jutting ledges of his cheekbones, and the strong thrust of his chin, now angled up to catch the falling rays of the setting sun while he seemed to scent, or seek to scent, some fragrance or taste on the wind. His dark skin against the leaking light of evening turned tightly round his temples, as if it had been hammered into place by sledges, or as if he had moulded it there himself, cramming and jamming it into place like the viscous sludge of clay with the tough thumbs and balls of his hands that now hung ready at his sides. Everything about his posture was pointed and directed; the set of his hips grounded his arching spine, on which was set the yoke of his shoulders, vaulting forth that head, those brows that scanned the island for signs, for clues, for any least mark of distinction that might bring their search and his journey to an end.

Navy had gone to join him, but Fitz in his reverie stood by the stone distracted and disturbed. Something was ruffling at the periphery of his gaze, just as the wind played at Mr Ahmadi's cape. He looked down, and saw it.

'No,' he said, then louder, calling: 'No.' He ran along the border of the shadow even as it seemed to shudder and unravel in the weakening horizontal light, to a place where new lights, lying further off the others, and shining more faintly in the shade of the stone, now gleamed into shape.

They sickled away from the others, describing a pattern that curved back towards the north, revealing that the shape they had seen earlier was no line, but the beginning of a wide arc pointing to the north-east.

'It's down here,' Fitz called. He was standing on the lip of the height, looking down towards the whirlpool they had passed earlier. From this vantage, it was hard to see how they had missed it: following the spiralling arm patterned out by the stone's windowed lights, a ruined set of stairs circled in an anticlockwise arc from the summit of the island down to a sort of platform or ledge cut out of the island's tough basalt. As the others reached him, Fitz had but to wave his arm to the left, and they saw it instantly.

'This must have been very beautiful, once,' said Navy.

'And as obvious as the day itself,' said Mr Ahmadi. 'I doubt we'll find anything that hasn't been found before.'

They set off down the slope, almost skipping from one to another of the heavy stone slabs that had once formed the steps of a grand and sloping stairway, cut or shaped from the rock of the cliffside. Now that they knew where they were, and what they were seeing, they recognized on many of the slabs of stone the same curious and cursive carving, now largely eroded, that covered the menhir at the island's summit. Here and there, too, a socket lay empty, and some of these sockets were cracked, where perhaps a gem had been set, or a metal or polished stud. Fitz's eyes took it all in, greedily, as they passed in the sloping shadow. The evening thickened around them, cooling and congealing, while they descended, until at last they stood beside the ledge they had glimpsed from above – a sandstone platform grooved with wide trenches and sockets that seemed to suggest it had once been the site of a substantial structure, nestled against the cliff.

'It's gone,' said Mr Ahmadi. The tight weave of his temples had slackened, and his skin, like his cape, seemed to drag at his shoulders.

Navy was eyeing the approach to the platform. The edge of the cliff where they stood dropped in a smooth cascade away, steep and almost polished by the wind and rain. This perilous drop sloped round the platform and out of sight, sliding into the sea near the centre of the whirlpool they had seen churning on their ascent. They could still hear its ominous purr from below. Before them, access to the platform was nearly impossible; a three-metre chunk of the cliff had been washed away, and that which remained, so narrow a path as to be almost impassable, lay across a plinth of dark rock riven by a menacing crack.

'I don't think so,' said Navy. 'There are markings there, on the inner wall.' She gestured round to the left, where on the cliff face the remnants of stone carving might – could it? – be seen in the diminishing light.

She tried her foot on the stone plinth. It held.

'Navy,' barked Mr Ahmadi. Severe and monitory, his voice drove through the air like a mallet.

Navy seemed not to notice. She was already out of reach, placing one foot directly in front of the other as she inched across the narrow path. Mr Ahmadi didn't dare follow her; his own weight might be enough to break the unsteady ledge, but combined with Navy's it would certainly send them both plunging on to the rocks below. Fitz stood paralysed. He wanted to reach out to pull her back, and yet knew that his arms would come back filled only with air.

'I'm nearly there,' she said, half-trying to reassure them as she closed the last part of the gap, half-trying to reassure herself. Fitz didn't dare look down.

The stone made no noise at all as it gave way. Massive and solid, it operated by those laws reserved for slow and silent things. It didn't drop but gave itself away, not falling but almost floating into the chasm that yawned beneath it.

But Navy made noise. With a tremendous yell, a barbaric holler that she seemed to summon from her feet, at once she pushed with her legs and against the cliff wall with her arms, trying to launch herself on to the high part of the polished slope that lay just beneath them. She half succeeded, clearing the path of the tumbling stone, and landing almost flat against the steep slide. For a moment she hung there, trying somehow to dig in for purchase, clawing with her nails.

Fitz dropped to his stomach and pushed his arm down the slope as far as it would reach. His fingertips were inches from Navy's. Without looking at him, breathing in big and effortful gasps, she coiled on her legs and unleashed her hand at his, wildly, like a whip's end. He caught it. With the tips of his fingers he caught it. With the last hyperextended yearning of his arm he caught it. The pain seared through his shoulder, his elbow and his wrist, but he caught it.

He caught it, but he couldn't hold it.

Beneath the surface of his nails, his skin blanched. The joints of his fingers, which at first had curled tight and muscular against Navy's wrist, began to draw open under the weight of her body. She scrambled against the cliff face as Mr Ahmadi gently tried to pull Fitz's own shoulders and chest back from the edge, stabilizing him even as he also ground his ribs and sternum into the sharp stone below.

'Don't let me go,' she whispered, the words hissing through her exertion like the steam from an old piston. With a desperate lunge, she gave up trying to hold to the surface of the cliff and instead threw her second arm towards Fitz. If he had been ready, he might have tried to grab at it, to clutch it, with his free hand. But he wasn't ready; he missed it – he missed it, and as her weight shifted, she slipped, pulling free of the pale tips of his fingers, to the last digging at his skin with her tearing nails.

They watched her slide down the cliff face, silent and stubborn, keeping her body flat as it slipped round the curve of the stone and out of sight, her red curls bright against the slick dark rock.

By the time they had climbed up to the path, where they could see the whirlpool, all trace of Navy had vanished.

# 18

# The Giant's Almanac

O nce when he was small, climbing on a rock at high tide by the sea, Fitz had fallen several metres on to the tide pools below, landing heavily on his back and smashing his head against flat stones, pebbles and limpets. He had bled from his head in thick swells, and he wasn't able to move his arm – but until Clare had found him and picked him up, he had felt none of it. Numb, tired, as empty as a cloth hanging from a line in a full wind, he had seemed to himself not so much paralysed as pliant. The rush of the surf that crashed on nearby rocks, the calls of gulls and guillemots, Clare's cries when she found him – everything had seemed in his shock distant, as if a story told him about his life, rather than his own experience. It had seemed to befall him as if already, in the happening, a memory.

As Fitz and Mr Ahmadi stood on the short cliff above the swirling water, the dark mountains in the darkening east could have crumbled and sunk in the sea, and Fitz wouldn't have noticed, or cared. The old shock, the familiar sense of unfamiliarity, stole over him as the chill before a fever, both sudden and profound.

*She's gone.*

It was then he heard a reedy whine, as of an engine.

Mr Ahmadi seized his arm, pinching it so tight that his fingers seemed to press the bone. He shoved Fitz south along the ledge.

'Run.'

Fitz fumbled for words as he staggered on the loose rocks of the ledge. 'Why?' he managed. Or perhaps it was, 'What?'

'Run,' repeated Mr Ahmadi. He was close behind, too close, as if he were ready to run straight through the boy blocking his way. 'And keep your head low. They might not have seen us.'

*Who might not have seen us?*

And then Fitz realized that the sound was the drone of a motor, skipping through the sea swells, and that it was near, driving at them across the water, with red and white lights like eyes searching for them, blazing at them with anger through the enveloping dusk.

'Who is it?' he shouted through the wind. The rhythmic noise, broken by waves, was resolving in the chill, wet air, rebounding off the cliffside with growing intensity. As they passed beneath an overhang slick with dark earth, a few small rocks shuddered from above and rained around their feet.

'I don't know,' answered Mr Ahmadi, breathing hard. 'But I'd rather not find out.'

The boat was very close now – fifteen, maybe ten seconds from the shore. Fitz tried to lengthen his stride, leaping from one sure footing to another, watching them unfold before him in the gloom. At this speed, everything depended on hitting stable, dry footholds with every step, so he gave the ground his full attention, blind and deaf to anything else happening around him.

Mr Ahmadi had to call him twice before he heard.

'Stop.'

Pulling Fitz down to the ground, Mr Ahmadi cast his cape over their faces as the boat came round the island's shore. Fitz was aware of a searching light, but it wasn't particularly close to them.

'Now, go. We're almost at the south slope. The tide is down, and the boat should be high on the sand by now.' Mr Ahmadi placed his hands on Fitz's shoulders, and gave him a gentle shove.

That was when they heard her.

It was Navy's voice – high, thin, distant, but unmistakable. She was calling for help.

They didn't exchange a single word. Without pausing to breathe, much less take their bearings, both Mr Ahmadi and Fitz scrambled downslope, staying low and gripping anything that would hold. Leg over leg they shimmied and shuffled, scraping and bruising themselves in their haste to get to the sea.

Her voice came again, more distant this time. They were standing on the rocks, metres from the lapping sea.

Fitz looked south, towards the warm red light of the sun setting beyond a little south-facing bluff. Mr Ahmadi had immediately started north. They both froze, listening.

The horizon had burst into flame, and over a low band of clouds great pools of colour – orange, blue, yellow, pinks and purples that pulsed in and out of one another – rioted in the sky. Great open-winged gliders soared in the slate heights of the evening, birds undulating the vague distance between the ocean's deep phrase and the sky's deeper silence, between the day's bright things and the night's inestimable voids. Fitz's ears yearned into that space and action, striving to hover everywhere at once, to lie listening upon the whole vault of the island as sensitive to its every rustle and twitch as the wings of those birds, coasting on the invisible engines of the air.

*Albatross. The diver.*

Again she cried. Her voice seemed to bounce on the water, dispersing like the faint light on the small waves.

'I don't know,' said Fitz. His heart was heaving, and his tongue hung in his mouth like a withered thing. He felt terrified.

'What did you hear?' asked Mr Ahmadi.

'It can't be,' said Fitz.

Mr Ahmadi took him by both arms. 'Tell me what you heard,' he said.

'It sounds as if she's up there,' said Fitz, pointing.

*She's at the top of the island.*

'That's what I heard, as well,' said Mr Ahmadi. The noise of the boat's engine had cut out, or gone behind the island. They both feared what that might mean. 'Come on.'

Side by side, hand over hand, they climbed. There were moments when Fitz thought he might tumble backwards, or lose his grip on the rocks or plants round which his fingers, perhaps too lightly, perhaps too hastily, had closed. There were moments when the pain in his thighs, which seared with hot cramps at each new push, nearly threatened to overwhelm him. There were moments when he couldn't pant fast enough, couldn't force his mouth and throat open wide enough, to take in the air that his body demanded in order to go on. But he did go on, hardly slipping behind

Mr Ahmadi's big lunges as he raced back up the rocky slope. In his thought, again with every step, with every handhold, was the sight of her fingers slipping from his, the sight of his joints, white and exhausted, relaxing.

When they next heard Navy's voice, it seemed to come from beneath their hands.

'Quickly,' said Mr Ahmadi.

They had stopped abruptly on a rough section of tumbled and shattered stone, the debris left behind from an ancient rockfall. Above them, the clear line of the island's summit in this place lay broken, as if a huge chunk had slid down the face of the slope. In the falling light it wasn't easy to distinguish loose from fixed material, the basalt from the seam of sandstone that in places lay beneath it. Mr Ahmadi crammed and inveigled his fingers as deep as he could inside the complex texture of pebble, rock, boulder and slab, over and over searching for purchase before yanking with the full power of his back whatever he could release. Again and again he found himself pulling against the solid fabric of the cliff, and was forced to release it, to try again. Fitz followed him, trying to prise little, then larger pieces from the puzzled lattice of sharp and unyielding stuff. They clawed and picked, probing and catching at impossibilities. Fitz pulled with his legs, straining alike at both little and weighty things; sometimes he found his fingers locked as if in concrete, while at other times he heaved only to sprawl backwards with almost empty hands. He longed to find *that* stone, the one that would unlock the whole riddle of the scree, the one that, plucked from its matrix, would open the others as a key might a lock.

And then it happened on him, as an arrow long feathering the shifting air at last, somehow, hits its mark. It was the pattern of the pieces on the board, the last *mansūba* the Master had shown him before his arrest: the Giant's Almanac.

*Al-manac: the place where the camel kneels, and the end of the journey.*

*The stone that holds the others will not be a free stone. It will sit at the centre, at the base, and every other stone will weigh down on it. If I am to move that stone, it will have to be small, and very, very tightly wedged.*

'Stop,' he said to Mr Ahmadi. 'Stop.'

'What is it?' Mr Ahmadi looked up, still, sensing some danger. His eyes roved fast to the high ground above them.

'Step back. Step to the side. I have an idea.'

Mr Ahmadi looked at him from very close. In his eyes Fitz saw the light of the setting sun, tumultuous and searing. Without a word he clambered away, and crouched half-hidden in the evening, low, furled in his cape.

Fitz closed his eyes for an instant. He pictured himself a spider, long legs and arms jointed, stable, and fast. Almost without looking, but feeling his way, he scuttled downslope, pulling his gaze back in the dim light so that it seemed to centre in him, so that he seemed to see with his touch, sensitive to the tension in the rocks beneath his hands and feet as if he were stepping not on scattered rocks, but on wound and woven threads, feeling their twist and their twining, noticing with his eyes but much more with the rippling nervous sense of his spine the story that the rocks were telling, the debts that each owed the next, their weights and angles, their manifest and hidden energies, the way they passed the rain between them and withstood the screaming winds, their basking radiance in the sun as the heat cracked through them, their gravity, their song, their silence, their cold nights and their lichen faces. He felt for the lucky place, for the navel, letting his body be the judge of their body, his centre the measure of their inwardness.

*Let me be lucky.*

He didn't see the stone. He knew it, and his hands closed round it as the mind might close on an idea, or the mouth on a word, composing it even in the breath of its delivery. He pulled it, wishing and believing. He pulled it, willing the cliff to speak its mind, and in the same motion – lithe as a cat – sprang away.

A heavy stone crunched into another with a short, sharp, thud. For a brief interval, no more than a breath, nothing else happened. But then another rock turned, as if revolving in its mind with long and grating deliberation on some matter of immense weight and pressure. As it turned, the slope came alive. Fitz clambered further back as the big slabs began to shift and slip, fractured shears of stone settling old imbalances and answering questions that had long hung slung and depending between them.

It was all over in a few seconds. Mr Ahmadi had lost no time, not even seconds; the moment the stones began to move, he had climbed, searching with his eyes and then with his hands for openings. In the shadows and crevices they might have missed a thousand things, but they couldn't miss Navy's head and bright, sky-snatching eyes.

'I'm here,' she said.

Mr Ahmadi all but pounced on her. Gently pushing her back down into the dark gap between two huge piers of basalt, with limber and sinuous strength he dropped himself in after her. By the time Fitz found a safe path across the fall and had climbed down into the crevice, he found the others had already pushed further down, inside a kind of tunnel or passage that – from somewhere in its recess, seemed to be bathed in the yellow glow of the sea's evening.

Mr Ahmadi was helping Navy pull off her wet clothes. She was shaking violently. Almost bare, her teeth clattering against one another, Navy in the near darkness seemed scrawny and battered, but vital.

Mr Ahmadi unfastened the pin at his neck, and drew his heavy cape from off his shoulders. Its inner lining, thick and furred, would make a terrific towel. 'Take this,' he said to Navy, 'and get yourself dry.' He signalled to Fitz to help her, while he climbed – with absolute caution and silence, picking his way as if over broken glass – back towards the sky.

'It's a good thing he had his cape,' said Fitz, embarrassed as he helped wring the water out of Navy's jumper, then her trousers.

'Always handy to have a dry cape – for wrapping round half-drowned girls – in underground caves,' she said, shooting out the phrases with her usual levity, between racking shudders. She started to laugh.

Mr Ahmadi turned suddenly, hushing them, his finger pointing up towards the rocks above.

'Someone's here,' Fitz whispered to Navy, clapping his hand over her mouth. He thought he had heard voices just as he was easing himself down into the tunnel. 'There was another boat. We don't know who it is.'

'But we were seen, and so we can guess,' whispered Mr Ahmadi, rejoining them, 'so we'll stay down here, out of sight, and wait.' He pulled the cape tight round Navy's shoulders and back. She sat beside Fitz on a stone, still shivering, and put her head to his. For a few minutes, with Navy's chin and draggled hair nestled on his shoulder, he began to feel as safe and solid as the island itself.

'I'm sorry for dropping you,' said Fitz.

Navy's eyes had closed, but now they popped open, serious and solicitous. She drew back.

'You didn't,' she said. She pulled the cape ever more tightly round her. 'I let go.'

Fitz shook his head, trying to shed this thought the way a cow, cumbered by flies, will wag and twitch its ears. He remembered Navy's arm swinging up – the look in her eyes.

*Don't let go.*

'I let go,' she repeated. 'And I'm glad I did. Otherwise I wouldn't have found it.'

Navy stopped shivering. With a darting, familiar motion, she tucked her orange curls, stained brown by the saltwater, behind her right ear, then behind her left. For a moment she held her lip in her teeth.

'I remembered where we are. What this place is. This is where the Heresy *began*. This place, what they did here, entombing the *shāh*, after such a journey –' She broke off. 'Everything they taught us, everything *you* taught us at the Heresy – all our lessons – they started from this idea, that you have to accept your death. And there, on the edge of that cliff –' here she shook again, once, in a violent spasm – 'I was fighting to hold on to my life. I suddenly realized that that wasn't going to be the way to find anything at all. We came to an island in the sea, in the middle of a storm. Night is falling. We were looking for a tomb in a shadow. Come on,' she said, and cocked her head, as if in disappointment. 'There was only ever one way we were going to find it. I had to let go.'

'And the whirlpool –?' Mr Ahmadi was whispering still, but his voice was no less urgent for that.

'The current there was amazing. Terrifying. It felt like I was being pummelled with hammers. With anvils. Falling into the water I had taken a huge breath. I really filled my lungs. I guessed that that pool was going to spit me out somewhere interesting, but maybe it would take a while. I held my breath. I covered my head with my arms. And I let myself be pulled by the current. Wherever it was going, I went. All the while I counted, steady, trying to match my pulse to a slow beat, to stay calm. All the while I could feel myself going down, being sucked *under*, and I started to get scared because I could feel the pressure rising, and the pain in my chest. I had this almost uncontrollable urge to open my mouth and take it all in – whatever was there – the rush of foam and air and water and surge that was all around me. But I didn't. I died in it, let myself be carried. And then, all of a sudden, with no explanation – and I never came up at all – I was in the air. I was breathing. All around me things were swirling in the water, like fish or slimy things circling round me, touching me everywhere – and then I realized that it was air, bubbles, rising in the water all around me, and that they had been pushing me up, making me float. I didn't even have to swim. And then I saw that, although I was in the dark, above me there was a kind of cavern, and it was bright with sunlight, and there were *steps* – a whole staircase, carved in the stone, leading up. When I walked up it –'

A rock shifted above their heads, sending a little cascade of pebbles scattering down the slope outside. From far away, there was a shout, as of someone in pain.

'We have to move,' said Mr Ahmadi. 'In.'

'Come,' Navy said, her voice an eager whisper. 'I don't need to tell you the rest, anyway. I'll show you.'

The tunnel down which they ran, as fast as Navy's closely caped legs would allow, was narrow, but high. It seemed to have been carved; the scalloping trace of chisels became ever more visible as they hurried downslope and the air began to lighten – and Fitz wanted to stop, to make sense of it, to run his hands along the grit of the stone ground beneath him, to feel the cool, wet surface of the walls, with their crazy veins of bright quartz gleaming. His gaze was still lingering on the tunnel walls, as they passed, when suddenly they opened into a broad cavern. He nearly crashed into Navy's shoulder.

They stood there, breathing by the moment in fast, thick pants. Still catching his balance, Fitz tried, and failed, to take it all in. Around them slouched in gaudy luxury the most unlikely vision he had ever seen, or dreamed: a high-domed cavern, circular, gave out to the west by myriad windows cut in the cliff's steep face on to the sea and the evening sun; but it was not the sun that irradiated and warmed its glowing air, or not the sun merely – for the cavern's walls and ceiling were spread with beaten gold, gold that amplified and spun what little light it was given into threads and braids and sheets of spangled, scintillating fire, so that all the air seemed to hum and drone with honeyed metal. Around the cavern dim and burning ran a balustraded path cut from the stone that looked down on a pool of seawater, dimly visible but clearly audible – seething with tiny bubbles that frothed and exploded in the dark air. Fitz stared out over the darkness, but not at the water, nor at the circular stairs cut in the inner stone wall of the cavern, that circled and ascended from it, nor at the elaborate carving on the inner walls, inlaid with gold and studded with diamonds that palely glittered in the weak and failing light that was still shafting in through the western windows; but at the island at the pool's centre, a circular platform all of basalt that writhed out of the water on the five muscular fingers of a huge, single stone hand, on which was set beneath a canopy of gold a simple, squared tomb, all of white sandstone veined with quartz and set with a border of rubies and emeralds. If the cavern had taken his breath away, by the tomb – by its strangeness, by its size – Fitz found himself wholly moved, even to tears, and as he felt them gather in his eyes and tip at intervals down his cheeks, he felt also a kind of knot twisting in the base of his throat, a compression in which was combined not only joy and relief, but sorrow.

*It has been for this.*

Directly in the middle of the flat sandstone cover of the tomb, set in a simple carved niche, lay the Giant's Almanac.

Mr Ahmadi had seen it, and was already circling to the head of the steps, where a gap in the retaining wall would allow him down to the water and there, by a little skiff chained to a landing, to the island of the tomb. Without even thinking about it, Fitz ran after him.

He caught up with him just at the bottom of the steps. Navy wasn't far behind.

'No,' said Fitz, setting his hand to Mr Ahmadi's arm.

Mr Ahmadi stopped. He turned.

'The light is falling,' he answered. 'There isn't much time.' *Please*, said his eyes.

Fitz realized that he was right. Even as they had stood in the chamber, the lustrous honeyed light had begun to dissipate, and the chamber to take on a pale, almost green gleam; nonetheless, Fitz stood there, his hand still on Mr Ahmadi's arm, his face turned up in supplication, no words issuing from his heart.

'Why?' asked Mr Ahmadi.

'I don't want to know,' said Fitz.

Their voices reverberated in the chamber, echoing from the metalled dome, the smooth and coated walls, the little rippling water.

'I don't want to find out that I'm not myself,' said Fitz.

From behind him, Navy trained her arms through his, and bound them close round his chest, holding him to her, and burying her head in his shoulder. He smelled the salt on her, felt the clinging skin and bone of her beneath the cape and her shirt, sensed the blood beating in her wrists and neck. His own answered it.

*You're alive. I want to be alive.*

'All my life,' said Mr Ahmadi, 'the Heresy has owned me. When I was a boy, it took my childhood. When I became a man, it stole my thoughts. For the briefest time, for a blink, a breath, three beats that my heart will never forget, I escaped – to a world of *dreams*, to a world richer than my imagination, to a place where children weren't despised but prized, where gold wasn't just saved for gilding a man's grave – it was *drunk*, it was *spoken*, we *breathed* it. In that freedom, what was not possible to me? What goodness did I not enjoy, like fruit on the lips, like sugar on the tongue? Child, the Heresy dragged me back. It wrecked my love, everything that was dear to me in this world. One child I lost, the other they took, and I know the Heresiarch plans to use her to hold me forever. Let me break that hold. Help me. Let me give them the Almanac. Let me buy my freedom.'

Navy's arms had tightened round Fitz's chest. He almost couldn't breathe.

*He doesn't know.*

'Mr Ahmadi,' he began. 'Habi. There's something –'

'No,' said Mr Ahmadi. 'I won't let you say it.' He turned to step into the boat.

'Let him say it, Habi.'

The voice came from above. It was a deep, reedy voice, tight as a twisted wire and thick as a slug of iron. Now it was Fitz's turn to tighten.

It was the Rack.

He stood ten or fifteen metres away, at the cavern's head, not far from the stairs. Fingal stood by his side.

Mr Ahmadi slipped into the stern of the skiff and began to set the oars. Fitz and Navy, keeping low, settled nimbly in the bow. His back to them, Mr Ahmadi was already turning the boat before Fingal reached the stairs.

'Go on, Habi!' The Rack hadn't moved. 'Let him tell you. Let him tell you the thing that will break your heart. Let him tell you that, one way or another, you'll die in my prison. Let him tell you that I, personally, will tear every last dream out of your double-crossing heart, and leave them to wither in the sun. Let him tell you that the Great Loom is broken. Let him tell you that the Deplorable Society of Second-Rates and Freaktasms is no more. It's done. It's wound up. I – personally – have broken the fool Sassani, turned him, and he is now on his way to the Mountain – to form an *alliance*. They'll be working for the Heresy now, Habi.'

Fingal had taken the steps two at a time, his long legs loping for the landing; but he didn't make it. By the time he reached the shore of the pool, they were three lengths into the foaming water. Short of leaping in after them, he was stuck.

'Let him tell you, Habi!' thundered the Rack. 'Let him tell you that Dina will never leave the Heresy.'

The skiff pulled up at the bank of the little island. Mr Ahmadi had finessed the landing so that the boat drew perfectly alongside, and had already shipped his oars. He leaped lightly out, and the others followed.

'Let him tell you that the game is already ended. Let him tell you that the age of stories is over.'

The Rack was leaning against the low stone wall of the gallery. His whole head was a red ball of fury, and he spat his words into the cavern with a venom that rang on the dome and ran across the water as shots might, fired from a rifle. He was so absorbed in his own rage that he didn't hear, or see, Phantastes behind him.

The struggle was over before it began. The old Imaginer's knife lay at the Rack's throat, and he let his body slacken as Clare bound his wrists with cord. Ned stood on the stairs. Fingal – still the coward – chose not to fight, but gave himself up to be bound with his master. Phantastes draped their bodies on the wall over the pool while Mr Ahmadi and Fitz went to the tomb. Fingal resisted and struggled awhile, before he accepted the indignity; the Rack simply lay there.

The tomb sat on a raised plinth, accessible by three steps cut into the stone at either end. Under the flowing canopy of hammered gold, the tomb itself stood less than a foot high, and was about six feet in length. As they approached it, Fitz saw in the light from the Rack's lanterns that the jewels encrusting its base were few, but enormous – six giant rubies on each length, interspersed with five emeralds, and on the ends two, and three, respectively. The heavy cover, two inches thick of solid sandstone, hung proud of the case by about a finger's breadth around the whole. But they had not come to the island, or the chamber, or the tomb itself, for that. They had come for one thing only.

Mr Ahmadi knelt beside the centre of the tomb. Fitz dropped beside him. His hands were cold on the cold stone. Before them, under Mr Ahmadi's fingers as they hovered, unwilling to touch it, lay the Giant's Almanac. A perfectly round bronze plate, elaborately figured and marked with intricate cursive writing, it seemed about a foot in diameter. This, Fitz knew, was the *mater*, and on its back was fixed a gnomon by which, according to the readings taken against the stars by night, certain astronomical calculations could be made. But they had not come for that, either, and below the *mater* he knew other plates must be stacked, the three interlocking shells of the Giant's ingenious map, along with a fourth and final plate – the key to the proportions of the Great Loom of the Muses, possibly the most sacred and valuable object in the world.

Mr Ahmadi let his fingers fall delicately on the Almanac's surface. He traced the cool metal with his fingertips, brushing them as lightly as a bird might fan the air with its wings. Fitz knew he almost didn't dare to disturb something so ancient, something so *finished*.

*But it's not finished.*

With sudden decision Mr Ahmadi slid his finger beneath the bronze plate, and lifted it. Heavy, fragile, inestimably valuable, it seemed to lift him rather than he it, as he stood and raised it into the air before him. Taking it firmly in both hands, he turned it over.

He stopped.

'It's just the *mater*,' he called to Phantastes.

The old wraith leaned against the wall beside his prisoners, staring down with ancient gravity at the tomb. He was thinking.

'He wouldn't have let those plates out of his sight,' said Phantastes. 'They're here, somewhere.'

*Out of his sight.*

'The manuscript that the professor – that Phantastes – showed us – it said – in order to regain the Kingdom, the heir would have to stand before the eyes of the *shāh*.' Fitz broke off. He didn't know what he meant to say.

'And so you think –' began Mr Ahmadi.

'Is he – in there?' asked Fitz.

'There's only one way to find out,' answered Mr Ahmadi.

Navy took one end and Mr Ahmadi the other; Fitz stood behind, to hold the cover as they raised it. He didn't want to look, so concentrated on his fingers where they gripped the stone slab as it rose towards him. It must have been heavy; they lifted it so slowly, and with such concentration on their faces – concentration and something else.

*Horror. They're horrified.*

When the cover stood vertical, Fitz held it as Mr Ahmadi and Navy repositioned themselves beside him. Together they lowered the cover to the ground, so that it landed with no more than a tiny scraping – which nonetheless resounded around the expectant cavern.

The tomb was empty.

It wasn't just empty of a body. It was *empty*.

So far as the eye could see into the darkness that it contained, it dropped and dropped, a chasm and an abyss that, for all that one could dream or divine, stretched beyond fathom into the earth.

But it wasn't *quite* empty. On each of the four internal walls, positioned a little more than a metre below the level of the floor, hung one of the missing plates. To retrieve them, someone was going to have to climb down into the tomb.

Mr Ahmadi was already rolling up his sleeves. Navy had bound his cape round her waist like a skirt. Seeing Mr Ahmadi preparing himself, she turned back her own cuffs, and stepped forward.

'I'm lighter,' she said, 'and more agile.'

'This is my fight,' Mr Ahmadi answered.

Navy put out her hand. Mr Ahmadi hesitated, then took it in a full bind round her wrist. Her fingers enfolded his. Stepping backwards, never taking her eyes from his, she positioned the tips of her toes on the short edge of the tomb, then took a step down, pushing against the wall hard with her toes while arching her foot. Step after step, she walked herself down, her right arm rigid in the air like an iron rod, the look of concentration on her face so severe it seemed to etch lines in her skin. Sweat gathered on her brow as she inched with her free arm towards the first plate – even as she threw her weight backwards, leaning against the force holding her legs to the wall. Mr Ahmadi had at first allowed his knees to bend towards a squat, then dropped one knee to kneel by the side of the opening. Now, with the plate in Navy's fingers, he began to lift her, breathing hard as she skipped up the wall. She cleared the edge, and rolled, curling the plate into her chest and cradling it there as she came to a rest.

For a moment neither of them moved. Then Navy got to her feet, handed Fitz the plate, and shook out her arms. She tucked the hair behind her right ear, then her left, and smiled.

'One down,' she said.

Fitz set the first *rete* on the *mater*, and put them both by. Navy had taken Mr Ahmadi's hand again. Once more, this time on the first of the longer sides, she began to step down the inside wall. First her legs, then her torso, then finally her head dropped below the level of the floor as she descended. Fitz heard her touch, then take the plate, and with his eyes closed marked the intensification of Mr Ahmadi's breathing above Navy's light footwork as she pulled herself a second time up. The third descent was faster still, this time on the far, long side, and now she had recovered three of the four plates.

But the last, Fitz could see, would be a problem. Both Mr Ahmadi and Navy were exhausted. As she reached for his hand, her own trembled; he was putting a brave face on the pain that had seized his own arm, shoulder and back, but Fitz could see the signs of it palpably enough – his wincing, the kink in his posture, the hobbled way in which he tried to shake out, then stretch his back before the final push. Fitz didn't dare close his eyes.

Navy went down. Mr Ahmadi dropped to his knees. Fitz listened for the report of her contact with the plate. There was nothing.

'It's stuck,' she said at last. 'I can't get it off.'

Mr Ahmadi groaned. His eyes were turning into the tops of their sockets.

'Give me another few seconds. I can see it. I can do it,' Navy called.

Mr Ahmadi was leaning as low as he could, without losing his balance. Suddenly, without warning, his back seemed to spasm, and he fell forward towards the opening. His left hand shot out, and as he fell he clutched at the far edge of the floor, catching himself even as his body flexed, concave against his spine, into the opening.

Navy shouted unintelligibly, flailing with her free arm and kicking with her feet – but through it all, regardless of the commotion and his own excruciating pain, Mr Ahmadi held his grip. Somehow, against all reason, he ended up lying athwart the opening, one hand on the far side, along with a shoulder and his head, while his shins and feet remained beside Fitz. He began to lift Navy, but without the ability to sit up, he couldn't pull her very far.

Fitz had been watching, helpless. Now, seeing Mr Ahmadi's back start to flex, sagging under the weight of the girl on his arm, Fitz jumped to his feet and sprinted to the boat. Mr Ahmadi had shipped the oars, and Fitz was able to lean in, pulling one into each hand. He was back under the canopy in seconds, and laid the first of the oars next to Mr Ahmadi. It took his weight, and immediately he pushed against it to lift Navy – but the distance was just too far, the angle too shallow, and their strength already entirely spent.

Fitz dropped the handle of the second oar down towards Navy.

'My hands are full!' she shouted. 'I'll have to drop it!'

'Then drop it,' commanded Phantastes from across the cavern.

Fitz tried to reach down, but there was no way he could make his arm meet Navy's.

She looked up at him from the void shaft. Pale whiteness soaked her straining face in the gloom. Her eyes searched his.

Somehow, in that instant, they reached an agreement. Maybe he had seen a flick in her eyes, or perhaps her arm had twitched. Fitz stood up. In the moment he had left, he breathed deeply, and set his shoulders.

A second later, the plate came spinning into the air, directly through the gap between Mr Ahmadi's torso and the end of the tomb. Navy had sent it up turning fast, like a discus, so when it glanced off the edge of the stone, it only skipped, hardly changing direction. But she had sent it high, too high – and it was sailing through the air away from him, towards the far steps, and below them, the foaming sea.

Fitz didn't hesitate. He felt the compression and power in his thighs before he knew he was going to jump. On another day, it would have been nothing, but here, over that void, under that canopy, with that sea lying on every side – and above all, with this precious, singular disc sailing through the air – his whole body charged for the instant like a thunderbolt. The plate seemed to hang for an instant suspended in the air, and Fitz thought briefly that he would be too late, that his arcing jump over Mr Ahmadi's prone frame was too shallow. He almost flailed, and would have missed it – but he held his nerve and it sank, dropping as it spun just below its peak, and settled as he passed, directly between his thumb and forefinger. He closed on it just as his foot hit the far side of the stone plinth.

Only, his foot hadn't hit the stone plinth – instead, he had landed on the corner of the tomb's heavy stone cover. His weight on the corner was too much, or maybe a flaw lay hidden in the stone; as he landed, and the full pressure of his weight pointed

497

into the touch of his toe, the sandstone cracked and gave way. Fitz caught his balance, stepping lightly on to the plinth, and laid the plate with the others. Behind him, a loud and skin-blanching crack ripped through the air of the cavern, and he lunged, scooping up the second oar. Somehow he angled it, handle first, down the opening in time for Navy to grab hold of it, first with one and then with both hands, while Mr Ahmadi rolled away from the other, broken oar. As he heaved at the wood, holding it firm while Navy hauled herself hand over hand up its length, Fitz watched the splintered wood give way and tumble into the chasm.

If it ever hit the bottom, it never made a sound.

'I didn't let go this time,' said Navy, when she was standing again beside him on the plinth. She gave Fitz a sharp elbow in his side. His body tried to smile and cry at once.

Fitz was putting the sound oar back into the boat when something dark appeared in the foaming water between the landing and the island of the tomb. Everyone had seen it – even the Rack, who though still doubled over and gasping for breath, began to laugh.

She didn't surface until she had reached the landing on the island of the tomb. There, pushing herself from the water, and climbing easily on to the plinth, she squeezed the water from her long, dark hair while she turned her head very slowly round the chamber. She took it all in before she said a word. Shocked, they allowed her.

'Dina,' said Mr Ahmadi at last. He smiled, and the years dropped from him like an old skin.

'Dad,' she answered, and fell into his open arms.

19

# *The diver*

'The Kingdom,' Dina said. She had pulled away from her father's arms, and was looking with curiosity at the great golden dome, the stone and gem-work of the chamber, its elaborate tomb, the little boat. She seemed almost delighted. 'What sort of madman begins a story he doesn't mean to finish? Who plays a game he knows he can't win?'

'Dina,' said Mr Ahmadi, 'I have the Almanac.' He held it up, fanning the four plates against the *mater*. 'I will give them to the Heresiarch, and ask to be relieved of my office.'

Dina ignored him. She turned to Phantastes, and called to him across the chamber.

'Hožir. Let them go. We all want the same thing.'

Phantastes already had his knife in his hand. He cut the cords binding the wrists of Fingal and the Rack. They both stood up, slowly and with difficulty, wary.

'The knife,' said Dina.

'Dina,' said Mr Ahmadi.

'Mr Ahmadi,' tried Fitz.

*He doesn't know. How can he still not know?*

'The knife, Hožir.'

Phantastes drew back his arm over his shoulder, and launched the knife into the air. It sailed across the chamber, end over end, the tip of the blade revolving so close to the dome of the ceiling that Fitz was sure it had nicked the gold. The arc dropped, and it seemed to fall into Dina's outstretched hand. As if it was meant to be. Her grip tightened on its handle with a finality that might have ended anything.

'Kneel,' she said to Fitz.

'This is madness – Dina, stop.' Mr Ahmadi tried to take the knife from her arm, which was still raised in a fist, but she turned away, putting it beyond his reach. Her wrist swivelled, and the long, flowing knife seemed suddenly very sharp. Mr Ahmadi backed away.

'Kneel,' she said to Fitz. 'We're all in this story together, little brother. And you chose me. Your time has come. Kneel.'

Fitz understood. He stood in front of Dina, as close to her face as he had been the night before, when in the frenzy of the Black Wedding she had kissed him. Her eyes hadn't flinched then; by now they had, if anything, hardened. He searched them for her assurance, for any tenderness, for any warmth at all. He thought of the interminable mornings they had passed together, side by side and often arm in arm, in the Keep, painting; under the Jack's lofty plane, swapping paradoxes and impossibilities, hyperboles and formulae; in the Registry, telling stories as they leafed through the atlases and inventories, the herbals and the encyclopedias, the endless catalogues and indices of learning. He looked for some memory of those happy hours, of the attachment they had formed, of the hands they had joined in the work of their learning.

But the only thing in Dina's eyes was the end of the story.

*Al-manac. The end of the journey. Burden's close. The place of kneeling.*

'Kneel,' she said again. Still her voice was iron.

Fitz kneeled. Beside the water he knelt. Crowned with a crown of beaten gold, with his friends gathered to see him glorified, he knelt. He knelt for a thousand years, for two, for the cities whose walls had been thrown down and for their people, for the desert and the mountains, for the sea and for the sky, for the Sad King and for Hožir his brother, for the tears that watered the tamarisk trees and for the wood of the Great Loom, smoking on the fire, he knelt. He knelt for the Giant, and he knelt for a thousand kings, for a thousand captains dead and sorrowing beneath the sands. He knelt for the game, and he knelt for the story. He knelt for the end.

She put her hand into his hair, kneading it with her fingers, running her grasp through its thick texture – closing, opening her hold, until she had touched every part of his scalp, felt every ridge and hidden mole. Then she began to cut. The knife was sharp, and the hair came away in thick clumps, easily and without pain. Again and again she held it, ran the knife through with a scything cut, and dropped the hair on the stone below. When she had made it short – very short – she pointed the blade of the knife towards the water beside Fitz. It was only a matter of leaning over, and he could rinse his whole scalp in the cold, foaming sea.

As he came upright again, she took the blade in both hands and worked it gently across his scalp like a razor, cutting against the angle of the bristles. She moved fast and dexterously, and within a couple of minutes she had finished. She stood back, and appraised him where he knelt beside the tomb.

Now she looked at her father, as if for the first time.

'I am the Heresiarch,' she said.

Mr Ahmadi buckled. His body hardly moved, but the courage and determination that had propelled him through every adversity, and carried him unbroken over every obstacle, now broke. His eyes foamed like suds washing harmless on the sand.

'You.' It wasn't a question, or an accusation.

'Grandfather chose me. The choice is mine. All the moves are mine. Now take the reading and end the game, for this is the heir and the Kingdom is now.'

Fitz bowed his head. Phantastes gasped. His awe filled the chamber.

Navy stepped forward, and put her hand to Fitz's head.

'It is strange that you cannot see this,' she said.

'You can be my eyes,' answered Fitz.

'There is a beautiful design on your head,' said Navy. 'There are shapes in red, and in green, like a constellation –'

'It is the Giant,' said Fitz.

'It is the Great Loom,' said Phantastes.

'It is the Almanac,' said Mr Ahmadi. 'That day, in the Mastery, when I showed you the last problem on my father's *shatranj* board, which was his father's before him, the board that once belonged to the *shāh* himself. That problem is called the Giant's Almanac.

'And that is the state,' said Phantastes from across the chamber, 'in which the *shāh* and his brother abandoned their game, so long ago. And there is but one solution.'

'I know,' said Fitz.

'It is time to take the reading,' said Dina. 'It is past time.'

Mr Ahmadi stood back. They all watched him. Clare and Ned, standing beside Fingal and the Rack, looked over the stone railing beyond the foaming pool, Phantastes behind; nearer at hand, Navy stared, spellbound.

'Little brother,' called Dina – imperious, solicitous. 'The words grandfather taught you.'

With eyes like moons, like empty dishes, Fitz stared at her, uncomprehending. He staggered to his feet.

'The words of your heart, little brother. Now.'

Fitz gibbered. His heart yearned, and his cheeks, hot, shook. He felt he was reaching into the innermost emptiness of a huge void, that he was tunnelling through a world of pure air, throwing nothing to every side as he dug through his memory for those words that were nearest to his heart. At the very centre, he found them.

'*Zenith*,' he said. It whispered from him as soft as a breeze in summer, in which the petals of the rose do not stir.

Dina drew up her arm in a sweep. Fitz, seeing her hand describe the gold dome above them, stood at the tip of the little island, beneath the dome's very centre. On the stone beneath him, where his eyes were fixed, a cross laid in diamonds marked the spot. He fell again to one knee, and closed his eyes, presenting to Mr Ahmadi the top of his head, and the great mark with which he was marked.

'*Zenith*,' he said again. A sob choked in his throat. Tears began to stream on his cheek.

Before him, Mr Ahmadi held up the *mater*.

503

'*Zenith*,' insisted Fitz. He held his body straight as a wand, his head like a fixed mark in the green, green sea.

Mr Ahmadi set the first plate and turned it.

'*Nadir*,' Fitz said. The earth seemed to open, time to open, as the words dawned over him with a new light, and the sobs rose in his chest, forcing their way from his heart to his throat. Mr Ahmadi set the second plate.

'*Algorithm*,' he called. Mr Ahmadi fumbled, muttered, and then set the third of the plates upon the *mater*.

Fitz paused, and breathed, tensing every muscle in his chest and stomach in order to hold the breath steady. Here, last of all, most delicate of all – the final plate – the final word. He could not stumble –

'*Almanac*.' He couldn't look. He didn't need to look. Mr Ahmadi laid the fourth plate in the *mater*, the fourth plate inscribed on its snaking spiral arms with a thousand numbers and measurements, the secrets of the dimensions of the Great Loom of the Honourable Society of Wraiths and Phantasms.

'It's done,' said Mr Ahmadi.

From outside the chamber – almost now in darkness save for the high, shedding glare of the Rack's two lanterns – there came a low, ominous rumbling. They all froze. A little cloud of dust floated, high up, from the passage where they had all entered.

Clare and Ned sprinted for the passage. Almost immediately, they disappeared into a darkness both of night and dust. Everyone waited. Cracks they hadn't noticed in the ceiling, here and there, began to widen, shooting like fracturing stars across a sky of lamp-burnished gold.

'It's the cliffside,' said Clare, panting and coughing, from within the cloud of dust that still engulfed the passage. Ned came to her side. His face and body were coated in white powder. 'The tunnel's sealed off, and the slide – it's picking up.'

Dina turned to Mr Ahmadi, and took the Giant's Almanac from his hands, careful not to allow any of the plates to turn against the others. She placed it on the floor and, with the heel of the heavy knife, struck four hard blows into its beaten bronze surface, denting it. Then she seized one of the slender spiral ornaments that radiated from the centre of the first plate, and bent it back across the others. The bronze was sharp and heavy; her fingers bled. She took another arm, and again with huge effort bent it back.

'Dina,' said Mr Ahmadi, his voice a tangled knot of anguish, rebuke and dismay. 'What are you doing?'

'I don't want it,' she said. 'Only he does.' Getting to her feet, she hurled the Almanac at Phantastes; her arm was as good as his own, and he caught it with ease.

'But the Great Hoard of the *shāh*? The treasure? The Joy of the Heart?'

'How do you feel?' Dina asked Fitz. She put out her hand, and lifted him to his feet.

Above them the ceiling shuddered, and thunderous cracks, each jarring the very body of the island's rock, began to spread across the dome. Dina didn't seem to notice.

*The game is already ended.*

'I want to go home,' said Fitz.

'This is your home, little brother,' Dina answered. 'The Heresy is your home.'

Fitz looked at Clare, who was straining over the stone railing, twenty metres away – less. Her eyes said she was his mother.

'Her love for you is just a story she tells herself,' said Dina. 'She told herself this story because it made her feel good, at a time when she had lost everything. My father told himself this story because he wanted to leave the Heresy. Hožir told himself this story because he wanted the Great Loom back. They all loved you for themselves, little brother. They used you.'

'And you – don't you want me for the map? For the Giant's Almanac?'

Fitz stood before her. They were eye to eye as the ceiling began to fall, in great gold chunks, splashing into the foaming water. Mr Ahmadi leaped for the skiff, and Navy too. They called for Fitz and Dina, cried for them, stretched out their arms.

But Fitz and Dina stood on the plinth, each measuring the other.

Mr Ahmadi pushed the skiff into the water, then began to paddle with the single oar. The water, still bubbling around him, surged as chunks of stone fell into it from above. The two passengers rocked perilously.

'Don't you understand?' said Dina. She was speaking very softly, but Fitz didn't need to hear the words that he could read just as easily on her lips. They moved silently like words in a book, long written. *Burden's close. The place of kneeling.* Her eyes were on him, only on him. They encompassed him, held him. 'You are the Blank Eye itself,' she said, 'the diamond on which everything else turns. You are the treasure. You are the whole hoard. You are the gold. You are the emeralds and the sapphires and the rubies as big as a man. You are the myrrh and the amber, the silver, the precious tapestries and metalwork forged from falling stars, you are every rich thing stolen from a thousand kingdoms and the cost never counted, you are twenty thousand days in the saddle, the blood on the sword, you are the sea and the fire, the moon and the dust. You are the game, and you are the end of the story. It was told for you and it was told for no one else.'

The chamber had begun to collapse from the centre. Now the pieces that fell were large, each one a metre or two in length, heavy, and dangerous. Mr Ahmadi and Navy had nearly reached the other side of the water. He was reaching for the heavy iron chain. Fitz and Dina watched him.

He was reaching for the heavy iron chain. He couldn't put his hand to it.

The water level was dropping. It was draining from the pool. As it fell, the little boat began to sink.

Clare screamed. Navy leaped for the chain, and caught it. Hand over hand she climbed, never looking back. At the top of the landing, Ned took her by the wrists and hoisted her to safety.

Mr Ahmadi still stood in the skiff. His head had already sunk below the level of the floor. It continued to sink. Somehow, as the ceiling fell in, every huge slab of it seemed to miss him, to fall here and there to every side, never near enough to capsize him, never near enough even to shake him. And still, he dropped.

The Rack and Fingal had disappeared. Fitz saw that the passage must have cleared again, or that some new hole had opened in the island's face. Cool air was flooding the dark chamber, and the dust like genies swirled in the planes of light cast from the lanterns.

'Fitz,' called Clare. 'We have to go.'

She leaned over the railing and put her arms down to Navy, pulling her up from the landing. The stairs, impassable, had been crushed by falling rocks. When Navy had scrambled to safety, Clare leaned back down for Ned. He was heavier. She almost couldn't bear his weight.

'There is one word more,' said Fitz to Dina, 'one that I missed out.'

'Say it,' she said. Her eyes were locked on his.

'*Albatross*,' he answered, and the breath flooded from him like centuries, like the vast swells of ocean and its roaring tempests as they subside beneath wings alighting. 'The diver,' he whispered. She took his hands.

'Oh, little brother,' she said.

*There are holes worlds deeper than those dug in the earth.*

The foaming water had disappeared entirely, and with it Mr Ahmadi. From the western end of the chamber, where the light of the dying sun had collapsed to a purple bruise, a char-crusted ember, through the open gap in the wall came a hideous shriek – and, behind it, the king of the albatrosses. With a balletic swiftness marked by no one, coasting on its broad wings it covered the length of the chamber in an instant, turned on a pin, and – gathering its wings around it – plummeted after Mr Ahmadi into the empty hole in the sea, and was gone.

Now the whole of the island of the tomb seemed to sway, and whatever the pillar or foundation on which it stood, it toppled.

The tomb leaned across the void, moving very slowly, and with a heavy, seismic crunch crashed into the wall at the chamber's side. From above, rocks tumbled down upon them – huge, shifting slabs and boulders of basalt. Fitz and Dina, thrown back against the wall but still on their feet, found themselves holding hands. As the dust settled in the light of the Rack's two lanterns, they could see the dark night sky above them.

'Fitz,' called Clare from somewhere above. 'I can get to you.'

He looked for her, through the swirls and rockfall. For a moment, no longer than a moment, the swirls of dust parted. Like a sea before a prophet they parted, and in that parting his eyes met Clare's. *Don't you understand*, said his eyes, *that they will always come for me, and that as long as they are coming for me, you will never be safe? That you will never be safe from the loss of my love? Don't you understand*, said his eyes, *that the kindest thing I can do is to leave you to think that I chose this?*

He looked at Dina.

*I will always love you anyway.*

'Aren't you forgetting something?' she asked. 'All this time.'

She brushed the skin around his neck. Fitz felt for the strap. But where he thought his fingers would close on the jaybird, they closed on something else.

He had forgotten. He had forgotten all this time.

It was a little bell. The little bell from the boat. It had always been there, from the beginning.

*How did I forget? How did I forget all this time?*

Dina reached behind his neck with both hands. She untied the knot.

'The bell I gave you, that day. From the boat. That day when I found you hiding behind the broken mast, that day when our mother died, that day, little brother, when we made it to the shore alive. When we survived.'

She placed the little bell in his hands, and his palm closed round it.

'And I tied it round your neck, so that I would never lose you again.'

Fitz looked at Dina through the dark swirling of dust, through the night and its thousands of years, through the tangled limbs of the living and the dead, and he saw the far blue of her eyes, that it was the blue of the horizon, the blue of the edge where the air and the water join.

'Yes, I remember,' he said. 'I remember it all now.'

*Love is a fact of the blood.*

'No,' said Clare, as Fitz and Dina began to climb. Phantastes put his arms round her, and gently began to draw her from the cavern, up the tunnel to safety.

'No, no, no, no, no.' Clare's voice – flat and refusing – fell among the stones falling across the cavern, thudding into rock, vanishing into the void of the fathomless tomb.

'Let him go,' Phantastes said, as he pulled and guided Clare through the debris, out towards the cool clarity of the evening, and to Ned and the boat already half-rigged. 'This is the end of his story.'

The two children climbed through the dust and confusion, setting their feet carefully among the fallen slabs. As they scrambled together into the clear night air, Fitz opened his hand, and the little bell fell between the stones.

# Acknowledgements

I am grateful to my agent at Peters, Fraser and Dunlop, Adam Gauntlett, and to my editor at Penguin Random House, Ruth Knowles, for their patience, their support, and above all their guidance; although it must be said it's not their fault that things turned out this way. To the skill, forbearance and good humour of Stephanie Barrett I owe the catching of many slips. The Mughal emperor Babur, Sinbad the Sailor, H. J. R. Murray, Ibn Sina, Emily Dickinson and Anne Carson were my constant companions in the writing of this book, and I thank them, too, for their words' company. My colleague Andrew Marsham on several occasions gave me expert advice, which I have sought to follow, along with much indispensable information on bandits and crucifixion. My friend Davara Bennett has heard me out and read me through more often than I deserve. To my wife Emily I am and will be ever indebted for a music that alone makes every kind of movement possible.